Mischief
And
Mistletoe

Also available by Mary Jo Putney

The Lost Lords series

Loving a Lost Lord
Never Less Than a Lady
Nowhere Near Respectable
No Longer a Gentleman
Sometimes a Rogue

Other titles

One Perfect Rose
The Bargain
The Rake

Also available by Jo Beverley

An Arranged Marriage
Christmas Angel
Dangerous Joy
The Shattered Rose
An Unwilling Bride
Forbidden
Tempting Fortune
An Invitation to Sin (anthology)

Also available by Patricia Rice

Love's First Surrender
Moonlight Mistress
Surrender

Published by Kensington Publishing Corporation

MARY JO PUTNEY
JO BEVERLEY

Mischief And Mistletoe

*Joanna Bourne * Patricia Rice*
*Nicola Cornick * Cara Elliott*
*Anne Gracie * Susan King*

ZEBRA BOOKS
KENSINGTON PUBLISHING CORP.
htttp://www.kensingtonbooks.com

ZEBRA BOOKS are published by

Kensington Publishing Corp.
119 West 40th Street
New York, NY 10018

All Kensington titles, imprints, and distributed lines are available at special quantity discounts for bulk purchases for sales promotion, premiums, fund-raising, educational, or institutional use.

Special book excerpts or customized printings can also be created to fit specific needs. For details, write or phone the office of the Kensington Special Sales Manager: Attn. Special Sales Department. Kensington Publishing Corp., 119 West 40th Street, New York, NY 10018. Phone: 1-800-221-2647.

Zebra and the Z logo Reg. U.S. Pat. & TM Off.

First Zebra Books Trade Paperback Printing: October 2012
First Zebra Books Mass-Market Paperback Printing: October 2013
ISBN-13: 978-1-4201-3786-6
ISBN-10: 1-4201-3786-7

10 9 8 7 6 5 4 3

Printed in the United States of America

*To our dear friends Sherrie Holmes and Eileen Buckholtz—
and That Unforgettable Layton Woman*

CONTENTS

ABOUT THE WORD WENCHES

A lunch among friends and a barrage of e-mails generated the Word Wenches blog. In 2006, authors Mary Jo Putney, Patricia Rice, and Susan King readily agreed that creating an author blog to share their love of historical fiction and research was a great idea—but the prospect was daunting for three busy authors. Over lunch, Web site guru and author Eileen Buckholtz suggested expanding the number of authors to offer a greater variety of writing and author experience—and to better share the work of running a truly interesting blog. E-mails and ideas flew, and soon Jo Beverley, Edith Layton, Susan Holloway Scott, and Loretta Chase agreed to join the effort. With Sherrie Holmes in place as "whipster," meeting the challenge of setting up and maintaining the blog (while keeping the Wenches organized), Word Wenches launched in May 2006.

Since then, the Word Wenches have blogged on a fascinating range of topics. They have interviewed dozens of authors, experts, artists, and historians; given away scads of books; bestowed dozens of Honorary Word Wench/Wizard titles; and have welcomed a large and loyal blog readership—all while continuing to write new novels. The Wench roster has evolved as well, first with the passing of Edith Layton in 2009, and then with the stepping down of original Wenches Susan Holloway Scott and Loretta Chase. Soon after, Australian author Anne Gracie and British novelist Nicola Cornick joined the blog, adding to the international presence of the Word Wenches. With the addition of Cara Elliott and Joanna Bourne, the blog has grown even more. Word Wenches continues to be one of the most successful and longest lasting group author blogs on the Internet—and the Wenches know that the true heart of the blog exists in their wonderful readers.

She Stoops to Wenchdom

Mary Jo Putney

Chapter 1

As the carriage rumbled to a stop in front of their destination, Lucinda Richards craned to look out the window at the manor, but her view was blocked by her companions. "Roscombe Manor looks just like it used to!" Lady Bridges said as she peered outside. "I'm so glad that Major Randall and his wife have renewed the custom of a holiday ball. How long has it been, Geoffrey?"

"It must be over twenty-five years since Randall's parents died and he was sent away to his uncle." Sir Geoffrey Bridges smiled at his daughter and Lucy, who were sitting on the back facing seat. "I met your mother at a Roscombe holiday ball, Chloe."

"I shall look about to see if I can do equally well," his daughter assured him.

Lucy said nothing, but she was bubbling with pleasure that her parents had allowed her to attend with her best friend's family. Her father was vicar of St. Michael's, the parish church, and busy with Advent services. But he and her mother hadn't wanted to deprive Lucy of a treat like the Roscombe ball.

A footman opened the door and lowered the steps so the

passengers could descend from the Bridges' coach. Lucille was last out, and she caught her breath at the sight of the manor house. Roscombe was the grandest house in the area and she'd seen it from a distance, but never before had she visited. No one had lived in it for years, so it was good for the whole community that the house had come alive again.

Night fell early in December, but the moon was full, casting silvery light over the house and the park. Every window had a welcoming candle burning, and faint music could be heard inside.

As they climbed the steps, Chloe said, "Shall we see if we can both find husbands tonight? The holiday ball worked for my mother!"

Lucy laughed. "I'll settle for an evening of dancing. Finding a husband is too much to expect. But you might find one. You look amazingly pretty in that green gown."

"I do, don't I?" Chloe agreed with a grin. "We should stay side by side since our coloring complements so well."

"Though you're my dearest friend, I'd rather dance with men than you," Lucy said firmly. But it was true that ever since they were in the schoolroom, people had remarked on the charming contrast of Lucy's angelic blond looks and Chloe's glossy dark hair and green eyes.

The personalities were different, too. Lucy was the quiet vicar's daughter, Chloe the vivacious youngest child of a baronet. She'd make a good match when she traveled to London for her Season in the spring. There would be no London Season for Lucy, but that was all right. She had a wonderful family and friends, and she felt quite grand enough in the white gown Chloe had lent her.

They entered Roscombe and were greeted with warmth, light, music, and delicious scents. The tang of winter greens twined with the fragrances of mincemeat pies and spiced cider. The scents of the holidays.

After their cloaks were taken, their party followed the

music and laughter. Adjoining rooms had been opened up to create a surprisingly large ballroom that was already well filled. Chandeliers illuminated the beribboned greenery and the colorful gowns of the ladies, while musicians played a country dance that made Lucy's toes tap.

Lucy sighed happily. How could London be any finer than this? And she'd know most of the guests, so this ball would be even better than fashionable London. She hoped the Randalls would have an annual ball like this every year for the rest of her life.

A receiving line led into the ballroom. It was headed by their hosts, Major Alexander and Lady Julia Randall, with others Lucy couldn't see clearly beyond. As Major Randall greeted the Bridges, Chloe whispered, "My mother said some of Lady Julia's family are here for the ball and the holidays. That very handsome young fellow must be her brother, Lord Stoneleigh. Single and heir to a dukedom!"

Lucy laughed. "Then he won't be interested in me, but you might wish to study him at closer range. Who is that beautiful white-haired woman? She looks like royalty."

"Close. She must be Lady Julia's grandmother, the Duchess of Charente. The two of them look very alike, don't they?"

Lucy nodded absent agreement as she glanced along the receiving line. Her gaze stopped at the young man dressed in scarlet regimentals and she gasped, feeling as if she'd been struck a physical blow. A wave of heat swept through her, followed by chill. On the verge of falling, she frantically whispered, "Chloe!"

Her friend took one look and led her out of the throng of guests to a room on the other side of the foyer, which had been turned into a cloakroom. "Are you ill?" Chloe said anxiously. "Shall I tell my mother? Or see if Dr. Jones is here? My mother said he'd be coming."

Lucy sank onto a cloak-draped chair, fighting for composure. "No. I . . . I saw *him*. In the army uniform."

Chloe's brow furrowed. "The one at the end of the line looking uncomfortable? That was Gregory Kenmore, wasn't it? Heavens, I haven't seen him in years! He's a captain, I see. He just sold out of the army, so I suppose he'll be putting away his regimentals soon. A pity. He looks very fine in that uniform." Her voice lowered. "My mother said he's refusing all invitations. I wonder how the Randalls coaxed him out?"

"I wish I'd known he'd be here so I could prepare myself." Lucy bent and hid her face in her hands as she fought for composure.

Chloe knelt beside her, her expression worried. "Did Captain Kenmore behave badly to you before he left for the army? If he's hurt you . . ."

"Oh, no, no, not that at all." Lucy straightened up in the chair, telling herself that she was a young lady of twenty-two, not a child. "You'll laugh at me . . . but I fell most horribly in love with Gregory when he took lessons from my father at the vicarage."

"That was years ago!" her friend exclaimed. "Calf love."

Lucy's mouth twisted. "That's why I've never spoken of him. No one would take me seriously. But it felt—feels—very real."

Chloe cocked her head to one side. "Is this why you've never paid attention to any of the young men hanging about you? Because you were wearing the willow for Gregory Kenmore?"

Lucy nodded. "Everyone has assumed that I want to remain single and be a support to my parents in their old age, but the real reason is that I can't fall in love with anyone else when Gregory fills my heart."

Chloe looked like she thought Lucy was an idiot, but she

was too good a friend to say so. "Captain Kenmore has been in the army for five years or so, hasn't he? Have you seen him in that time?"

Lucy shook her head. "He was home on leave once, but I was staying with my sister when she had her first baby. By the time I came home, he'd returned to Spain." She had wept when she learned that she'd missed him.

"It's common to become infatuated with attractive young men, but you should be over it after five years without seeing him," Chloe observed. "How was he so special?"

"He was . . . kind," Lucy replied. "Papa has tutored any number of young men over the years to prepare them for school or university, but none of the others took the time to talk to me. When Gregory recognized how interested I was in learning, he persuaded my father to let me sit in on tutorials. At Christmas, he gave me a book of poetry." It was Lucy's most treasured possession.

"Kindness is always good, but what else?"

"He was intelligent and funny. He made me laugh. He called me the vicar's little angel." She sighed. "I found him madly attractive, while he thought of me as a child, even when I was almost seventeen."

"You were late to blossom," Chloe pointed out. "Though you've made up for it since! He sounds like a lovely fellow, and this is your chance to see if he's still what you want. And if he isn't, there are plenty of other handsome young men here to flirt with."

"I know." Steeling herself, Lucy rose to her feet and smoothed down her skirt. "You're right, there is nothing between us but my case of calf love, which has lasted far too long. It was just such a shock to see him unexpectedly." She tried a smile. "I shall meet him and exchange pleasantries and then dance."

"You won't lack for partners," Chloe predicted. "Come

along, now. If my parents ask where we were, I'll say I stepped on your hem and tore the lace and I had to pin it up again."

Lucy raised her chin and donned an expression of cool composure. "Since I'm the one that held us up, I should be the one labeled clumsy."

"But my parents will believe it of me much more quickly!" Chloe pointed out.

Very true. It was always Chloe who got them into trouble and Lucy who got them out. Chuckling, the girls left the cloakroom and joined the receiving line again.

Major Randall was grave and thoughtful and quite shockingly handsome. The Duchess of Charente stood between Major Randall and his wife. The old lady was very grand, but her eyes had a friendly twinkle. Lady Julia, Lucy's hostess, was petite and warm and sounded as if she meant it when she said she was glad that Lucy could come.

Next was Lord Stoneleigh, Lady Julia's brother. Very courteous and handsome, though reserved. A future duke needed reserve to protect himself, Lucy suspected.

Then—Gregory. Heart hammering, she stepped down to him. His face was drawn and his light brown hair a little too long. There was bone-deep fatigue in his gray eyes. He looked as if he wished he was somewhere else—and he was dearer than any other man Lucy had ever seen. She wanted to melt, or run.

Blast it, she was supposed to get over him, not want to kiss him! But a vicar's daughter learned to control her expression, and she managed to say calmly, "Welcome home, Captain Kenmore." She offered her hand.

Ignoring her hand, he just stared, his gaze flat and forbidding.

Her heart sinking, she said, "I'm Reverend Richards's daughter, Lucinda. I often plagued you when you were attending tutorials at the vicarage."

His gaze moved down her, and he gave a stiff little bow. "Miss Richards."

He didn't recognize her. *He didn't recognize her!* The knowledge was like a dagger in her heart. Yes, she'd been young when he left for the army, but they had talked often. Taken walks, laughed. He'd welcomed her when she'd brought tea and cakes into the study to refresh her father and his student.

She hadn't changed that much. She was taller and had grown a figure, but otherwise she looked much the same. Blond hair, bland face, modest white gown.

But he had changed, and not in a comfortable way. After too long a pause, he said, "I'm glad to see you well, Miss Richards. Are your parents here?"

"No, they were engaged elsewhere, so I came with the Bridges." Remnants of pride forced her to pull herself together. "I'd heard you were avoiding society, Captain. What brings you out tonight?"

"Major Randall was my commanding officer in Spain," Gregory explained. "He ordered me to come. He said people were curious to meet me again, so I could take care of all my social obligations at once."

"Very practical." She inclined her head. "I hope I shall see you at church." She glided away, glad that she hadn't collapsed and howled. It had been foolish of her to think there could be anything between them after all these years.

Yet damnably, she'd felt drawn to him. That spark of connection, of rightness, still burned in her breast.

How long would it take for her to get over him?

Gregory stared after Lucinda Richards, stunned to the marrow. She'd always been the sweetest and prettiest of little girls, but even so, he couldn't have predicted that she would grow into such a beauty. The vicar's little angel.

Now she was an angel in truth, all golden and innocent and pure. As he watched her laughing with a friend, he knew that she would haunt his dreams.

But there could be no more than dreams between them. Not when he wasn't fit to touch the hem of her gown.

Chapter 2

The turning of the doorknob was followed by a hissed, "Lucy, are you awake?"

"Of course." Lucy had expected Chloe would come to her room after the ball. She always did when Lucy spent the night, and tonight there was much to discuss. Listening to Chloe's chatter was better than staring at the ceiling and trying not to cry.

Chloe slipped in, stopped to build up the fire, then slipped under the covers of the bed next to Lucy. As she propped pillows behind her, she said breathlessly, "Lucy, I think it happened! I think I found my future husband tonight!"

Lucy blinked. "I saw that you were having a good time, but a future husband? Who, Lord Stoneleigh? You danced with him twice."

"Not Stoneleigh. He seems a decent fellow, but rather stiff." Chloe positively bounced, making the bed shake. "Jeremy Beckett!"

"You didn't just meet him, though," Lucy pointed out. "You probably met in the nursery. You used to complain how he teased you."

"Yes, but I liked it even then," Chloe said with a chuckle. "I haven't seen him in a couple of years, but now he's down from Cambridge, and he's changed. Grown. Become quite, *quite* irresistible."

"He is a fine-looking fellow," Lucy agreed. "And the Beckett estate is a good one. It would be a very suitable match." Thinking of her own situation, she asked, "Did he show evidence of interest?"

"He did indeed! We were flirting madly when I said that I was going to have a London Season to find a husband. He said that in that case, he must come to London in the spring. And then"—her voice dropped—"he drew me under the mistletoe and kissed me. A kiss like I've never known before. It was a . . . a lightning strike that shocked us both. Then Jeremy kissed my hand and said he would certainly be calling at my house long before spring!" Chloe sighed rapturously.

No longer able to control herself, Lucy burst into tears.

"What's wrong?" Chloe exclaimed. "I thought you'd be happy for me."

"I am!" Lucy wiped her eyes with the edge of the sheet. "He's lovely and almost good enough for you. I don't want to spoil your happiness. But . . ." She drew a ragged breath. "Gregory didn't want to talk to me. Or touch me. When changing partners brought us together in a dance, he looked like he wanted to run away rather than take my hand for a few moments. He did run away after the dance. Paid his respects to the Randalls and left immediately after. I . . . I knew his feelings were unengaged, but it hurts that he hates me."

"How very odd," Chloe said thoughtfully. "If he'd half forgotten you, his most likely reaction would be indifference, but his behavior was not indifferent. He has no reason to hate you. No one hates you. You are the rarest of creatures, a beautiful girl who is universally liked. Perhaps he likes you too much?"

Lucy swallowed a hiccup. "That makes no sense whatsoever."

"No? The man has spent years at war, doing dark and dreadful deeds that we can only imagine. He comes home and sees a girl he's always liked all grown up into a woman, but she looks so innocent and refined that he feels wholly unworthy." Chloe paused dramatically. "Afraid of his own passions, he flees for the sake of honor!"

"That is absurd!" Lucy exclaimed.

"Is it?" Chloe retorted. "He might not want to touch you, but I hear he doesn't mind touching the barmaids at the Willing Wench." Then she clapped her hand over her mouth, her eyes rounding.

"I beg your pardon?" Lucy stared at her friend. "Gregory is doing what?"

Chloe sighed. "I'm sorry, I didn't mean to tell you. I must still be suffering from the champagne. In the retiring room I chatted with Helen Merchant. She's Gregory's cousin, you know. She said the whole family is worried about him. Since coming back from Spain, he hardly talks to anyone. Polite, but he just slides away. Rides or walks all day, and spends his evenings at the Willing Wench. He can apparently relax with the barmaids, if nowhere else."

"Drinking and risking the pox?" Lucy said icily. "He won't even touch my gloved hand, but he'll have a jolly time with a tavern wench?"

Her tone was so menacing that Chloe said soothingly, "It's just how men are, Lucy. You're a lady. You belong on a pedestal. With you, he'd have to be a gentleman, and he's just not ready for that."

"That is insulting to both ladies and wenches!" Lucy exclaimed. "Barmaids from the Willing Wench have called on my father for help or spiritual guidance. They are women just like we are. Some are mothers trying to raise their babes. Others need to work if they're to eat. They deserve to be treated with respect." Her head swung around to Chloe, her eyes glittering. "And I deserve to be treated like a woman, not a *lady!*"

"What does that mean?" Chloe asked warily. "The last time I saw that look in your eyes, you sold the pearls you inherited from your grandmother to buy winter garments for the inhabitants of the parish workhouse."

"Yes, and I'm not sorry." Lucy's parents had been shocked, then understanding. Her father had thanked her for the lesson in charity and organized a parish committee to improve workhouse conditions. Then he bought back the necklace and said he'd give it to his first granddaughter when he had one, in the hopes that she'd think twice before selling a family treasure.

"How do you plan to administer justice this time?" Chloe asked, even warier.

"I am going to dress like a barmaid, kiss him in a way he'll never forget, and then walk away from . . ." Her voice faltered. "I'll walk away from my dreams of him and move forward with my life. I want to marry and have children, and I've had several suitors who would have been worth closer study if my interest hadn't been elsewhere."

"Every eligible young man in the shire would come running if you dropped your handkerchief," Chloe said. "Just don't toss the handkerchief in Jeremy's direction!"

"I'd never do that! And if I did, he wouldn't even notice. I saw how he looked at you tonight. Since you're now looking at him the same way, it's just a matter of time."

"I hope you're right! But let us return to your comment about going to the tavern and kissing Gregory Kenmore. You were joking, weren't you?"

"I was not!" Lucy's jaw set stubbornly. "Kissing has a

great deal to do with love and marriage, and I think I need to do this if I am to stop pining for Gregory." She'd dreamed of him in ways an innocent vicar's daughter shouldn't. Those dreams would haunt her if she didn't prove to herself that there had never been a true attraction, only girlish fantasy.

"That is a truly bad idea," Chloe said, shocked. "You can't go to the tavern without being recognized! What would people think? Your reputation might be tarnished beyond repair!"

"I'll disguise myself. Remember how we used to play dress-up with the old clothes in your attic? One of those gowns and a wig will change my appearance out of all recognition." She grimaced. "It isn't as if Gregory looked at me closely enough that he'd recognize me even if I came in my usual garb."

Chloe pursed her lips thoughtfully. "It's possible that you can disguise yourself well enough to pass as a barmaid, but still, a tavern!"

"The Willing Wench might be no place for ladies, but it's safe enough. Just about every man in the parish stops by now and then to have a pint. Our maid Anne's cousin is in charge of the barmaids there. I'm sure she'll tell me how to go on. Will you stay at my house one night and help me with the clothing?"

Chloe sighed. "Very well, since you're determined. We can choose a suitable costume in the morning before you go home. But please, be careful!"

"I'll be as careful as I want to be," Lucy replied. Which wasn't at all the same thing.

"Ouch!" Lucy gasped as Chloe tightened the laces on her old-fashioned corset. Two nights had passed since the holiday ball, and this was the night when she would put her plan into action. "This corset is much tighter than my usual stays."

"It needs to be tight if you're to fit into this properly." Chloe lifted the blue cotton brocade gown and dropped it over Lucy's head and started lacing up the back.

Lucy smoothed the skirts down, enjoying the fullness. The gown had belonged to one of Chloe's great-aunts, and the medium blue shade went well with her blue eyes. The style was simple enough that it didn't look too horribly out of date, and it had dramatically low décolletage. She studied herself with some dismay. "This gown was designed to be worn with a fichu tucked around the neckline. If I don't wear one, I risk lung fever."

"You will *not* wear a fichu! You need to show enough of yourself that men won't look at your face." Chloe's voice changed. "You don't have to do this. You can change into your nightgown and we can giggle until your mother comes to tell us to be quiet."

"I *do* have to do this," Lucy said immediately. Even to herself, she had trouble explaining her reasons, but going to the tavern and inducing Gregory Kenmore to flirt with her seemed like some necessary rite of passage. She needed to be more than the vicar's obedient daughter if she was to cut Gregory from her heart and mind. And she needed to believe that she was a desirable woman, not just a prim girl on a pedestal.

"At least the Willing Wench is only a short walk away," Chloe said with resignation. "But I feel I should go with you."

"I won't be alone. Anne's cousin Daisy has promised to keep an eye on me and intervene if I get into trouble." Lucy practiced breathing and decided that she could move well enough to carry tankards of ale. "Now for the wig."

Chloe carefully settled the dark wig on her head again and pinned it in place. It was a provocative tumble of dark waves and curls. Lucy muttered, "It's hard to believe that people used to wear wigs all the time from choice."

"At least this wig never had mice living in it. Some of the hairstyle stories my grandmother told me would make strong men faint."

Lucy shuddered. "Time to see if I look suitably wenchly." She stepped in front of the long mirror and saw . . . a stranger. A dark-haired and very exposed stranger. Her hands flew up to cover the upper curves of her breasts. "I look like a trollop!"

"That's what you wanted." Chloe studied her critically. "That décolletage is truly impressive. Your usual clothing disguises what a fine figure you have."

Lucy stared at herself in horrified fascination. She had no idea how *much* of her there was! "It's the corset, not me."

"The corset has to have something to push up," Chloe pointed out with a chuckle. "You need some cosmetics. Your complexion is too pale for the hair, and you look too innocent." She opened a pouch and produced a hare's foot. After she brushed color on Lucy's cheeks, she said, "Use that pot of red salve for your lips."

Lucy stroked on salve, then considered her more colorful image. Clearly she was painted. Nice women didn't paint. "There's no mistaking what I am now."

Chloe bit her lip. "Please don't go, Lucy. Gregory Kenmore isn't worth your humiliating yourself like this."

"Humiliating?" Lucy put a hand on her hip and wriggled. The mirror reflected a brassy, confident woman. Vulgar, but strong. A woman very different from the vicar's daughter. "I think looking like this is . . . is very freeing." Turning from the mirror, she donned the plain navy blue cloak she would wear. "It's going to be an interesting night!"

Chapter 3

Despite her bold words to her friend, Lucy's nerves were tied in knots as she approached the Willing Wench. It stood near at the intersection of the main London road and the small road that led into Roscombe Village. Only fifteen minutes' brisk walk from the vicarage, yet she'd never set foot inside.

A lamp hung over the open door of the livery stable. She could see it was well populated with horses, though most of the patrons would have walked here from the village or nearby farms.

Daisy had said to come in the back door, through the kitchen. As soon as Lucy opened the door, she heard boisterous talk and laughter. Not threatening, but . . . very different from what she was used to.

This was her last chance to turn back.

She stepped inside and closed the door behind her.

A sweating female cook said, "You must be Daisy's friend come to help out. We need more girls. The place is powerful busy this time of year. What's your name?"

Thinking quickly as she removed her cloak, Lucy said, "Lacey."

The cook barked a laugh. "A good name." She scanned

her new barmaid and gave a nod. "You'll be popular even if you spill ale on the customers' heads. To work with you, now. Casks of beer and ale at the bar, they're the most popular. Hot whiskey punch in the cauldron over the taproom fire. Daisy will tell you the rest." She gestured toward the taproom door, then returned to her own work.

Warily Lucy opened the door, and was met with smoke, noise, and the scent of food, sweat, and hops. Suppressing her desire to bolt, she scanned the room. Men were in groups at tables or standing along the bar. A noisy game of darts was being played in one corner with the bottom of a wine barrel for a target. No sign of Gregory, though he might be blocked by someone else.

Three barmaids were moving around the room, deftly sliding between groups while balancing trays of drinks. There was a real skill to this, Lucy realized. The girls seemed to be enjoying themselves, but they were working hard.

Daisy spotted Lucy in the door. After delivering a tray of drinks, along with a comment that made the men at the table roar with laughter, she came over to Lucy. Her admiring gaze went head to foot. "I can scarcely recognize you even though I knew you were coming!" She nodded at the taproom. "Is all this too much for a well-brought-up young lady like you?"

"I'm no young lady, just Lacey the tavern wench. Tell me what to do, and I'll do it," Lucy said with nervous determination. In order to secure Daisy's help, she'd explained why she wanted to pretend to be a tavern wench. Daisy had rolled her eyes and made a comment about how women were fools for men, but she'd been helpful. Lucy continued, "Is . . . is Gregory Kenmore here?"

"Not yet, lass." Seeing Lucy's crestfallen expression, Daisy said, "He usually comes later."

"What is he like? How does he behave?"

"Very polite. Comes in with his dog, smiles at the regulars, flirts with the barmaids, and then drinks to forget," Daisy said succinctly.

"Drinks to forget?"

"You see that with men who've been to war." Daisy sighed, looking older than her years. "Work here long enough and you'll see everything. But you're here just for tonight, and it's time to put you to work. You can see we need the help! Follow me." Daisy led the way to the bar, tossing over her shoulder, "Do your best to keep your bottom out of pinching range! Our lads do like a pretty lass."

Daisy's warning was too late. Lucy jumped with a squeak when a man pinched her bottom. Whirling with shock, she saw a farm laborer give her a wide, mildly inebriated smile. "Bring me another pint of bitter, there's a good girl!"

Lucy managed a quick duck of her head, then took off after Daisy. When she reached the other woman at the bar, she gasped, "How do you stand the pinching?"

"A girl learns to dodge. And it's not so bad to be admired for a perky rump." Daisy studied Lucy's face. "Are you *sure* you want to do this?"

If she left now, she could be home with Chloe in fifteen minutes. . . .

Then she thought of Gregory. If she was ever to be free of her dreams of him, she must meet him. Talk to him. Kiss him. None of which he wanted to do with Miss Lucinda Richards. "I'm sure, even if my bottom does end up black and blue!"

"You'll develop fancy footwork soon enough," Daisy assured her. "But most of our regulars are good fellows. They work hard, and this is their bit of fun. If any of 'em kick up too much, their mates quiet them down. We get a few travelers from the London road, and now and then one will cause trouble, but this is a safe place to work. And the money is better than being in service somewhere."

"Can I pour ale on a man's head if he's too much trouble?"

Daisy grinned. "Yes, but if you do it too often, Mrs. Brown, the landlady, will charge you for the ale. Come along now, and I'll show you what's where. The lads are getting thirsty."

The next hour was the most educational of Lucy's life. She learned that a smile and a quip would gain forgiveness for her inexperience and that gently teasing an old man would bring a spark of pleasure to the gaffer's eyes. She learned how much bread and cheese, or boiled meat and potatoes, to serve when a man wanted food; where the clean tankards were kept; and how to wipe off the mouth of a tankard with a rag if there wasn't time for a proper washing.

Rushing back and forth was exhausting, but she felt pride in getting better as the evening progressed. She also realized that Daisy was right. The customers were good fellows who liked a pretty lass and wanted to have a bit of fun at the end of a long, hard day of work. There were laborers, tradesmen, and servants, with some more educated patrons as well. They teased the barmaids, but there was no threat to it.

Then Gregory entered and Lucy dropped a tray of full pewter tankards.

It was always a relief to enter the Willing Wench. The name alone made Gregory smile. The hum of men enjoying themselves helped drown out his thoughts, and dogs were welcome as long as they behaved. Santa Cruz was always well behaved. He might be a scruffy brown and white mutt of low birth and unknown breeding, but he was an honorable veteran of the Peninsular War with better discipline than most soldiers.

Gregory nodded toward men he knew, which was most of them. He was draping his cloak over a chair in the corner when one of the barmaids dropped a tray of drinks. He winced at the sound, fighting the urge to throw himself to the ground. It wasn't artillery fire, only clanging tankards.

The offending barmaid was new, he noticed. A pretty, dark-haired young thing with a figure that even a dead man would notice. Gregory liked the barmaids, who weren't innocents but weren't Haymarket ware, either. They were friendly, tolerant women who worked hard and liked a good time.

They weren't mothers who watched with barely concealed anxiety and disappointment in their eyes. They weren't idealistic maidens with wide, hopeful eyes like Lucinda Richards. He'd been shocked numb when he saw her at the Randalls' holiday ball. So delectable. So innocent. So hurt when he pulled away from her.

No, not for him, respectable women who expected more of a gentleman than a well-tailored coat. The coat he could manage, but nothing else.

He settled into the chair and waited for a barmaid to approach. When Santa Cruz rested his chin on Gregory's knee, he ruffled the dog's floppy ears. It was worth the effort required to bring him back from Spain. Dogs accepted their imperfect masters.

Acceptance was why Gregory liked the tavern. If he wanted to talk, there were people to talk to. More often he didn't, and no one bothered him. Not like home, where his family's silent worry about his mental health was palpable.

At some point, Gregory would have to pull himself together and act like a responsible adult. But he couldn't imagine when that day might come.

"Your usual, sir?"

He glanced up at the musical voice and saw the new barmaid with a tankard in her hand. He blinked. When she was across the room, he hadn't recognized how very, *very* good her figure was. A man could bury himself forever in that décolletage and count the world well lost.

With a jolt, he realized that for the first time in longer than he could remember, he was feeling a buzz of sexual response. He wasn't dead after all.

"Sir?" The musical voice was pitched higher to cut through the noisy voices. "Daisy said a pint of bitter is your usual. Would you like something different tonight?"

Pulling himself together, he said, "No, a pint of bitter is just right." Taking the tankard from her, he said, "You're new here, aren't you? Surely I'd recognize such a pretty face if I'd seen it before."

Her exquisite pale complexion turned an enchanting pink. "This is my first night, sir. The tavern is shorthanded, so I said I'd help out."

He smiled at the girl, realizing how rusty that smile was. "What's your name?"

"Lacey, sir." She bobbed a little curtsy, which did pleasant things to her dramatic curves. "Would you like anything to eat tonight?"

Usually he just drank, but with mild surprise, he recognized that he was hungry. And if he ordered something, Lacey would have to come back. "Some bread and cheese and some of Mrs. Brown's fine pickled onions would be a pleasure."

Her smile was bewitching. "Then you shall have them, sir."

She slipped away, picking her way between tables and chairs and patrons. The rear view was every bit as fine as the front.

With such a busy crowd, it was a few minutes until Lacey returned with his bread and cheese and pickled onions. "Here you are, sir."

Santa Cruz took an interest in the proceedings, pushing his long snout against the cheese board and almost knocking it out of the barmaid's hand. Before Gregory could order his dog down, Lacey crooned, "Poor pup! It must be dull for you here."

She stroked the dog's head, her slim fingers scratching his ears and sliding down his neck. "If you behave like a proper gentlepup, I'll bring you a bit of sausage."

Cruz leaned into her hand with a low moan of pleasure. Gregory understood entirely.

Lacey glanced up, her blue eyes captivating. "He's a handsome fellow. What's his name?"

"Santa Cruz, but calling him handsome is stretching the truth to breaking point."

"Santa Cruz?" Her brows furrowed. "Spanish for Holy Cross? Why that?"

"I didn't name him," Gregory explained. "He was an ugly stray puppy who wandered into our military camp in Spain and attached himself to Major Randall, the man who owns Roscombe Manor on the other side of town. When Major Randall sold out, he gave Santa Cruz to me." Gregory patted the dog affectionately. "He's not handsome, but he's a good dog."

"You brought him all the way from Spain!" Lacey exclaimed. "That can't have been easy."

"It wasn't. But I owed Cruz too much to leave him behind."

"You owed him?" the girl asked, puzzled.

Realizing he'd revealed more than he should, Gregory said, "No need to bring Cruz sausage. I'll give him a bit of my cheese. I don't want to get you in trouble by keeping you from your work."

She nodded and turned, swaying her way toward the bar. Gregory sighed with pleasure. Lacey was a definite asset for the Willing Wench.

Chapter 4

Lucy's heart was hammering as she returned to work. Gregory had spoken with her as easily as he used to! He admired her, too. A single evening in a tavern had taught her to recognize the glint of unabashed male appreciation.

As she pulled more tankards of beer, she thought about what she'd learned. Daisy, a shrewd judge of character, said that Gregory drank to forget. He'd mentioned owing the dog too much to leave him in Spain. Clearly war had marked his soul.

She supposed that wasn't surprising, but the idea left her feeling helpless. Her anger toward him had dissolved, leaving the tenderness she'd always felt. She wanted to help him recover from his experiences, but how? She had absolutely no useful experiences of her own. She supposed that time would gradually heal whatever wounds of the spirit he'd suffered. But other than pray for him, there was nothing she could do.

Three noisy strangers entered and glanced around disdainfully. Jane, one of the other barmaids, snorted. "Fancy fellows who were traveling the London road, I'll be bound.

They're taking seats in your corner, Lacey. Can you manage, or would you rather I took their orders?"

Lucy would have preferred Jane do it, but that didn't seem fair. "I'll go. If they're too rude, I'll cry and make them ashamed of themselves."

Jane gave a crack of laughter. "That might work, but don't count on it. We're almost out of boiled beef if they're hungry, but there's plenty of cold sliced ham."

Lacey made her way across the taproom. The hour was growing late and the crowd had thinned, though there were a fair number of customers still. The newcomers had taken the table right in front of the fireplace, which had recently been vacated.

Gregory was in his corner not far from the fireplace, staring broodingly into his tankard. She'd have to ask if he needed a refill after she'd taken care of the newcomers. They were expensively dressed but disheveled, and as she neared the rank smell of old alcohol became obvious. They'd probably been drinking all the way from London.

Lucy approached the table and bobbed a curtsy. "What would you gentlemen like? We have . . ."

Before she could say what food was available, the man nearest her swiveled in his chair. He had crooked teeth and whiskey on his breath. "I'll have a little of you," he said drunkenly. He grabbed at Lucy and pulled her onto his lap. "Aren't you the pretty little pullet! How much will half an hour with you cost?"

One of his friends, a mean-faced dandy, said, "I'll take her for ten minutes first!"

Panicked, Lucy struggled to free herself, but Whiskey Breath had a grip like iron. She opened her mouth to scream and he plastered a sour, smothering kiss on her. Mentally swearing with language that would have shocked her father, she tried again to break free, but Whiskey Breath's response was to grab her breast.

Suddenly it was over. Lucy was yanked free and tumbled to the floor. She looked up to see that Gregory Kenmore had wrestled Whiskey Breath to the ground and had the man's arm twisted up behind his back.

His companions leaped to their feet, shouting with outrage. The dandy was reaching inside his coat when a pistol magically appeared in Gregory's free hand. "I wouldn't advise that," he said coolly. "I suggest the three of you return to your carriage and head on down the road. We don't want your kind here."

As the dandy hesitated, there was a shuffling of chairs as other local patrons stood and drew close to the fracas, faces threatening. Lucy could see they were ready to fall on the strangers and beat them to a pulp. Santa Cruz came to his master's side and stared at the men with a growl rumbling in his throat.

In a voice of command, Gregory said, "Leave now and no one will get hurt." He twisted Whiskey Breath's arm, eliciting a gasp of pain. "That will be best all around, don't you agree?"

"Yes, damn you!" the man gasped. "Now, let go of me!"

Gregory released the arm and Whiskey Breath scrambled to his feet, trying to look belligerent and instead looking frightened. "I didn't mean any harm to the slut," he snapped. "I'd have paid her well."

Gregory raised his pistol until it was pointed directly at the man's heart. "Do not call our girls sluts. Now *go!*"

As the strangers hastened to the exit, Gregory offered Lucy a hand up. "Are you all right?"

When they'd touched briefly during the dance at the ball, gloves had separated their hands. Now they touched skin to skin, his warm, bare hand enclosing hers. She felt a wave of sensation unlike any she'd ever known—a combination of melting and the electrical shock one felt on cold winter days.

"I . . . I'm all right," she said feebly as she got to her feet, but being assaulted, then rescued by the man of her dreams left her shaking. Even though the strangers were gone and she was surrounded by protective men, the smoke and heat and noise of the tavern made her want to flee if she'd had the strength.

Daisy appeared beside her, a tumbler in her hand. "You've had a bad fright, Lacey! Can you take her outside for some air, Captain Kenmore? Here's some brandy for the shock." As she handed the tumbler to Lucy, one eye closed in a slow wink.

Lucy would have laughed if she wasn't so upset. Daisy was certainly giving her opportunities to improve her acquaintance with Gregory. And the idea was a good one. "I *would* like some fresh air," she said with a quaver that was genuine.

"Then come along, now," Gregory said kindly. "We can sit out front until you feel more the thing." He took her elbow and guided her toward the front door, pausing by his chair to collect his cloak and drape it over her shoulders.

The cloak reached to her ankles and carried Gregory's scent. It felt like the warm embrace of loving arms. She wrapped it around herself with murmured thanks, but when they stepped outside and she felt the bite of the winter air, she started to take the garment off. "You'll freeze without this, sir."

He tucked the cloak more closely around her, hooking it at the throat. "I've campaigned in all weather and I'm wearing warmer clothing than you, so don't worry about me. Here, relax on this bench and have some of that brandy."

Lucy obediently settled on the bench at the far end of the tavern. In better weather, the old gaffers sat here with their clay pipes and watched the traffic. The only traffic visible now was the coach of the drunken strangers. As it disappeared around a bend in the road, Lucy asked, "Do you think they might come back and cause trouble?"

Gregory sat down on her left so close she could feel the warmth of his body. "By the time they sober up, they'll convince themselves it never happened."

Cruz had followed them out and now lay across both sets of human feet with a contented sigh. Lucy ruffled his ears. "You're a good, brave dog, Cruz." She sipped at her brandy and promptly broke into a coughing fit.

"Are you all right?" Gregory asked with concern.

"I'm . . . fine." She managed to clear her throat. "I'm just not used to spirits."

"Shall I get you something else? A cup of hot tea, perhaps?"

"No need. Just being outside in the peace and quiet is calming." The moon was two days past full, still strong enough to silver the bare trees and fallow fields. She took a very small sip of the brandy. This time she didn't cough, but she wrinkled her nose. "People drink this for pleasure?"

Gregory laughed. She hadn't heard him laugh in . . . years. "Brandy is an acquired taste. Is it steadying your nerves? You had a bad experience in there."

She took a third careful sip. "My nerves are steadier, but my wits will be scrambled if I drink much more. You take it." She handed him the tumbler.

Their fingers touched again as he accepted the glass, and she was startled to feel a tremor in his hand. As he took a swallow of brandy, she said, "You're somewhat unnerved, too, aren't you?"

He lowered the tumbler with a grimace. "That always happens after action. I was surprised to find how automatically I snapped into using military force."

"You were *wonderful!*" She let her admiration and gratitude show in her voice. "I can't thank you enough for saving me from that horrible brute."

He made a deprecatory gesture. "The taproom was full of men who would have come to your rescue."

"But you were first, and believe me, I appreciated how quickly you acted. Every moment of his touching me . . ." She shuddered, unable to complete the sentence.

Gregory's right arm came around her, warm and protective. "I'm so sorry you had to endure that! Believe me, I was tempted to break the fellow's neck."

"Probably just as well you didn't since that might have got you into trouble." She nestled against his side as her upset faded. "You used exactly the right amount of force. It was very impressive to watch."

Not responding to her compliment, he drank more from the tumbler in his left hand. "I'm glad Daisy was generous with the brandy. It does steady nerves."

Lucy relaxed, not just because she was safe now but because of the way things had changed with Gregory. Now that she'd recognized that he was suffering from wounds beyond her understanding, she could once again think of him as an old and dear friend. It had been terrible to think they couldn't be friends.

Tilting her head back, she studied the sky. The bright moon obscured the dimmer stars, but others still sparkled. "Are the stars the same in Spain?"

He raised his gaze. "Yes, you'd have to go much farther south to see different skies. Below the equator, I think."

"What is Spain like?"

"I didn't see the country at its best because there have been years of fighting," he replied. "But there is great beauty there, and fierce, honorable people."

"They say the war will end soon. All countries have wars, but surely the land and people will endure."

"I hope so." He made an effort to lighten his voice. "Tell me about yourself, Lacey. Are you from around here?"

She nodded. "I'm a local girl with a very uninteresting life."

He hesitated, and she guessed that he was trying to learn

more about her without being rudely intrusive. "Will you be working here regularly? You've had a difficult first night."

She shrugged noncommittally. "We all do what we have to."

"I suppose we do. But I'd think a girl as pretty as you would be married by now. Surely you've had suitors."

It was her turn to hesitate as she wondered how to tell the truth without saying too much. "Aye, there have been suitors. But the lad I wanted went into the army and . . . didn't come home." Which was sadly true. The uncomplicated young Gregory who had enchanted her when she was a girl was gone forever.

His arm tightened around her. "I'm so sorry," he said softly. "War is such a waste. Such a terrible, terrible waste."

"Please tell me what war is like," she said softly, daring in darkness a question that would have been impossible in the light.

Chapter 5

He withdrew so abruptly that he didn't realize he'd removed his arm from her shoulders until the cold returned. "One doesn't speak of such things."

"Why not?" Her lovely, sweet voice was like honey. He had the irrelevant thought that honey was a very effective wound dressing. Healing.

"It's . . . it's not fitting," he said, knowing he sounded pompous.

"Why not?" There was a frown in her voice. "How can those of us back home understand if no one will tell us?"

"Why would you want to understand?"

"No one is improved by ignorance," she pointed out. "I want to learn. To know. To hope for wisdom."

"Is wisdom necessary for barmaids?" he asked, an edge to his voice.

He wouldn't have blamed her if she'd stalked off in a temper, but instead she laughed. "Wisdom is good for everyone if they can develop it. Barmaids have more than their fair share because they meet so many kinds of men." Her voice softened. "Speaking of dark things can let in light. I'm a safe listener. You're not likely to ever see me again, and I'm good at keeping silence."

He didn't doubt it. She was good at keeping silence about herself. There was also something about her that inspired trust. Maybe . . . maybe he should speak of what haunted his nights. He couldn't talk to his parents. Their opinion mattered too much for him to reveal what lay within his shadows.

If she'd tried to coax him he would have withdrawn, but her peaceful presence made talking possible. "War is so many things. Boredom. Fear. Fellowship. A hard world of men without the softening presence of women."

"Is that why you sold out?"

"My father was not well. It was my duty to return home and take over much of the estate management." Which was true, but not the real reason.

She must have sensed he was speaking less than the whole truth because she asked, "There was no deeper reason? You weren't wounded?"

"A few nicks here and there but nothing serious." He fell silent, then surprised himself by blurting out, "The dirty secret of battle is that it's exciting. When the fighting is fiercest, there's mad exhilaration. A wildness beyond fear, a feeling that you're immortal, and if you're not, death doesn't matter." He wiped his damp palms on his trouser legs. "The intensity of it is like a drug. Regular life can seem gray and dull by comparison."

"No wonder war is eternal," she said with wonder. "Men like it."

"Sometimes. Victory is sweet when the stakes are life and death."

"But surely there are bad times as well?"

He shuddered. "The only thing worse than a battle won is a battle lost. To look at a field of broken bodies and know how much has been destroyed. All the dreams, the hopes, the loves, that have died. Some men don't feel that, and they are the ones who can soldier on for a lifetime. I am not one of them."

"What were the worst things that happened to you?" she asked, her voice a soft, seductive invitation to unburden his soul.

He'd spoken of his experiences to no one, but perhaps he should. Maybe that would end the nightmares. Though he couldn't imagine talking about war to a sheltered young lady like Lucinda Richards, he had the strange feeling that this tavern wench with the sympathetic heart would understand. "I stopped feeling immortal when my best friend was killed in battle," he said haltingly.

"I'm so sorry." She took his hand in her warm clasp. "Tell me about him."

"Jack Dawson and I met when we were the newest ensigns in the regiment. He was from the north. Lancashire. We became friends in an instant." Gregory thought of his friend's laughing face. "He was so exuberant. So full of life. He feared nothing. He was a fine officer, too."

Her hand tightened on his. "What a tragedy that he's gone."

"His death was so random. He wasn't shot down while leading a charge or anything grand and noble. A French cannonball exploded and killed him and several of his men." Gregory swallowed convulsively. He had been in charge of collecting the pieces of soldiers for burial. Most hadn't been identifiable. A few, horribly, were.

"A great, great waste," she said sorrowfully. "It would have been far better if you could have been friends for the next fifty years and sat in front of the fire and told each other lies about the glorious days of your youth."

Gregory was surprised into laughter. "We would have,

too. They'd have to be lies, because much of daily life in an army campaign is dam . . . very uncomfortable."

"At least he died quickly and not in lingering pain," Lacey said. "And his spirit is intact even if his body is gone."

"Do you truly believe that?" Gregory had been unable to go to church since he returned from Spain.

"Oh, yes. Without question." After a dozen heartbeats, she continued shyly, "I've not seen war, but I've sat with the sick and dying. I have seen and felt things that have given me faith."

He'd underestimated her, he realized. The fact that she had lived a quiet life in the country didn't mean that she was sheltered. As a girl from a lower order of society, she'd had to be stronger than the more cosseted girls of his own class.

Cruz shifted on their feet, his body twitching. Lacey smiled and scratched his neck. "At least one loyal friend came home with you. You said you owed Cruz too much to leave him in Spain. Was there a particular reason, or just that he was a good companion?"

Gregory's hand spasmed tightly on Lacey's. When she made a small sound, he relaxed his grip. "Sorry. There was one particular occasion." Even thinking about that caused his heart to pound.

She waited, clasping his hand but silent. Finally he managed to say, "Not long after Jack was killed, the French were bombarding us again, and . . . and I was buried alive in dirt. Couldn't move, couldn't *breathe*. I knew I was dying.

"Then I heard Santa Cruz barking nearby. He found where I was buried and started barking and digging. My men joined him and they pulled me out." He swallowed hard. "Barely in time. I was unconscious when they rescued me."

"So Cruz saved your life, but what a dreadful experience! To be buried alive and face helplessness and death," she said compassionately. "Though you survived, that kind of experience is the stuff of nightmares."

"Exactly. But . . . there's worse." He hated to reveal his weakness, but he felt compelled to tell her the whole sordid truth. "It turned me into a . . . a coward. I realized that I no longer had the strength and courage to lead my men. My presence was endangering them. That's the real reason why I sold my commission."

"How long was it between being buried and your returning home?"

"About six months." It had felt like six years. "When my mother wrote that my father wasn't well, I seized on the excuse instantly."

"Six months of heavy fighting, if the newspapers are to be believed. During that time, did you lose more men than might be expected?"

"No, thank God."

"Did any of your superior officers say you weren't doing your job? That you were a disgrace to the uniform?"

He laughed humorlessly. "They were all too busy fighting to notice my failings."

"Perhaps. But perhaps you were doing your job well and honorably but had lost the desire for it," she said thoughtfully. "That's not cowardice. It's moving from one stage of life to another. Going from heedless youth to maturity. From feeling immortal to . . . to recognizing mortality. You were brave enough to protect a barmaid from three beastly drunks without thinking twice about it."

Lacey's words struck like a bolt of lightning. Because she was right: After being buried alive, he'd lost all his interest in soldiering. Yet looking back, he realized that he'd managed to behave like a decent officer despite his inner horror. He'd even done some things that an observer might have called brave. He'd lived and slept with fear and wanted desperately to go home, but he hadn't actually acted like a coward.

"You were right that barmaids have more than their share of wisdom," he said with wonder. "How did you become so wise?"

"The hard way. I'm not sure wisdom comes any other way. We learn by our mistakes, not our successes." Moonlight limned her delicate, flawless profile. She looked very young, but also calm. Strong. "I've suffered nothing dramatic. Just the usual errors of judgment. Times when I wasn't kind. Times I didn't help someone who needed help. Enough small mistakes to have a large effect."

"You don't give yourself enough credit. Plenty of people make mistakes like that, and it never improves them."

"Thereby giving those of us who are wise a chance to suffer the sin of pride," she said with a laugh. She rose to her feet. "Time for me to go back to work."

He stood also, reluctant to end the intimacy of their conversation. "Do you feel well enough? I can walk you home."

"Truly, I'm fine." She stood on her tiptoes and placed her hands on his shoulders as she brushed a kiss on his mouth.

The sweetness of her lips paralyzed him. He kissed her back, forcing himself to be gentle, but her mouth opened eagerly under his. Her uninhibited response struck fire through his numbed body. His kiss deepened, and he enfolded her in his arms.

Her soft, lusciously female form pressed into him, sending his heart hammering and his wits scrambling. Sweeter than honey, more stimulating than brandy. . . . "Lacey," he murmured. "Lovely, lovely Lacey . . ."

She turned rigid in his arms, then pushed away from him, her eyes wild in the moonlight. "No!" she gasped. "No, I mustn't!"

The cold air slapped him to his senses. Dear heaven, how

could he behave so to a young woman who had just been mauled by a drunken stranger? Gregory was no better than the man he'd saved her from. He reached out an apologetic hand. "Lacey . . ."

Before he could apologize, she bolted around the tavern. By the time he pulled himself together, she'd disappeared. She was *fast!* He followed, wondering if she'd darted into the kitchen, but he heard no sound of a door opening or closing.

A cluster of pines were behind the inn, and a path to the village ran through it. He saw a branch shaking though there was no wind. She must be running back to Roscombe. Swearing at himself, he moved into the path. In the moonlight, he saw a dark mass caught on the head-high pine branch.

Had Lacey been wearing a scarf or hat that had been tugged off? He lifted the object from the branch, disconcerted because it felt like a dead animal.

It was a wig. A black, curly wig. His sweet little Lacey was a liar.

Chapter 6

Lucy ran until a stitch in her side forced her to stop. She leaned panting against a tree, hand pressed to her ribs. Only then did she realize how chilled her head felt. She'd lost the blasted wig when she ran through the pines. And she'd stolen Gregory's cloak. She was turning into a hardened criminal.

Would he follow her? She wanted and feared that.

He didn't follow. At least she wouldn't have to explain herself. She continued home at a walk, his cloak wrapped around her like warm arms.

When she slipped quietly into the vicarage, she heard the living room clock striking. Midnight. Wearily she returned to her room, where Chloe was tucked under the covers reading the family's worn copy of *Robinson Crusoe*.

Her friend looked up, bright-eyed with curiosity. "How did it go? Was he there? Did you get to talk to him?" Her brows furrowed. "Whose cloak are you wearing? It's almost dragging on the ground."

Lucy collapsed into her shabby wing chair. "Yes, Gregory was there, I talked to him, I lost your wig and stole his cloak, and now everything is much more complicated!"

Chloe's brows arched. "It sounds like you had an interesting evening. Did it include a kiss so you can forget him and move on?"

Lucy began unpinning her hair, which had been flattened to go under the wig. "I got my kiss. That's why everything is so complicated." Briefly she explained the drunk who'd grabbed her, Gregory's rescue, and their long conversation, though she didn't say what they talked about. That was private.

She ended by saying, "Now I know him so much better, I had a kiss I will never, ever forget—and I realize how foolish I was to think he could ever be interested in me."

"Why do you say that?" Chloe asked. "It sounds like the two of you got on really well. A good discussion and a good kiss."

"Yes, but in the course of it, I realized that he is no longer a boy, but a man. He has been shaped by experiences beyond anything I'll ever know," Lucy said slowly. "I'm just a country girl and not very interesting. It wasn't me he kissed, it was Lacey the barmaid. He isn't interested in *me*. And his interest in Lacey was of the temporary sort."

Their conversation had been real and valuable to them both, she was sure of that. But it was a passing moment, nothing more.

Lucy wanted more than a moment. But she wasn't going to get it.

Baffled by the wig, Gregory made his way back to the Willing Wench, Santa Cruz at his side. Maybe Lacey wore the wig because her own hair was bad, perhaps shorn off if she'd suffered a bad fever. Or maybe she thought that looking dramatic and a little wicked would help her earn more money as she served drinks. Whatever her reasons, they undermined the sweetness and trust between them.

But he'd responded to her unlike any woman he'd ever

met in ways both physical and emotional. He wanted to see her again.

He *needed* to see her again.

The tavern was almost empty when he returned. He and Lacey must have talked for a long time, though it hadn't seemed that way.

Daisy and another barmaid were cleaning the taproom, their movements and faces weary. The girls here were a jolly lot who created a warm, welcoming atmosphere, which was why he was a regular. He'd never thought about what a tiring job it must be.

He approached Daisy, and she glanced up from the table she was wiping. "A bit late for another drink, Captain," she observed.

He handed her the empty brandy tumbler he'd been carrying. "I wanted to return this." He lifted the wildly curling black wig. "Also this. It became snagged in a branch after Lacey left me."

"Fancy that," Daisy said noncommittally.

"Where does she live?"

Daisy shrugged. "I don't rightly know."

"Then what is her last name?"

The barmaid shrugged again. "No idea."

Gregory said with exasperation, "You hired a young woman and don't even know her full name?"

"She was a friend of a friend who came to help out and maybe see if she'd like to work here regularly." Daisy stretched as if her back was aching. "She was pleasant and pretty, so I decided to give her a chance."

Daisy was flat out lying, Gregory was sure of it. But if she didn't want to talk, there wasn't much he could do about it. Maybe there was some good reason why it would be better if he didn't find the elusive Lacey. "If she comes searching for her wig, let her know that she can retrieve it at Naughton Grange."

"I'll do that." Daisy's voice was still bland, but there was a spark of amusement in her eyes. "I do know Lacey is a local girl. If you keep your eyes open, you might see her around."

He eyed her suspiciously. "Are you trying to get me out and about?"

"Isn't it time?" she asked tartly.

He felt a stab of irritation at the implied criticism. But Daisy had been kind to him over the last weeks when he'd been unable to face the normal world. And she was right— he'd gone to ground to lick his emotional wounds long enough. "Yes, it's time. Thank you, Daisy."

He left the tavern, mentally listing all the things he needed to do. His father wanted him to take over management of the estate, and that meant going over the account books with the steward. He must ride the property, visit the tenants, check the condition of estate-owned houses to make sure they were right and tight for winter.

He must also visit family friends and all the others who had the right to expect him to call. He hadn't wanted to before, yet he found that now he did.

And while he was doing all that, he'd keep his eyes open for Lacey. He owed her an apology for kissing her when she'd just been mauled by a drunk. She didn't seem to mind at first, but it was badly done.

And he needed to discover if she was as alluring as she'd seemed tonight.

With Christmas fast approaching, Lucy was kept busy helping with the preparations. She and her mother made up gift baskets for the poor, gathered greens to decorate the church and the vicarage, and helped the cook with the holiday dishes that would be served at the vicarage open house held after the Christmas Eve children's service.

Her biggest task was organizing the traditional St. Michael's Christmas Eve pageant, which featured young members of the congregation acting out the story of the nativity. The service was more playful than the solemn celebration of Christmas morning.

The pageant was popular with children and adults alike, but herding the young actors into some semblance of order was not for the faint of heart. Lucy's mother had directed the pageant for years, and Lucy had been her assistant. When Lucy turned twenty-one, her mother handed the production over to her daughter, sheep and goats and all. The job was a challenge, but the results were worth it.

Lucy hoped busyness would help drive away thoughts of Gregory Kenmore, but she wasn't entirely successful. Actually, she wasn't successful at all. As she chopped dried fruit in the kitchen and adjusted costumes to fit the pageant players, she said all the right things and managed to get her mother's recipes right, but she couldn't stop thinking about Gregory. About the conversation that had taught her so much. About the kiss that curled her toes and taught her even more.

Her only return visit to the Willing Wench was to give Gregory's brushed and folded cloak to Daisy. Daisy told her that Gregory had the wig and she could retrieve it from Naughton Grange, the Kenmore estate. Luckily, Chloe said it didn't matter if the wig was gone since no one else had touched it in years.

Lucy didn't see Gregory, but she heard about him. He had emerged from his seclusion and rejoined the Roscombe community. He made calls on friends and neighbors, and was reportedly pleasant and sociable. Perhaps not as outgoing as he'd once been, but no one suggested that he was behaving badly.

He even called on her parents one day, *and Lucy wasn't there!* Her first reaction was to howl. Her second was relief.

If he recognized her, she'd faint of pure embarrassment. It would be horribly awkward for both of them.

Luckily, he wouldn't recognize her. Prim, blond Lucinda Richards, the vicar's daughter, was nothing like saucy, raven-haired Lacey with No Last Name.

But she wistfully hoped that he would come to the Christmas Eve service. She'd like to at least see him. To make sure that he was really all right.

To mentally say good-bye to the charming Gregory she'd yearned for, and to the complex man he'd become.

Gregory had always enjoyed the children's Christmas service at St. Michael's. The church was packed to overflowing, warming the cold winter's night. Garlands of greens and clusters of candles created a festive air.

His brother, Roger, who was studying at Oxford and planned to enter the church, was home for the holiday. As they made their way to the Kenmore family pew, his mother said happily, "I am rich beyond measure to be here with my two handsome sons."

"Don't I count?" his father, Sir James Kenmore, said with twinkling eyes.

She patted her husband's arm. "You I can always count on. Sons are more unpredictable."

Which was as close as she would come to saying how worried she'd been about Gregory. The morning after he met the elusive Lacey at the tavern, he'd come out of his room, announced plans to sit down with the estate steward, and eaten a hearty breakfast. His mother had looked ready to weep with happiness.

Gregory felt a surprising sense of rightness as he settled into managing the estate. This was his home, his place. If he hadn't been away for five years, he wouldn't have recognized just how much he loved Naughton Grange.

His father was available if advice was needed, but Sir James was getting along in years and a riding accident had left him in need of a cane. He was delighted to hand over the daily work to his son. Gregory realized he'd learned something about command when he was at war, for he had no trouble with older tenants treating him as too callow to be taken seriously.

Life was good and getting better—except that he'd found no trace of Lacey. He hadn't seen her, and discreet inquiries didn't produce anyone who recognized the name. It didn't help that he couldn't describe her except to say that she was so high, amazingly pretty, and her hair probably wasn't black. Perhaps she wasn't really local.

He settled down at the end of the Kenmore pew, his mother on his right and his father and brother beyond. On the other side of the church, Major Randall and his wife and their family filed into their pew. The major smiled at Gregory before helping his wife's grandmother into her seat.

When everyone was seated, leaving the main aisle clear so players could come and go, the Reverend Richards called his congregation to order. The vicar loved the pageant because he loved children. That was probably why he'd been such a good tutor when Gregory needed help preparing to attend Rugby, the school that Kenmores had attended for the last century or two.

The early part of the service was short because everyone was eager for the main event. The pageant began with the vicar reading the beginning of the nativity story, his sonorous voice filling the church. *"And it came to pass in those days, that there went out a decree from Caesar Augustus, that all the world should be taxed. . . ."*

Gregory settled back with a happy sigh as the children took over and the familiar words rolled over him. The angel Gabriel was played by Major Randall's foster son, who was actually some kind of cousin. Bursting with pride, the boy announced the coming birth to an adorable blond Mary. Gregory had played Gabriel himself one year, having worked his way up from the role of a sheep.

A choir of very small angels sang a carol in sweetly angelic voices. A shepherd's headdress fell over his eyes and he walked into the kneeling rail. A wise man led in a goat disguised to look like a camel, and the goat tried to eat the embroidered altarpiece.

As laughter rippled through the church, the altarpiece was saved by the deft actions of Lucinda Richards, director of the pageant. With her golden hair pulled back in a simple knot, she was as serene and lovely as an angel herself.

The pageant ended with the baby Jesus being laid in the manger. The moment of sweet solemnity ended when it turned out that the baby was being played by a light-colored puppy. It was sleeping as only puppies sleep when laid in the manger, but it woke up abruptly, looked at the children surrounding it, and leaped to the floor.

As the puppy ran yipping down the aisle, the goat bolted, baaing, and the whole congregation burst into laughter. Gregory saw Lucinda Richards sigh ruefully at the collapse of the pageant, but she knew better than to attempt to create order out of chaos. If all the players performed properly, the pageant wouldn't be half so much fun.

The vicar raised his voice in a hymn of celebration that the savior was born. The congregation joined in, singing jubilation until the stone walls shivered. People rose and streamed from the chapel, voices still raised in song. Families with small children would go home, while others would stop by the vicarage open house.

Gregory was the last to file out of the Kenmore pew. As he waited for his father to rise with the aid of the cane, he glanced around the candlelit church. Lady Julia Randall was hugging her young angel Gabriel, and a very small sheep was perched and giggling on her proud father's shoulder.

Gregory's gaze moved back behind the altar where Lucinda Richards was collecting halos and sorting out her pageant players. She really was the loveliest girl, as refined and delicate as spun glass.

Laughing, she turned her head and said something to her father, and the sight of her pure profile was like a blow to his midriff. He stared at her.

No, it wasn't possible. *It wasn't possible!*

Lacey. Lucy.

A black wig lost.

The same flawless, delicate profile.

Lucinda Richards was the elusive Lacey.

Chapter 7

Lucy had sent all her players back to their families and was reaching for her cloak when she saw Gregory Kenmore cutting through the crowd with a purposeful look on his face. Merciful heavens, he'd recognized her as Lacey!

She wrapped her cloak around her shoulders and bolted out the rear entrance of the church into the graveyard. But where could she go? The vicarage was close, but it was already filling with guests, and as daughter of the house, she'd have to help.

Could she flee to Chloe's house? No, on Christmas Eve she couldn't invite herself over even if Chloe was her best friend.

The church bells were ringing with jubilation, a soft, pretty snow was falling, and she was about to be cornered by a man who could turn her brain to porridge. A man she'd deceived.

She saw his broad-shouldered form emerge from the church. With an embarrassing squeak, she took off, thinking she could circle the church and lose herself among the departing worshippers.

But it was too late. By the time she'd darted through the

lych-gate that led from the graveyard, he'd overtaken her. He caught her shoulder in a firm grip. "So the elusive Lacey is really the very proper Miss Lucinda Richards."

She wished the ground would open up and swallow her, but the frozen earth didn't cooperate. "Yes," she whispered. "I'm sorry."

"Why did you do it?" His voice was stern, male, and utterly clueless.

"Because I was angry!" she said with sudden exasperation. "I'd thought we were friends when we were younger. In my evening prayers, I always asked for your safe return. Then you returned and didn't even call on my father, as would have been proper. I was delighted to finally see you at the Randalls' ball, until you looked at me like I was a *leper!* You scarcely managed a polite hello, you didn't want to touch my gloved hand in a dance, and after the dance you took off like a scared hare!"

He winced. "I suppose I did. You were so lovely, so refined. I didn't feel worthy of touching you."

But he'd touch a different sort of girl, she thought resentfully. "I heard you had jolly times at the Willing Wench, so I decided to see if you'd talk to me there. You did." He'd touched her, too.

"It never occurred to me that a well-bred young lady would work as a barmaid. You looked so different." Lucy's high-necked gown and heavy cloak disguised her figure, but his gaze dropped involuntarily to where Lacey's décolletage would have been.

"An old gown from the Bridges' attic assured you wouldn't look at my face and recognize me," she said tartly.

He wrenched his gaze back to her face. "So which is real—angelic Lucy who directs the Christmas pageant, or playful Lacey who listens so well?"

She bit her lip. "Both are. I was raised well and I enjoy working with the children, but I'm no bloodless angel. I liked being Lacey and having the men at the tavern think I was pretty. And . . . and I liked being kissed. Too much."

"A girl as lovely as you needn't lack for kisses."

With sharp clarity, she recognized that this was a critical moment. If she didn't show him her heart—and risk having it stamped on—she might never have a chance to be more than a baffling female to him. Voice shaking, she said, "I want only one man's kisses. Yours."

He rocked back on his heels, shocked to the bone that she could want him. But her hopeful, terrified expression was utterly convincing. "Lucy," he said, using the name he'd called her in simpler days. "Are you saying that you . . . you care for me?"

"I've been in love with you since you started coming to the vicarage so my father could teach you Latin and Greek," she whispered. Tears slid silently down her cheeks. "I knew I was too young, that I must wait until I was grown up. So when I prayed that you would come home safely, I also selfishly prayed that you wouldn't find someone else before I had a chance to persuade you to look at me."

"My darling, darling girl." He brushed the tears from her cheeks, then cupped her exquisite heart-shaped face in his hands. "You didn't really know me. I am not worthy of such devotion."

"I knew that you were kind and patient with a little girl, intelligent in your studies, respectful to my parents, and that you had a sense of humor," she retorted. "You were a young man worthy of any woman's regard."

He sighed. "Perhaps I was then. I'm not now. You learned that when we talked outside the tavern."

"I learned that you are a man who has suffered and survived and become stronger in the mended places," she said quietly. "I know you better now than I did, and care for you even more."

She was both Lucy and Lacey, he realized. A warm-hearted, well-raised vicar's daughter and a young woman who had seen enough of the dark side of life to learn wisdom and compassion. The connection he'd felt with her at the tavern was real and strengthened now that he saw her more clearly.

"Lucy." He bent and kissed her lips tenderly, tasting her sweet honesty. "Lacey." He kissed her again more deeply, feeling her strength and compassion.

She responded with innocent, intoxicating enthusiasm. He embraced her so that her soft body molded against him. He wanted to merge with her, protect her, worship her. *So this is love,* he thought dazedly, sliding his hands down her back.

He hadn't realized how far his hands had slid until she shoved him away and took off into the snow. After an instant of ice water shock, Gregory followed, catching up with her in a few strides. He caught her and drew her close, her back to his chest and his arms around her waist and shoulders. "Please don't run away!"

Before he could apologize for moving too quickly, she said tearfully, "I had to run. I'm a *trollop!*"

"Nonsense!" he retorted. "What gave you such an absurd idea?"

"I dressed like a trollop and went to a tavern and enjoyed it when men flirted with me." She gulped. "And I enjoyed kissing you far too much! My parents would be so disappointed in me."

He realized that Lucy, the vicar's daughter, was talking, and she didn't approve of Lacey's innocent but real enthusiasm. "Your parents enjoy kissing, or they wouldn't have had four children," he said soothingly. "While they wouldn't want you to kiss too casually, my kiss wasn't casual. I don't think yours was, either."

After a long silence, she whispered, "It wasn't. But I'm so ashamed of my behavior that I can't look you in the face."

He kissed the edge of her right ear, and she shivered deliciously. "Don't you know that every man's dream is to find a woman who is kind and good, but also passionate and beautiful? A woman just like you."

"I don't have any idea what men dream of," she retorted. "I certainly didn't understand why you were so rude at the Randalls' ball."

"I was rude because I cared what you thought." He cast about for an example to persuade her that she had nothing to be ashamed of. "I'm no expert on women, but my guess is that a girl interested in marriage would like to find a man who is devoted and faithful and will take good care of her and their children."

He kissed her other ear. "But she'd also want him to think she's the loveliest, most desirable woman on earth, and to be anxious to prove it. Am I right?" He slid his hand inside her cloak and rested it on her waist, careful not to move too high or low.

"That's what I want," she admitted shyly. "A man I can trust, but who also excites me. A man . . . rather like you."

"May I apply for the position?" he asked. "Just tell me what you want. A year's restrained courtship with no kisses? That would be difficult, but if it's what you want, I'll do my best to oblige."

She turned in his arms and gazed up at him, snowflakes frosting the dark hood of her cloak. "A courtship with no kisses wouldn't be very amusing, but are you sure, Gregory? I am young and inexperienced compared to you."

Knowing he must persuade her of her worth, he said gravely, "But you have learned wisdom at sickbeds and in helping with your father's parishioners. The other night your wisdom started the process of mending my broken places. I'm still not sure I'm worthy of your regard, but I am not fool enough to turn away from the most entrancing girl I've ever known."

Her eyes were wistful. "Does it cancel out if we each think we're unworthy of the other's regard?"

"I do believe it does," he said thoughtfully. "And now that we have that settled, shall we go to your parents' reception with enough stars in our eyes that everyone will immediately start forecasting wedding bells?"

"If you mean that," she said with a shining smile, "I'll be almost the happiest girl in England when we go inside."

He imagined seeing that smile across the breakfast table, and thought his heart might burst with joy. "Can I do anything that will make you the very happiest girl in England?"

She gestured at the tree above them. "This is an oak tree, you know."

"And . . . ?" he asked, not understanding.

She grinned and was pure mischievous Lacey. "And it's absolutely full of mistletoe!"

Miss Brockhurst's Christmas Campaign

Jo Beverley

Chapter 1

"It's going to be a sad Christmas with William so far away."

Penelope Brockhurst heard her mother's complaint, but couldn't look up from her quill work at that moment. "We'll do well enough with our friends here, Mama, and Prague is an excellent opportunity for him."

"Oh, yes, and at only twenty-six. I am very proud of him, but I understand they have a great deal of snow there in winter. I do worry about the children."

Pen's mother worried about all children—her own four, even though they were grown; her two grandchildren; a cluster of godchildren; and any other youngsters she met. She was the epitome of motherly, with an apple-cheeked face, a round figure, and soft graying hair under a large, frilled cap. She often wondered aloud how she'd come to have a daughter like Pen—lacking in curves, lean of face, and recently with her dark hair cropped into short curls.

"They'll revel in it," Pen said. "I remember when there was all that snow at Christmas . . ."

"And your father was home that time, and ordered sleds made. Such a shrieking and a yelling, and a wonder no bones were broken. Especially yours, Pen."

Pen glued the curl of paper in place and could look up. "My bones are no weaker than my brothers', Mama."

"I'm sure that can't be true, dear. Men are stronger in all respects, which is why ladies do not do such things as hurtle down icy slopes on a piece of wood . . ."

"I wasn't a lady then. I was only thirteen."

". . . or gallop horses, or climb trees."

"I don't climb trees anymore." Pen returned to her work, first pinching a thin strip of paper in the middle, then wrapping one end around a fine rod. That done, she wrapped the other half around another stick, striving to make both halves equal in tightness.

She had no idea why this fiddly work entertained her, for she'd never enjoyed stitchery or watercolors, or any other ladylike pastime, but it did, and it passed time on a cold November day. London presented endless amusements, even at this time of year, but one had to venture out to enjoy them. The cozy drawing room and a lively fire were much to be preferred.

"Christmas is so much more pleasant in the country," her mother said, returning to her theme. "I suppose we could remove to Lowell Manor. . . ."

She sounded hesitant, and no wonder.

"Without William and the family there, what would be the point, Mama? We are so much more comfortable here, and can enjoy the shops, amusements and our friends at the expense of a stroll or short hackney ride."

"I suppose that's true, dear," her mother said, but a few moments later she sighed. "I will miss Christmas in the country."

Pen thought that was the end of it, but a few days later her mother almost ran into the drawing room. "Pen! A letter from Mary Skerries!"

After a second, Pen put down the very complex curl she was attempting and smiled at her mother. Pray God she looked only bright with curiosity, that there was no sign of how her heart had thumped at the name Skerries.

"Is there exciting news?" she managed.

"What? No, no, not particularly. All is well at Cherryholt."

No deaths. Why Pen had first thought of a death, she had no idea.

"Marianne is married," her mother said. "You'll remember Marianne, dear, for she is only three years younger than you. Married to Lord Montdown. A very good match."

Her mother resisted a reproachful glance, which was noble of her. Marianne was twenty to Pen's twenty-three, but Pen languished unwed. She'd tried to do as she ought—three times. Which only meant she'd jilted three men, and was now apparently known in some quarters as Miss Breakheart.

Her mother had fallen silent.

"You seemed excited?" Pen prompted.

"Ah, yes." Her mother refolded the letter, looking uneasy. No, guilty? "I wondered . . . Pen, do you think it would be very incorrect to ask Mary to invite us to Cherryholt for Christmas?"

Pen's heart pounded again, and kept up the pace in a way that threatened her senses.

Mary, Viscountess Skerries, had been her mother's dearest friend since girlhood. Pen's father had been a diplomat, but her mother hadn't cared for distant travel, and in those situations she'd often removed herself and her children for a month or more to Cherryholt in Hampshire.

Pen had many fond memories of those times, but the ones that threatened her senses were of a person, not a place. Ross Skerries, heir to the viscountcy, almost the same age as she, and once her very best friend.

Go to Cherryholt?

Where Ross Skerries now was, to the best of her knowledge?

Oh, yes.

"I'm sure you could phrase it well, Mama."

"Perhaps . . ." But her mother peered at her. "Are you quite well, dear? You sound a little hoarse."

Pen swallowed and did better. "Quite well, Mama. We never spent a Christmas at Cherryholt, did we? I'm sure it would be delightful."

"Then I'll do it. I really can't bear to be in Town for Christmas."

Chapter 2

On December twenty-third Pen sat in a coach that approached Cherryholt, fighting to show only appropriate expectation of seasonal amusement and pleasant company. In reality, her heart and dreams sped ahead so brightly she was surprised they didn't light the way through the evening gloom.

"How lovely Cherryholt looks," her mother said, full of innocent delight. "It is a most gracious house, and with so many windows lit. . . ."

"Yes."

Ross might be in one of those lit rooms. Not all had curtains drawn, and Pen couldn't help looking, seeking.

She'd last visited here five years ago. Shortly after that, her father had retired, his health broken by some foreign fever. She and her mother had lived at Lowell Manor, caring for him, until his death nearly two years ago.

The boys had flown the nest to careers in diplomacy, the army, and the church, but there could be no career for a daughter other than marriage.

Mourning over, Pen's mother had set out to find her a husband, taking her to London, Brighton, Bath, and various house parties where eligible gentlemen might be found. The campaign had worked, except for Pen getting icy feet after the engagement was made.

Three times.

Miss Breakheart.

There'd be no more of that, she'd resolved, not now that she understood why she had been unable to go through with the engagements. The truth had struck one November day in Oxford Street.

She hadn't seen Ross in years. She'd been at Lowell, but she might not have encountered him, anyway. Mary Skerries's letters to her mother had told her he'd been enjoying manly pursuits—hunting in the shires, shooting at various estates around Britain, and managing the Irish estate traditionally allocated to the Skerries heir.

Even if nearby, they could be worlds apart. She'd visited Epsom racecourse in the summer, but she'd sat with the ladies far from the muddy areas where the men inspected horses and laid bets.

She'd missed her friend, but hadn't thought it more than that until that encounter in Oxford Street. He'd been carrying a number of packages, which he'd explained as commissions for his mother.

"Just back from Ireland," he'd said.

She supposed she'd made a sensible response, but something odd had been happening inside her.

He'd seemed older, in a way that improved a man of twenty-four. His cheeks had been leaner, and something or someone had polished him a little. He'd been wearing a cravat instead of a simple knotted cloth, and his boots had been polished.

They'd chatted about family and old times, but he'd not delayed. He was to set out for Cherryholt in a few hours.

Pen hoped she'd shown none of the turmoil inside, but a week later she'd broken off her third and, she vowed, last engagement to wed. How could she marry another when she'd been in love with Ross Skerries since girlhood? But how was she to attempt to win Ross, especially when he didn't seem to feel the same way about her? He'd shown no interest in lingering in Oxford Street, said nothing about meeting again in the future.

Now she was approaching Cherryholt, which would give her an opportunity, and she was resolved to capture the prize if it was at all possible. After all, some men, especially the sporting types, seemed slow to arrange marital matters themselves but happy enough when settled.

It was do or die. If she left here uncommitted, she would remain a spinster all her days. But by the Lord Harry, she'd be an adventurous one. Quill work could fill only a small part of a life. If England didn't offer her enough scope, she'd travel. Europe had to open to English tourists one day soon, and there were ever more distant places—Canada, India, Egypt, Araby.

Anywhere that was far enough from the Honorable Cardross Skerries.

The coach drew up beneath a porte cochere, and servants waited. Pen braced herself. She must show nothing of her thoughts and feelings, nothing.

As soon as they were inside the house, petite Lady Skerries rushed forward. "Ellie! It's been far too long since we were together, and even longer since we enjoyed your company here. And Pen, dear Pen. My, how you've grown!"

Pen smiled and accepted a hug, but inside she winced. She was rather tall, so perhaps she shouldn't have purchased a new bonnet as they were very high-crowned this season. Thank heavens she'd brought some French berets and turbans.

Lady Skerries and her mother chattered all the way to a handsome bedroom. "Here you are! I'll have washing water and tea brought to you, and of course you must command anything you desire. We dine at seven, but if you're fatigued . . ."

"Of course not," Pen's mother said. "I don't want to miss a minute of this pleasure."

Indeed, she looked younger, and in a way even young, as did Mary Skerries, despite the gray in her blond hair. There was an alchemy in long friendship.

Pen untied her foot-high bonnet, wishing she had a friendship like that, forged in childhood and strengthened by lives that followed a similar pattern. She had some childhood friends, but they were all married now, and with children, which seemed to fracture the bond.

But above all, from childhood the friend of her heart had been Ross. They'd been apart more than they'd been together, but it hadn't seemed to matter. Whenever they were apart she'd written him long letters, and he'd replied, if only briefly, with stories of school pranks, horses, or guns.

As they'd grown older, the letters had seemed to shuttle between different worlds, and when Pen's mother had hinted that she was too grown up to bother a young man that way, she'd ceased writing. She'd hoped that would inspire him to write of his own accord, but it hadn't. All connection had ceased except for the occasional mention in a letter from Mary Skerries to her mother.

But he was here now, somewhere nearby. When they met, when they talked, would it become like the old times, as it had with her mother and her old friend? Pen hoped so, but she wanted more. She didn't only want a friend.

Lady Skerries left, and Pen sat to comb her hair.

"I do wish you'd not cropped your hair, dear. It was such a lovely mass of curls."

"And tiresome to care for. See, a comb and I'm done." She surrendered the chair to her mother. "Shall I brush it for you?"

"Thank you, dear. I miss Peggy, but I didn't want to burden Mary with another servant, and Peggy will enjoy Christmas with her family."

"We can fasten each other's laces and buttons," Pen said, unpinning her mother's rather thin hair.

It had once been thick, she remembered, and dark like her own. Was this her future, but without husband, children and home? She might not look womanly, or always behave as society thought a woman should, but she wanted all those womanly things as much as others did.

But only, it would seem, with one man.

She drew the brush carefully through her mother's hair, making sure not to tug on a knot, and then recoiled it and pinned it in place before replacing the cap. If this venture failed, perhaps she should take to a cap herself. Oh, no, not that. A turban, perhaps, of rich silk with a cockade, but not a spinster's cap.

She'd look foolish in one, anyway.

She wasn't sure why she was different, but she always had been. Tomboy had excused it for years, but as she approached and then passed twenty she'd been described as an original. Soon, without doubt, she'd be an eccentric.

She liked her short hair, and she wasn't the only lady to adopt the style. Some ladies looked positively enchanting with a crop—like Sophie Ashby with her pretty, heart-shaped face and big eyes, or Miss Willoughby, who was considered a beauty.

Pen's face was not heart shaped or beautiful, however, and in truth would better suit a man. Her jaw was square, her nose long, and her lips did not form a cupid bow. Her mother chose to believe that a mass of hair would make her a beauty, but it wasn't so.

It had never mattered before, but suddenly it did.

Dreadfully.

No wonder Ross Skerries had never thought of her with

marriage in mind. If it would work magic she might have purchased a wig, but she remembered how she'd looked if she'd let her long hair hang loose—like a Restoration rake in full periwig.

She wasn't an antidote, she reminded herself. Three men had sought her hand in marriage, each expressing intense admiration. When she'd regretfully broken her commitment, each had claimed a broken heart.

Yet Ross Skerries had spoken to her in Oxford Street without looking slain by love, and he'd not sought her out afterward, in person or by letter.

Why was she even hoping?

Because when it felt as if life itself depended upon the matter, she had no choice.

Two maids arrived, one with hot water and the other with a tea tray. They set about unpacking as Pen went behind the screen to take off her traveling gown and wash. She'd worn no corset for the journey, for the dress was substantially made and she really didn't need one. Her small breasts sat high without needing to be forced up, and no amount of padding could make them look believably plump.

Setting aside the doldrums, she put on her robe and went out to enjoy her tea, but in truth she wanted to dress in her most becoming gown and begin her hunt.

Where was he?

How would he react when they met?

What would she do if he seemed hardly to notice her?

Behave as if nothing was amiss, she told herself sternly. She might not emerge from Christmas a bride, but she was determined to retain her pride.

She dressed for dinner and battle in a bronze silk gown delicately embroidered in gold. She'd put off whites and pastels years ago, for they'd never suited her, especially as she'd never taken enough care of her complexion to keep it pale.

Lord Thretford, in wooing her, had called her a pagan goddess in this gown. He'd called her a heartless harpy when she'd dismissed him, and she'd truly regretted any pain she'd caused.

She was heartily glad to be done with that business, even if she did remain a spinster all her days.

Chapter 3

Pen entered the drawing room with her mother, and again Lady Skerries hurried to them, this time with her tall, thin husband by her side. He greeted them both warmly and teased Pen, "Are you still as fearless a rider, Penelope?"

He probably expected a laughing denial, but Pen had abandoned polite lies with her whites and pastels. "Almost, Lord Skerries. Age makes us more aware of what there is to fear, so I'm perhaps a little less heedless."

He didn't seem upset. "Then we will have some fine rides as long as the weather stays clear, and you must make free use of the stables as you wish."

Lady Skerries took them off to meet her youngest daughter, Julia, who was still unmarried. Julia Skerries looked uneasy despite an elegant pale green gown, pearls, and an elaborate arrangement of her brown hair. Perhaps too elaborate for comfort.

When Lady Skerries took her mother off to speak with an old friend, Pen realized she'd been allocated to the young hopefuls. Where else did a twenty-three-year-old spinster fit, but Julia Skerries, only just seventeen, was staring at her as if she were indeed a pagan.

"That's a wonderful gown, Miss Brockhurst."

"Thank you. Yours is very pretty."

"But very conventional."

Pen smiled. "Time to be unconventional when you're older."

"Oh, I hope to be married well before then," Julia said, innocent of any intent to wound.

Pen had very carefully not searched the room, but now, as Julia chattered nervously about the Christmas festivities, and mistletoe, and the mummers who would come up from the village the next day, she allowed herself to look.

She almost didn't see him, for he was sitting down—beside a blond young lady in sprigged white. On the other side of the virtuous maiden sat a proud, beaming mama.

There might as well be a label over them.

Couple engaged to wed.

Bile rose in Pen's throat, and she quickly looked away before she disgraced herself. But by Hades—she was stuck here for twelve days in the torture of the damned.

". . . don't you think, Miss Brockhurst?"

She stared at Julia. "I'm sorry. I missed that. It is a little loud in here, isn't it?"

Julia Skerries surprised her. "I beg your pardon. I was chattering on about nothing. I'm terribly shy, you see. I know you used to come here in the past, but I paid little attention to older visitors, so you seem a stranger."

Pen admired honesty, being fond of it herself. "You've learned to cover it well."

"By chattering. I'm dreading going to London. I know it's nonsensical," Julia said in a confiding whisper, "but I sometimes can scarce bear to enter a room if it contains mostly strangers."

This was distraction, and Pen clamped onto it. "There's no way to avoid it, however, short of being a recluse. I don't think you'd like that."

"Not at all! I want to marry. I wish I were confident and vivacious, but wishing creates no miracles, does it? It's like the time I wanted to jump across the Cutty Brook. I wanted to so much, but I just couldn't."

"I almost failed at that, too," Pen said. "It's such a short distance, but the water flows so fast and deep, and people will tell stories about those who've slipped and drowned."

"True stories. A lad died there a few months ago. So it's really more sensible not to jump, isn't it?"

"Probably, but if we only do what's sensible, life's a dead bore."

Julia raised a hand to cover a giggle. "Mother said you had a reputation for being outrageous."

Pen felt her cheeks heat, and despite all her efforts, she was aware of Ross across the room as if he were calling her name.

"Oh, I'm sorry," Julia gasped. "My unruly tongue!"

"Nonsense, I am outrageous, as often as I can be. For example, my riding habit's cut in a manly style, complete with breeches." When Julia's mouth formed an O, Pen grinned. "I wear a skirt over them, but I like to ride astride."

The "Oh" escaped.

It was no good. She had to go over to Ross and the horrible chit by his side and discover the worst.

"If you're still willing to be seen in my company," Pen said, "perhaps you would take me around and introduce me to old and new acquaintances. I do remember Squire Purdue, though I'm amazed he's still alive."

"Ninety-two and still inclined to pinch the maids' bottoms. Very well, then."

Julia rose as if facing ravenous lions, but she did well enough at taking Pen around. Slowly they approached the sofa upon which Ross sat, smiling at his fair bride.

Pen felt able to ask, "Who's that with your brother?"

"Cassandra Gable-Gore," Julia said. "Ross may be marrying her."

May! Despite sanity, it filled Pen's head like a paean of hope. There was no commitment yet.

"Ross," Julia said, "you'll remember Miss Brockhurst, so I'll introduce her to Mrs. Gable-Gore and Miss Gable-Gore. Miss Brockhurst, ladies, an old family friend."

Pen did not appreciate the "old." The Gable-Gore chit looked no older than Julia and had a round-cheeked, short-nosed face that resembled a toddler's.

Both the Gable-Gore ladies were polite, but treated Pen as a strange creature—a Mohawk from Canada, perhaps, or a princess of India.

Ross had risen, and his smile was open and friendly—but not the tiniest bit loverlike. "It's good to see you here again, Pen."

First names. Was that promising, or a sign he saw her as a sister?

"I delight to be here, Ross. Cherryholt has always been one of my favorite houses."

"It is a very handsome house," Mrs. Gable-Gore said, managing to make it proprietal.

Pen turned to the infant. "Where do you usually make your home, Miss Gable-Gore?"

For some reason she'd expected the same shy style as Julia's, but Miss Gable-Gore was perfectly composed. "In Northamptonshire, ma'am, near Chipping Warden. My father's estate is called Shearing Manor. And you, ma'am?"

The "ma'am" was becoming an irritant. Pen wasn't a matron yet. "Our family home is Lowell Manor in Kent. We would have been Christmasing there if my brother had not been abroad with his wife and children."

Miss Gable-Gore's finely arched brows—plucked, Pen was sure—twitched. "Do you have a large family, ma'am? I am an only child."

"Three brothers," Pen said. "Alas, no sisters."

She hoped she was sounding cheerfully unaffected, but Miss Gable-Gore, only child, was a formidable challenge. Whatever the family had set aside for children would all come to her, and Pen suspected it was a handsome amount. The pearls the girl was wearing were very fine.

What sensible man would reject a pretty heiress in favor of an eccentric, aging spinster with a portion of only two thousand pounds?

What was more, Gable-Gore was the family name of the Earls of Maybury. No matter how far this branch lay from the main trunk, Miss Gable-Gore had aristocratic blood to match Ross's own.

"Do please excuse me," Pen said. "We must go on if I'm to meet the company before we dine." She dipped a curtsy and escaped. "What a cold fish," she murmured to Julia.

"She's a pattern card of respectability."

"A pattern card being a rectangle of cardboard. Flat and dry."

Julia giggled, but Pen reminded herself not to sink to spite, which would only reveal her feelings.

People were paired for dinner by precedence, so neither Pen nor Miss Gable-Gore secured the heir to Cherryholt. When seated at the table, Pen could have grinned with triumph. She was opposite him, whereas her rival was on the same side. Only two people separated Ross from Miss Gable-Gore, but it might as well have been a mile.

Of course the width of the grand table made conversation across it unlikely, but they could share smiles and other reactions throughout the meal. Crumbs for the starving, on her side at least. She fought the need to watch him constantly, trying to interpret every flicker of expression, but she succumbed enough to see how he had changed yet again.

When they'd met in Oxford Street, his hair had been carelessly trimmed, but now a neat Brutus cut revealed a noble forehead and gave his whole face more dignity. His dark evening clothes were impeccable; his cravat beautifully tied and secured with a glittering bronzish stone, which she knew would match his eyes if she could see them from here.

It also matched her gown. Had his eye color informed her choice of material? She feared she was heading for defeat here, but she wanted no one to know it other than herself.

She made herself pay lively attention to the gentlemen on either side, and could only feel relief when Lady Skerries signaled for the ladies to leave. She'd quite like to seek the sanctuary of her room, but the only way to survive this disaster was boldly, all pennants flying.

Chapter 4

Pen found herself again shepherded to the unmarried young, which now included the inconvenient heiress. She must *not* show how much she loathed the poor girl, for Miss Gable-Gore was not to blame for stealing Pen's man.

The youthful spinster group also included a rather monkeyish Lady Azure Finchley and a quiet Miss Cavendish. Lady Azure immediately insisted that everyone use first names, "For as I must use mine, absurd as it is, you must all suffer yours."

Miss Cavendish admitted to Caroline, Pen to hers—"and not Penelope, please!"—and Miss Gable-Gore, perhaps reluctantly, to Cassandra.

Though she must be under twenty, there was no hint of shyness about Lady Azure. "My mother's of a poetical disposition, and no one seems able to cure it. I have a sister Viridian and a brother called Madder. My father insisted on normal names as well, so Madder uses his second—George, though we all tease him by using the other. I like Azure," she declared, "little though it suits me."

"I don't think I'd care for such an unusual name," Cassandra said.

"Do you think Cassandra commonplace?" Pen asked. "A predictor of disasters, was she not?" *Stop it, Pen.* Quickly she added, "Not so bad as Clytemnestra, which besides being a mouthful is the name of a wife no better than she ought to be."

"Clytemnestra Ashby," Miss Gable-Gore said, flourishing her familiarity with the great, for the Ashbys were the family of the Duke of Tyne. "Sadly, she goes by Clytie."

Julia spoke up. "She could hardly insist on the whole of such an unwieldy name. I'm grateful to have a simple one. Have you ever thought of being Cassie, Cassandra?"

Pen bit her lip. She was sure Julia was innocent of all intent, but Miss Gable-Gore looked as if she'd bitten into an unripe gooseberry.

"I prefer complete names," she said. "After all, they must be what our parents intended. I will . . ." She accepted tea from a maidservant. "I much prefer Cardross to Ross."

Had she been about to say, I will insist . . . ? Perhaps there was more steel to the little Gable-Gore than at first seemed, and Pen didn't like the sound of that.

Lady Azure was asked to play the pianoforte and did so excellently. Julia followed suit. The Gable-Gore went next, choosing the harp. Competent but not gifted, Pen assessed, but far better than any performance she could supply. She'd never been willing to practice any instrument and declined when invited to play.

Cards were another matter.

Two tables were set up, and eight of the matrons sat to play whist. Pen enjoyed whist, but her group of spinsters numbered five, which would leave someone out. "We could play loo," she suggested.

Cassandra swayed backward. *"Gamble?"*

"Only for fish," Pen said "There was always a box of them in that cabinet there. Very pretty ones of mother of pearl."

"The principle is the same," Cassandra said. "Gambling is vice, pure and simple, no matter what the stakes."

"They're playing whist for tokens," Pen pointed out. "I do think it unwise to criticize one's hosts, don't you?"

Cassandra, cheeks red, rose and went to sit by her mother.

"Oh, dear," said Pen, sipping her own tea, "I only meant to advise."

Julia suppressed a giggle, and Caroline bit her lip.

Lady Azure asked the question. "Is she truly a candidate for your brother's hand, Julia?"

"I fear so."

Pen said, "Ross used to be very fond of gambling games, though never for high stakes."

"He still is. We all are."

Pen raised her brows in a question.

Julia shrugged, but unhappily.

Azure said, "Perhaps he seeks an antidote? I don't mean as in ugly, I assure you. Only that my brother married a very studious woman, when he never opens a book. It was as if he were trying to balance his lack."

"How goes the marriage?" Pen asked.

"Well, I suppose, but they are rarely in one another's company."

"Which is the key in many marriages, but it seems a shame to me."

"And me," Caroline said. "I will only marry where there is true communion of souls."

That seemed to Pen to be the opposite extreme, but she toasted Caroline with her cup. "Then I hope you find it."

Cassandra had returned to the harp. It was a pleasant enough noise, but when the men shortly entered the drawing room, Pen wondered if she'd deliberately presented herself well. She certainly sent Ross a sweet, blushing invitation.

For all her youthful sweetness, Cassandra Gable-Gore was as much on the hunt as a fox in the night, but she wouldn't catch Ross unless he well and truly wanted to be caught. Pen was resolved on that. She watched his reaction to the blushing smile. He smiled back and even gave a slight bow, but then wandered over to watch one of the games of whist.

Pen had the fight of her life not to cheer at Cassandra's momentary lapse into glaring fury. The girl was smiling again within a second, but she was all harpy underneath.

As was usual at Cherryholt, the men had arrived cheerfully awash with port and brandy, and brought the decanters with them, including one of Madeira, which Pen knew to be Lady Skerries's favorite. Lady Skerries had done the conventional thing and served tea, but now she accepted a glass of Madeira, as did Pen's mother. Even Julia took a small glass.

The Gable-Gores declined all the offerings, frostily. What pleasures did they approve of?

Pen requested brandy, which was on the edge of scandalous, for it was definitely a man's drink, but it was her declaration of war.

Love could take strange paths, but she couldn't imagine Ross being happy with sanctimonious Cassandra Gable-Gore. Even more importantly, she couldn't imagine Cassandra would be a comfortable addition to Cherryholt. As the heir's wife, this would be her home, and in time she would rule here.

Lord Skerries called for more tables to be set, and the players shuffled around so that the partners were a man and a woman. Pen watched as Ross went to the harp to invite Cassandra to play, concealing a smile as he received a reproachful refusal.

Instead of sitting beside his lady, as she was sure was the plan, he came over to her. "Pen, you enjoy whist, don't you? Come and partner me."

"When so masterfully commanded," she said rising, "how can I refuse?"

He grinned. "Did I command? Your apologies, my dear Miss Brockhurst. Of your kindness please partner me in the game. You know how much I enjoy it, and there's a table awaiting another couple."

Pen went with him, and with extraordinary willpower she did not glance toward the harp, which was now being played in rather ferocious style. She was sure that if it had suddenly become a bow, an arrow would transfix her, and perhaps him.

"Do you still do archery here, Ross?" she asked.

"Of course. Might be a bit nippy for it, though."

"It wouldn't deter me," she said as she sat.

"Did anything ever?" he said, and took the seat opposite, happily oblivious to all danger.

Chapter 5

Pen woke early the next morning and slipped out of bed without disturbing her mother. A glance outside showed a clear day with only a light frost. Splendid for riding. And the fact that Ross might feel the same was only part of the reason that she put on her habit, glad not to need help. Not wearing a corset could sometimes be a great advantage.

She carried her boots downstairs so as not to wake anyone and only put them on in the hall, sitting on the steps.

Ross caught her at it, coming down the stairs behind, dressed for riding.

"Two minds with but a single thought," he said, grasping the heel of the right boot to help her stamp fully into it. They'd done this sort of thing for each other in the past, but Pen was aware of her light skirt falling back to expose her leg. A leg covered in breeches, but all the same . . .

He might, she thought resentfully, notice.

He picked up the left boot and held it for her as she put that one on, then offered a hand to help her rise. She didn't need it, but she took it, relishing the firm grip.

"I see you clomped through the house without a thought for others," she said.

"Heir's privilege."

They walked to the back of the house, and as they passed near cellars and storerooms the familiarity of Cherryholt wrapped around Pen like a shawl.

"I do like this house," she said spontaneously. "I always have."

"It is pleasant, isn't it? I count my blessings for being the heir."

"There's a responsibility, too, isn't there? To preserve it."

"Just as it is?" he asked as they walked down the flagstoned corridor by the kitchen. "It's not a museum."

"No, not that. But the cozy warmth. The welcome to all."

In other words, you dolt, not to bring a wife here who'll curdle it.

"Ah, that, yes," he said, opening the door for her, but then he paused to inhale. "Crisp fresh air."

Pen gave up the campaign for now. "It's going to be an excellent Christmastide," Pen agreed as they walked on toward the stables. "Clear starry nights and crisp sunny days for greenery gathering. I gather the mummers are to come tonight?"

"It wouldn't be Christmas Eve without them. You've never been here for Christmas, have you?"

"No."

"That seems odd. You're such a part of the family. I think you'll enjoy our Christmas. We do it in the old style."

What does "family" mean?

"Do the Gable-Gores know that?" Pen asked. "About the old-style Christmas?"

"I don't know. Why?"

"Miss Gable-Gore seems to have some strict principles."

"She does, doesn't she?" he said. With approval?

Caroline Cavendish might have told a relevant story. Was Ross choosing a bride to balance his lack, in this case a lack of sobriety and high principles? What a disaster that could turn out to be.

They entered the stable yard, and grooms ran out to take their requests.

"Side or astride?" he asked her.

"Astride, of course."

He grinned. "You haven't changed. I'm glad." He called for two horses, both with regular saddles. Pen knew hers would be a match for his so they could race.

"I'm sadly out of practice," she said. "We've lived in Town for four months since Will went abroad. Mother doesn't much care for an empty Lowell."

"Not surprising. Your brother's set on a diplomatic career like your father's, then?"

"Yes, and it doesn't fit well with being a landowner. Father bought Lowell for his later years, but then didn't enjoy many, and none in good health. It was never a family home like Cherryholt."

A thickness in her throat startled her. By Hades, she wouldn't cry, but why had she never realized how much she loved this place? How in a way it had always seemed her real home?

"What is it?" he asked. "You look sad."

Pen swallowed, shaking her head. "Silliness. Just that Lowell needs better. It should be cherished as your home is."

"True enough," he said as the horses were led out. A rangy bay for him and a white-socked chestnut for her. She stroked the chestnut's nose, greeting it. He boosted her into the saddle, where she settled, getting the feel of the horse and its nature. Well behaved, but ready to go.

They walked the horses out of the stable yard, then trotted past the kitchen gardens out onto the sweeping grass of the estate, where they loosed them into a canter.

Pen was so exhilarated by the perfect ride that all other thoughts blew away, until they reined in on a rise, with Cherryholt below, comfortably solid with smoke rising from the many chimneys.

"What would you change?" she asked him.

"Change?"

"You said it wasn't a museum. What would you change?"

"The water supply. There are many improvements available. And I'd like to find space for some indoor toilets. Not in my father's lifetime, however. He thinks that extremely unhygienic."

"I agree."

"More so than chamber pots?" he challenged.

"They are emptied and cleaned outside."

"An unpleasant job."

"Many are."

"Shouldn't we reduce the number of unpleasant jobs?"

"Goodness, have you become a reformer?" she asked.

He smiled. "Not politically. I've become interested in some practical matters. Farming ones, too."

Pen couldn't resist, though she knew she should. "What does Miss Gable-Gore think of indoor toilets?"

"No need for her to be involved in such sordid stuff."

But no concern over talking to me about it?

Pen managed not to say it, and indeed, she was glad he could talk to her about the things that interested him. That didn't, apparently, have anything to do with whom he married, which was ridiculous.

"She does favor a wall," he said as they walked the horses back down the slope.

"Around the estate?" Pen asked.

"With a wrought iron gate."

"I like the openness."

"There's a couple of rights of way pass through, anyway, so I don't see the point."

Pen suspected that Cassandra would wall them off, too, if she had her way. Many landowners were trying to cut off access to their land, but Pen didn't like the idea, and she doubted Ross did, either.

They picked up speed again and raced back to the stables. They were soon strolling back through the kitchen area shouting orders for a hearty breakfast before heading for the morning room.

Pen halted in the doorway. The Gable-Gores were there, partaking of tea and toast.

Ross gave them a hearty good morning, which seemed to pain both. Pen did the same, wishing them to the devil. She had no doubt that the ladies normally breakfasted in their room, at home and away, as most people did. This room was small, and the table could only seat eight.

The only explanation for their presence here was that they'd seen her and Ross out riding and taken measures.

Coffee arrived, and she poured some for herself and Ross, who'd taken a seat beside her, opposite the Gable-Gores.

"You must come out riding tomorrow, Cassandra," Pen said. "Glorious weather for it."

"I don't ride," Cassandra replied.

"What a shame. We must start your lessons."

Mrs. Gable-Gore entered the fray, stating, "My daughter *does not ride.*"

"No reason why she should," Ross said agreeably. "Carriages and roads are so improved, many people don't care for it these days."

"But there's riding for pleasure," Pen said. "I know you enjoy that, Ross. And it's the best way to go around an estate."

Servants came in with two beefsteaks and a mountain of toast that would mostly be eaten by Ross. The steaks were nicely bloody in the middle, and Pen ate her first mouthful with appreciation, also relishing a slight shudder from Cassandra.

What else would make her shudder?

"Christmas Eve," Pen said. "So exciting. When do we go out to gather the greenery, Ross?"

"In the afternoon, so the light will be going as we return." He smiled at Cassandra. "We light lanterns and carry them back, singing 'The Holly and the Ivy,' which builds the Christmas atmosphere."

Cassandra's smile was slight, and Mrs. Gable-Gore was unreadable.

"Light in the dark is such an important part of *Yuletide*," Pen said, tossing in the pagan name as if tossing sticks on a fire. "Do you bring in a Yule log?"

"Not as such," he said. "We don't have a big enough fireplace for a real one that would burn the whole twelve days, but we light a large log in the drawing room after the mummers leave, and when it burns down, it's replaced."

"Perhaps you should enlarge the fireplace in the hall," Pen said. "A true Yule log is supposed to bring good fortune to the house all the year long."

Mrs. Gable-Gore spoke up. "I'm afraid that is superstition, Miss Brockhurst."

"Tradition," Pen corrected cheerfully. "Where would we be without the old ways?"

"I doubt anyone will enlarge the fireplace," Ross said. "It would need structural changes to the house."

"Alas," Pen said, "but Cherryholt is so perfect it would be a sin to change anything. Anything at all. Don't you agree?" she asked the two Gable-Gores.

"Nothing can remain unchanged forever," Mrs. Gable-Gore said. "Only think of bells. In my girlhood most houses had only handbells and it was necessary to bellow for a servant. The pulls that ring a bell in the servants' hall are a great improvement."

Pen had to grant her the right of that, and switched back to traditions. "Do your mummers here do Saint George and the Dragon?" she asked Ross.

"No, the local tradition is Robin Hood and the Turkish Knight."

"Wonderful."

"Especially when well fueled by punch and mince pies, both mummers and audience. What mumming traditions hold in your part of the country, Miss Gable-Gore?"

Cassandra sat dumbstruck.

"There are no such practices at Shearing Manor," her mother said, "and I'm not surprised that Cassandra is distressed. I have to say, Mr. Skerries, that many of the practices here seem pagan."

"Pagan?" he asked, surprised.

"The mummers don't go back so far," Pen put in, "but mistletoe is connected to the Druids, Ross. I think that's what's meant. And holly and ivy, too, I believe. Of course Yule is the ancient festival of light in midwinter, with practices to ensure spring and summer will come again."

"And a good thing, too," Ross said. "Wouldn't care for never-ending winter, now, would we? In any case, Christmas was popped on top of the Roman Saturnalia, which was a very racy affair. At least we don't re-create that."

The Gable-Gores excused themselves and departed.

"I don't think they're too comfortable with your traditions," Pen pointed out.

Ross cut into the remains of his steak. "Once they've enjoyed it, they'll be charmed. What's Christmas without a bit of fun?"

"Pagan fun in particular," Pen said, well satisfied with her work. "More coffee?"

She filled his cup, imagining future mornings like this, if she married Ross. A brisk ride, a hearty breakfast, and the two of them, talking about everyday matters.

As for her rival, surely Cassandra Gable-Gore must be realizing that Cherryholt would not suit her at all.

Chapter 6

When Pen returned to her bedchamber, her mother was sitting in bed, enjoying her breakfast from a tray. "Riding, dear? I know how much you enjoy it, but I wish you wouldn't go out alone."

"I rode with Ross." Hot water arrived, so Pen went behind the screen to undress and wash. "Cherryholt seems to observe all the old Christmas traditions."

"Lovely, dear, as long as I don't have to go out into the cold to take part."

"I'm sure you'll be excused. But when we bring back all the greenery, you can help arrange it. You've always been clever at such things."

Pen washed, put on her robe, and came out from behind the screen to find a suitable gown for the day.

Her mother said, "We did have some pleasant Christmases when your father was home, didn't we?"

"And when he wasn't. You always made a merry Christmas for us when we were young."

"A family Christmas is so important. Such a shame there aren't any children here. When Ross marries a new cycle will begin."

Pen hunted for a clean shift, considering stays or no stays. She might as well be conventional. She added those to the shift, then chose a green woolen gown.

Her mother had finished her breakfast, so she climbed out of bed. "Let me help you, dear, and then you can help me."

"The Gable-Gores don't approve of Christmas traditions," Pen said, wanting her mother's reaction. "Yule logs, mummers, mistletoe boughs."

"Then why are they here?"

"I think Miss Gable-Gore has hopes of Ross Skerries."

Her mother tugged on laces. "I wondered about that, but I don't think they'd suit."

"She plays the harp well."

"That hardly contributes to a happy marriage. I noticed that neither joined in the card games."

"They don't play cards," Pen said, imitating Mrs. Gable-Gore's tone.

"How very odd." Pen's mother knotted the laces. "I'm sure Ross has too much sense to choose a bride who won't enjoy his home. After all, he is the heir."

Pen put on her green gown, which overlapped and fastened at the front, and then helped her mother dress in a pretty lilac shade. With the addition of warm shawls, they were soon ready for the day, and set out for the drawing room.

They found all twelve of the ladies in the house party were gathered there. It was well warmed by the large fire, but the distant corners remained chilly, so everyone gathered in the center.

Conversation was general and cheerful, but most ladies had needlework to occupy their hands. Pen wished she'd brought her quilling, though it would have sent her off to the table in a chilly corner.

Cassandra smiled at her. "Do you not have your stitchery with you, Miss Brockhurst?"

"I'm no hand at it, I'm afraid."

"What a shame," Cassandra said. "I could teach you."

So, she was a worthy opponent. Pen was glad of it, for she intended to rout her completely.

"How kind," Pen said, "but *I do not sew.*"

Cassandra flushed. "How is that possible?"

"I never cared for it."

"Perhaps you paint," Mrs. Gable-Gore suggested.

"Only walls," Pen replied. "I achieved a lacquered room at Lowell."

"I much admire the Chinese style," Lady Azure said. "When I have a home to decorate, I shall attempt that."

"It's a dilemma," Pen said, "isn't it? Whether to respect the way a house is or change it to suit fashion. The room I painted was a bare one with no pleasing features at all. There's such a fashion now for tearing out paneling. Of course, it is always dark. . . ."

As she'd hoped, Cassandra took the bait. "We are in agreement there, Penelope. I have seen cases where it's been painted a pale shade to a much lighter effect."

What a shame Lady Skerries wasn't here to note that.

"Yet the patina of old wood is of value," Pen said. "Once painted over, it would be lost forever. As I said, a dilemma. But I see no uncertainty over a handsomely plastered ceiling such as this one."

Everyone agreed on that, and talk wandered the ways of house design and decoration, ancient and modern.

Pen felt satisfied with her small skirmish, and after luncheon would come the gathering of the greenery. She had great hopes of that.

* * *

As it played out, battle began at the informal meal, for Cassandra won the seat beside Ross and said all the right things about the delights of Cherryholt, both building and company.

Yes, a worthy opponent.

When the meal ended, she kept hold of his arm, and her mother went up to get her cloak. Pen wouldn't put her mother to such trouble, so she went for her own. When she returned to the hall she had one satisfaction. Her own cloak was red, lined with fur as dark as her hair. Cassandra's was a soft fawn color lined with gray. It made her look rather like a mouse.

All the same, Ross showed no sign of minding, or of admiring Pen's bolder style.

Damn him.

There were ten in the party when they left the house, agreeably balanced, two by two, with the five unmarried ladies, each carrying a basket, escorted by five bachelors. Cassandra had Ross, and Pen was with a Mr. Hawley, a Skerries cousin.

Lady Azure seemed pleased with a military man, Captain Skerries, and Julia by a neighbor only a little older than herself, Mr. Passmore. Quiet Caroline seemed well suited by Doctor Scott, even though he must be in his thirties and the oldest of the unmarried group.

Pen was well enough with Mr. Hawley, who was cheerful and amiable, but she made sure to walk just behind Ross and Cassandra so she could hear some of their conversation. It seemed bland at the moment, and she was sure Cassandra was being very careful, but perhaps the pagan merriment would lead her to dig her own grave.

As they entered the orchard, Ross began a traditional song.

> *"Hey ho, the mistletoe*
> *It's off to the greenwood we do go.*
> *My lady fine and I."*

Unfortunately he sang it to Cassandra, who smiled up at him as if he'd declared eternal love.

Mr. Hawley sang the next verse to Pen.

> *"Hey ho, the mistletoe bough,*
> *That a daring lass stands under now*
> *To tempt the man in her eye."*

She looked up and saw that she was indeed beneath a spray of berries. It would only be in fun, but she didn't want to kiss Mr. Hawley here, in front of Ross. . . .

"Now, now," Lady Azure said, "mistletoe only gives kissing privileges when it's hung indoors, sir. Then, we'll all be willing to tempt, for it is our duty, isn't it, ladies?"

There was a carol of agreement, but Pen noticed that Cassandra didn't join in.

Time to strike. "You don't agree, Cassandra?"

"Agree?" Cassandra asked, smiling with lips only.

"That it is every single lady's duty to grant mistletoe kisses."

"As you push me, Penelope, I must admit, I think kisses sacred to marriage."

"You don't think them proper between a betrothed couple?" Pen asked, trying to sound simply surprised.

"A firm engagement to wed allows for more intimacy," Cassandra agreed. "Of course that presents problems if such an engagement is broken."

Oh, a neat shot.

"Three times," Pen said, choosing a bold defense, "which does mean three intimacies. But I cannot hold mistletoe kisses in the same respect. They are public, light, and only for amusement. I do hope you change your mind, Cassandra, as I'm sure do all the gentlemen."

A couple of the men, insensitive to nuance, agreed heartily. Ross was unreadable, but said, "We need ladders, gentlemen. Ladies, baskets at the ready."

He propped his ladder against one tree and climbed up. "Now, Miss Gable-Gore, which sprig of mistletoe may I cut for you?"

Pen gave Cassandra credit. She pointed to a branch that was heavy with berries, and as the afternoon progressed, she added holly, ivy, and laurel without complaint.

Yes, a formidable opponent, and very determined to catch Ross Skerries as husband. It seemed strange to Pen that any lady chase a husband whose life and pleasures were so at odds with her own, but she supposed a viscount was a viscount, and a coronet a coronet.

They paused to gather up some pine boughs that had already been cut, and finished in the herb garden, snipping rosemary. The gentlemen had already lit the lanterns, for the sun had set, and they did make a warm light as the party began the procession back to the house, singing "The Holly and the Ivy." Cassandra did seem to join in, perhaps because the traditions had been given a Christian twist.

> "The holly bears a blossom as white as any
>   flower,
> And Mary bore sweet Jesus Christ for to be our
>   sweet savior.
> Oh the rising of the sun and the running of the
>   deer,
> The playing of the merry organ, sweet singing
>   in the choir."

As they crossed the open lawn, Pen moved herself and Hawley alongside Ross and Cassandra. "How is Christmas observed at your home, Cassandra?"

Pen sensed she'd scored a hit, but Cassandra answered. "More quietly, I must confess. We do not decorate."

"Not at all?" asked Hawley. "Shame, that. Adds to the spirit of Christmastide. I'm sure you enjoy a jolly dinner, though."

"Of course. Roast beef and goose, and the company of the vicar and his wife."

"You'll find it much more fun here, Miss Gable-Gore. You'll be able to take the traditions back with you for next year."

Pen struggled with laughter. Unawares, he'd fired a cannonade, for Cassandra was surely thinking of the sobriety she could bring to Cherryholt next Christmas—as Ross's wife.

Chapter 7

Once back in the house, everyone welcomed the cups of hot punch offered to warm their bones, and soon the indoor party was helping to spread the greenery around and constructing mistletoe boughs.

"At least three," Lady Skerries declared. "One for the hall, one for the drawing room, and one for the servants' hall. Ah, mince pies!" she declared, as a footman came in bearing a huge platter. "Hot from the oven and well laced with brandy. Pen, come and have one."

Pen bit into it carefully, but it was just warm enough rather than hot enough to burn. "Delicious, Lady Skerries. The best I've ever tasted."

"It's the brandy, dear." Lady Skerries hurried over to Cassandra, who was waving the platter by. "You must try one, dear. It's tradition."

Cassandra obeyed, but there was something in the way she bit into it that promised retribution one day. Mrs. Gable-Gore was sitting as audience, smiling blandly, but she waved on the platter of pies. Such a fear of inebriation! It was surprising that they drank wine with dinner.

Ross was organizing the hanging of holly high on the

walls, ignoring the pall that hung over the future of his home. As Cassandra had lost her grip on him, however, Pen took her place.

"I like the addition of pine," she said. "Along with the rosemary, it gives such a lovely smell."

He smiled. "It's always Christmas to me. Are you enjoying yourself?"

"Splendidly."

"Where did you spend last Christmas?"

"At Lowell, and it was lovely, because there was William, Anne, and the little ones, and a few neighbors up for Christmas dinner. My father only bought the place twenty years ago, however, so we don't have deep roots. We were invited to other houses around the area during Christmastide, however. That's where I met . . ."

She bit that off.

"Lord Thretford, your most recent conquest."

"Yes. Christmas can make fools of us all, so be wary, if you please."

"Did you recover your wits on Twelfth Night?"

"Hardly, as I persisted past Halloween." *When I met you again.* To break the silence, she said, "I'm done with such follies, however. No more foolish commitments for me."

"A sad loss to men everywhere," he said, and she longed to take her words back, or to say, *"Not you."*

And here came Cassandra, brightly smiling. "How lovely all this is, and evergreens are a symbol of eternal life, aren't they?"

Pen went off to help make the kissing boughs, afraid that her future was slithering through her fingers, beyond any power of hers to halt and grasp. What if Ross didn't feel anything other than friendship for her? What if he truly loved Cassandra, despite her prissy ways?

The punch kept coming around, and Pen kept drinking.

Eventually, all the greenery had been placed around the

main rooms, and the three kissing boughs were finished, each heavy with berries and entwined with red and green ribbons.

Lord Skerries made a great business of hanging one in the drawing room, and then tugging his wife beneath it for the first kiss. "And thus," he declared, "the bough is rightly brought to life!"

Amid laughter, Ross carried the other into the hall, where it would hang from the bottom of the chandelier.

"I'm like to get dripped on by wax," he complained as he climbed the stepladder and tied the ribbons.

Pen watched, realizing he would now choose some lady for the first kiss. Cassandra had positioned herself nearby, and her eyes were bright with expectation. Pen couldn't bring herself to fight for the honor.

Ross descended and looked around. "Miss Gable-Gore, I won't offend you by proposing an unmarried kiss. Now, who won't mind such a thing?" He looked around. "A sister? That will not do. An aunt?" he asked, stepping toward one laughing lady. "No, no." He turned to Pen. "You won't be offended, will you, Pen?"

He tugged her beneath the mistletoe and put a firm, warm kiss on her lips.

Their first kiss.

Offended? Pen felt completely overset, but as they stepped apart, she made sure to smile brightly. "Thus the bough is rightly brought to life?" she said.

"Vividly," he said, smiling around. "Come, ladies and gentlemen, make merry with it until the berries are all gone."

There was much dancing around as ladies young and old pretended to try to avoid the mistletoe but allowed themselves to be caught, but the Gable-Gores had disappeared.

Soon everyone went up to the drawing room, where a light supper was laid out, along with wine and more punch. There was also tea, perhaps especially ordered by the Gable-

Gores, who sat, safely distanced from the mistletoe, sipping in sober virtue.

Pen couldn't settle to this conventional gathering.

She'd been kissed by other men, and more thoroughly, too, and often enjoyed it. None of those kisses had had the electrical power of that brief press of lips to lips, and she was finding it hard not to follow Ross with her eyes as he went around, chatting to one and all.

Even though it left the field to her rival, she escaped. She went toward her room, but feared someone might look for her. She walked past the door and to the end of the corridor, but almost collided with a maidservant on an errand. Cherryholt wasn't a large house, and it was full of guests and servants.

Then she remembered the roof. She returned to her room to get her cloak, then found the narrow stairs that led up to the attics. There was a door there that led onto a walkway around the roof.

She stepped out into crisp cold that made her breath puff white, but it was lovely up here, and completely safe despite the dark. The walkway was wide enough for two, and a waist-high wall stood between her and a fall.

She looked up at a sky full of stars, many as bright as diamonds. She knew some must be planets, but she didn't know which. Was it stars that twinkled or planets? There was the Christmas star, brightest diamond of them all, guiding all true hearts to Christ's birthplace.

This was a Christian festival, but it was a pagan one, too, and rightly so. Now, in the darkest time of the year, when night fell upon them at four and held its grip until eight, without the moon and the stars people might give up hope. No wonder they embraced fire, with its golden warmth from lantern, candle, or log, and had so since ancient times.

Yule, the great festival of faith and hope, along with the

evergreens, a reminder that life existed even in the cold and dark.

The Gable-Gores and their like were wrong. People like them would strangle the true spirit out of Christmas and leave everyone the worse for it. She wouldn't let it happen here.

She was startled out of her thoughts by singing and the ringing of small bells, and then she saw bobbing lights coming up the drive. The mummers were approaching.

Chapter 8

Pen paused in her room to shed her cloak and make sure she was tidy, then ran down to the hall where the mummers were just arriving. Everyone at Cherryholt had gathered to see the performance, including the servants, who lined the walls.

There were some chairs for the older people, but most guests stood, and some were on the stairs for a better view. Pen spotted Julia, Azure, and Caroline and joined them.

"Splendid costumes," she said.

"They're treasured and augmented over generations," Julia said. "The Turk's helmet is a real one, brought back from some travels by one of my ancestors."

The Turkish Knight was a splendid figure in long black robes, the pointed helmet, and a sword on an embroidered belt. He wore a dark beard and mustache and a long, dark wig. His magnificence was just a little undermined by him being mounted on a hobby horse.

Robin Hood was a fine young man in Lincoln Green, with a longbow and quiver of arrows.

"That's Tom Fletcher," Julia said, "and his bow's real. He wins championships."

"Excellent. He can kill the dragon."

There was one—a small dragon attached to the Turk by a chain, and clearly a man on all fours with a long snout on front and a very long tail behind.

Robin Hood had a Maid Marian in tow—a lad in a long flaxen wig and a vastly overstuffed gown.

"Why is Maid Marian wearing a helmet?" Pen asked.

"Because she's also Britannia."

As the play began, recited in rhyming couplets, Pen let herself look for Ross and for her rival. Cassandra was sitting beside her mother, which was bad of her, for she hardly needed the comfort of a chair. She looked delightfully peevish, probably because Ross was nowhere near her. Where was he?

Then the Turk approached her, declaring,

> *"Now here's an English maiden, it would seem*
> *Ideally suited for my infidel hareem!"*

He made to grab her, and Cassandra screamed, flailing at his hand.

Amid laughter, Robin Hood leapt to the rescue.

> *"Unhand the wench, you dragon-loving beast!*
> *You'll take no Englishwoman to your hareem feast."*

The play moved on to interact with others, but Cassandra was in tears and her mother led her away.

"What a widgeon," Julia said. "As if she was in any danger."

"Serves her right for sitting with the older people," Azure said, "presenting such a juicy treat. I wish he'd tried to raid up here."

"He normally does," Julia said, "and we make a play of it, the chosen maiden pretending to be afraid and calling for help. It goes on a little while."

Pen felt sorry for Cassandra, who hadn't been prepared, but if she'd ended up in that situation she wouldn't have re-acted so foolishly.

"Here comes Robin Hood's song," Julia said. "We all join in the refrain."

All the mummers, in their motley costumes, began a stamping dance in a circle around the knight.

> *"So here's a knight from distant lands*
> *Come here to eat us all-oh!*
> *But Robin Hood so bravely stands*
> *To defend us all, forever-oh!"*

Robin Hood turned to the audience to encourage every-one to join in.

> *"And it matters naught who assails our land,*
> *French, Dutch, or Spanish, or dragons-oh!*
> *True men of England will always stand,*
> *To defend us from invasion-oh!"*

Next came a verse about the French, with references to Napoleon worked in, and everyone belted out the refrain with particular vigor. Pen realized that Azure was singing *"true women of England,"* so in the next refrain, after a verse about the Armada, she did the same.

But then she whispered to Julia, "Where's Ross?"

"Gone to soothe Miss Gable-Gore?"

Pen searched the room frantically. Could he really be doing that, and perhaps being inveigled into a formal pro-posal? She shifted to work backward and escape. Ross wasn't going to be caught in Cassandra Gable-Gore's sticky web. . . .

Julia grabbed her arm. "Don't leave now. It's the fight!"

Insisting would create another scene, and surely minutes wouldn't matter.

Robin and the Turk were fighting with a great clashing of wooden swords. Robin slew the dragon, which rolled to lie on its back, legs in the air. The Turk fought on, however, until Robin tripped him and drove his sword through his heart. Or, in fact, between arm and chest.

Everyone applauded, the dead came to life, and the mummers began their begging song to end the event.

> *"At Christmas be merry and thank God for all,*
> *And feast thy poor neighbors, the great and the small.*
> *Yea, all the year long have an eye to the poor,*
> *And God shall send luck to keep open thy door."*

Baskets were passed and the gentlemen all tossed in coins—Lord Skerries was particularly generous. . . .

But then Pen noticed the Turkish Knight. He'd taken off his helmet, which had the black hair attached, and was peeling off the mustache and beard. It was Ross!

Julia laughed. "I knew you'd not want to miss that. He's been playing that part for years. Come on."

She led the way down the stairs and through the crowd where guests were admiring and rewarding the mummers, but by the time they reached the other side, Ross had gone.

"He'll be changing back to English gentleman," Julia said. "Come along to the drawing room. We'll play charades soon."

Pen smiled, but said, "I really do need to go to my room."

She saw Julia understand that she needed the chamber pot and not try to delay her, then she was free to hurry upstairs. There was no enduring this longer.

> *True women of England will always stand*
> *To defend us from invasion-oh!*

Cassandra Gable-Gore was a vile invader to Cherryholt and must be opposed. Ross Skerries was Pen's man, and must be won. After that kiss, there was only one way to bring the matter to the point—another, and much more passionate, kiss.

Pen knew which room was Ross's, for as the heir and only son he'd moved down from the schoolroom area at twelve. In innocent youth they'd often gone to his room to discuss a plan, or inspect a captured insect with his microscope.

Perhaps it was those memories that made her walk in without knocking. "What on earth were you doing to upset . . . ?"

She froze, dry-mouthed, at sight of his bare chest. He still wore his breeches, fair enough, and stockings below, but he was stark naked from the waist up.

Chapter 9

"What on earth are *you* doing?" he asked, but mildly. Then he added, "If you're coming in, come in."

Dazed and dumbstruck, Pen shut the door behind her.

"You have a complaint?" he prompted. Was he looking amused, damn him?

Pen straightened and pulled herself together. "You should have known better than to terrify Cassandra Gable-Gore like that."

"I'm surprised you leap to her defense."

"I . . ." Pen abruptly remembered her purpose in coming here. It was a great deal harder when confronted by a half-naked man, especially one whose half-nakedness was so splendidly . . . masculine, with the outline of muscles and . . .

She jerked her eyes up to his. He was laughing at her!

"You can't marry her," she said, then winced. That wasn't how she'd meant to put it.

"Why not?" he asked, picking up his shirt from the bed.

No, don't put it on yet.

"She doesn't suit Cherryholt."

"Is that my main duty?" he asked, simply holding the shirt.

"It has to be a principal duty, yes. I don't know why you're even considering her."

"Temporary madness."

He'd spoken softly, and she wasn't quite sure she'd understood.

"Temporary?" she asked.

"Perhaps a different madness," he amended thoughtfully. "Why is this your cause, Pen?"

She remembered her purpose, her bold purpose. It had seemed simple when it had shot into her mind like lightning. Now, here, it wasn't simple at all, but it was the only way. She couldn't endure uncertainty anymore.

She walked up to him. "Kiss me."

He glanced up. "No mistletoe."

"We don't need mistletoe. Kiss me, Ross."

"No," he said. "You kiss me."

She frowned into his eyes, surprised to find them guarded.

Very well. It wasn't so huge a challenge, except that she felt she should put a hand on his arm or shoulder, but they were bare, and she couldn't.

She went on tiptoe and kissed him.

"A mistletoe kiss," he said, but smiling now. "You can do better than that."

That was a challenge, a true challenge. She put one hand on his shoulder, his warm naked shoulder, and the other at his nape to draw down his head. Then she tilted her head as she put her lips to his, parting her lips in invitation.

He accepted, pulling her tight against him and deepening the kiss so they seemed sealed together. Plighted. Betrothed.

She'd never been kissed so passionately in her life.

He tumbled them onto the bed and was over her, between her sprawled legs but with layers of cloth safely between them. The position made hot kisses even more delicious, though, and when they rolled so she was on top, it was even better.

She looked down at his bright, bronze eyes and ran fingers through his short, springy hair. "You see. You can't marry her. It wouldn't be right."

"After this, the only right course would be for me to marry you."

"Yes!" But then she had qualms. "No, Ross. I'll never tell, and we've not done anything truly . . . committed. So you mustn't feel . . ."

"Idiot," he said, and pulled her head down so he could kiss her again, rolling them again until she was trapped beneath him. He gripped her wrists on either side of her head.

"It seems to me we should do something that would be truly committed."

Pen felt her eyes stretch wide. *"What?"*

"We're going to marry, yes?"

"That's not quite . . ."

"Backing out already, Miss Breakheart?"

Hurt, she struggled, but she couldn't get free. "Let me go!"

"No, never. That's the point, Penelope Brockhurst. You said yes, you agreed that we should marry, and this time you're not getting cold feet about it."

"I will if I want," she spat, "and there's nothing you can do about it!" His earlier meaning suddenly struck her. "Even if you rape me, you . . . you . . ."

He let her go and rolled off the bed. "Of course I wouldn't do that."

Pen scrambled to a kneeling position. "No? What else did you mean, then?"

"That we could do what we want so much to do, that's all! Admit it, Pen. Why else did you come here?"

She tried to hold the glare, but he knew her too well, and she was too honest to fight it. "I came here to win you, yes. You've been driving me mad these past days."

He surged forward to lean arms on the bed, his face only

inches from hers. "You've been driving me mad for years! I'd pluck up my courage to try my luck, and you'd commit yourself to some other man!"

"I . . . Why did you never *say* anything?"

"I do have some honor, you know. I couldn't pursue a woman pledged to another."

"What about Miss Gable-Gore?"

"I have a duty to the line, to fill a legitimate nursery, so I decided to put an end to the madness. She seemed suitable."

Pen sat back on her heels. "I've been very slow, Ross. I'm sorry. I chose men who seemed suitable, and then I couldn't do it, but I didn't know why. I hardly ever saw you in the past years," she added in defense.

"And I couldn't believe you'd be interested in a rough-and-ready type like me. Is it my improved appearance that's made the difference?"

"What? No! I do like your hair short, but it makes no difference to me." He'd opened his heart to her, and she knew she must take the same brave step. "You weren't so elegantly turned out in Oxford Street, but that's when I really knew."

"You were betrothed to Thretford."

"I broke it off the next day."

"Before I heard that, I invited the Gable-Gores here for Christmas."

"I resolved never to accept another man's offer."

"Does that include mine?"

She smiled. "No."

He touched her chin. "Another broken promise."

"That's not fair!"

"Fair or not, I'll have your word, Pen. Here, now, just the two of us. That from this moment it will be as if we were married, till death do us part, with no possibility of breaking the bond."

"Ross!" she objected, tears in her eyes. "I'd never jilt you."

"You can't blame a man for being nervous about it. Your promise, Pen."

"In blood, then," she said. "Remember how we did that once—made a blood pact over something? We'll seal it in blood."

He laughed and went to his desk to return with a pen knife. "Just as we did before?"

Pen remembered, and went hot at the thought. At thirteen their toes had often been naked as they waded in streams or even ran across dewy grass, and a nick in a toe would only be what adults were always warning about.

Toes were still not terribly risqué, but she continued to blush as she untied a garter and rolled down her right stocking.

"Green stripes," he said, "and a red garter. How deliciously Yulish—and bold."

Pen glared at him, still hot-faced, but at the look in his eyes she couldn't help but grin. "And even pagan?"

"A man can always hope."

He pulled a chair close to the bed and took off the white stocking on his right leg. Then he jabbed the point of the blade in the outside of his big toe. He held out his hand and she put her heel into it. She winced as he stabbed her, but then they pressed their cuts together.

"Bound in blood," he said, as he had in the past, "never to be parted."

Pen smiled at him. "A bit tricky to dance if we stick together like this."

"And tricky to do other things." He had his handkerchief at the ready, and when they parted he dabbed the blood away on both.

Pen pulled up her foot to look at the wound. "Stopped bleeding, but if it starts again, how do I explain it?"

"A pin in your shoe."

He was smiling in a particular way, however, and Pen realized she was sitting on the edge of the bed, right ankle on left knee, showing a great deal that a gentleman wouldn't normally see. She smiled back before slowly restoring decency.

"And thereto we plight our troth?" he said.

Pen slid off the bed. "Stop this, Ross. I only jilted those other men because they weren't you! It's always been you."

He took her hands. "It's always been you, but we men are often even slower than you women. My parents will be delighted. I hope your mother will be, too."

"Of course. She adores your mother and Cherryholt."

"I was thinking that she might like to come to live here once we're married. I know there's Lowell Manor, but I don't have the impression it's a true home."

"Oh, I'm sure she'd love that! Bother it, you've made me cry, you wretch. I'm not a watery sort of female."

He hugged her. "I know that. You see, everything falls into place when the central pin is inserted. We are that pin."

"What of Cassandra?"

"I'm sorry for any dashed hopes, but she'll find a man more in tune with her nature, especially with her handsome portion."

"You don't mind that mine's small?"

"I'd take you without a shilling and consider myself the most fortunate of men."

"Tears again! But you surprise me with your eloquence, indeed you do!"

"You bring out the gift in me. But we really should return to the company before a search party is sent."

Smiling, they separated to restore their clothing. Pen delighted in adjusting his cravat, even though he probably didn't need her help.

"Do we tell anyone?" she asked.

"What better way to celebrate Christmas? Anyway, love, I doubt we can hide it as we both have stars in our eyes."

She went into his arms, simply resting there, in the most perfect place in the world. "I'm not sure I deserve to be this happy. I came here to win you."

"Did you?" He tilted her chin up to his. "Then may I claim a forfeit?"

"That depends what it is." But then she said, "No, I'll not constrain you. I deserve a penance."

"I hope it won't be that, but will you grow your hair again?"

"My hair? It makes me look like a Restoration rake."

"Then perhaps I have a taste for Restoration rakes."

"That, sir, would be decidedly off. But if you insist, then yes. It'll take years, but I'll grow it down my back again and suffer the consequences."

"And the pleasures. I'll adore your hair, all tangled around your enchanting, naked splendor."

Pen was dry-mouthed again, and hot in a different way, with a burning desire she'd never experienced before. She glanced toward the bed.

He took her hand and dragged her to the door. "Come, wench, but of your mercy, name a date soon."

Pen let him tow her out into the corridor. "With a Special License, we could be wed by Twelfth Night."

And so they were, and the mummers returned to celebrate the union, playing lovers' parts this time. Robin Hood had his Marian, and King Arthur his Guinevere. Saint George had his princess, and King Edward his Eleanor.

Pen and Ross said their vows beneath the mistletoe in the hall, on which one berry had been preserved to permit the couple's first married kiss.

The company enjoyed the Twelfth Night feast, and everyone was in the merriest spirits because the sour note—the Gable-Gores—had left on Saint Stephen's Day, complaining that they found the pagan nature of Cherryholt uncomfortable.

After the feast, Lord Skerries and some of the other men went out to fire guns in the orchard to salute the trees and ensure good harvest in the coming year, but by then Pen and Ross were in their marriage bed, hoping for a harvest of another side.

"Perhaps there'll be a child here next year," Pen said, contentedly in her husband's arms. "The perfect addition to Christmastide in the country."

INTRIGUE AND
MISTLETOE

Joanna Bourne

Chapter 1

Snow came down in flakes the size of cake crumbs. Determined snow. Heavy, abundant, enthusiastic snow that had finally blocked the progress of the York-to-London coach with drifts the height of a full-grown man. Stubborn snow that showed no signs of stopping.

Elinor Pennington followed the dark shape of Mr. Broadleigh's back down the narrow path cleared to the front door of the inn, watched her step on the packed ice, and sought consolation in the classical philosophers. Despite extensive acquaintance with Seneca and Marcus Aurelius, no useful quotations came to mind. The Romans didn't have much to say about snow.

Maybe she should use her ill-gotten gains to move to Italy. It was warm there.

The inn was close-fitted, ancient gray stone. It looked old enough to have been in place when Roman legions marched up this road, planning mayhem on the Picts. She'd lay money the oldest parts were here in the Middle Ages, serving monks and King's messengers and cattle drovers headed for points south. It was a ghost of a building this afternoon, the stones only a shade darker than the falling snow, the windows black squares that seemed to float in the general white. Someone had twined evergreen and holly around the iron post that held the lantern beside the door, a reminder it was only three days to Christmas.

She entered the inn called the Laughing Wench with a cold wind behind her and noisy confusion ahead.

The hall was crowded with unhappy people and haphazardly stacked luggage. One of the maidservants, in cap and apron, climbed the stairs, balancing the weight of a heavy pitcher. A bow of red ribbon decorated the newel post.

Elinor tucked her hands under her cloak. Miss Trimm and Jeanne Dumont, the other two women from the coach, sidled in behind her.

A male voice snapped, "Out of my way." A gentleman in a fashionable driving coat elbowed her in the back. He pushed past and stomped snow down the hall to confront the plump innkeeper. It was a young man, barely in his twenties. "What a Hell of a day. I want your best chamber and the private parlor. Be quick about it."

A proud and exigent gentleman. His carriage had barreled into the yard while the common stage was unloading. He'd barely missed running down the passengers as his carriage jockeyed into place at the door. Now it seemed he had no intention of waiting in line.

"Don't you worry. I'll find a place for you, sir. We'll find a place for everyone. Ned, take that red case to the Crescent Chamber. We'll put—"

"What are you standing around for? Show me to my room. God save me from a pack of country idiots." The gentleman took his hat off and slapped it against his side, scattering snow. "I want dinner early. Chicken or pheasant, if you have it. And send some brandy up."

"Well, now . . . If I had a room, it would be yours." The innkeeper spread his hands expressively. "We're full up, as you can see. More than full. We're bursting at the seams, but

I'll fit you in. You'll be sharing with the gentlemen from the coach. Inside passengers, sir. Only the—"

"I do not intend to share my chamber with a pack of louse-ridden clodhoppers and greasy clerks."

The front door slammed open. Sharp wind sent fingers of cold down her neck. Everyone shuffled aside to let a pair of the inn's servingmen stagger past, carrying a trunk between them. Cries of "Close the blasted door" came from the public room to her left.

"That goes in the Star bedroom." The innkeeper pointed. "Same for the bags of them other men off the coach. That's the black bag and t'other one beside it. The ladies' bags go in the front—"

"If this filthy hovel doesn't have enough rooms, you can damned well evict the rabble." The young gentleman would have a private room or know the reason why. He didn't give a devil's farthing what a plaguey innkeeper wanted. "Do you know who I am?" he demanded.

"That I don't, sir. I never seen you stop at the house before. You'll be in the Star room, on the right at the top of the stairs. Just follow yer trunk up." The innkeeper turned away, still imperturbably polite, to deal with Mr. Broadleigh, another demanding patron. The fashionable gentleman's trunk bumped up the stairs to a room he would share with four or five of the clodhoppers and greasy clerks gathered around him. A neat serving maid crossed the hall from some kitchen in the back to the public rooms at the front, carrying a tray with bowls stacked on it.

"He is very tiresome, is he not?" The French girl, Jeanne Dumont, came to stand beside Elinor. "The so-demanding gentleman of such importance who travels without a valet."

"I noticed. He has debts in London, I should think."

Jeanne patted her workbag carefully, checking that her stitchery was safe inside, and tucked it under her arm. "One can always tell."

"The innkeeper can too. No fool."

They exchanged grins. They'd become Jeanne and Elinor to each other during the journey. When passengers are stuffed in a coach like neighboring herring in a barrel, they reach a certain informality.

She liked Jeanne, who had a sly, cynical sense of humor. She was very young, no more than sixteen, surely. She was one of the many desperate French émigrés who had come to England in the last few years, fleeing disorder and the guillotine in France. Jeanne was to take up work in London, she'd said. "I shall be a nursery governess, not a full complete governess. I am very ignorant, you understand. I know nothing of this business. But, then, the children do not either, so we may struggle along together."

The other woman in the party, stiff, fierce, white-haired Miss Trimm, joined them. "There is no private parlor," she announced. "To be more precise, there is one, but it's being used by three gentlemen to sleep in. However much I approve of the practicality of this, I deplore the lack of propriety. We must take our meals in the public room. The place seems respectable enough at first inspection. We will sit together." She nodded. "There. He's taking our bags up. We should wash before dinner. In any case, our presence is not needed here."

Miss Trimm, having laid down the law, followed the inn servant up the stairs, keeping an eye on her valise.

"I am entirely intimidated by that woman," Jeanne said. "It is very cowardly of me, is it not?"

"Not at all. She'd intimidate the North Wind."

"It is a good day to do that." Jeanne glanced to where the inn door had opened again, letting in weather and the thump of boots. She paused infinitesimally. Then she said, "That is a handsome man, I think."

Oh, to be so young and lighthearted that one was still struck by a handsome stranger. Jeanne showed her extreme youth sometimes, and her Frenchness. Would it be one of the servants who caught her eye or another traveler, stranded by the storm?

She turned to see the man Jeanne admired.

She wouldn't have called him handsome, herself. Impressive was a better word. He was just closing the door behind him, a tall man with square features and ordinary brown hair. His eyes were the deepest possible blue. She didn't have to see them to know that. He brushed snow off the shoulders of his greatcoat and came around to survey the hall as if he owned the establishment and were making one of his periodic inspections. He looked from face to face, piercing in his attention, till his gaze came to her.

Her heart hit in big thumps in the hollow of her chest. She would have sworn every sound in the room went silent.

She didn't look away. He wouldn't make her look away.

Maybe some spark of emotion crept into his bland expression. It was . . . what? Triumph? Relief? It didn't matter. He was a genius at putting lies on his face.

His interest moved smoothly onward around the room. She realized only a second had passed.

Jeanne said, "It is not a bad thing to have a handsome man to look at during breakfast. I am fatigued beyond words with the grim scenery of this countryside. And our fellow travelers are not prepossessing, are they? I wonder who he will turn out to be."

"We'll never know." She didn't wait for Jack to strip out of his gloves and take his hat off and stroll calmly over to confront her. "I'm going upstairs."

In the background, the young fop continued, "I am Mr. Rossiter, nephew to Lord Brampten. I could buy your sordid little pigsty of an inn and not notice the cost. Do you realize that? I'll have your name, my good man. We'll see whether . . ."

There must have been fops and fools of exactly that type in the Roman provinces, two thousand years ago, and innkeepers as imperturbable. And perhaps a young poet. He'd be poor, like the shabby student who'd taken an outside seat for the journey to London. There would be a pretty young wife involved in this somewhere.

She began rewriting that exchange between Mr. Rossiter and the innkeeper in her head, in Latin, as she climbed the steps.

Chapter 2

Snow fell in her dreams. They were deep, confused dreams where she felt herself still moving. She swayed and bumped endlessly in a coach and the other passengers were animals wearing frock coats and bonnets. They changed from dog to wolf. Wolf into bear. Bear to leopard. Outside, the landscape was composed of vast piles of Belgian lace.

On the seat beside her, the leopard became a fox, knitting a long scarf in many colors, holding the needles in neat red paws. "You tell lies," the fox said softly, "in Latin. I admire that." It had a French accent.

The stork spoke with Miss Trimm's voice. "The place seems respectable enough at first inspection, but nobody can be trusted." In the dream, this seemed rational for a stork to say.

In the dream, Elinor's hair writhed around her as if it were blown by the wind. Her pale, straw-yellow hair grew till it was a curtain she hid behind. She had to part it with her hands to look out. "Nugator tells lies. It's not me. It doesn't count."

The fox laughed, already changing. Already half a cat. The mouth and whiskers were a cat's mouth and whiskers.

"I'm the one who says what counts." The bear on the forward seat reached the great pad of his forepaw across the carriage. He covered her face and she couldn't breathe.

She fell out of the dream, thumping down, cold and trembling, into reality and night.

A hand clamped over her mouth. A body, heavy as lead, held her down, muffled her in the blankets so tightly she couldn't break loose. Couldn't get her hands free to claw at him. The strength was huge, hard, unfightable, male, infinitely strong, and it surrounded her everywhere.

He muttered into her ear. "It's me, dammit. It's Jack. Hold still and listen!" The fire had died low and orange. She saw images of it in his eyes.

It had been two years since they touched, but her body remembered. She went still.

The timbers of the old inn creaked and groaned like the hull of a ship in high seas. Outside, winds twisted and howled and pulled at the glass of the window. The draft up the chimney was a shrill, intermittent whine. In the big bed in the corner, Miss Trimm snored determinedly. The French girl slept silently in the trundle bed.

"You know me now," Jack said. "You'll be quiet?"

She nodded. Oh, she knew him, all right.

His hand went away, but he didn't. He stayed, covering her with his weight, looking down. He had the same hard eyes. Even when she'd been in love with him, she'd always seen the hardness in his eyes and wondered about it.

When he was satisfied she'd be silent, he jerked his head once in the direction of the door and let her go. Noiseless, he lifted himself away from her and was gone into the dark of the hallway.

She didn't stop for decent clothing and modesty. That was a barn door that couldn't be locked again. She took up her wool dressing gown from where it lay across the end of the cot, put her feet into her slippers that were keeping warm next to the fire, and followed him.

The floorboards were ice cold. She could feel it through the soles of her shoes. The hall was darker than the room. At the far end of the corridor, the window was a gray square of light. The innkeeper had left a lantern burning at the front window of the inn. A little light filtered a story upward through the snow.

Jack wasn't even an outline in the blackness. He sank into it somehow.

She said, "You practice hiding in the dark, I suppose."

"Constantly."

No way to tell where the man began and the darkness ended. She didn't even hear him breathing. She followed where his voice had been and her outstretched hand touched the soft of his clothes. This was a sleeve. This, the front of his jacket. His hand, when it came up to cover hers, was warm.

She drew back. "How did you find me?"

"I asked the maidservant an innocent question about who was sleeping where tonight. You'll be pleased to know she said you were a respectable lady and I'd best not trifle with you. I didn't say I knew—"

She closed her fist and punched, hard. It was pure, uncalculated impulse.

She wasn't fast enough. Her fist slapped into the palm of his hand, not his belly. He caught the blow before it landed. His hand closed around her fist and held her.

"That's new," he said. "There was a time you wouldn't have hit a man. You've changed." He sounded calm about it. Thoughtful.

"I'm not trusting and naive anymore. You made me very, very wise. I'll ask again, how did you find me?"

"The coaching company. You're listed as a passenger."

"What?" She shook her head.

"In York, six days ago, I sent men to look at the names of everybody who'd booked passage to London. And there you were. Elinor Pennington." She felt him move. Even knowing exactly where he was, she didn't see it. "What have you done, Elinor? What are you mixed up in?"

Of all possibilities in the world, this was one she hadn't expected. Jack, hunting her down, full of suspicion. A huge shiver grabbed hold and shook her. Her dressing gown was warm enough in her snug rooms in London but no match for the countryside in the dead of December. "I don't even know what you're talking about. I'm going back to bed. Don't sneak into my room again."

He shifted his hold on her. Took her wrist and didn't let go. "I was so sure you weren't involved. Was I wrong? Were you part of that business, all along, working with your uncle?" He didn't give her a chance to answer. "We can't talk here. Come downstairs."

"Give me one reason to go with you."

"You can't yell at me here."

Oh, but he was so bloody sure of himself. She knew, just knew, he was smiling. "Fine." She twisted her hand free—he didn't stop her—and stalked ahead, skimming the backs of her fingers along the wall to find her way. She tripped a little on the first step. Stumbled again where the stairs turned at the landing. She ignored Jack's hand on her arm. She didn't need him to help her.

On the ground floor, there was light, a long strip of it under the door to the public room. That was where they were headed. Jack skirted round her and opened the door. "In here."

It was marginally less cold. She walked down a long, narrow, white-washed room, reeking of smoke and ale, ancient and recent. The ceiling was low and crossed by black oak beams. At the far end, where the fire was banked on the hearth, Jack knelt to pile bricks of peat into the ash, on top of the live coals.

He didn't look up as she came close, just went on with building up the fire. He said, "I looked for you, Elinor. There is not one corner of this kingdom I didn't have men out, combing the bushes for you."

"I was in London."

"Where there are few bushes indeed. That accounts for it." He rearranged chunks of peat, laying them on the flames that licked upward, using his fingers as if the fire didn't dare burn him. "I looked in London."

"It's a big place." And he wouldn't have thought to look for Elinor Pennington in the rookeries of Whitechapel.

The warmth drew her to the fire. Maybe the chance to talk to Jack drew her just as much. She edged forward to the stones of the hearth and wrapped her arms around her. The cold pressed in from every direction. "I spent hours planning what I was going to say to you if ever we met again."

"I had a few choice comments saved up myself. Maybe we'll get around to them."

Jack rose to his feet. He hadn't changed at all in these two years. He was a solid, muscular man of wide shoulders and narrow hips. He still wore his hair a little too long, as if he couldn't be bothered to keep it tidy. Stark lines marked out his cheek and jaw and a wide forehead. It was an ascetic, intelligent face. He'd passed himself off as a scholar when she knew him in Oxford.

He pulled off his coat and settled it over her shoulders before she figured out what he was up to. "Put this on."

It was dark gray wool, warm on the inside. Jack had always given off heat like a stove. "I don't want this."

He set one of his boots on the iron fire basket and scowled at the fire. "Humor me. You're more eloquent when your teeth aren't chattering."

She didn't want to accept even this small kindness from

him. But she didn't follow her first impulse and let the coat slide off and fall to the floor. That would be silly and melodramatic. It was a cold night. Somebody should make use of a perfectly good coat, and Jack wasn't going to. He knew she was too sensible to let it go to waste. He was a master at manipulating people.

Even when she'd been in love with him he had really, really annoyed her.

"You ran from me in Oxford." He hacked the words out in little blocks of anger and set them down in a neat row. "I told you to stay put. I told you I'd come back and explain."

"I had a full collection of lies from you, Mr. Tyler. Bushels full. Quite sufficient, thank you." That was her own careful array of sarcasm. He'd left himself in shirtsleeves and waistcoat. He must be freezing. Good.

He looked at her sideways. "After everything we'd done, you couldn't wait three days to hear what I had to say."

"You were going to tell me you were a spy for the government. You would explain that you'd used me to worm your way near my uncle. You'd say how very important it was. Maybe you'd thank me for helping you."

That silenced him for a full three seconds. He stood glaring. "Your uncle was the center of as vicious a nest of French spies as I've ever seen. He might be harmless, but they weren't. I was disposing of that lot, some of them armed, when you took off. I told you, 'Give me a day or two.' I said, 'I'll explain every damn, bloody thing you want.' "

"You came to arrest my uncle. If he hadn't got away, you'd have dragged him off to the gallows."

"Don't be ridiculous." He pushed away from the fireplace and began pacing back and forth behind her. "We don't kill men for being political idiots. We leave that to the French. Do you think the government wants the most respected Latin scholar in England thrown in a London prison, churning out political tracts and writing letters to the *Times*? Sending him to France was the smartest thing I ever did."

"Hah!"

"Who do you think warned him? I sent that boy to get him out of Oxford. How do you think an idiot like your uncle crossed the Channel in the middle of a war?" He stopped behind her and talked to her back. "When you disappeared, I thought you'd followed him to Paris. I thought you were alone, trying to get across France through the fighting."

She'd braided her hair for the night. It hung down in front of her in two long plaits of pale, nothing-colored hair. She tucked the braids, one and then the other, under the coat that covered her. "My uncle didn't want me with him. My political opinions are commonplace, you see. He explained that while I was packing for him."

Her uncle had emptied every penny from the bank. He'd taken the housekeeping money. And the rent. And the change in her purse. The landlady evicted her that afternoon. It had been a difficult day.

"You should have waited," Jack said. "You should have trusted me to take care of you."

"Oddly enough, I didn't believe you." The fire was making a determined fizzing sound as steam blew off. Smoke crouched in gray hillocks, hugging the sharp edges of the cut peat, before the draft took it up the chimney.

Memories were insubstantial as that smoke. Jack Tyler wasn't going to hurt her again. The Jack Tyler she'd believed in had never existed.

She looked up and found him watching her steadily. She was wrong in thinking he hadn't changed. The features lit by the fire were the same, but he'd stripped a layer of disguise off his expression, now that it wasn't needed anymore. His voice sounded rougher at the edges.

Jack Tyler, in Oxford, had been diffident and a little shy. He'd been so charming. She would never trust charm again.

This man looked ruthless as barren countryside.

"How did you survive?" he asked softly. "You were alone. I know your uncle took every penny of your inheritance with him when he ran to France. Now I find you prosperous, well dressed, traveling comfortably. Who pays for this?"

She could have laughed. The girl he'd lied to so easily was gone. He was dealing with a wickeder woman. He wasn't ever going to know how she made her living. "I pay my own way."

"What were you doing in the north?"

There was tension in the words that didn't match the simple question. Uneasiness crept along her nerves. "I had business there."

"Which is?"

"My own. It doesn't concern you."

"I'm not your enemy, Elinor."

The coat, pulled around her, suddenly felt like being held in Jack's arms. Memory rose up everywhere in her body. Being held by this man had been so easy. So completely natural. She remembered feeling his strength through the linen of his shirt. Remembered rubbing her cheek against his hand while he stroked her and they lay together, side by side, in the fields near Oxford.

Damn him for smudging even that small, pretty dream, the one lovely image she'd rescued from the debacle. "You didn't rouse me from a warm bed to ask why I went to York. What do you want?" She shrugged, and Jack's coat caressed her on every side, making all kinds of promises of warmth and protection. Even his clothing lied. "You're not going to apologize. I'm not going to forgive you. What can you possibly have to say after all this time?"

In a single sleek movement he closed the space between

them. He set his fingers to turn her face so the firelight would fall on it. "Willen Castle. Lord MacClaren. The list."

"I don't understand."

Heartbeats passed, flowing through her in a moment that stretched long. His expression held and held, then subtly changed. He said, "That means nothing to you. Your eyes are clear as glass."

"After all this time, I'm still a transparent fool. Thank you."

He wore a heavy gold signet ring. He hadn't had that in Oxford. When he lifted his hand and set her hair back from her forehead, reddish light slid along the band of the ring. The palm of his hand was warm and dry where it touched her skin. The gold was like ice. "You cannot imagine my relief, *Amica*."

"Don't call me that." *Amica* meant friend in Latin. Hearing it now was unendurable. "Don't pretend we're still friends."

"We are, though, whatever I've done to you." He stroked through her hair. "You're made of loyalty. Did you know that? You can't turn it off like a tap when you want to. I need your help."

"No." She ducked her head away from where he touched her.

"Let me tell you why I'm here. There's a message in code. We know it's headed south, right now, written in a book or on paper. It'll be a long string of number or letters. I need to intercept that."

She didn't care.

He went on, just as if she'd answered. "I've been chasing French agents up and down Yorkshire. There's a party in Paris that thinks we're on the verge of a homegrown English revolution. They're sure if they put an invasion force ashore, the countryside will rise and march on London."

"The Stuart prince thought the same. He was wrong."

"I have most of the Frenchmen arrested, but they made a list of sympathizers in the north . . . and men the French thought they might convince. Innocent men and guilty ones and a number in between. We know the list left York on the sixteenth, on the London coach."

Her coach. "You thought I had it." Pain closed in.

"Stop that." He tapped her shoulder impatiently. "I saw your name. I've ridden three days without stopping to get to you."

"You think I'm a traitor, working for the French."

"Not for one minute. Not for a bloody instant. But I had to get to you." He looked unutterably weary. "For so many reasons." Her mind filled up with imagining him, his coat collar turned up, leaning into the wind, and the storm getting worse. York·was a long, hard ride away from here, even in good weather.

He whispered, "I was afraid one of your uncle's damned French friends had talked you into running an errand for him. A harmless errand, delivering a letter. You would have handed it over to another French agent who wouldn't have one reason to leave you alive."

"You think I'm a fool."

"I think you're frighteningly intelligent. Lying to you took all my considerable reserves of cunning, and that was when you were nineteen. I hate to think what it would take now. But you're trusting."

"Not anymore. I've finished with that."

"You're an untrusting woman who meets me in the middle of the night. Alone. Unprotected." He surprised her then. Amazed her, in fact. Swiftly, lightly, he leaned toward her. Kissed her on the lips. It was a brief clap of thunder wrapped in a great astonishment. It left not one single thought in her mind. Not one.

He said, "Go. Get back to bed. You better leave the coat

behind. You don't want to explain how you got it. And lock your damn door. There's a French agent in this place."

She still couldn't think. She held the back of her hand to her mouth and rubbed. "Don't do that again."

"I won't do it in a public room in the middle of the night. Not when I'm exhausted and you're freezing."

This seemed a good time to retreat in disorder. So she did.

She thought he muttered, "I can wait," but she was halfway to the door, and she might not have heard him correctly.

Chapter 3

She woke to knocking on the door. Since her cot was closest, she dragged herself out of bed. Jeanne Dumont, on the trundle bed, was a blanket of two rounded humps and a graceful hand extended over the side of the bed. Miss Trimm slept on her back in the main bed with her mouth wide open, snoring magnificently.

It was dawn. It was, if anything, colder than it had been in the night. Her bare toes curled up from the floorboards, protesting, as she crossed to the door. Her breath frosted out as she leaned over to turn the key in the lock.

The door flung open to the maid and clopping footsteps and a country dialect. There was a breathless, "Oh, miss, I'm so sorry," and "Ever so sorry, mum" for Miss Trimm. "The landlord asks, could you please come to the kitchen." Yes. All of them. Something had been found in the kitchen fire. Ever so strange.

The maid disappeared to tap on the next door down the hall and deliver the same message.

So much for lying abed in the quiet and frigid dawn, brooding. She'd planned that for this morning—a long session in bed, cocooned in blankets, feeling resentful and mis-used. It was not to be.

They'd left the pitcher of water in the corner of the hearth, the warmest spot in the room, but still had to break ice on the surface. This time of year, the washing water was melted snow, not drawn from the well. It had a wild, piney scent to it.

Miss Trimm washed first, sponging herself off under a voluminous nightgown. But Jeanne nonchalantly stripped naked in front of the fire. That made it easy to follow suit. Then it was fumble into a cold shift and her blue dress that stuck to her damp skin. She turned to let Jeanne fasten up the buttons in back. Then it was wool shawls all round.

The kitchen was at the back of the inn in a separate wing, down a dogleg in the hall and past a thick oak door. Inside was overwhelming noise, heat, and the smell of bacon.

A dozen men, including all her fellow passengers from the coach, were gathered at the long central worktable. Burned papers lay in a row on a ragged bedsheet—a rolled newspaper, quite black and unreadable, half-burned books, and a charred letter. There were perhaps ten specimens in all. The innkeeper stood at the far end, frowning down at the piles of black, shaking his head and muttering.

Jack stood behind him, leaning on the bricks surrounding the hearth. He looked as if he'd wandered in to ask for an early cup of tea. As if he had no part in the proceedings. But the list he'd come seeking must lie, destroyed, in one of those piles of burned paper.

The coachman held his hat, turning the brim around and around. ". . . make no sense of it. Why'd somebody do that? What's it for?"

"Mad. That's what it is. Has to be a madman," a kitchen-maid whispered.

"I don't understand. This is mine." One of the outside

passengers claimed what was left of a red leather binding. "It's my *Elements of Chemistry*." He picked it up gingerly, holding the cover by one corner, but still getting smeared with black. He was the university student from Edinburgh, Timothy Fleet, a long, thin, red-haired stripling, poor enough to travel as an outside passenger on top of the coach in the middle of winter. "How did it get here? I left this in my bag last night."

Mr. Broadleigh sensibly fetched a toasting fork and used it to poke in a pile of blackened pages. "My accounts," he said shortly. "I want to know who's had hold of this." He stirred, and columns of numbers fell apart across the tines of the fork till he had nothing but a pile of ash. "Who's been snooping in my papers? Who's seen this?" He glared around the kitchen, impartially suspicious of the innkeeper, Jack, a nine-year-old scullery boy, Jeanne, and Miss Trimm.

Broadleigh was a London merchant, closemouthed as to what he traded in. He'd spent the seven days from York fuming at the delay caused by the snow. He had important business in London, he said. He'd established himself in the desirable forward-facing seat, taking up most of Miss Trimm's half, shuffling papers from one folder to another, spreading this one or that over his lap, pursing his lips importantly and making penciled notes.

She'd sat across the coach from him. He had bony knees for such a plump man.

Miss Trimm marched stiffly down the row to the crumbling remains of a letter. She snapped, "A napkin, please." Such was the force of her personality that one of the kitchen-maids hurried over with a freshly ironed napkin.

"Thank you." Without dirtying her gloves, Miss Trimm retrieved the letter and wrapped it up neatly. "I left this in my coat that's been hanging next to the door in our bedroom since I entered the inn last night. Anyone who had a key could have gained access to it while we ate dinner. Or during the night, when we slept, I suppose." Her eyes dismissed the innkeeper and went directly to Jack, where he lounged by the fire, interested but uninvolved.

No fool, Miss Trimm. If anybody got up to mischief in the night, it would be Jack.

"That's the strangest of all, isn't it?" Broadleigh said. "Who'd go after your letter? Nothing in it of any interest, I shouldn't think."

"Then I suggest you refrain from thinking." Miss Trimm directed a pointed glance from one kitchen minion to another. "If there is any reason breakfast should be indefinitely delayed, I'd like to hear of it. In the meantime . . . Jeanne. Elinor. I will be upstairs in our room. After you have located your belongings, I suggest you go to the common room and await me. I will join you shortly." She swept out.

"Regular old Tartar, ain't she?" Broadleigh muttered. But he'd waited till she was out of earshot. "I want to know who did this. Why? I want answers. What happened?"

The innkeeper raised his voice over the others. "Katie—" A young maid, well scrubbed and pink with excitement, stopped in the middle of swinging a kettle over the fire. "Katie here come down first in the morning, like always, to put water on and build up the fire. She found all this"—he gestured down the table—"heaped up higgledy-piggledy on the old coals. Burned, like you see. She run and called me, and we pulled out what we could." He made half a motion, as if he'd include Jack in this history, then decided not to. "What they were burned for, I can't say. No reason to it."

Everybody started talking nineteen to the dozen, arguing, commenting, demanding the innkeeper find out who'd done this. Maidservants, the innkeeper's wife, and a tall, gaunt woman who seemed to be the cook carried on preparing breakfast as best they could, around the corners of the room.

Jeanne slid through the chatter. She chose a charred black book midway along the row, then wrinkled her nose at the soot left on her fingers. They all knew this particular volume. She'd been sharing it with them in the coach, mile after mile, for the last three days. Lettering on the cover read . . . *oetry for Young Ladi* . . . Most of the pages were gone.

"So. I will not practice my English in this book anymore, I think." She held the volume away from her skirts, walked to the fireplace, and tossed the book on the flames. "I have spent good moneys upon it and barely memorized three of the poems, which were very dull. And now I must wash my hands. Is all the country of Lincolnshire full of madmen? It is bad enough that one must freeze in this place without the burning of the books."

She went to the sink in the scullery. Timothy, the university student, laid the pitiful remains of his chemistry book on the fire and followed after her, a few respectful but interested paces behind. Broadleigh gave the ashes of his accounts one final whack with the toasting fork that sent showers of ash in all direction and strode out, demanding breakfast.

Jack said, "Anybody else? We have some prime literature still laid out on the table."

His eyes rested on Elinor. Nothing stood between her and the force of Jack Tyler's curiosity. She'd thought, once upon a time, that his focused intent, his unswerving demand for answers, showed the mind of a serious scholar. It was the mind of a spy, instead. His patience was that of a cat at the mouse hole.

The other two outside passengers, brothers from York, carpenters, disclaimed all knowledge of the written word. The driver admitted he didn't read, "much."

That left her, didn't it? So many curious, expectant eyes.

The table held another letter, newspapers, and a copybook, such as a student might fill with schoolwork. The cover of the copybook was intact and the pages burned, as if it had been laid facedown on the fire.

The copybook was hers, of course. Her next poem. Some Latin already written. Some English. She'd drafted dozens of stanzas.

All that work, gone. Hours of jiggling words, searching for exactly the right phrase. Lines of poetry she'd never get back. Notes on the Latin that would take hours to resurrect. She felt like pounding on the table with a toasting fork herself.

And now, every page of that book was ready to betray her. She'd even made some rough sketches to show the illustrator. She wanted to blush, thinking about them. She wasn't about to go over there and lay claim to it. She said, "The newspaper is mine. You may dump it unceremoniously into the fire."

Jack studied her narrowly, being enigmatic.

It was no madman who found a way into her room to rifle through her belongings, who dared to invade luggage a few feet away from men who slept uneasily to the music of one another's snores. That kind of theft called for quiet feet and light hands and an intimate acquaintance with lockpicks.

The French agent Jack was hunting would be that skilled. Jack would too.

What did it all mean? Maybe the Frenchman realized he was cornered in this snowstorm and burned his secrets before they could be found. Maybe all these other papers were gathered in and sacrificed to disguise that one destruction.

Maybe it was just meant to look that way.

Or Jack could be in the middle of some deep game of his own. Laying snares for the unwary. He could have set this stage to watch how everyone reacted. It was far too early in the day to sort this out.

They put Jack on the trail of hard, violent men, but she was willing to bet he was more dangerous than any of them.

I have to get out of here. She left a veritable Greek chorus behind her, deploring and remarking at length.

Chapter 4

The innkeeper had given the most comfortable table in the public room, the one cozily close to the fire, to the three women traveling on the coach. Chivalry was found in the oddest corners of life. There was a blunt, imperturbable solidity to the innkeeper. His well-run inn with its bustling, cheerful maids spoke of a simple decency in the master of the house. He took a watchful care of the respectable single women sheltering under his roof.

And he was probably afraid of Miss Trimm.

Elinor sat on the long bench that put her nearest to the fire, leaving the high-backed settle and soft cushions for Jeanne and Mrs. Trimm. The round-faced maid, Kate, circled the room laying the tables with cups and saucers, spoons, and bowls of sugar lumps. Mr. Broadleigh followed Kate, complaining about his ruined account papers till the girl bobbed a curtsy and fled.

"It is sad to consider"—Jeanne slid into the wooden enclosure of the settle—"how many men are fussy idiots. Do you suppose that one has a wife?"

It felt good to laugh. "If he does, she says, 'Yes, dear,' and 'No, dear,' and dreams of strangling him in his sleep."

"The perfect marriage, in short." Jeanne shuffled across so they were close to each other. The ever-present workbag was on her arm, half-finished embroidery peeking out the top. "This is excellent. The good Kate returns with teapots. She placates the Monsieur Broadleigh and comes to us. We will drink tea now and exchange wild speculation about the madman who stalks this inn and is such an enemy of literacy." To Kate, "We are all thunderstruck, no?"

"Oh, yes, miss. Who'd do such a thing? Those beautiful books. And dear, I daresay." Kate set the china pot on the table and a pitcher of milk. The pretty, blue-and-white pattern had a look of Delftware. "Mrs. Tharpe—she's the cook—she has a book her son sent her from London. Cost every penny of three shillings. She's hid it under her mattress."

"I have a small volume of Monsieur Milton still. The madman is welcome to it," Jeanne said. "Though I am sorry about the chemistry text of the young man. Now I will ask you to bring me toast. Only toast. But also some of the jam of great excellence I am sure you have in your cupboards. I am not yet English enough to embark upon anything more ambitious in the morning. I have the greatest respect for those who can face the bacon and the ham in the earliest morning. It argues a remarkable endurance. I will drink tea, because there is no least sign of chocolate and Mademoiselle Pennington shall pour for me in the English manner. We are old chums now, she and I."

Jeanne's company was exactly what Elinor needed this morning. She didn't want to consider all the many possibilities that arose from Jack's inspection of her notebook.

She turned a pair of cups right way up and poured tea. She would take buttered eggs and toast, please. Yes. That would be enough. She tipped a bit of cream into both cups and agreed with Kate that it was worrisome, all those papers burned. No, she'd never heard of such a thing. She was fair taken aback herself. No, she didn't think it was Gypsies.

"That's what your Miss Trimm said." Kate polished the tray with a corner of her apron. "When I met her in the hall. Said it weren't Gypsies. It'll be one of the guests, being daft, most like. Maybe that London gentleman." London gentlemen were notoriously unpredictable. She left, reminding them the kitchen was all at sixes and sevens and everyone was that upset.

"They will tell tales of this mystery for a hundred years." Jeanne plumped the cushions behind herself and leaned placidly into their embrace. "It will become a fable to frighten children. I do not think we will be in those stories at all, unless we are murdered in our beds by a madman."

In the doorway, Timothy Fleet had stopped to blink and pull at his ear, trying to decide whether he'd come into the room or just stand on the threshold.

"Perhaps it is the good young Timothy," Jeanne said. "Much learning hath made him mad. That is Shakespeare." She took her cross-stitch out of her bag and unrolled it. Bright threads spilled across the white linen. "I do not like Shakespeare. He does not spell correctly."

"You've started on the flowers."

"I will use three threads for a while. Red and two pinks. This and this. I will pick up yet another pink on the next row and the design becomes complicated in the extreme. But I skip ahead to work on the interesting parts for a while, since I am not being jolted in the coach. As well, I am tired of making an endless background of white thread and cream-colored thread and also looking out upon white snow. I indulge myself with flowers. And now look. Your mad scholar comes toward us."

They watched the young man approach.

"Will he talk to us?" Jeanne began stitching. "I think not, but the suspense is almost unendurable."

He passed close by and went to the fire to warm his hands, standing two feet away. He slipped a glance in Jeanne's direction now and then. They waited.

Finally he edged over to their table. He ventured that it was a nice day.

Gravely, Jeanne agreed that it was. Outside the many-paned front window, snow fell. Wind picked up more from the branches of trees and threw it at the glass to hit in tiny, soft, individual thumps.

"Except for the snow," Timothy corrected himself. "Sorry about the snow. I know it's hard to get around in skirts. I mean to say . . ." He became entangled in a sentence. Trying to break out, he gestured hugely, lost his balance and grabbed the table. Tea slopped into saucers. Spoons rattled. The cream jug wobbled. He overturned the sugar bowl.

Twenty or thirty apologies later, he retreated to a seat in the far corner of the room.

"That is a young man who badly needs a visit to the women of London," Jeanne said, when he was beyond earshot. "One wishes to mother him. What woman desires a man she must mother?"

"A great truth." Even when she'd thought Jack was an unworldly scholar, she'd never felt the least impulse to mother him. She retrieved sugar lumps and put them back in the bowl. Why did she immediately think of Jack when Jeanne talked about desiring a man?

"But you do not drink your tea." Jeanne tasted her own. "It is a time of trouble. We are in a snowstorm, surrounded by madmen. We will be English and drink tea."

Elinor picked up her cup and wrapped her hands around it, feeling the warmth. This time last year, she and her publisher were counting sales one by one. She'd lived in an attic room and skipped meals to pay for paper and ink. Tea had been an unthinkable indulgence. She would never take the simple pleasure of drinking tea for granted. She lifted her cup and poured some onto the hearthstone behind her as a libation to Mercury, god of travelers.

When she turned back, Jack stood in the doorway. It was a reminder that Mercury was also the god of those who lived by cunning.

"He looks our way." Jeanne's eyes were bright and observant. "Excellent. That is a man one feels no least instinct to mother."

"None whatsoever."

"It would seem he knows one of us. Not me, I think."

Jack strolled the length of the room. Slowly. Toward her.

"He is much interested in you, Elinor." Jeanne found this amusing. "He is also, oh, so serious. And perhaps angry. Will we have the small wager, you and I, over what it is he wishes to set his teeth into this morning? It is perhaps breakfast, but I think it is also you."

Jack, having taken his time, arrived. She set her cup into her saucer and ignored him.

Jeanne peeped up at him through her eyelashes. "We are discussing the life of a student of chemistry. You see him? He takes only bread this morning, as if he were French. The storm delays us and adds two days or three days to our journey, so he counts his pennies and worries. He must buy himself a new chemistry book, as well. I am very sorry. Sometimes the world is difficult. I am Jeanne Dumont, once of Paris. This is Elinor Pennington. The student of chemistry who must count his pennies is Timothy Fleet."

"I'll see to him. I'm Jack Tyler. Hello, Elinor." Jack chose the short bench across from her and sat himself down. He collected one of the teacups and turned it over, and he was established.

"I didn't invite you to join us." She could have saved her breath. One might as well scold the tomcat curled by the fire. One might as well scold the fire.

"If I waited for an invitation from you, I'd be standing here till doomsday."

"But I am happy that he sits with us," Jeanne said. "Miss Trimm is not here to make me proper, so I will flirt with Monsieur Tyler. He will not take me seriously."

"There." Jack smiled. "An invitation."

Jeanne laughed with her eyes. She stuffed her sewing away and shifted her embroidery bag from one side to the other so he might make his elbows comfortable on the table. She poured him tea and lifted the cream jug. She had given him enough? A little more, then. She chose sugar lumps. She stirred his tea with pretty deference. She could have been entertaining a favorite and elderly uncle. In return, he was lightly gallant. They both enjoyed the game.

All of them knew Jack's attention was fixed on Elinor, not Jeanne. The hard, alert eyes were for Elinor Pennington. The little smile was for Jeanne.

Jack, being charming. She kicked him under the table and he winced.

"I will tell you what is planned for this morning, Monsieur," Jeanne said brightly. "So you are warned. I have not told Elinor yet. I was waiting until she has eaten and is strong enough to bear the shock."

"She's tougher than she looks," Jack said. "What are we doing?"

"Miss Trimm plans that we go out into the woods at the first small break in the weather. She and I and Miss Pennington and some of the grooms to push a path through the snow. Now you also. We will take Mr. Fleet as well, if he does not hide himself quickly. He does not look strong enough to resist Miss Trimm."

"Hey ho, to the greenwood let us go. With Miss Trimm wandering in the snow. Why? Or should it be obvious?"

"It is to bring holly to the house, of course. This is an ancient English custom to do, and you should know it very well. She is enamored of a wood across the road full of red berries. One sees it from our window upstairs, though I had not seen it myself until she opened the window and pointed it out. The branches will be full of many small, sharp leaves, which we will put"—Jeanne added more cream to his teacup and used the pitcher to indicate the mantel—"there. It is a pointless thing to do, the bringing of greenery into the house. I did not explain that to her."

"Wise choice," Jack said.

"As you say. Holly is a very English twig. One decorates the English pudding with such leaves, but one does not eat them. One also does not—" She saw something on the other side of the room and her eyes lost their laughter.

They shifted to look. It was the fashionable gentleman, Mr. Rossiter, who was so very unhappy with this country inn. Elinor set her cup down in its saucer, next to Jeanne's. "He's up early for a London fop."

"I'm afraid I woke him," Jack said. "There are some men who do not appreciate voices uplifted in song first thing in the morning."

Jeanne said, "I will warn you of that man, Elinor. I poke the fun at Miss Trimm, which is not well done of me. But consider this. Twice this morning she has chanced to be between me and Monsieur Rossiter when he would rub himself up against me in passing and pretend it was by accident." She made a little grimace of distaste. "Because she does this, I will gather any number of prickly branches for her. I only wish I might stuff hollies into the smallclothes of that *caboche.*"

I can use that. The slave girl Chloe puts burrs in her master's subligaculum when he goes to visit her rival. She can—

In her poems, Roman senators met their comeuppance at the hands of clever slave girls. Handsome young poets dallied with the wives of fat merchants. True love conquered all.

The real world was full of conceited fools like Rossiter. He was exactly the sort who would buy her books and not read them. He would only look at the pictures.

Rossiter swaggered to their table. "Damned cold in this godforsaken hovel. Morning, girls. You've slipped the leash from Miss Trimm, I see. Hoped you would."

"Find somewhere else to sit, Rossiter," Jack said evenly.

"And leave you with both pretty ones? I don't think so, my friend. Make room."

Rossiter didn't pull up the empty bench. He leaned over Jeanne, taking hold of the back of the settle behind her. "Let's squeeze in here and get warm, eh, girl? The old trout isn't here to spoil the fun." He let his hand slip down to Jeanne's shoulder, under her shawl, feeling for bare skin.

Jack shifted his weight and brought his boots in under him. A small, significant motion that signaled violence to come. Elinor recognized the signs and prepared to pull Jeanne out of the path of a fight. Two years ago, at the lowest ebb of fortune, she'd scrubbed floors in a tavern in Whitechapel. It was honest work, and she'd learned to keep out of the way of fights.

Jeanne upended the cream pitcher, right down Rossiter's silk waistcoat.

"The hell!" He grabbed at his trousers and stumbled back. "You stupid slut. Look what you've done. You—"

Jack applied his boot to the man's buttocks. Rossiter sprawled to his hands and knees on the floorboards. The cream pitcher splashed its last drops on him as it rolled to the floor.

The room went silent. Every head snapped in their direction—Broadleigh, Timothy Fleet, the maid Kate, another maid carrying a pile of napkins, the innkeeper with a tankard of ale.

"How dare you?" Rossiter scrambled to his feet, panting and brushing futilely at his clothes. "You jumped-up clod-hopper. I'll have the magistrate on you for this. Who do you think you are?"

"I know who he is, Mr. Rossiter." Elinor grabbed his attention with her voice and an upraised hand. "Who are you?"

"You insolent, little tuppence of a governess. When my uncle, Lord Brampten, hears about this, you'll be lucky to get a job licking chamber pots. My uncle—"

"Lord Brampten's nephew is twelve years old and studying at Eton." She said it with absolute and calm authority. She'd heard that tone often enough in Oxford, making some pronouncement or other. The dons might be wrong, but they were never uncertain.

The crackling of the fire was the loudest sound in the room. A huge marmalade tomcat appeared from a corner by the hearth and padded over to lick up the spilled cream.

Rossiter took a step back. And another. And, with that, admitted everything. "You must be mad."

Jack threw his head back and laughed. A big, deep, genuine laugh. Nothing could have been more devastating.

"You . . . You . . ." Rossiter spat, then spun on his heel. "You're lucky I was taught to be polite to women. Even women like you." He stalked away, white-faced and stiff-legged. Fury wrapped in ruined clothes.

Jack said, "And she sweeps the board."

"She is more than capable of routing five or six of that variety of pig." Jeanne folded her hands placidly,

"She is," Jack said. "Nicely done, Elinor. How did you know?"

"Well . . . I didn't."

It took a long second. Then Jeanne began to giggle. Jack raised his hands and clapped, slow and deliberate.

He admired that. He liked stripping away lies. Digging up secrets was his life's work.

And she had secrets to hide. Lies to protect.

Miss Trimm arrived, full of plans to assault the holly trees across the road. The snow had delayed them. They would not reach their destinations. They must celebrate the holiday where they were. The holiday custom of decking the house with evergreen boughs was of considerable antiquity. The ancient Saxons . . .

Chapter 5

"I can't claim to be an expert on the weather of Lincolnshire. If this were Somerset, I wouldn't call it a lull." Jack studied the particular snowy tree he'd chosen, satisfied with it.

"Miss Trimm has declared this is a lull. The weather does not contradict Miss Trimm." Elinor stood in the snow with her arms full of holly. This was a scratchy and uncomfortable business. Holly does not love humankind. Every so often a little flurry of flakes swirled past her face, emphasizing how temporary the break in the storm was. A pair of crows sat on a high branch, shoulders hunched—if crows had shoulders. Wings hunched, in any case. They looked no better pleased with the weather than she was.

Jack scooped snow into a ball and hardened it, pressing and turning again and again. "I read that copybook."

She'd been afraid of that. "I was hoping it had burned to unreadable ashes."

"I'm glad it didn't. You write clever verse. I knew it was yours the minute I pulled it out of the fire."

"The Latin."

"Your handwriting. Now I know how you earn a living." He finished the snowball to his satisfaction, tilted his head back, considering distances and angles, and threw, fast and full out. Cascades of snow fell from branch to branch. Thirty feet above them, high in the birch tree, a clump of mistletoe shuddered and hung on. The crows flapped off into the deeper woods. "I can't tell you how relieved I was."

"That I'm writing naughty Latin verse."

"Instead of selling your body? Yes."

In this path Jack had made for them out to this solitary tall birch, the snow was higher than her knees on either side. She could go forward or back, but there was no room for maneuvering sideways. Maybe that was symbolic. In any case, she spoke frankly. "If I were desperate for money, I suppose I could have become a spy."

"I didn't waste time worrying about that." He threw again and hit mistletoe. Nothing dislodged but more snow. "I have your book wrapped up tight and safe in my baggage. You'll be able to salvage a good bit of that writing."

She wasn't grateful to him. She wouldn't be grateful.

Jack reached deep into the snow where it was damper and easier to mold and made the next snowball. He threw again. He was a fine, accurate bowler at cricket, unpredictable and strategic. Back in Oxford, she'd watched his matches. If she'd had any sense she'd have learned to distrust him then.

He never gave up. She knew that about him too.

A dozen snowballs later, and a dozen hits in the target of mistletoe, a cluster of green, frozen hard and weighted with ice, broke and tumbled. "Got it," he said.

It hung up in the vee of a branch ten feet above their heads.

"Are you going to climb up and pull it out of the branches?"

"I will if you want me to." He was already packing another ball, but he was looking at her. Between them, snow descended slowly in distinct points. His eyes were startlingly blue in the colorless white. "I like your work, Nugator."

He truly did know everything. "You read my book *Im-proba*?"

"And *Criso,* the second book. I enjoyed them immensely. The part where Laia locks Terentius out of the bathhouse, naked. And the scene with the lettuce . . ." He shook his head, shedding snowflakes. "You're a delight."

For more than a year she'd written very naughty verse, in Latin, under the name Sutela Nugator. Verse that pretended to be previously undiscovered classical writing. She gave an English translation and provided footnotes in stuffy academic language. Her publisher illustrated with tasteful lithographs of the more explicit Roman statuary.

That was why she'd been in York. She'd spent the last two weeks with the artist, discussing illustrations for the next book.

"I'm still getting used to the idea." He grinned, looking boyish. "All that wonderful, scandalous verse. Yours."

"It's not scandalous." She thought that over. "Well, the Latin is, but the English half is formal and sedate and uses the Latin words when it isn't. My publisher says men buy the books for the lithographs, anyway. The Latin is there to make the pictures respectable, so he can sell them."

"Every Latin scholar in the kingdom owns *Improba.*"

"It's a hoax. We all but admit it in the preface."

"Maybe, but every student at university has it, and every schoolboy who can get his hands on a copy." He was chuckling, so his shoulders shook, but his aim was straight. He caught the mistletoe in his hands as it fell. "That's it. We've collected the magic of the holiday and scooped it up before it hit the ground. Our mistletoe is just full of pagan power. Here, give me that." He dropped mistletoe onto the pile of holly she carried, then relieved her of the lot. "This is surprisingly prickly. Let's get inside. If you're not freezing, I am."

"We will return to the inn and strew every flat surface

with holly. We will drink wassail, which I think is rum punch at this particular inn. Possibly we will sing."

"Always something exciting." He talked over his shoulder. "Everyone in Oxford thought you were the quiet, deep sort, Elinor Sutela Nugator."

"It's classical Latin. With footnotes."

"I think, all that time in Oxford, you were pretending to be something you aren't." He sounded pleased. He walked in front of her, so she couldn't see his face.

The others, back in the stand of hollies, stacked branches red with berries, calling advice and triumph back and forth. Miss Trimm and Jeanne were there and the shy Timothy, housemaids and servants, even Mr. Broadleigh, who was particularly full of admonition. Jack stopped to send two husky fellows after more mistletoe, then took the path back to the inn.

She followed him. Out of the woods, out in the open again, they were small beneath the tremendous, hovering sky. They crossed the smooth indentation that was the road. There were no wheel ruts here, but a few horses had passed in the last few hours. She didn't envy whoever had to be out on horseback today.

In the inn yard, dozens of journeys from stable to house marked the snow. A well-beaten track veered off to the back wall, where peats were stacked in a long battlement, high as the withers of a horse.

Jack didn't head for the front door and the fire in the common room and the bowl of hot punch the innkeeper had promised. He led her around to the back of the inn.

The Laughing Wench sprouted additions like so many mushrooms. The shed-roofed room at the back was an example. Jack shoved snow from the step with his boot and managed, despite all that prickly holly, to pull the door open. He leaned against it, holding it back for her to walk by.

It was a small familiar act, Jack holding the door for her.

She had a sudden, vivid memory of Jack kissing her in the doorway of the house in Oxford. It had been the long, warm twilight of summer, and neither of them willing to let go and say goodnight.

Cold wind pushed at her back. When she brushed past Jack, he was close enough that she felt his breath on her face.

Inside it was a few degrees warmer. This was a narrow room, empty and utilitarian, with flagged floor, a long, wooden bench, and one high window set asymmetrically in the wall. Boots and clogs lined up on one side under the pegs where maids hung their cloaks.

Jack lifted his armful of greenery to the shelf above the bench and stowed it out of the way. Dark green and red of the holly jumbled with the oval leaves and white berry of mistletoe.

"We used to do this when I was growing up," Jack said. "Holly and ivy and a Christmas pudding in the rectory. A Yule log up at the manor." He brushed the sleeves of his coat, where the holly had been. "Life was a good deal less complicated before I started chasing spies. One of them's disporting himself out in the snow right now. I wish I knew who. And somewhere about the place, I have a coded message to find."

She could say this much: "It wasn't in the bonfire this morning. He burned everything else in sight, but not the code."

"Not a chance. That was pure theater, for my benefit. Since he left York he's had time to move the list from the paper it was on. Now it's something we won't recognize." He had his gloves off while she still tugged at the fingers of hers. He shrugged out of his greatcoat and slung it casually on a peg. Dropped his hat on top of that. He came over and began work on the buttons down the front of her coat, slipping them loose as fast as a maid shelling peas.

She said, "It will be a new code altogether maybe. Numbers, if it was letters. Letters, if it was numbers. He'll write it in the lining of a coat or roll it up and hide it in the sole of his shoe. He's walking around on it even now."

He opened another button. "Give me six months and I'll make a first-rate spy out of you. I went through everybody's luggage after breakfast and didn't find anything. It's here somewhere."

"He's clever, whoever he is. He knows what you are. The minute you walked into the inn, something you did, something you said, gave you away."

"I don't think so. I'm careful." He worked his way down her coat. Bits of snow fell where the buttons had frozen in place.

"Then he knows you by sight."

"That's possible. He might have seen me in France, or testifying in court in London. I don't spend all my time in Oxford, betraying classical scholars. No, you don't." He grabbed her. "Don't push away from me."

She would have stalked off, wrapped in dignity and anger. Strong hands held her. Turned her to him impatiently. "You're the only woman I've ever betrayed. You're also the only woman I've ever loved. One woman. You."

"I don't want to talk about it."

"We're going to finish this." He didn't let go.

"I 'finished this' a long time ago."

"I didn't. I never had the chance. I wasn't even sure you were alive." The pain in his voice swept right into her. There was no distance between them. He'd taken it all away. All the barriers, gone. "There's no bloody corner in this inn where we can be alone. I have to say all this in a miserable little closet. Lift your chin."

"No."

He tapped her under the chin. "Yes." And he was picking

at her bonnet strings where they'd frozen together. "I betrayed you. That's where we start."

"What do you want me to say?" She'd thought he couldn't hurt her any more. She was wrong. "You did what you had to do. You want me to forgive you? Fine. I forgive you."

"And you say I tell lies. Elinor, Elinor, I'm an amateur next to you."

"What do you want from me?"

"I don't want you to forgive me in that tight little voice, dammit. Be angry if you want to. Be furious. Find a knife and carve my heart out. Hate me, but stop being polite. Why do they make these ribbons all small and fiddly this way?"

No words. There were no words in her, just rage and ragged breathing. If she'd had a knife handy, she might have obliged him with that hole in his chest.

He said, "Nobody can get your hat off once this tying-on affair gets wet. I can take a gun apart, clean it, and reload with my eyes closed. There's no reason I can't . . . ah . . . That's got it." A few brisk tugs and he tossed her hat down on the bench. "I'm the same man I always was. Look at me, for God's sake."

She wouldn't be cowardly. She raised her head.

He hadn't changed. A tanned face. Brown hair. A heavy brow and emphatic nose. Feature by feature, he was the same, except that his eyes were grim and tired. The Jack Tyler of Oxford had always been laughing.

This was Jack, the man she'd loved . . . and he was more. Strength she'd only guessed at. Hardness and power. Experiences she'd never imagined. This was Jack Tyler without the mask, freed from acting a lie. What she'd felt for him once seemed pale compared to these new possibilities.

"No more being polite." He stripped her coat off her, peeling it down her arms. He tossed that on the bench behind her. "No more smiling and counting the minutes till you get back in the coach and roll away and never see me again." Behind him a black wool shawl hung on one of the pegs. He flicked it free. "Borrow this. Don't freeze while I talk to you." He wrapped her inside, and his hands stayed on her when he was done.

She shook her head. She wasn't sure what it meant when she did that.

He said, "I'm sorry. Not just for the lies. I should have stayed your friend back in Oxford. Just a friend. I shouldn't have loved you and let you love me back. It wasn't the right time for either of us."

"I didn't love you."

The ghost of a smile crossed his face. "Yes, you did. We were honest about that, you and I. What we had . . ." He set two fingers where the black shawl crossed over her heart. "It's still here, waiting for us to take it back. This time, it's going to be better. We can make this right."

He let his fingers rest there, rising and falling with her breath. It was more intimate than a kiss. Only lovers touched each other this way.

Tension built inside her. It wasn't anger. It was a restless, hungry need to pull him to her and consume him, mouth to mouth. She hadn't stopped wanting him.

The moment to push him away came and passed.

He smoothed his knuckles across her cheek. "Look up there. Do you see? The mistletoe."

She looked up and saw tightly furled, glossy green leaves. Waxy white berries.

"Do you know why couples kiss under mistletoe? When you bring mistletoe down to the earth, that's the first time it's ever touched anything but the air and the branches of a tree. It's magic. They've known that for a thousand years. Let me start over with you, Elinor."

She didn't say "yes." But it was there, somewhere inside her.

She watched Jack read the nuances of her face and body

and understand the featherweight of that small, almost "yes." She'd missed that more than anything else—the absolute certainty that Jack understood her.

The shawl was cold from hanging in the hall here. He fed warmth through it where he stroked smoothly up and down her arms. She recognized persuasion. Softly, he kissed her.

Her hands tightened in the fabric of his jacket and she kissed back.

She had the strange feeling that time hung suspended. It was as if past and future had released their hold on her. As if she were free to be anything she chose.

Deliberately, she let the anger drain away. She lost herself in the sensation of Jack's warmth and strength. His jaw was rough with bristle even a few hours after he had shaved. His skin was still cold from being out in the wind. His teeth nipped at her lips. This Jack, the real one, was more demanding than the man she remembered. More exigent. More sure of himself.

And she was no longer the sheltered girl she had been. Shuddering, she took every kiss and gave it back. Traded back every caress.

The inn filled with raucous whistles and cries of a dozen voices. Everyone had returned.

He held her face between his palms. "You take my breath away."

Someone yelled for Jack. Someone else called her name. There was laughter and speculation and more laughter.

He said, "Pretty soon, I'll get you someplace we can exchange ten words in private. Here. Take some of the greenery. I'll carry the stickery stuff."

They went toward the jollity, reluctantly, before it came looking for them.

Chapter 6

Elinor carried the last of the ivy upstairs to the bedchamber she shared with the others. Jeanne, hidden behind her own armload of holly and mistletoe, said, "Let us toss this on the mantel as if it were feed scattered for chickens and consider the matter done."

"Properly." Elinor imitated Miss Trimm's voice. "It must be proper."

"Whatever we do, she will come and change it around."

"Very true. Set it down here." Elinor tossed ivy onto the coverlet of the bed.

"You will get your blanket dirty." But Jeanne let the holly fall beside the ivy. Ivy to the left, holly to the right.

Downstairs, they were singing noisily. There were meat pies and ale and the smell of dinner cooking. Miss Trimm was in the kitchen making elaborate decorations from gilt paper that had been dug up from the attic. Jack had made himself comfortable near the fire. He'd watched her like a hawk, waiting for . . . she didn't know what. Some sign. He wanted that "yes" she felt bobbing around inside her, nearly ready to emerge.

When she'd wandered close to Jack, every eye in the

place fastened on them. So she'd avoided him, and that was watched just as carefully.

She laid ivy across the mantel, turning it here and there so the leaves pointed outward, all neatly in the same direction. Organized ivy.

Jeanne went to the dresser and took her hair down to brush. "I will take a small nap, I think. I have had an exhausting day. There was much to be accomplished."

"Holly and ivy," she said. "Like the song." Long, floppy sprays of ivy made the background. The holly was a more complex beast, all brown twigs, leaves that were not cooperative, and red berries scattered at random. She put some up and took it down again. Shifted a little branch to the left. Set another one just so.

Jeanne said, "You were alone with Monsieur Jack for some time. We are all interested. No. Do not say anything. I do not pry. I will admire your art of greenery instead."

"The trick is to use all of it. If I don't, Miss Trimm is going to find something else that needs holly on it." She didn't have the least idea what to say about Jack. "Is that even on both sides, do you think?"

Jeanne looked in the mirror, braiding her hair tight. "It needs more on the left."

My left, or hers? Or the left in the mirror? Life was full of such conundrums. "I'll put the mistletoe here. And . . . here. We don't want it exactly even. It's more interesting if we make a pattern. What do you think?" She stepped back and considered it from left to right, reading the pattern, as it were.

A pattern of leaves and berries. Different colors make a pattern.

A pattern. Jeanne's workbag lay on the trundle bed, casually tossed down.

What was it Jack said? "He'll move the list from the paper it's on and put it in some other code." She drew Jeanne's bag toward her and opened it. Inside was linen cloth and thread with the needles hanging. A woman's handwork. What could be more open and obvious? She'd watched Jeanne hour after hour in the coach, reading her book and stitching away at her needlework and thought nothing of it.

The code is here. In the embroidery. It had been laid down, stitch by stitch, right under her nose. There would be tiny variations in the direction the thread was set. In the choice of color. The background was an expanse of white and cream in a pretty, rich, stippling effect. No one would be surprised that the threads seemed laid at random.

Jeanne said softly, "This is very tiresome."

When she looked up, Jeanne held a small pistol.

Oh, dear. Cold fear pierced her stomach, sharp as an icicle. "You assume I've discovered you. You could have been wrong."

"I am not. You are the only one I watched. The one I stayed close to. If anyone were to uncover and expose me, it would be you. Even the very clever Monsieur Jack Tyler would not see this. Only a woman would have the combination of intelligence and an understanding of matters such as"—the gun indicated the embroidery on the bed—"needlework."

"It really is exquisite."

"Thank you. My mother taught me to sew. I have practiced it for exactly such a use. It is not the first time I have used this device, though generally I am not forced to produce my little masterpieces under the watchful eye of half a dozen people."

"If you shoot me, everyone will hear."

"That is one of many reasons not to shoot you. I like you, most honestly, and it is Christmas Eve. Also, I have no wish to face an enraged Jack Tyler after I have shot his chosen lady."

"He'd track you to the ends of the earth." *Jack would do that.*

"Very true. And I have only a single shot. Given a choice, I would reserve it for him."

"I'd rather you didn't shoot either of us."

Downstairs, everyone was hoping gentlemen would rest merry and undismayed. She could have used some of that herself.

"Perhaps you will give me my needlework, and allow yourself to be tied up, and I will depart. That will assure that no one at all gets shot." Jeanne's eyes were sober. "You understand? I cannot remain, trying to convince you. I swear to you in great seriousness that I could stab you as you stand, nearly as quickly as I could shoot, and in absolute silence. Do not think otherwise."

A cold shiver trembled down her spine. She backed toward the fireplace.

"I do not wish to earn the enmity of the organization Monsieur Tyler represents. I am trying to think of a way out of this impasse, frankly."

She felt the heat of the hearth at her back. Her heel touched the hearthstones. In a single movement, she threw the embroidery behind her, onto the fire.

"No." Jeanne started forward.

"Let it burn."

The gun poised between them, unwavering. Jeanne's eyes narrowed. "I did not expect this."

Downstairs, they sang about tidings of comfort and joy. Upstairs, Elinor said, "If you run, Jeanne, and leave this behind to burn, I promise to stay silent until you have a chance to get away." She risked a glance at the fire. "I'm gambling you won't shoot me to get the cloth back."

"That is a very great gamble," Jeanne said.

Chapter 7

"You did what?" Jack wasn't a man to shout. He compressed outrage into a low, reasonable voice. His hands opened and closed convulsively.

"I promised her ten minutes' head start. I kept the promise."

"She stole my horse."

"I didn't really think about the details of horse stealing." She considered the matter. "It wouldn't have made any difference."

"She stole my damn horse and rode off into the snow."

"She's strong and warmly dressed and clever. She'll be safe enough until she reaches shelter."

Jack brought his anger over close to her, so they could both examine it. When she put her hand on his forearm, his muscles were hard as carved wood. He said, "I'm not worried about her being safe. She's a French agent."

"And she stole your horse. Yes. I understand. I'll buy you another horse. I'm not rich, exactly, but I make a good living."

"I can buy my own damn horses. That's not the point."

"If you're determined to chase after her, there are other horses in the stable. Steal one of them."

"She took the ten minutes you gave her to cut every saddle girth in the place. They're patching something up for me. It'll be a while." Jack took her shoulders into his big hands. His fingers shaped to her, firm and strong, with the careful control that was exactly Jack Tyler. "What did she say to you?"

Jeanne's embroidery, pulled from the fire, lay on the hearth. The linen backing was brown and burned all the way through in spots. The threads had fared worse. They were curled and crinkled and gone black. There was nothing left. The code and the names were gone.

Good riddance, in her opinion. "She said she was glad to be dealing with me and not some male idiot. She was sorry we had never had a chance to play cards against each other. She said the French would find these same sympathizers again, or others, and this was only an inconvenience. We agreed, in fact, that such lists are useless because very few men have the resolution to carry through on promises. Most of those supposed traitors will turn out to be only loyal Englishmen who like to grumble. I don't like lists with so many innocent people on them."

"You stood and chatted." His hand shook a little when it came up to touch her hair.

"While the code was burning busily on the fire. She wouldn't leave till she was certain that list wouldn't fall into your hands. Oh. And she said her scruples against killing me were transient and fragile as soap bubbles. I thought that was rather pretty."

Minute by minute, he found new places to touch her. To hold onto her. His hands were not entirely steady. "You could have been killed."

"I thought about that possibility."

"Nothing in that message was worth risking your life for.

You should have given it to her and stayed quiet and let her go. If that girl is who I think she is . . . You don't—" He took a deep, deep breath. "You don't realize how much danger you were in."

"I knew. I considered the—"

"You're alive. You bargained for your life, and you won. Do you have any idea how wonderful and remarkable you are?" He wrapped her to him, tightly, body to body, as if he were joining them, heart to heart. As if he were settling them together just right, because it was going to last for a long time. He took her mouth under his and came down for a long, slow kiss.

It roused a hundred intriguing sensations inside her. She couldn't wait to explore them.

Another kiss. Jack said, "Two years ago I tore Oxford apart, looking for you, wanting to say this. Marry me, Elinor."

"I—"

"I'll show you all the mischief the classical Romans got up to between the sheets. I'll write love poems to you. In Latin." Close to her cheek, he whispered, "*Amo te,* Elinor Pennington. I love you."

She loved him. Outside, Christmas Eve settled around the inn, wrapping it in peace. The new year was coming. They'd been given a second chance. What could she say but yes?

WENCH IN WONDERLAND

Patricia Rice

The wretched snow would not stop falling. What a miserable Christmastide this promised to be. Damaris Bedloe gazed out the frosted coach window at the Lancashire countryside and knew it wasn't the snow creating the gloom, but the ache in her own heart.

What she was doing was wrong. After years of propriety, she was severing her relationship with all she knew and loved, for the right reason perhaps, but in the wrong way. She should never have let Lady Alice persuade her to this foolish charade, but loving her young cousin like the sister she'd never had, Damaris couldn't deny Alice in the matter of her entire future.

She supposed that Alice's father, Lord Reidland, had his good points. After all, he'd taken her in after Damaris's parents died when she was only twelve. Her uncle had made it clear, though, that her purpose was to keep his young daughter company in his all-male household. His temper had left her trembling in fear of being thrown from his home for years.

Alice was less inclined to fear her father's wrath. She'd stalwartly rejected all offers for three Seasons because her father refused to countenance a match with Theodore

Harley, a promising young barrister and the man Alice loved. But in the end, Alice had not been able to fight back when Lord Reidland had thundered that it was time for his daughter to stop mooning over a penniless nobody. He'd accepted the next of her suitors to ask for her hand—Jonathan Trevelyan, younger brother of a wealthy viscount.

Alice was not the sort given to hysterics. But as soon as her father accepted an invitation for her to travel to her fiancé's family home in rural Lancashire for Christmas, Alice had realized that this was a perfect opportunity to elope with Theodore. All she had to do was leave the coach in a town where Theodore would meet her with a special license in hand. Damaris would continue the rest of the journey alone, covering up Alice's escape until the young lovers were safely married—although none of them had anticipated she'd be riding into a blizzard.

Having helped Alice slip away in Banbury, Damaris understood and accepted that once the earl discovered her part in the deception, he would never want her to darken his door again. At least she was too old to be placed in an orphanage for her one act of defiance.

She despised deceit, but any sacrifice was worth saving Alice from a life without love. That misery was more easily endured by a twenty-seven-year-old spinster who lacked backbone or dreams.

Damaris sighed, and her warm breath cleared a small spot on the frosted window. Alice had promised that her cousin would always be welcome in her new household, but Damaris doubted that even good-natured Theodore would want her underfoot forever.

Too late for second thoughts now. Surely she could find some sort of work. Perhaps as a teacher. She'd always enjoyed children, and she'd had ample experience with Alice's younger brothers.

The coach swayed through an icy rut, and the driver

shouted curses at his horses. Damaris's death grip on the leather strap was all that prevented her from landing on the floor. She rubbed her bruised shoulder, glad Alice had escaped before the blizzard hit.

The luggage-laden rear of the coach sank into a hole, abruptly heaving the front upward. Damaris bounced off the wall again, the door frame connecting painfully with her head. The horses whinnied frantically. The driver shouted and cracked his whip. The jarring upheaval slammed her against the door. This time, the frozen lock split open, and she tumbled out into the snowy night, head over heels.

"I did not think Mack would accept a plain girl," a woman whispered in the hazy way of dreams. "Her dowry must be large indeed."

"That's very cynical of you, Mother," a dry, deep voice responded. "Perhaps she's very good at gambling."

She wanted to join in the chuckles that followed, but she did not quite understand the joke. Who was Mack? And who was the plain girl with the large dowry? Her head ached abominably, but she thought it rude not to join the conversation.

She struggled against the downy weight covering her, and instantly, strong, masculine hands adjusted the pillow she'd just discovered she was lying against. Why was she in a bed with a man about? She froze in horror.

"Don't try to do too much just yet, Lady Alice," a pleasant baritone warned. "You are fortunate that pretty head of yours is still on your shoulders after the blow you took."

Confused, she wondered if he was addressing her, but her eyes could not quite open. Her head pounded as if a dozen blacksmiths beat upon it. The pillow adjustment felt wonderful.

Her woozy mind tried to remember a moment when

she'd felt such comforting strength, but she could not recall ever having a man's hands on her. She struggled with her memory but there appeared to be holes in it, brought on by the pounding in her head, no doubt.

"The doctor said you must drink this, dear. It might relieve the pain a little." The feminine voice that had sounded so caustic earlier switched to syrupy softness while fragrant hands held a cup to her lips.

She couldn't quite tilt her head to sip. The strong hand returned to ease her a little higher, and she drank greedily. Once the cup was empty, she fell back against satiny soft sheets scented with lavender. She couldn't remember ever sleeping in such luxury. There must be a very large gap in her memory.

"Do you think Mack forgot we invited her?" the woman whispered as she slipped toward sleep.

"More likely, he got her with child and is fleeing responsibility," the man retorted. "Otherwise, she wouldn't be traveling without a chaperone. I'd thought it odd that an earl would accept a reprobate like Mack. This could all be a hoax. I'll send Fred to look for the rascal once the snow clears. I'll have him dragged home to do the proper thing."

"Oh, dear, really, Trev, another child in the Hall. I don't believe I can bear it."

Slipping into sleep, she tried to picture a Mack but couldn't. The sensation of strong hands holding her had replaced all fears with comforting dreams of security.

Adam, Viscount Trevelyan, looked up from the estate map as the housekeeper marched his oldest son into the study, pinching the boy by the ear as if he were a disobedient pup. Which he was.

"What now, Mrs. Worth?" Trev asked, gesturing for her to release the brat.

"He stole the tart Cook baked for you, my lord. He and those other heathens ate all of it."

"Blackberry jam, I take it?" Trev observed, the evidence smeared across his heir's face. "My favorite, too."

Georgie had the grace to look guilty. He scuffed his toe on the plush Aubusson carpet. "We was hungry. Nanny *starves* us."

"Nanny does no such thing. She merely deprives you of your pudding when you've behaved wretchedly. What did you do to irritate her today?"

Georgie screwed up his eight-year-old face, looking a great deal like his scapegrace Uncle Mack. "We didn't do our sums. It's *snowing* out," he protested, as if that were the greatest excuse in the world.

"And had you done your sums, Nanny would no doubt have let you go out to play in it. As it is, now you will have to stay inside and do twice the work, with no pudding for you tonight."

"That's not fair!" his little scoundrel shouted. "We're just babies. We should be let to play."

Out of the mouths of babes . . . spoke the idiotish excuses of Uncle Mack, by way of Violet, Lady Trevelyan, his frivolous mother. Trev rubbed his brow and gestured at the housekeeper. "Take him back to Nanny and tell her what I said," he told the housekeeper.

Trev had no other idea how to deal with his motherless brood. That's what nannies and nursery maids were for. There were days Trev longed for a cheerful, obedient wife to rein in his troublesome family, but it had been his madcap wife who had created these straits. Disorder had ruled from the moment he'd brought Louise home as a bride. Never again. He could dismiss bad help. It was impossible to dismiss a bad wife. Or a bad mother, but that was another topic.

He had an estate to run or there would be no blackberry tarts in anyone's future. Years of paying off his younger brother's gambling debts and his mother's profligate spending had drained the home farm's cash until he'd finally played the part of ogre and refused to cover more than their allowances. He'd offered to buy Mack colors or find him a position in a foreign office. He should have known his brother would find an heiress instead.

Knowing Mack had no wherewithal to take a bride anywhere except here to the Hall, Trev didn't dare hope that he had found a meek, obedient wife, one who would quietly organize his disorderly home. Admittedly, the patient upstairs appeared older and possibly more mature than the silly chit he'd anticipated. Still, Mack did not typically choose older women. Perhaps the purple bump on her brow sallowed her complexion.

The dowry Mack had promised to hand over to Trev for housing his bride would go a long way toward making up for the gambling debts Trev had paid over the years. Perhaps Mack was finally growing up and accepting his obligations.

Once he had the extra funds, Trev could plow them into improving some of the fallow grounds, and with the profits maybe set Mack up with his own house here on the estate. He could hope the chit was with child and had no choice but to marry the wretch quickly, before she realized what kind of ramshackle household she was marrying into.

A footman summoned him to the sickroom. Hopes rising for the first time in years, Trev took the stairs two at a time.

Damaris savored the smoky Darjeeling tea. Alice detested tea and preferred hot chocolate in the mornings, and as her companion, Damaris had always drunk whatever was offered. Tea was a rare pleasure.

Her memory was returning. She recollected wishing wistfully for tea while sipping sweet chocolate. Still, she couldn't remember how she'd come to be in this strange place. With the realization that her mind wasn't whole came uneasiness and confusion, which caused her head to throb. So she simply enjoyed the treat and the sinfully wicked scones and the wonderful pillows and tried not to wonder why a mere servant was being gifted with such luxury.

Two pairs of curious green eyes appraised her from beside the bed. That might be sufficient cause for confusion, she thought, as she studied them back. Twins, would be her guess, although the one had luxurious brown ringlets hanging to her shoulders and the other appeared to have butchered her curls with a carving knife. The one with ringlets wore an immaculate pinafore. The one with short hair appeared to have been crawling in mud.

"I'm Mina and she's Tina," the rumpled one said, before they seated themselves on the carpet. Damaris guessed them to be about five. She would offer them some of her tea and scones, but they produced some lint-coated candies from their pockets and sucked on them.

"Uncle Mack said he'd marry a dragon who would breathe fire on us if we're bad," the ragged twin declared.

"You don't look like a dragon," the other explained. "Dragons eat children, not scones."

The mysterious *Mack* again. Damaris thought if she was meant to marry him, she ought to remember someone of that name, but it hurt to try. "Dragons aren't real. Only hungry wolves eat children," she added teasingly.

"The nanny before this one said there's wolves in the forest," Mina—the ragged one—said with a frown. "But Georgie just sneaked out there to play in the snow."

Oh, dear. Damaris cast a glance to the maid standing by, who dipped an obedient curtsy and hurried out. Apparently the entire staff was needed to deal with the scamps.

"He won't get eaten, will he?" Tina asked worriedly.

"I'm sorry, I was only teasing about the wolves. England doesn't have wolves anymore. I think Georgie may need to be afraid of what your nanny will do when she catches him."

"Oh, she'll just yell, *I don't know what I'll do with you, Master Georgie, I simply don't.* And then she'll go to her room and slam the door. She smells funny when she comes out of her room." Mina sprawled on her skinny belly to peer under the bed. "Grandmere says there's dust bunnies under here because Mrs. Worth doesn't make the maids work worth a farthing. Are dust bunnies big as real bunnies?"

"We got real bunnies in the garden," Tina offered.

Damaris's head was definitely spinning. She almost sympathized with their nanny. "I don't think you ought to be crawling under the bed if there are bunnies there. You'll scare them," she suggested. "Do you have any books I could read to you?"

"I don't see no bunnies," Mina said, backing out covered in even more filth. Their grandmother was right about the maids. "And Georgie burned my bunny book."

"I've gots . . . I have a fairy book," Tina said eagerly. "Will you read that?"

"Certainly, although Mina might want to wash her face and hands before she touches anything else." Damaris suppressed a smile as the imps jumped up—and almost collided with a pair of long legs elegantly encased in knit pantaloons.

She winced as she lifted her aching head to follow the legs upward, skimming past his narrow hips and embarrassing maleness to a formidably broad chest in a gold-embroidered brocade vest. She didn't dare look higher.

This was no footman come to fetch the miscreants.

"You were told to leave our guest alone," the new arrival said sternly. "She is ill and needs to rest. Where is your nanny?"

"Nanny's taking a rest. The lady says dragons don't really eat children and Georgie won't get eaten by wolves but we shouldn't scare the bunnies under the bed so we're fetching books."

This run-together speech tumbled from both twins at once. Damaris dared to lift her gaze a little higher to see how the stern stranger took the stream of information—and forgot how to breathe.

Besides being exceedingly tall, the gentleman had shoulders that nearly filled the doorway, a head of chestnut curls as rich as that on the twins, and a heavy-lidded look that almost had her swooning. In fact, she was quite sure she did swoon. She couldn't remember any man ever looking at her in quite that way—as if she were a plum ripe for savoring.

"I'm sorry you've been bothered with my urchins, Lady Alice." He caught the twins before they escaped and turned them around. "Make your curtsies and begone, heathens."

Lady Alice? She had thought she was starting to recall . . . But she didn't know this man or this place or how she had come here. Fear froze any further thought. While the twins bobbed curtsies and escaped, Damaris tested the bump on her forehead. It was quite a large bump. She must truly have scrambled her brains.

How could she possibly contradict a gentleman? She didn't feel like the kind of person who could maintain a lively banter.

"I'm sorry to have intruded, but the nanny seems to have vanished along with my son. May I have someone bring you something for the pain?" he said sympathetically, apparently noticing her exploration of the bump.

"If your son is Georgie, then he is playing in the woods. And your nanny is in her room, no doubt tippling if I'm translating correctly." She wasn't entirely certain she was the kind of person who said things like that, either, but someone ought to see to the safety of the children, even if she had no memory of this man or his family. "And no, I think I'll suffer the pain until my head is clearer. I cannot remember how I came to be here. It's like stepping into a new country."

He raised his thick eyebrows. "You cannot remember anything? That's quite a nasty blow you've taken. Let me fetch my mother while I throw a nanny into the blizzard."

With that astonishing statement, he followed the twins down the hall.

Would he really throw the nanny into the blizzard? She most certainly was inhabiting some book she must have read. Or she was dreaming. She was fairly certain her name was Damaris. Damaris Bedloe, not Lady Alice. Lady Alice was . . . *her cousin!*

Oh, dear.

Trev sent a footman in search of Georgie, dragged the nanny out of her hiding place, sent her to the kitchen to drink a pot of coffee, and watched over Mina as she scrubbed her filthy face and hands. Despite this latest contretemps, he was nearly giddy with anticipation.

Lady Alice liked children! Mack's wife could stay here and help with the household, and maybe even Mack would settle down to the pleasures of the marriage bed. He could use Mack's help with the damned paperwork. Mack had an excellent mathematical mind when he applied it. Besides, the last steward had left the office in disarray after Trev had sent him packing for pressing unwanted attention on a kitchen maid.

Finding good help who wanted to live in the isolation of the Lancashire moors was not simple. Lady Alice was a stroke of genius on Mack's part. Perhaps the lad had more Trevelyan in him than he'd shown thus far.

Keeping his hands firmly on small shoulders, Trev steered his daughters toward their grandmother's suite. They protested, wanting to take a book to Lady Alice, but he'd seen the pain in their guest's eyes as she rubbed her fore-head.

His mother was lounging beside the fire, reading one of the gossip sheets and sipping tea. After the episode with Nanny, he could only hope it was tea.

She looked up with a sigh at the sight of her granddaughters. "Can you not look like respectable young ladies instead of Gypsies just once?"

"The nanny needs to be dismissed," Trev said. "Meanwhile, I have to prevent these two from driving off our guest. Could you entertain them for a while? I want to find a switch to take to that eldest brat of mine."

"You can't beat Georgie for being a boy," his mother protested, changing her tune as she always did when she was not directly involved. "He'll be fine. Have one of the parlor maids teach the girls to sew. They should be able to embroider their initials by now."

The last time anyone had given the twins needles, Mina had sewn her sister to a Restoration-era footstool. They had both thought it quite amusing. "Just watch them, Mother. Read them a book. And if you have anything for an aching head, I believe Lady Alice could use it. She's refusing to take any more laudanum."

"She's young. She'll be fine, too." Vi waved a dismissive hand. "Go on. But if I hear young Georgie crying, it will be on your head."

Every responsibility in the household had been on his head since his father's death when he was ten. He had taken his duties seriously, even if his mother never followed through on her threats. Perhaps he should have been the one to run around London, leaving his younger brother to deal with the estate. Then Mack might have had a chance to learn responsibility.

But that had never been an option. If Mack didn't show

up soon, Trev would have to ride out on his own to box his brother's ears.

He wondered if it would be horrifically inappropriate to ask the lady's family if they would mind if she married immediately.

Although why the lady was alone was a bothersome question. The Earl of Reidland was a busy man, a widower, but surely he would have sent some relation with his daughter? Trev needed to question the lady—once she was feeling better, and maybe after he strangled Mack.

The effects of the laudanum wore off as the hours passed. Damaris's head still ached, but she was considerably more clear on who she was and where she might be, although the accident remained murky, and without proper introductions, she couldn't be positive of anyone's identity.

The children didn't return, and she spent the rest of that day idling in bed, alternately sleeping and eating and wishing for a good book. She didn't have much experience at the life of the idle rich and grew restless with nothing constructive to do. But without her trunk, she had no clothes, or even any mending to keep her occupied.

She needed to explain to the large, scary gentleman that she wasn't Lady Alice. That kept her fretting. A man who would throw a nanny into a blizzard was likely to send minions to the corners of the earth to drag Alice back here if he wanted her dowry. Although this mix-up was rather fortuitous, now that she thought about it. If she didn't reveal the charade yet, then Alice might have a better prospect of escaping the gentleman and her father's wrath. Since Damaris had little chance of receiving a reference from the earl, she was free to do as she pleased, she supposed. Independence came at a high cost, though, if it meant being flung into the bitter cold. She'd rather postpone the pleasure.

By morning, though, she really needed to "recover" her memory and give the viscount Alice's regrets.

She was still pretty unclear on most of the accident. When a maid arrived to restore the fire, Damaris attempted conversation. "Excuse me, but could you tell me how I came to arrive here? I cannot remember anything except the blizzard."

The very young maid looked startled to be thus addressed. Not more than twelve or thirteen, the girl dipped her gaze to the floor and returned to building the fire without answering.

Belatedly, Damaris remembered that ladies only addressed upper servants, and she was supposed to be an earl's daughter. She had an impolite thought or two about that, but she didn't want the girl to get in trouble. At least the staff must be well trained, even if the children weren't.

Shivering, Damaris was still debating whether a partial loss of memory justified pretending she was who she wasn't a while longer when an elegant older woman with graying hair and high cheekbones entered. Wearing billowing silk skirts fashionable in a prior century, she came bearing gossip sheets and a box of sweets.

"You're looking better, my dear," she said in the syrupy voice Damaris recalled hearing earlier. "I apologize for our harum-scarum ways, but I don't believe we've been properly introduced. Mack has apparently been delayed by the blizzard or I'm sure he would have organized us much better. I'm Violet, Lady Trevelyan, Mack's mother."

This *Mack* still had her puzzled, but Damaris responded politely. "Pleased to meet you."

Lady Trevelyan continued with her own order of business. "Now that the snow is done, we'll send men to fetch your trunks. Your driver elected to stay at the inn rather than risk his horses in the drifts on unpaved road. Shall we tell him to return south to your father, where the roads are better? We'll see that you're safely returned home."

It would very definitely be a good idea to send the driver home, Damaris decided. She nodded, trying not to panic and wonder how she would leave. But she couldn't ask for the earl's valuable cattle to be risked for her sake when the roads south would be much safer.

"I've asked Mrs. Worth to bring you a tisane for your poor head," the lady continued, apparently not needing more reply than that. "And I've brought you something to read and some sweets to soothe your spirits until our Mack returns. Cook makes a delicious Swiss chocolate fondant mixed with caramelized sugar. Positively decadent. You simply must try one." She offered both box and newssheets.

Damaris silently accepted the sweets. Perhaps if she never spoke, she would never have to explain who she was. But she'd been raised properly and couldn't avoid offering her gratitude. "Thank you, my lady. That is most kind."

"Violet, you simply must call me Violet. And I shall call you Alice, shall I? We are going to be the best of friends! I do hope your father won't object to an early wedding. Dear Mack is most impatient! Now I'll let you rest. Perhaps in the morning, after your trunk arrives, you can join me for a lovely coze!" Without waiting for agreement, she smiled benevolently and swept from the room.

Damaris thought she might have just experienced a whirlwind. Did they expect Alice to be speechless and obedient and without a brain in her head? From the reports she'd heard of Jonathan Trevelyan, that was possible. He would most likely prefer an empty-headed coquette with a large dowry so he might continue his dissolute ways. Or so Alice had said.

But *Jonathan* had asked for Alice's hand. Was there another brother called Mack? Not the one who'd offered for Alice.

Her head hurt to think about it. She eased the pain by tasting one of the chocolate sweets, and thought she just might swoon again. Alice had always shared her sweets, but Damaris had never tasted anything so decadently delicious. For chocolate like this, she would pretend to be Alice forever. She could grow quite accustomed to luxury if it wasn't so boring.

With nothing better to do, she picked up the gossip sheet. It was over a month old, and she had no idea to whom all the initials belonged in the chatty columns. She could follow what the Prince Regent was doing from the HRH, of course, but Alice hadn't traveled in his circles.

Here was mention of an MT, a Visct T's brother. Could that be Mack? If so, he'd apparently played a good game at White's last month, if she understood the slang correctly. He'd bought a pair of new bays. Apparently the new horses weren't sufficient to bring him home in winter.

Could E of R be Alice's father, the Earl of Reidland? If so, he was apparently courting a lady half his age. Oh, dear. No wonder the earl had been so preoccupied lately and wasn't returning home for Christmas! Alice hadn't told her that. Did she know?

If so, it might explain her haste to escape. That hurt a bit. They used to share everything.

Feeling very lonely, she ate another chocolate.

Even knowing the pandemonium that would reign without any authority in the nursery, Trev informed the nanny she was dismissed and would be leaving in the morning when the men fetched Lady Alice's trunks. A drunken authority was more dangerous than none at all, and he had a low tolerance for deception.

Leaving behind a weeping nanny, he grabbed his greatcoat and led the footmen in search of Georgie. After finding his protesting son in the woods and banishing him to his room, Trev dealt with two of his tenants over a cattle dispute, grabbed some cold meat and bread off the dinner buffet and finished the accounting for the day. By then, he had almost forgotten their guest. Almost.

The hope she'd brought had carried him through his tasks with a spring in his step that he hadn't felt in years. She was a slender thing, and the ugly bruise on her brow hadn't helped her appearance, but in his eyes, she was absolutely perfect, if only because she'd conversed pleasantly with his daughters instead of criticizing them.

It was only then that he realized he hadn't introduced himself. She'd think him a cowhanded chub and this a very improper household.

He sent a maid up to see if the lady was still awake and would accept a few minutes of company. He was fairly certain that was how it was supposed to be done, although living out here in the wilds most of his life, his experience was secondhand at best. His mother had long since given up any pretense at propriety that would disturb her comfort.

He'd visited with school friends in London before he'd married, knew proper ladies had an etiquette all their own, but left with three children and an estate, he was out of practice.

He stopped in his room and checked a mirror to be certain his neckcloth was still tied and to comb his unruly hair. He really should have it cut, or he would deserve the *barbarian* epithet his mother frequently cast at him. At this hour, he needed a shave as well, but their guest would fall asleep before he could manage that.

All he needed to do was convince an earl's daughter that this was a dignified household and that she would be welcome here. The second part was far easier than the first.

She was sitting up against the pillows, reading his mother's gossip sheets, when he arrived. The maids had burned her torn and bloody gown and dressed her in one of his mother's bed sacques. She'd apparently brushed out her lovely fair hair and pulled it into a braid. At least she hadn't thrown a hysterical fit when she'd discovered she had nothing to wear. His mother and his late wife would have been sending footmen out in the blizzard to fetch their trunks.

Before knocking, Trev stole a moment to study this woman his brother had chosen. She had kind eyes, he'd already noted. A wide brow, good teeth, and clear skin. She was no ravishing beauty, but once the bruises faded and she was properly dressed, she'd shine like a subtle ornament.

Which immediately made him suspicious. Mack wasn't into subtlety. Mack liked flashy jewels. He could only hope that Mack had finally turned a leaf and accepted his duties by choosing a sensible wife. Was that too much to hope?

Probably. Trev hadn't done so well in that area in his youth, so he was skeptical of Mack succeeding where he'd failed.

He rapped on the door jamb, and she looked up warily. The bruise looked quite painful and seemed to be spreading down her delicate jaw. He was grateful her injuries were not any more serious.

"I'm afraid I was quite rude earlier," he said, "and failed to introduce myself. I'm Adam Trevelyan, Mack's brother, and I'm very pleased to meet you. How does your head feel?"

She touched a hand to the worst bump. "I think it is a little better. I'm sorry I was so foggy at our first meeting. Do you mind telling me how I came to be here?"

She didn't introduce herself, he noticed. Perhaps she thought she already had if her head was still muzzy. He hoped she hadn't addled her brains. Sitting there in his mother's bedjacket, she looked delicate enough to snap with a single blow. They were blamed lucky she hadn't been killed!

"Your carriage went off the road not too far from a local inn," he told her. "A farmer discovered your plight, wrapped you up and took you in while your driver settled the horses. Your driver told them your destination, so the innkeeper sent for me. I'm very sorry that our invitation has led to this mishap."

"A storm this early in the season is unusual," she said agreeably, not pointing a finger of blame. "We were equally responsible for accepting."

She seemed to be guarding her words, perhaps because of her memory? He was simply relieved not to be called to task. "I'll send word to your father of your arrival once the road clears. Is he in London?"

"Yes. He had other plans for Christmas, which is why we thought this visit might be agreeable."

She kept speaking of *we*. Uneasily, Trev attempted to find out more without disturbing her. "My men did not mention your maid or companion. Should I be looking for her?"

She closed her eyes and seemed to struggle with herself, crumpling the newssheet in her hands. He wanted to tell her not to worry, that he'd ride out and look for the wench himself, but he needed to know who he was looking for.

"She ran away," the lady whispered. "At the last inn. I'm so sorry to arrive this way."

"You can hardly be faulted for the actions of others," Trev said reassuringly, while fretting at the oddity. Lady's maids did not generally run away. He hoped Mack was not perpetrating some fraud by sending an impostor, but he failed to see the purpose. "I will assign one of the parlor maids to you. She will be thrilled with the opportunity, but I fear she will be inadequate compared to your own maid."

"That is kind of you. I dislike leaving your housekeeper shorthanded, though. Perhaps your mother would not mind sharing her maid if I promise not to ask for her too frequently?"

She worried about his housekeeper more than a viscountess? Trev shivered at the possibility of more chaos in the household as the servants jockeyed for her good will and ignored his mother. But he supposed the important thing was that Mack was settling down with a good woman. He wished he was better at winkling information out of ladies. He'd love to spend an evening conversing with someone just for the pleasure, and Lady Alice seemed to have a good head on her shoulders.

"An excellent idea, thank you. Mack must be extremely proud that you have consented to be his wife. I hope he has been all that he should be as a suitor?"

She clasped her hands and blinked long lashes, then replied with care, "As far as I'm aware, my lord."

That was not precisely the satisfactory answer he was seeking, and Trev's worry knot twisted tighter. Should not a romantic blushing bride extol the virtues of her groom? Was she having second thoughts already? "Did he warn you that we were likely at sixes and sevens out here? I hope our country ways have not frightened you."

She looked quite surprised at that. Trev would have to wring his brother's neck if he'd promised her roses. Trev didn't want to be the one to explain to this demure lady that the household lacked the sophistication, decorum, and society to which she was accustomed. That they expected the young couple to live here, within their means, had to be sufficiently daunting. He really didn't want the lady to run screaming into the night.

"I have been treated with extreme kindness, my lord," was her mild reply.

Trev took a deep breath and decided if Lady Alice wasn't the shining gem she appeared, he didn't want to know. "I don't wish to disturb you any longer. I hope your stay will be less eventful from here on out. Trevelyans are sound riders, and Jonathan MacOwen Trevelyan one of the best. He will arrive as soon as the road clears. Good night, my lady."

He bowed out, still a trifle confused but hopeful. The snow had stopped. He'd have messengers galloping to London in the morning in search of his lout of a sibling.

The viscount had truly not seemed to be an ogre last night, Damaris thought, running her fingers across the fine fabric of Alice's gown. She had found him breathtakingly gracious and kind. Or perhaps that had just been his charming dimple to which she reacted. He still had every right to fling her into the snow if he discovered she wasn't an earl's daughter and brought no money to his coffers. Which he would learn as soon as *Jonathan MacOwen* arrived. The last of the confusion had been sorted out.

Despite being perfectly clear that she was a fraud who needed to figure out how to leave as quickly as possible, Damaris hadn't argued when the luggage arrived and the maid had disdained her practical gray bombazines. Instead, Lady Trevelyan's maid had delighted in picking through Alice's fine muslins and choosing a confection in white. The girlish puffed sleeves and pink ribbons looked a trifle silly on Damaris, but she'd covered them up with a colorful kashmir shawl. She was feeling dauntingly rebellious and unlike her usual self.

"Help! Hide me! She'll kill me!"

A blur of blue and soot dashed under Damaris's bed, leaving the bed curtains swaying. Sitting in a fireside chair, Damaris stopped examining her bruised face in Alice's hand mirror to stare in dismay from bed to door. She already knew to expect still another visitor to follow. A maid had chased the twins from the room twice this morning. She didn't think she'd been introduced to the imp now hiding under the bed.

A scullery lad, perhaps? What kind of household was this that threatened mayhem on children and servants alike?

A harried maid arrived in the doorway as expected. "Did Master Georgie come this way, my lady?" she asked with a bob.

"Would that be the young man covered in soot?" Damaris asked.

"That would be the rascal, miss," the maid said. "After his lordship sent Nanny packing, Master Georgie tried to climb the chimney to escape the nursery, and now there's soot everywhere."

He really had thrown out the nanny! Oh, dear. Still, Damaris could not fight the disobedient twitch of her lips. She had often wished she could climb a chimney and fly away. She supposed the scamp ought to be punished, but if *she* was being willfully deceptive, then she could scarcely condemn a *boy* for a much more minor infraction. "Did he leave a trail of soot you can follow?"

"He's been all up and down the hall and stairs," the girl said in exasperation. "There's soot everywhere."

"Then when I see him, I shall tell him he must sweep it up." That was no lie. Perhaps evasions were equal to lies, but Damaris had learned evasion in her first days as a companion. The earl had been difficult, the servants hadn't accepted her, and she'd had trouble adjusting to her in-between position. Evasion and subservience had made life easier.

What she would really like was to tell the truth, but that never worked out well in her experience.

The maid bobbed another curtsy and ran off.

"Do you know where to find a broom, Master Georgie?" Damaris asked the seemingly empty room.

"No, ma'am," the boy said from under the bed. "Papa banished me to my room, and I'm bored!"

"Yes, well, that may be, but it might have been more responsible to apologize for your infraction and ask politely if you might come out of your room instead of climbing a chimney. Now you must pay the price of your foolishness. There should be a broom in the kitchen. Go down, make your apologies to Mrs. Worth, and ask if you might have a broom and dustpan. She'll be so shocked, she'll forget to kill you."

A small chestnut head popped out from beneath the bed skirt. "Really? You promise?"

"I promise," she said rashly. "Tell her I sent you."

"Should he change from his filth first?" a dry male voice asked from the doorway.

The boy popped back under the bed.

"If he has anything he doesn't need to wear again," Damaris replied in the same tone. "He will be all filth either way."

The viscount was dressed in country drab this morning. From the ruddy color on his cheeks, she surmised he'd been outside in the cold for quite a while and had just returned.

"You have some experience with young boys?" he asked, so obviously suppressing eagerness that Damaris had to bite back a smile.

And just a frisson of hope. Could she offer to be taken on as nanny? Not if she continued to pretend she was Lady Alice. The next question—Did she wish to be thought of as a servant for the rest of her life?

Of course. What else did the future have to offer?

But gazing at the handsome viscount . . . She sighed in wistfulness. She could never dream to capture a man of his consequence, and if she told him who she really was, he'd throw her out into the blizzard, too. She was enjoying her brief respite much too well to wish for that.

"Three brothers, my lord," she said, condemning herself with the lie. Alice had three younger brothers in school. Damaris had no one. "But he is your son. You know him best."

"Georgie, remove yourself from the bed at once," the viscount thundered in a voice that could command troops. "You owe Mrs. Worth an apology. Go change and then do as Lady Alice says."

"She'll kill me," a small voice whispered.

Damaris almost melted at sight of her host's stern visage softening into a grin with a dimple that disappeared the moment his son peered out from under the bed.

"She cannot kill you, even if she might wish," he said. "So take your punishment like a man."

The boy sighed and wriggled out of his hiding place. "But I am not a man," he protested. "I am only a little boy."

"You are master of this household," the viscount said sternly. "You must learn to take responsibility for your actions."

The boy stuck out his bottom lip and marched off, sending Damaris a last look of hope, as if she could free him from his burdens. She hid her smile and nodded solemnly in approval. He sighed and dragged out.

"He *is* a little boy," she pointed out the instant the child was gone. If she was about to be thrown into the blizzard, she might as well say what she thought. It wasn't a freedom she'd be granted again. "Telling him he is a master may be too heavy a burden for small shoulders."

"It's what I was told when I was his age. He is pandered to by every other soul in the house. Someone must teach him his duties." He frowned at her, as if she'd accused him of making the boy into a slave.

Had her uncle frowned at her like that, she would have quaked in her shoes. It was amazing how fearless she could be when she had nothing left to lose. "I agree, but perhaps the duties should be small ones, like finishing his schoolwork. It must be rather daunting to believe he must take care of an entire estate. Children are very literal."

The viscount's brow dragged down in a heavy frown, but

he did not yell. "Literal? Perhaps." He brushed off the argument and was again the cheerful host. "How are you this morning? You are looking much better."

"I am feeling much better, thanks to your kindness. I'm still a little vague on how I came to be here, but I'm most grateful to be rescued." Here is where she ought to say, *But there seems to be a misunderstanding. . . .*

She could not bring herself to do it. She wanted to stay here for as long as possible. If they were waiting for irresponsible Jonathan to come claim Lady Alice, Damaris wagered they'd have a long wait. Of course, once he showed up, her game was all over.

"You took quite a bad blow. It is not unusual to forget the accident that caused it," the viscount said sympathetically. "Sufficient to say that your coachman and horses are safe and well, and you were the only victim. I've sent your carriage home, and you are welcome to stay for as long as you like, although with no nanny and Christmas only weeks away, the children are likely to be wild, I fear."

Damaris thought longingly of childhood Christmases. Her parents had not been wealthy, but they'd been happy. She remembered the lovely scents of pine boughs, oranges, and boiling puddings, the happy laughter filling the halls as her parents hid presents from each other. That had been so very long ago . . . before the influenza epidemic that had snatched them away.

Sniffing back a tear, she smiled weakly. She had no chance of sharing that happiness again, unless rakehell Jonathan refused to leave London, and even then, her stay could only be temporary.

She could live with temporary. Perhaps Alice would have found a place for her by then.

"I will gladly help with the children while I am here," she offered, holding back her hopes. Perhaps they would not be too angry at her pretense if she was helpful.

"I cannot ask that of you!" he said, genuinely shocked. "Even experienced nannies cannot deal with the brats. They've been dreadfully spoiled, I fear."

"Children do not spoil in the same way milk sours," she pointed out. "They simply need love, attention, consistent rules, and occupation that suits them. It is rather difficult for one person to provide all that, but if everyone agrees on what they should be doing and when, and enforces the rules, they'll learn quickly."

"That was the nanny's job," he protested. "I cannot be expected to spend my days tracking them, and my mother has always been inconsistent in her treatment. Perhaps I should hire two nannies."

"A governess," Damaris boldly suggested, wishing she could be the one he hired. "The children have active minds and they are not toddlers. I'm surprised your son is not at school already."

"My mother did not allow us to go to school until we were much older, and we survived. But if I keep him home instead of sending him to school, I need both a tutor for Georgie and a governess for the twins. I have difficulty keeping even a nanny."

Damaris was thoroughly enjoying having a real conversation with a man who respected her intelligence instead of ignoring her as if she were invisible. The sensation was so heady that she did not hold her tongue as she ought. "You need to know the right people and ask the right questions to find good servants. I suppose, if you were married, your wife might do that. But I can write . . ." She hesitated, trying to think and speak like Alice. "I can write to my brothers' former tutor and ask for suggestions."

He nodded gravely. "I would be most appreciative. I've not had time for visiting London, and my man of business is in Manchester. Most of our servants have been from that area. Perhaps it is time to look farther."

A loud thump, a terrifying screech, and a clamor of screams interrupted any more pleasant communication. The viscount dashed away without apology. Unable to bear staying idle, Damaris lifted her—Alice's—narrow skirt and rushed after him.

Trev tore into the morning salon from which the screams were emanating. A massive Jacobean bench blocked his view of the floor. A chandelier chain jack swung freely, but the massive chandelier no longer hung from the ceiling. The sight gave him heart palpitations.

Two doves distractedly flapped their wings on the enormous timber mantel amid a stack of evergreen boughs he didn't remember seeing earlier. The kitchen cat clung to the frayed medieval tapestry on the wall, wailing its fury. And for some reason, the goat the twins had adopted last summer was nibbling the fringe of his mother's upholstered chair.

Georgie was shouting and jumping up and down in an attempt to reach the chain jack that lifted the chandelier. Maids screamed uselessly. He could hear the twins but not see them. Not a good sign. Trev vaulted the bench and nearly fell over the ornate iron and crystal chandelier on the floor.

One twin lay beneath the heavy ring of iron, while the other desperately attempted to lift it with her chubby hands. Candles and crystals were scattered across the floor and thick carpet. Trev crushed them as he dropped to his knees to lift the chandelier from his daughter's crumpled form.

He didn't think he could breathe unless he knew Mina was breathing. Of course it was Mina. He could picture the entire episode from beginning to end—the children carrying in evergreens followed by doves and goat. Birds flying to roost on the chandelier. Georgie trying to lower the fixture to capture the birds. Mina reaching for them. . . . Trev wanted to close his eyes and gasp for breath, but he had to lift a half-ton wheel first.

And he needed someone to extricate Mina while he did. Now that he was here, she started to cry, and her big eyes stared at him pleadingly from her nest of ragged curls. She was alive. Trev heaved the wheel up and shouted to the room at large.

No one did the obvious.

His mother raced in and added her screeches to the maids'. The goat wandered over to taste his trousers. Georgie hauled on the chain reel—sensible but useless because he was much too small to wind it.

Where were the damned footmen? Trev couldn't hold the fixture forever, but he couldn't allow Mina to be crushed again!

Into his panic raced fragile Lady Alice, a single strand of fair hair falling from her coiffure, her delicate muslin clinging to her womanly curves. To Trev, she was a vision of an angel. Without a single shriek or question, she slid beneath the section of the chandelier he'd lifted. She shouted at one of the maids to kneel down and brace the weight so she might check Mina for broken bones before moving her. She ordered the other maid to fetch a footman.

And miraculously, everyone obeyed her crisp commands. She was sturdier than he'd thought when she'd been lying pale and listless in the bed. She was everything feminine on the outside but capable of thinking for herself. Where had women like this been all his life?

With someone to share his burden, Trev could think clearly again. "Georgie, wrap the chain around the ring in the fireplace to help hold it," he ordered. "Mother, help him, or at least call for a stable lad to help him. Tina, see how much of the glass you can sweep away with the chimney broom so we may move Mina from under here without scratching her."

With Lady Alice speaking reassuring words to his daughter, easing her from danger, Trev could have held the wheel for a century. It was as if the weight of the chandelier was as nothing compared to the weight of the household he'd been carrying all his life. He sent a footman running for a physician. Under Lady Alice's direction, another lifted Mina as if she were porcelain. Trev even managed a few comforting words for his other children as he lowered the wheel back to the carpet.

He hadn't wept since he was ten and his father had died, but he was on the verge now, only these were tears of gratitude. And perhaps a little of despair that Mack had found this gem and would never appreciate his good fortune.

Trev hugged Georgie and Tina and reassured them as they cried and tried to explain. He really didn't care what had happened. It would happen time and again if he did not gain control of his household. And he feared that would never come about as things stood. He needed help, he had to acknowledge. He could no longer convince himself that nannies and nursemaids were sufficient to watch over his children, but he could not do it alone.

Trev left Georgie and Tina in the hands of his mother, forcing Vi to take charge instead of retreating to her chamber. In her confusion, she actually ushered them upstairs without protest.

Then, drawing a deep breath and steeling himself for the worst, he entered the nursery where Lady Alice and a nursemaid were tending to Mina—who was chattering like a chickadee.

Trev nearly staggered with relief. Lady Alice glanced up and offered him a tentative smile. He probably looked like a towering tyrant to her, but he couldn't bring himself to relax just yet. He pulled a chair up close to the bed and took Mina's tiny hand. He adored his children. He just didn't know what to do with them. He despised being helpless.

"I think she may have tried to stop the fall with her arm. That appears to be the worst damage, but I'm no physician. I've asked your mother for some of the medicine she gave me, to ease the pain, but I think we must give her only a little bit since she's so small." Lady Alice didn't look up from binding Mina's swelling arm with a length of muslin.

Mina winced and looked at him tearfully. "I just wanted to shoo the birdies out," she whispered. "I knew you wouldn't like them."

"It's all right, sweetheart. You couldn't know how heavy the wheel is. Georgie shouldn't have lowered it, but he didn't know, either." Trev had known, but he hadn't been there. A nanny would have known, but he'd thrown her out. He wanted to howl his dismay to the moon, but that wouldn't help anyone.

"You should have called a footman, Miss Mina. That's why you have servants, to help. Perhaps you'll remember that next time the goat gets in the house." Lady Alice said this with such good cheer that even Mina smiled through her pain.

Trev wanted to hug the beautiful lady. He wanted to find Mack and drag him to the altar this very minute so she could not escape his Bedlam. But he stoically sat with his injured child and waited for the physician.

When the physician finally arrived, Lady Alice rose to give him her seat and step out of the way.

"Saw young Mack riding hell for leather in this direction," the elderly doctor said, competently testing Mina's arm. "I thought someone was dying."

Lady Alice blanched beneath her yellowing bruise, Trev noted. If she feared Mack's arrival, that did not bode well for their betrothal. But he could do nothing while his daughter was in pain.

"I'll see to Georgie and Tina," the lady whispered, fleeing the room before Trev could even form a question.

* * *

Oh, dear. Oh, my. What should she do now?

Panic rattled about inside Damaris's addled brain. She could only do what came naturally—seek out the children to reassure them that all was well, as promised. And pray a plan of escape would occur. She could no longer doubt that Jonathan and Mack were one and the same. He'd had plenty of time to arrive by now. Surely he would come looking for her at any moment.

She should have known her luck wouldn't last, that she could never linger in luxury under false pretenses. It had been foolish of her to believe anyone might want her.

She kneeled on Lady Violet's luxurious bedroom carpet and opened her arms to the weeping children. They laid their heads on her shoulders and tried to explain about goats and doves and wanting to decorate for the holidays. Damaris took as much comfort from holding them as they seemed to take from her. Perhaps she really should ask to be their nanny.

Lord Trevelyan could not possibly trust a nanny who posed as someone she was not.

And she could not bear to work for a man who was everything she had ever dreamed of in a man. He'd single-handedly raised that monstrous chandelier as if he were a mighty blacksmith! Her heart bled for him and his children. No, she could not be their nanny. She must leave, immediately.

Lady Violet hovered anxiously, then decided hot chocolate was the answer for everything and called to have a tray brought up. With the children settled at a table with pastries and chocolate, Damaris decided she must pack her trunk and then look for a footman to help her find a way back to the inn.

First, she returned to the morning room to tell the servants that all would be well and to be certain they were returning the room to rights. Lord Trevelyan had his hands full as it was. She could do him this last little courtesy for his kindness in rescuing her.

Someone had removed the goat, but the doves were still fluttering about, out of reach. A footman had hauled the chandelier chain to return it to the ceiling, although it looked sadly bent and lopsided from the fall. Damaris suggested placing bread crumbs in a bushel basket, then throwing a tablecloth over the top when the birds landed inside.

While one maid swept debris from the plush carpet, another raced off to find a basket. Having done all she could, Damaris started up the stairs to pack her—Alice's—trunk. She had her savings in her reticule. She could manage a night at the inn and a coach to . . . somewhere.

A dashing young man racing up the staircase nearly bowled her over. Looking grim, he apologized, righted her, then continued on as if she were nothing and nobody. And so she was.

Since she just barely recognized him, she supposed she had no right to expect Jonathan Trevelyan to recognize her, especially with a bruise on her face. Perhaps she could escape before there was a confrontation.

She packed the trunk herself rather than disturb Lady Violet and her maid. She offered the footman a coin to fetch a cart and driver and asked them to be brought around in an hour.

She could not leave without saying farewell, she discovered. She just could not. She might have learned meekness out of necessity, but apparently she did possess some backbone.

She stopped at Lady Violet's suite first, and froze when she saw Jonathan pacing the length of the room with Georgie on his shoulders.

"Of course she's not with child, Mother, what a dreadful thing to say. She's a sweet chit with a large dowry. I'll cease to be a drag on the estate once we're wedded. I hadn't thought to be leg-shackled immediately, though. I just won a great deal of blunt, but if you insist. . . ."

He reached the far end of the room and turned just as Lady Violet cried, "Lady Alice! Mack has arrived!"

A sweet chit with a large dowry, indeed! Damaris fixed the foolish young man with a frosty gaze. "Sorry to disappoint, sir," she said without the least bit of regret, before he could recover from his startlement. "But Lady Alice prefers to be loved for herself and not her dowry. By now, she is quite safely wedded by special license to a fine young man who worships her."

"Who the devil are you?" the Honorable Jonathan Trevelyan shouted.

"Lady Alice's companion. I don't expect you to have noticed me when you so obviously never noticed what a fine woman Alice is. Next time, choose someone who does not mind being married for her wealth. Better yet, take a position and earn your own." She could scarcely believe the words had come out of her mouth, but she had years of pent-up opinions that finally spilled forth with this astonishing freedom to speak her mind.

Ignoring the wicked blasphemies emitted by the spoiled young lord, Damaris dipped a respectful curtsy to the dowager viscountess. "My sincerest apologies, my lady. I did not deliberately set out to deceive you, but I was somewhat scrambled in my thoughts for a time. All is very plain now, and I must clear up any confusion I unwittingly caused. I am Lady Alice's cousin, Damaris Bedloe. I had come to give you and Jonathan her regrets. If you would be so good as to offer Lord Trevelyan my gratitude for his hospitality, I will leave now."

She swung on her heel and marched off, her heart weeping at leaving this home—and the man—that she could never have. It was beyond foolish to believe one could fall in love in the matter of a few days. He had just awakened her dreams, that's all.

But she was not to escape so easily. As the footman carried her trunk out the front door, heavy footsteps hit the stairs at a precarious pace behind her. She knew who it was without turning. She wished she could flee before she must see the disappointment, or worse yet the fury on his handsome visage.

But she had dug this hole and must face the consequences. Holding her chin up, she met Lord Trevelyan's fierce gaze. Her heart almost shattered and died at the sight, but she soldiered on. "My lord," she said grimly. "Again, I am sorry. I cannot say what came over me, and I cannot apologize enough. Let us leave it at that, please."

Whatever had been behind the wild-eyed look he'd first given her quickly shuttered. He nodded stiffly to match her cool tones. "Will you be returning to Lady Alice?"

The hole in her heart tore a little wider. "I do not know, my lord. My duty was to raise my cousin as if she were my own, and I have done so. She's a wife and on her own now."

"I can offer you a position here," he said gruffly. "I know we are not all that is proper, but the children . . ."

She held up her hand before he could finish offering her the position she wanted so much to accept and knew it would kill her to fill. "No, my lord. Your children are beyond adorable. I have told you what they need. Perhaps in time you will find a wife who can help you. Until then, I'll send you the names of a few tutors and governesses who might suit. I am not qualified. I give you good day, and once again, my apologies." She dipped a low curtsy and left before he could see her weep.

Trev sat with his brandy and his misery before a roaring fire that evening. Mina's arm had been set, and she'd been dosed with laudanum to keep her quiet. Mack was sulking in his room after Trev had given him a sharp set down. Would Mack have turned out better had he been sent to a strict school—away from their permissive mother—a little sooner? Should he send Georgie?

He had no way of knowing. He had built the estate into one that could support a dozen families. He could balance account books, choose what fields to plant with which crop, decide on the best horse or bull, and pick a fine wine, but he did not know how to be both a mother and father to his children. They were the most important part of his life, and he was failing them.

The blasted deceptive female he'd hoped would teach him what the children needed had said they should have rules and teachers and he ought to have a wife to help him, but there was another thing he was very bad at—choosing a woman. He'd thought this one perfect, and she'd been lying to him the whole time. So why should he believe anything she said? Like his late wife, she'd left all in chaos. The children were devastated to lose her. They were well rid of her, even if they didn't understand.

And yet, he missed her. After the day's events, his insides were hollow. She'd left a hollow where there had been hope and joy. She'd awakened a heart that he'd thought dormant, if not dead. The desire for a real family that he'd allowed to seep into him had been crushed, and he saw nothing to replace it on the horizon.

He was actually sitting here anticipating how long it would take for the deceptive chit to send him a letter with the names of tutors! As if that were likely to happen.

The study door creaked, and a small shadow crept into the room. Trev said nothing as Georgie sidled up and snuggled into the large seat beside him. The boy was supposed to be in bed. There was no one to keep him there. Trev couldn't think of a punishment the boy would believe should he threaten him with it.

He loved his children, but Miss Bedloe had been right. They needed rules, and they needed to be enforced.

"Are we ever going to have a mama?" Georgie whispered.

Leave it to a child to go straight to the crux of the problem. "I'd have to go to London to find one," Trev told him, putting the question aside. "I would be gone a very long time. You wouldn't want that. Now go on up to bed."

Miss Bedloe would probably have asked the boy why he wanted to know. But Trev knew and didn't want to hear it.

"The twins and I talked," Georgie said insistently. "We want the pretty lady to be our mama. She would be our Christmas present. You would never ever have to find us another present. You could give her our Christmas oranges, and we'd promise to be good forever."

Trev kept his curses to himself. He ruffled Georgie's hair and pried him out of the chair, pointing him to the door. "If it was as simple as that, I'd agree, but it's not. To bed with you or you'll never ever have another present."

Georgie pouted and refused to leave. "She *likes* us. You made her leave. It's all your fault!" he cried, before running off on stockinged feet.

Well, yes, it probably was his fault. If she was Lady Alice's cousin, she was of good family—and he'd offered to make her his servant. He deserved to have his face smacked.

What else was he supposed to do? He barely knew the woman except to know she'd lied and deceived.

And hugged his children and made them love her. And ordered his servants about and made them obey. And behaved sensibly and intelligently in every way except the one—and if she was protecting her cousin from a thoughtless lout like Mack, Trev couldn't really argue with that, either. Such a deception had taken courage.

Opportunity had knocked, and he'd closed the door because he'd been burned once. *Stupid, Trev, really cork-brained stupid.* He kneaded his forehead and fought back a wave of anguish.

With nowhere better to go, Damaris caught a coach heading south, out of the rapidly melting snow. Remembering the blizzard that had led her to Trevelyan Hall, she blinked back tears, desperately attempting not to think of the viscount. Discovering she could actually harbor a lovely dream was one thing, but losing her heart to a handsome, caring gentleman with too many burdens on his mind, whom she'd met only days before, no less. . . . Well, she'd been raised to be more practical than that. If only her heart would mend and the tears would go away.

At a lovely inn near Cheltenham, she dabbed at her eyes with a handkerchief and decided to stay awhile. The cost was cheaper than the city, and the food was good. She wrote Alice to ask if any of her friends might need a companion, and for the names of good governesses for the poor, deceived Trevelyans. She deserved a broken heart for what she'd done to them.

During the days, Damaris explored and made discreet inquiries about the wealthy families in the area, hoping she could find employment here.

She'd met many of the earl's acquaintants over the years, but she could not immediately think of one who would need her services, such as they were. And it would be best to wait until the bruise had completely faded before applying for any positions.

She had just received a reply from Alice and was scrubbing another tear from her eye when the innkeeper announced she had a gentleman caller. Alice had said she would send Theodore to fetch her to London, but Damaris had not thought he would arrive with the mail!

Not wishing to look as if she'd been crying, she tidied herself as best as she could and arranged her hair so the last of the bruise did not appear too grievous. Then she hastened downstairs to the private parlor to which the innkeeper directed her.

She froze at the sight of the tall gentleman pacing the room in travel-worn riding attire, slapping his boots anxiously with his crop. His hat looked as if it had wallowed in mud before he'd discarded it on the table. His tall boots were all filth as well. And when he turned around . . . she saw the dark circles beneath his eyes and the lines of weariness where his dimple should have been.

"Mina!" she said in dread. "Has something happened to Mina?"

His smile lit all the way to his eyes. "That is your very first thought when you see me?"

Flustered, she didn't know what to say. She clasped her hands and sought frantically for another reason for Lord Trevelyan to track her down. She could not even imagine how he had done so. "Unless you have come to arrest me for fraud, I cannot think why else you would be here."

His smile died, and he began smacking his boot again with his crop. "You must think me a bumblewit. Mina is doing well. The physician says he believes he only cracked a bone, and that children are very resilient."

Recovering from her shock, heart still pounding, Damaris nodded cautiously. "I am glad to hear it. Would you care for some tea? The innkeeper should have asked."

"Let me have my speech first. Then you may throw me out on my thick head." He hit said head with the heel of his hand and reached for a package on the mantel. "I brought you these."

In wonder, Damaris took the box, then smiled at the childish drawings adorning it. "The children painted this," she exclaimed. "How exquisite!"

He nervously shrugged broad shoulders. "I am crass enough to use all the persuasion I can muster. Open it. I had ordered them for the children, but they have assured me that you are more important than gifts."

She blinked in amazement, but he was staring fixedly at the box. With trembling fingers and no thought in her empty head, she opened the pretty box to find half a dozen fragrant oranges inside. "Oh, my, how wonderful! I used to have an orange every Christmas."

"It was all I had to say you're special to us. I do not have a hothouse full of flowers to provide a bouquet. I believe that is how London gentlemen woo their ladies. I thought you might be a trifle more practical and prefer the oranges."

"W-w-woo?" Damaris stuttered in disbelief. She feared her newly discovered dreams were filling her head and that she was reading more into his words than was there.

He nodded decisively, disturbing a handsome curl in the process, and Damaris almost lost her heart then. Except she knew it to be already lost.

"Woo," he said, his face set in determination. "I envied Mack when I thought you were his. But I've been so mired in despising marriage that I did not even consider it when you disclaimed him. First, let me apologize for offering a lady such as yourself a position as governess."

Clinging to the wonderful box with one hand, Damaris covered her mouth with the other. Surely she was not misunderstanding him. "Marriage?" she asked. "To me? I am not qualified to be so much as a governess." And even her uncle had never recognized her as a lady.

The viscount waved an impatient hand. "I don't want you to be a governess. I want to woo you so you will be assured that we suit and that I'm not a total empty-headed ninnyhammer. My mother has agreed to remove herself to the dower house and take you as a guest so all will be proper. I may go mad with waiting, but marriage is worth doing this properly."

"Me?" she asked again, unaccustomed to seeing silver linings in the dark cloud of her life. "Why me when you are free to court all the wealthy ladies in London?"

He looked slightly embarrassed as he ran his hand over his bristly cheek. "Do you really think I am interested in silly misses who flirt fans and titter? *Mack* needs to marry wealth and pay his own debts. I need to marry a sensible woman who can come to love me and my children. I want to marry someone who can hold her end of the conversation, someone I can love as I love my children. I never hoped I could find all of that in the same woman."

A tear streaked down her cheek, and Damaris thought this might be one of joy. "Could you come to love a woman who deceived you so badly?"

"You deceived me and everyone else quite well, actually," he said cheerfully. "I would never have believed you to be the meek, mild companion your cousin claims you are. Or the ungrateful termagant your uncle is currently shouting about. It seems you have hidden your true self for years. I want the intelligent, forthright woman I saw in my house, the one who knows what to do and does it. And the children have promised to never ask for another gift if I bring you home with me."

Damaris laughed. She actually laughed. She could not remember the last time she'd felt free enough to express her joy. Before she could recover her equilibrium, Viscount Trevelyan's big arms swept her from the floor, and a man's demanding lips covered hers.

The first crush of his mouth created more excitement than even her dreams could have produced. She reveled in the smell of horse, leather, and man, the scratch of bristles on her cheeks, the strength supporting her. She boldly wrapped her arms around his neck, showing him the thrill his words and his touch raised in her heart. He clasped her close, until their hearts beat as one, and she melted into his embrace. His kiss became fiercer, and she responded with all the courage she'd never known she possessed.

She did not know how it came about, but she knew deep in her soul that they were connected, that somehow guardian angels had brought them together.

And perhaps those angels resembled the three cherubs waiting impatiently for their return.

Damaris greedily claimed her first real kiss and vowed to be everything Adam Trevelyan needed, as long as she could be this woman he was kissing now.

It promised to be a merry Christmas, after all.

On a Wicked
Winter's Night

Nicola Cornick

Chapter 1

Newport, Pembrokeshire, Wales—December 1814

It was a stormy night, black as pitch, the wind high in the branches of the bare trees and the sleet drifting like a ghost across the road. Some way back they had passed an inn, the only sign of life in a landscape as bleak as the night. He had pulled aside the curtain and for one brief moment the carriage lamps had illuminated the sign swinging in the wind: THE SILENT WENCH. There had been a picture of Queen Anne Boleyn, smiling demurely, and behind her the shadow of the executioner. Someone in this godforsaken place, Johnny thought, had a dark sense of humor.

Surely it could not be much farther to Newport Castle. He had traveled for three days over roads that the mild winter rain had set awash, staying in execrable coaching inns with flea-infested beds, feeling as though he were journeying to the end of the world. The weather had turned colder as they traveled west. The driver was probably frozen to his box by now. They should have spent the night in St. David's and covered the final few miles in the morning. Or, preferably, stayed in London. He remembered with astonishment that only four days ago he had been filled with ennui for the city. London could be damnably tedious for a viscount who could buy anything he wanted and had done so, repeatedly, over the past few years. Nevertheless it was surely preferable to this wasteland.

It was his wasteland now. Conscience pricked him. His uncle had been an absentee landlord. He had no intention of following in the old man's footsteps.

The carriage was picking up speed as it rolled downhill, rocking, creaking, the axles straining. It was too fast. A notable whip, Johnny recognized the precise moment the coachman lost control. He braced himself for the crash, heard wood snap like a gunshot, felt the first dreadful lurch as coach and horses parted company, and then he was falling while the world smashed and broke around him, tumbling over like a cork in a stormy sea.

Johnny was not sure how long it took for the carriage to steady and come to rest, canted over at what felt like a dizzying angle. It was impossible to stand, for the floor sloped away sharply. Instead he slid with more speed than elegance out of the space where the door had once been.

Ice cracked. He landed in freezing water up to his knees. He swore, pulled himself out of the ditch and up onto the track. It was perishing cold and the snow swirled, thicker now. Almost at once he found himself surrounded.

"We've come to rescue you, sir, take you to the inn."

They swarmed around him, boys scarcely into their teens. How had they appeared so swiftly, so late, and in such a benighted place? Two of them were calming the horses with impressive efficiency. Another pair supported the dazed groom and coachman. Three more encircled Johnny, inspecting him.

"Have you broken your arm, sir?" The tallest, the ringleader, sounded eager.

"Or perhaps a leg?"

"Or hit your head?"

"I am quite well, thank you." Johnny was touched by their solicitude. He had been lucky; although he ached, there was nothing broken.

He could not see the boys well in the dark, but he sensed their reaction to his words. They seemed nonplussed. He could feel puzzlement rather than relief.

"You must be injured, sir." One of them, the smallest, sounded as though he would take it as a personal affront if Johnny proved to be in good health. "I'll fetch the doctor."

"I assure you there is no need."

The boys exchanged glances.

"Best for the doctor to check you over, sir," the ringleader said, assuming control once more.

"Best to come back to the inn." The others were an eager chorus. "There's hot water."

"Food."

"Good brandy."

They pressed closer, like a bodyguard, and started to shepherd Johnny down the road. There was no question about it. He had been kidnapped.

"I need a carriage to take me to Newport Castle."

She recognized that voice. It was deep and smooth but with an unconscious note of command. Unmistakeable.

Lydia Cole paused, one hand on the parlor door. She had heard what had happened that night. Despite what she had told them, the boys had been out again and stopped another carriage. Or wrecked another carriage, more to the point. She had heard that it was ruined and it was only by some miracle that coachman, groom and horses had not been hurt. The horses were now stabled in the yard and the coachman and groom were in the taproom, drunk as lords already with encouragement from the Silent Wench's barmaid, Tydfil.

They would remember nothing of the incident, nor would they have the slightest idea that it had been deliberate sabotage. In fact, both men were already boasting loudly in their cups, convinced they had been the heroes who had saved the day.

Which left the gentleman who now occupied her best parlor. Lydia had no idea how to deal with him.

She took a deep breath, smoothed her palms over her apron, straightened her shoulders and pushed open the parlor door. She nodded her thanks to the flustered servant and dismissed him with a jerk of the head. Only then did she turn to the man who was standing before the fire. He looked exactly as she remembered him. She wondered why she had expected him to have changed; perhaps because she herself had changed out of all recognition.

"I am sorry, my lord," she said. "The Silent Wench does not possess a carriage, but we can certainly provide you with a horse so that you may complete your journey."

The sooner the better, she thought. She looked at him and felt her stomach tighten into a knot of panic and the breath catch in her throat. When had that begun? When had the mere sight of John Jerrold been sufficient to scatter her wits? Certainly not when they had been neighbors in childhood, growing up together. Johnny had never caused her heart to miss a single beat then. Nor had he set her pulse awry when he had turned up unexpectedly at her come-out ball and danced with her on the terrace, beneath a summer moon and a dazzle of stars. It had been ridiculously romantic, yet she had been immune to his charm. She had shown Johnny off like a trophy that night because all her female acquaintances had been aflutter to meet him.

They had spent a lot of time together that summer, rediscovering their childhood friendship. Her mama had warned her that Johnny was a rake and was dangerous to her reputation, but Lydia had laughed at the mere idea of falling in love with him. A pity that she had guarded herself so carefully from Johnny only to fall in love with a man who had been twice the libertine he was with less than half his integrity. She had been a naive fool. The pang of regret she felt now was so sharp that for a moment it stole her breath.

He turned fully to face her. He had the same breadth of shoulder beneath a coat that was now soaked and stained and considerably less pristine than it must have been when he had first put it on. He had the same strong face, square jawed and clean-shaven. His fair hair fell across his brow above those narrowed blue eyes. Lydia remembered the way that his lips curved when he smiled and the way that smile crept into his eyes like sunshine rippling across water. Emotion stirred in her. She blinked; pushed the disturbing sensation away. It was too late for her and Johnny, far, far too late.

He was staring at her in blank astonishment.

"Lydia?" he said.

That neatly answered the question she had not quite dared to pose in her own mind—the question of whether Johnny had come to find her. He had not. Of course he had not. Four years before, she had rejected his offer of marriage. He would not be looking for her in order to renew it.

Lydia's heart did a sad little flop down into her slippers, and she was powerless to help it.

"Mrs. Cole," she corrected him with just the faintest hint of hauteur.

His brows rose. "You never were that."

"I am now."

His blue gaze was quizzical on her face. "Did you marry your cousin?"

"I don't have one. As well you know." He knew her family tree as well as she knew his.

"I thought you might have found one down the wrong side of the blanket." Fully in control of the situation now, Johnny strolled across to her with all the insolent grace she remembered. He put one hand under her chin and lifted her face to his. Those blue eyes appraised her thoroughly. The touch of his fingers against her skin made her tingle. She wanted to pull away but knew she could not, not without betraying too much of her feelings. Her face warmed beneath his scrutiny.

"You look well, Lydia." He was smiling now, that slow smile that she knew. Her cheeks heated. Her pulse tripped. She stepped back.

"I *am* well. Thank you."

"And how is Eliza?"

Lydia felt touched that Johnny had asked after her daughter. So many people had wanted to pretend that the child, the proof of her mother's fall from grace, did not exist. Not Johnny. He sounded as though he cared about her answer. He *did* care. She knew that. He had offered her the protection of his name out of sheer kindness. Which was one of the many reasons she had had to refuse him.

"Eliza is well too," she said. "She is happy here." She felt a clutch of fear. No one in Newport knew about Eliza's illegitimacy. They all thought her a widow. If Johnny said anything the fragile security she had built for herself and her daughter would be shattered and they would have to start all over again. She was not sure she could bear that.

She drew in a deep breath to calm herself. Johnny would never give her away. Besides, he could only be traveling through. He would be gone soon.

"What are you doing here?" She knew she sounded abrupt.

"I might ask you the same question." Johnny had started to unfasten his soaking jacket. Lydia, who had seen him wearing considerably fewer clothes than this over the years, nevertheless felt her throat dry to sand.

"I am the landlady of the Silent Wench," she said. Her

voice sounded odd, squeaky and husky at the same time. She cleared her throat. "This is my inn."

She saw Johnny's hands check on the buttons. "How enterprising you are." He looked up. "Did you choose the name? And the sign board?"

"I did."

Laughter crept into his eyes. "Your sense of humor. I like it." The smile fled. "We all wondered where you had gone after Eliza was born." He straightened, his hands falling to his sides. "I suppose you told Laura and Dexter and the others where you were?"

"I . . . Yes." Lydia could feel what was coming. She could feel his hurt.

"But not me." His voice was carefully devoid of expression. "I thought that we were friends."

"We were!" Lydia stopped. They *had* been friends, but that had changed when Johnny had offered to marry her. His offer, her refusal, had changed everything. "I didn't . . ." She floundered, searching for the words that would mend, not cause further hurt.

"You didn't trust me?" Johnny supplied the explanation with lethal politeness.

"No!" Lydia burst out. "Of course I trusted you, Johnny! I—" She gave a little despairing gesture. "I simply needed to get away, to start afresh."

It was inadequate, half an explanation, a quarter of one. When she had run from Johnny, she had been running not only from her past and the shame of her ruin but also from her feelings for him. She had come to value him too late, come to love him too late. Her hands trembled a little, and she pressed them together to still the shaking.

After a moment she saw Johnny nod his acceptance, saw the distant courtesy in his eyes, and knew it was too late to put matters right between them. The childhood friendship had gone. They were no more than acquaintances now.

"What are you doing here?" she repeated, trying desperately to bridge the gap that yawned between them. "No one comes to Newport."

"I do," Johnny said. "I am the new Baron of Newport." He smiled. "Quite a coincidence, is it not?"

Lydia sat down abruptly on one of the overstuffed parlor chairs. It was very far from a coincidence, but even so she had not anticipated it. Mr. Churchward, the family lawyer, had been the one to find her refuge in Newport, a tiny town on the Welsh coast. Mr. Churchward was also lawyer to Johnny's family, which was no doubt how he had known of Newport in the first place.

"Damnation," she said. "How extremely unfortunate."

Johnny shrugged his jacket off, revealing a soaked linen shirt that clung rather too closely to his muscular chest for Lydia's peace of mind. She swallowed hard and fixed her gaze on the beams of the ceiling where a cobweb drifted.

"I was not too pleased about it myself," Johnny said, "but why should you mind?"

"Because you are my landlord," Lydia said. "The Silent Wench belongs to the Newport estate."

"Really?" There was a smile in Johnny's voice now. "How piquant. I must check the ledgers to make sure you are not fleecing me."

"You would not know what to look for." Lydia risked another glance at him and regretted it immediately. He had removed the shirt now. The firelight ran over his shoulders and chest in slabs of bronze and red, burnishing his skin, picking out the tiny golden hairs on his forearms.

"You might have saved that for the privacy of your room." He had caught her staring and she had to say something. She tried to sound stern rather than breathless.

"You hadn't offered me one, and I was about to perish from the cold and wet." He smiled, boyish and rakish at the same time. "Besides, I've been taking my shirt off in front of you since we were children."

"We're not children now."

It had been the wrong thing to say. She realized it at once as his gaze fixed on her, darkened.

"Indeed we are not."

The air between them heated, fizzing with something sweet and fierce.

Lydia cleared her throat. "I did not offer you a room, but I did offer you a horse to take you to Newport Castle."

"I would rather stay here."

She would rather he left. Now, while the shreds of her composure were still intact and before he ruined the fragile existence she had carved out for herself and her daughter.

"You can't stay," she said.

"This is an inn," Johnny said. "You should be open for business."

"A moment ago you wanted to leave."

The gleam in his eyes was intense and disquieting. "And now I've changed my mind. I'd like to stay here tonight. Possibly longer."

There was more than a hint of challenge in his voice. Lydia's heart bumped against her ribs. Johnny had been challenging her since the nursery but not like this, not in a way that made the awareness shimmer down her spine.

"Besides," Johnny added, "the doctor tells me that it is dangerous for me to be left alone. I sustained a blow to the head in the accident. I need to be under constant supervision."

Damn Doctor Griffiths. He was a regular fixture in the taproom of the Silent Wench. The children, Lydia thought, must already have pressed him into service to assess Johnny's state of health and would have pocketed some shillings for their good work in putting business his way.

She sighed. "Dr. Griffiths was probably too drunk to give an accurate diagnosis." She surveyed Johnny critically from tousled fair hair to scuffed boots. "You look to me to be in fine health," she said dryly. "Certainly you do not have a concussion. If you did, my life would be a great deal easier—" She broke off, turning scarlet, aware that her tongue had run away with her.

She felt Johnny's fingers again against her hot cheek. "Are you wishing amnesia on me, Lydia? I am sorry to disoblige you."

Lydia stepped back, away from that provocative touch. "Of course not! Don't be foolish—" Her voice cracked. Suddenly tears seemed perilously close. Of course she did not wish that Johnny had been injured. If she had imagined it even for a moment it was an unworthy thought, borne only out of fear that his sudden appearance might endanger Eliza's future.

"Everyone here thinks I am a widow," she said, by way of excuse, unable to meet Johnny's gaze.

There was a silence. "Surely you know I would never do anything to hurt you, Lydia," Johnny said. All mockery was gone from his voice now. "I would never give you away."

"I know." Lydia risked a look at him. There was such tenderness in his eyes. It hurt her to see it, yet she could not look away. "You have always been everything that is kind," she whispered.

"I assure you that kindness was not what moved me to offer for you, Lydia," Johnny said. There was exasperation and ruefulness in his tone. He ran a hand through his hair, disordering the tousled locks still further. "It seems a little late to be having this conversation."

"Of course it is!" Lydia grabbed thankfully at the chance to get matters back on an even keel. "Now, I shall go to the stables and find a horse to take you to Newport—"

She stopped as Johnny put out a hand and caught her sleeve. "I do believe you were not attending," he said. "I am staying here." He slung both jacket and shirt over his shoulder and made for the door.

"You can't walk around like that!" Lydia knew she sounded like a maiden aunt, but the amount of naked man on display was rather overwhelming. She had seen one before, but she did not remember ever feeling like this, so hot and dizzy and confused.

"Someone might see you," she said. "The staff, the other guests . . ." There were none, but Johnny was not to know that.

He grinned, unrepentant. "What are you afraid of? That they will think they have stumbled into a bawdy house?"

"Oh!" He always had been able to drive her to madness. "You are infuriating."

"Of course. But may I have a room for the night, please?"

He asked so charmingly that Lydia could feel herself weakening. It would only be for one night and then she would be rid of him. The late Lord Newport had never troubled to deal directly with his tenants, sending his man of business to collect the rent and check the ledgers. Nothing would change under this new incumbent. Johnny was a man who had always appeared to prefer the entertainments of London to the dubious charms of the countryside. Once he had assumed control of his new estate, very likely they would never see him again. Everything would go back to the way it had been before. She felt the constriction in her chest ease as the thought brought relief.

"Where is your valet?" She eyed Johnny's state of undress with increasing disquiet.

"Valet and luggage went on ahead." Johnny spread his arms wide, which only served to give Lydia another fine view of his muscular chest. "I have only what I stand up in."

"Which is decreasing even as we speak." She hustled him out of the parlor and along the stone-flagged corridor to the crooked staircase. He stood aside with an ironic bow so that she might precede him. The treads creaked beneath her feet, and the beams bent low; Lydia was very aware of Johnny's presence behind her as they climbed the stair. She could feel his eyes on her every step of the way. The hair on the nape of her neck, beneath the sensible chignon, seemed to rise as though he had pressed his lips to her skin. She shivered. Such a foolish fancy when Johnny had never viewed her as anything other than a rather tiresome little sister he had wanted to help out of trouble.

They reached the landing, and Lydia threw open the door of the first chamber on the right. Darkness pressed on the diamond windowpanes. Winter wind blew down the chimney and raised the worn rugs on the bare floor. In that instant Lydia saw the room as Johnny would, not as a comfortable and familiar refuge but as a bare, cold and empty space. She put her candle down on the dresser, hurried across the room and drew the curtains shut with a clatter.

"But this is your room." Johnny had followed her in and closed the door behind him. The room seemed to shrink, the space dwarfed by his physical presence. Lydia felt a quiver of awareness pierce her again.

He picked up the battered novel that rested on her bedside table, examined the spine and put it down again. Her belongings were scattered about the room. They told a story, one that Lydia knew Johnny would understand. Darned stockings across the arm of a chair, starched caps and aprons stacked on the dresser, on the shelf a pottery vase she had made herself as a child, a ragged doll Eliza had dropped in a corner . . . This was her life now, Lady Lydia Cole, the daughter of a duke, fallen far in the eyes of the world and now landlady of the Silent Wench, a dubious hostelry at the back of beyond. She would not exchange it for all the salons in London. She had hated society even before it turned its back on her.

"The best guest chamber has a leaking roof, and the chimney of the second-best chamber smokes in a northerly wind," she said.

"And the rest of the rooms?" Johnny was watching her closely with that disconcertingly direct blue gaze.

"The beds are not aired." Lydia smoothed her palms self-consciously on her apron. "We do not have many visitors in the depths of winter." She started to gather up her belongings. Johnny put out a hand to stop her.

"Lydia," he said, "there is no need—"

"I insist." The guest chambers overlooked the courtyard, and tonight, despite the inclement weather, the men were due to bring in the latest consignment of contraband brandy, lace and tobacco. She certainly did not want Johnny to witness that. "I'll send a servant to light the fire," she added, "and fetch you soap and warm water. I'll share Eliza's chamber next door. It's no trouble—for one night."

Johnny did not move. He watched her for a long, long moment as she gathered up her meagre possessions in clumsy hands.

"Thank you," he said. A wicked light leapt in his blue eyes. "Do you know how long I have waited to be in your bed, Lydia?"

Lydia's heart gave an errant thump. Her hands shook. He had to be teasing her. There had never been anything other than friendship between them.

"A pity you had to suffer an accident to get there," she said sharply, to cover her self-consciousness. "Don't get used to it. The arrangement is entirely temporary." She whisked around the door and shut it firmly behind her before he could see how much she was blushing.

* * *

Lying alone in Lydia's bed was not conducive to a good night's sleep. Johnny slid deeper beneath the covers, smelling Lydia's scent on the sheets, feeling her presence wrap around his senses and his body harden in instinctive response. The realization that Lydia was in the next room, separated from him by the thin lath and plaster wall, did nothing to cool his blood. It was going to be a long, uncomfortable night.

He had not lost a moment's sleep over Lydia when they had been younger. He had never had siblings, so Lydia had been a substitute sister to him. It was only when he had finished at Oxford and then returned from a tour of the continent that he had met Lydia again and suffered some odd kind of reversal, as though everything had turned inside out and he was seeing her properly for the first time. The plainness he had previously seen in her he now realized was exquisite delicacy. Her quietness was tranquility. She was warm, generous and loving. She took his breath away.

And he was too late.

By then Lydia had been in love with someone else, an unworthy scoundrel called Tom Fortune who had abandoned her alone and unwed when she had fallen pregnant with Eliza.

When Johnny had heard that Tom had ruined Lydia, he had been possessed of such fury that he had not known what to do with it. He had wanted to kill the man, tear him apart with his bare hands. The wash of protective love he had felt for Lydia then had completely floored him. He had gone to her to offer her his protection but, betrayed and desperately unhappy, she had rejected his suit. Johnny had understood then that if he wanted Lydia, he would have to gain her trust slowly and carefully. He had been determined to do so, but Lydia had not waited for that to happen. Lydia had disappeared.

That had been four years ago. Now he had found her

again. Discovered as well that she had thought his proposal had been motivated by no more than kindness. How wrong she had been.

Restless, Johnny slid from the bed and crossed to the window, pulling back the heavy curtains to look out into the winter night. The inn sign swung in the wind. Hail spattered against the glass. The floor was icy cold beneath his bare feet.

The Silent Wench was precisely that, silent. Or was it? His ears caught the scrape of iron on stone, the rattle of a bridle, the rumble of a barrel, all sounds that were caught up by the wind and tossed aside. Shadows slipped by the window.

Johnny let the curtain fall back into place. So the Silent Wench was a haunt of smugglers. His mouth turned up at the corners. Lydia certainly had changed. Long gone was the respectable debutante daughter of the Duke of Cole.

He thought about her, the neat chignon that restrained all her rich chestnut hair, the sensible white apron and the plain woollen gown beneath. Lydia was bundled up tight, all passion restrained. How he wanted to undo her. He had wanted her for a very long time. He had loved her for a very long time.

But Lydia had made a very public mistake when it came to love, and society had punished her for it. Johnny doubted that she would willingly risk her heart again. It was down to him to persuade her that this time it would be no mistake. This time he would not let her run away.

Chapter 2

"There's a man I'd be willing to lead astray." Tydfil, the beautiful blond barmaid at the Silent Wench, set aside the cloth she had been using to polish the cutlery, leaned her elbows on the table and stared in rapt admiration across the taproom to the window seat where Johnny was reading to Eliza. Their heads were bent close, the dark and the fair, and Eliza was listening with a child's passionate concentration, her ragged doll clutched in one hand. Lydia blinked, feeling a surge of maternal love so strong it shook her. Behind it was another emotion, regret perhaps, or a fierce stab of wistfulness for what might have been.

"I don't think he would require a great deal of encouragement," she said. "Lord Jerrold is a very accomplished rake."

Tydfil's eyes lit with appreciation. "Is he so? When I first saw him I thought Christmas had come early. And there was me thinking that all the Newport barons were as ugly as sin."

"Clearly they are not," Lydia said shortly.

"He certainly takes his responsibilities seriously," Tydfil said.

"He does indeed," Lydia said. It was true; everywhere she

turned these days it seemed that Johnny was there, and even in his absence she could not escape him, since his name was on everyone's lips. It was difficult to believe that he had only been in Newport for two weeks. He had already arranged for repairs to be made to the tenants' cottages. He had discussed new forms of animal husbandry with Dai at the Home Farm. She had heard he planned to invest in the mines and to expand the village school. It seemed that the new Lord Newport was committed to spending a great deal of time on his estates, and that made Lydia extremely nervous. She had been convinced he would be back in London by now.

Johnny also had a disconcerting habit of turning up unexpectedly at the Silent Wench when Lydia had thought him safely elsewhere. He had strolled casually down the steps one day when she was helping the cellar man put the contraband brandy away. He had appeared in the kitchen when she had been making Christmas toffee and had flour on her nose. Most disconcerting of all, he had found her in the parlor decorating the mantel with green boughs of holly and ivy. He had lifted her down from the stool she was perched upon, then kept his arms about her.

"A pity it is not mistletoe," he had observed, before kissing her swiftly and soundly, arousing in her an earthquake of feeling from one brief touch of his lips. He had released her, smiled and walked away, leaving Lydia shaken and out of temper with herself for the rest of the day. She had not been able to look him in the eye since. She felt hot and disturbed in his company. And she was sure Johnny knew the effect he was having on her, damn him.

"It's very odd that he takes such an interest," she said now, watching Johnny smile as Eliza placed a confiding hand on his sleeve and tilted her head up to ask him a question. "Johnny was always extremely lazy. His most energetic occupation was seducing bored society women."

Tydfil shot her a sly glance. "Know him well, do you?"

"We were childhood friends," Lydia admitted, aware that she was blushing.

"Friends, was it?" Tydfil said dryly. "I see."

"He is in the way here," Lydia said, too quickly. "He pries into matters that don't concern him. The ledgers, the profits . . ." *The illegal transactions with the free traders, the dates on which the inn had been full with the travelers the boys had sabotaged on the road.*

"Well, if you need me to distract him . . ." Tydfil left the sentence hanging suggestively, and Lydia sighed. Tydfil's distractions were notorious in the district. So far she had distracted a dozen of the shepherds, several of the miners, plenty of visiting sailors and Mr. Jones the harbormaster, much to the fury of his wife. It brought plenty of business to the Silent Wench, but Lydia was not sure it was the sort of reputation they wanted.

Eliza had fallen asleep in the crook of Johnny's arm, her head resting against his shoulder. She was a very confiding child, trusting everyone because she had never been given reason not to do so. *Once,* Lydia thought, *I was the same as Eliza. I trusted too easily.* The love she had for Eliza coursed through her with a fierce spirit. No one would ever hurt Eliza the way she had been hurt. She was determined upon it.

Johnny looked up, and their eyes met. Lydia felt her stomach tumble away. She got quickly to her feet.

"I must put Eliza to bed," she said. She walked over to the window seat and took her daughter gently from Johnny's arms.

"I hope Eliza did not pester you too much," she said, smoothing the silky black hair away from Eliza's brow. "It was good of you to read to her."

"It was my pleasure," Johnny said. He smiled at her. "She

has your curiosity. I remember you were the same as a child, always asking questions."

"And you always pretended to know the answers," Lydia said, "even though you were only five years my senior." She pressed her lips to Eliza's soft cheek. "She looks like Tom," she said suddenly. She was not sure why she had raised it, other than the fact that Eliza looked so like her father that it could not be ignored and she wondered what Johnny thought of that.

Johnny's gaze was very clear as it rested on her face. "She has your eyes, Lydia," he said gently. "She's beautiful. But it doesn't really matter what she looks like. She's all yours."

Lydia was horrified to feel her eyes filling with tears. She hugged Eliza tighter. "Yes," she whispered. "Thank you."

When she came back downstairs an hour later, Johnny still occupied the corner seat by the fire and Tydfil was assiduously polishing his table and sweeping the flagstone floor around him, giving a splendid view of her bosoms as they fought to escape her low-cut neckline. If she edged any closer, Lydia thought, she would land on Johnny's lap. Johnny had his face politely averted from Tydfil's advancing cleavage and was reading a three-day-old copy of the *Times*.

"Tydfil," Lydia said, trying not to sound cross or jealous because of course she was neither, "there are customers waiting."

As the girl flounced off provocatively Johnny looked up, a twinkle in his eyes as he folded the paper and tossed it carelessly aside.

"Thank goodness you rescued me," he said. "I had no notion that cleaning was such a sensually charged activity. I was afraid I would not escape with my virtue."

"You should see the way in which she plays the harp," Lydia said. "It is positively indecent. Do you have any virtue left, Johnny?" she added tartly. "I cannot believe it, since you ran off with Lizzie Waterhouse when the ink was barely dry on her marriage certificate."

As soon as the words were out she wished them back, for she knew she had given away far too much of her feelings. Johnny's rash elopement with one of her dearest friends had happened years before; it had hurt her at the time and it still stung now. But how she wished she had not betrayed the fact.

She saw the amusement leap in Johnny's eyes. "Were you jealous, Lydia?" he murmured.

"No, of course not." Lydia tried to affect boredom, but the anger and resentment lacerated her again, shocking in its intensity, too extreme to hide. She fought a brief, vicious battle with it and lost.

"Lizzie said that you were the perfect rake," she said. She could not seem to help herself. The words were tumbling out now no matter how hard she tried to squash them down.

"Lizzie doesn't know that." Johnny's tone was expressionless.

"You spent the night with her!" Lydia burst out.

"We spent the night talking," Johnny said. He drew slow rings on the table with the base of his tankard. "We were unhappy." He looked up suddenly, and Lydia's heart lurched at the expression she saw in his eyes. "We were both in love with the wrong people."

The silence was thick with emotion. Lydia felt breathless, her chest as tight as though it were encased in a metal band. She had not thought Johnny had ever been in love. She felt jolted, her senses shaken out of kilter, as though she had missed a step in the dark.

"These things happen when you are young," she said, trying to sound light and uncaring but knowing that there was a forced note in her voice. "I should know that."

Johnny smiled at her. It was a smile of such warmth that it made her toes curl with longing.

"It doesn't matter, Lydia," he said gently. "The past doesn't matter."

The silence extended and extended again. There was such tenderness in Johnny's eyes that Lydia felt her mistrustful heart start to yield. Yet she knew Johnny was wrong. One could not escape the past.

The door of the taproom banged open in a jumble of cold air, sleet and loud voices. Lydia jumped. She thought she heard Johnny muffle a curse. The intimacy of the moment was broken, though, and she felt relief as well as a contrary pulse of disappointment. She leaned her palms on the table, feeling the wood cool and soothing against her skin.

"It's been two weeks now," she said. "Why are you still here, Johnny?"

Before she could move Johnny slid a hand across the table and encircled her wrist. His touch was light, but she felt it all the way through to her bones. "Sit with me and I'll tell you," he said.

Lydia hesitated. Then she sat. There did not seem to be much choice. Johnny withdrew his hand from her wrist. Lydia immediately missed the warmth of his touch. He gestured to Tydfil, and she came across with two glasses.

"Wassail cups," she said, with a saucy smile at Johnny. "Made by Mrs. Cole herself. Well known for their aphrodisiac qualities, my lord."

Lydia rolled her eyes. Johnny looked as though he was trying not to laugh. The aroma of spices and sharp cider filled the air. Johnny took an appreciative sip.

"It's strong," he said.

"My customers have hard heads," Lydia said. She took a mouthful. The hot, heady liquid fizzed through her veins like fire. "So," she repeated, "why are you still here, Johnny?"

Johnny slanted a mocking look at her. "Always so welcoming, Lydia." He shifted on the bench, settling more comfortably against the tapestry cushions. "Newport Castle is uninhabitable," he said. "I'll be staying here until it is ready."

Lydia felt a rush of apprehension. "Staying here at the Silent Wench? But the repairs could take weeks!"

"Months, more like," Johnny murmured. "It is in a dreadful state."

Lydia felt her panic rising. For the past fortnight she had told herself that Johnny would soon be gone and her life would resume its even tenor. Now she felt confused and disturbed.

"Surely it would be better for you to return to London?" she said. "You know that you prefer it to the country. Besides, it is almost Christmas! There must be people you want to see—" She broke off as she looked into Johnny's eyes and saw the brilliant amusement there. He could read her like a book. He knew she wanted him gone. More disturbingly he knew why, knew that his presence discomfited her. She felt a tremor of emotion shake her. Johnny was dangerous to her. Her feelings for him were too raw, too close to the surface. She had to be rid of him.

"There is more here that interests me than in London," he said gently.

Oh. That made her breath catch. But of course he must be referring to the estate.

A sudden gust of wind clattered down the chimney. The fire spat and hissed and the candles guttered.

Johnny picked up his glass of cider and tilted it to his lips. Lydia watched the muscles of his throat move as he swallowed. He needed a shave. His skin was rough with stubble. She could imagine the prickle of it against the tips of her fingers and gave a little shiver.

"Cold?" Johnny asked.

"Yes . . . no . . . a little." She felt hot, in fact; hot and confused, still bemused by that moment between them. "The Silent Wench is a little dilapidated, I fear," she said. She knew she was chattering in a vain attempt to ease the awareness between them. "It is an old building and there are lots of draughts and ill-fitting doors. Your predecessor did not invest in the upkeep of his properties, as you have already discovered for yourself. But then, he was seldom in Newport."

Johnny put down his glass with a sharp click. "My uncle belonged in the London clubs," he said. "Unlike me, he really did not care for the country."

"No one liked him very much," Lydia said, "so we did not really mind." She was aware of the alcohol loosening her tongue. Already her body was starting to feel heavy and relaxed with the lassitude the wassail cup brought. And yet it also brought awareness, sharp and sensual as a whetted blade.

Johnny laughed. "I confess I did not like my uncle either," he said. "Nor did I care for Roberts, his estate manager. I think he was lining his own pockets. I'm afraid I have dismissed him."

Lydia gaped. "You dismissed Mr. Roberts? Oh, how splendid!"

Johnny laughed again. "You did not care for him either, then?"

"No, indeed. He is an odious man, a bully and a cheat." Lydia frowned a little. "But who will run the Newport estate now he is gone?"

"I will," Johnny said. "At least until I can appoint someone else I trust."

"But . . ." Lydia boggled. "Viscounts do not run their own estates."

"I do not believe there is a law against it," Johnny said. He gave her the lopsided smile that creased the corners of his eyes and lit them with warmth. "Don't worry, Lydia. I swear I will not cramp your style here at the Silent Wench. I enjoy a good bottle of brandy as much as the next man."

Lydia jumped, spilling a few drops of cider on the table. "You know!"

Johnny's blue gaze was very steady on her. "I know that the Silent Wench is involved in smuggling," he agreed. "I heard the free traders last week." He raised his drink to her in mocking salute. "And there I was thinking you had given up your bedchamber to me out of kindness."

Lydia blushed. She threw a quick glance over her shoulder, but apart from a group of men in the corner playing at shove ha'penny, they were alone.

"Why the secrecy?" Johnny asked. "I'll wager everyone in Newport knows what goes on here." He settled his broad shoulders against the high back of the bench. "I thought that smuggling was long gone."

"Not in these parts," Lydia said. "The free traders resent having to pay what they see as English taxes. And the brandy is very fine. So are the laces—and the linen."

"I see." She could tell that Johnny was trying not to laugh. There was a spark of amusement deep in his eyes. "A fine justification for breaking the law." His gaze narrowed. "I suppose the Silent Wench houses a highwayman or two as well?"

"Certainly not," Lydia said. She hesitated. "Well, there was Thomas of Henfaes, but he was too poor a rider to make a career of highway robbery. The carriages refused to stop and then he could not catch them up."

"That would be a distinct disadvantage," Johnny agreed gravely. "What about wreckers?"

"Now you are being absurd," Lydia said severely. "You have read too many adventure novels. Here in Newport we value our sea trade too highly to try to wreck it."

"But you have no compunction about wrecking carriages if not ships?"

Lydia could feel her guilty blush deepening. In the days

since Johnny's arrival she had almost forgotten that his accident had in fact been no accident at all.

"I do not know what you mean," she said, hearing the woefully unconvincing note in her voice.

Johnny laughed derisively. "Cut line, Lydia. Those scapegrace children—Miss Evans's young brothers, I believe—habitually sabotage travelers on the turnpike road. Their father repairs the carriages or provides alternative transport, the doctor treats any injuries and the Silent Wench offers accommodation—and you all get paid for it. It's a brilliant piece of enterprise. It's also dangerous and illegal."

It sounded very bad when expressed like that, Lydia thought. "Smuggling is dangerous and illegal," she pointed out with a flash of spirit, "yet you condone that because you enjoy good brandy. Your moral code is somewhat flexible, Johnny."

"Touché," Johnny said. "It always has been, I fear." He leaned forward. "Nevertheless, this has to stop, Lydia, before someone is killed. I say that as Baron Newport and your new Justice of the Peace."

"I know it's dangerous!" Lydia burst out. "I've told the boys to stop, but they do it for the best of motives. Newport is impoverished and many people have no work, and so the villagers take matters into their own hands. We need work and we need investment in the estate. We need a landlord who cares!" She stopped as she ran out of breath.

Johnny's hand covered hers, warm and strong. "You have one now," he said.

Once again Lydia felt that tug of awareness combined with profound emotion, a pull deep within her. She wondered again how it had happened, when it had happened. When had friendship and familiarity transformed into this mysterious attraction? Not that it mattered. Explaining it, understanding it, would not change her feelings. And she was fooling herself if she pretended it was mere attraction. That was to demean what she felt for Johnny. She had loved him for years as a friend and somewhere along the line that emotion had transmuted into a different sort of love.

"I know you care," she admitted. "I have seen what you have already done to help us."

"Then trust me," Johnny said. His hand tightened over hers. In his eyes were both challenge and demand. "Trust me, Lydia," he repeated softly.

"I do." Lydia felt panic stifling her breath. She dropped her gaze. Johnny must not be allowed to guess her feelings. She jumped to her feet, sending her chair clattering back on the stone floor in her haste to escape.

"Excuse me," she said. "I need to check on Eliza."

Johnny stood up politely and bowed. "Of course." He came around the table, waiting for her to precede him to the door.

"There is no need to escort me," Lydia said. "I know my way."

There was a wicked glint in Johnny's eyes. "I find I need to fetch a book from my chamber. An adventure novel, perhaps, to inspire some more wild flights of imagination."

Lydia did not believe a word. She put her hands on her hips. "I will fetch it for you," she said.

"No, you will not," Johnny murmured, holding the taproom door open for her. "You are not to wait on me."

Out in the passageway it was cold and quiet. The light was dim. Lydia risked a glance up at Johnny's face and wished she had not. He was watching her, his blue eyes narrowed and intense in a look that sent the awareness cascading over her skin. His arm brushed hers and she almost flinched, so acute was her response to him.

"How did you know?" She grabbed quickly for conversation to ease the tension between them. "How did you know that the boys sabotaged travelers on the road?"

The shadows hid much of Johnny's expression, but she could see a faint smile tilt his lips. "They were so anxious for me to be hurt, so keen to escort me here, that it made me suspicious. I asked a few questions, and a pattern soon emerged. Too many people have had accidents on the road for it to be by chance."

"Please don't punish them," Lydia said. She pressed her hands together anxiously. "They are good boys. Truly they are. I teach them at the school."

She saw Johnny's smile deepen. "They told me that you teach here too," he said. "You are very generous to do that as well as run the Silent Wench."

"I found kindness in Newport," Lydia said. "I do no more than give it back."

She was about to start up the stairs when Johnny put out a hand and stopped her. She paused on the first step, her hand on the carved newel post. They were level; she could look directly into Johnny's eyes. What she saw there made her heart thump.

"It occurs to me that I know a great many of your secrets," Johnny said softly. "There is a price for my silence."

For a moment Lydia did not understand him, then comprehension broke over her and her head spun with the combination of knowledge and fierce, dizzy temptation.

"Oh!"

She had not expected it, not of Johnny. He had said he would protect her and it seemed that was exactly what he was offering, his protection. She knew she should be horrified, offended, any one of a dozen reactions. She waited to feel horrified, offended or some other suitable emotion. She did feel a flicker of disappointment that a man who had professed himself honorable should, after all, prove to be a complete rake. But she also felt more than a flicker of excitement. It slid through her veins like heady wine, wicked and wondrous. It was true, Lydia thought helplessly. All those people who had said she was wanton had not been mistaken. She might have lived like a nun since Eliza was born but place temptation before her—place Johnny before her—and she was lost to all respectability.

Johnny's gaze was watchful. It made her heart race and the breath flutter in her throat. His hand was still resting on her arm; she could feel his touch through the thick, practical worsted of the gown and she wanted to feel his hands on her bare skin beneath. The urge was so sudden and so fierce that it made her gasp. She bit her bottom lip to quell the sound, saw Johnny's gaze fix on her mouth and then she was in his arms and he was kissing her.

She had never kissed Johnny before, and now she found herself wondering what on earth had taken her so long because it felt perfect, tender and sweet, yet somehow so fiercely *right* that it shook her to her soul. She slid her hands up over his chest and about his neck, pressing closer to him, making a tiny sound of gratitude and gladness when he gently nudged her lips apart and deepened the kiss, touching his tongue to hers. The ground shifted beneath her feet; the familiar walls of the Silent Wench spun about her like a fairground ride. Desire, deep and turbulent, lit her blood, and it was as though all her senses, starved to barrenness for so long, had come alive again.

She pulled back abruptly as common sense intervened. She was tempted, she wanted Johnny, but it was impossible. She was mad even to contemplate it.

"No!" she said. "No, I can't do this."

Johnny ran a hand over his disordered hair. He was looking less than his usual immaculate self. "I thought you seemed to be managing quite well," he murmured.

"I can't be your mistress," Lydia stated baldly.

Johnny looked disconcerted. "I was not aware that I had asked you."

"You implied it," Lydia said. "You said there was a price for your silence."

She saw the understanding break in his eyes. He smiled. "I see," he said slowly. "I am flattered that you were prepared to consider it even for a moment, but . . ."

Mortification crashed over Lydia in a wave. She closed her eyes. "I misunderstood, didn't I?"

"I fear so." He was trying not to laugh, damn him.

"It would be more gentlemanly of you to pretend," she snapped. How embarrassing that he had not wanted her after all. And yet he had kissed her as though he desired her.

"I don't believe it would be more gentlemanly of me to blackmail an unprotected woman." Johnny sounded mildly offended. "What interests me, though, is why you would have agreed."

There was the rub. He knew she had at least given the matter consideration. She was certainly not prepared to admit that she found him infuriatingly attractive. Or, more importantly, that she loved him. There was no future in that when Johnny could look as high as he wished for a wife and when she was the least suitable bride in the whole of Wales.

"I would have done it for Eliza's sake," she lied. "I thought . . . I was afraid . . ."

"That I would betray you? When I had promised I would not?" Johnny sounded so hurt that she felt stricken.

"No, of course I did not think that!" She could not help herself; she pressed a hand to his cheek, feeling the roughness against her palm. "I'm sorry," she whispered. "I did not mean to hurt you."

Johnny's eyes had darkened again to the blue gray of a storm. "Lydia—"

This kiss was even better, intense, hungry from the first, sweeping her away. There was the tightest, most wicked spiral of heat in her belly that she had ever experienced. Her fingers itched to tear his clothes off, drag him into the skittle alley or the games room and make love to him on the billiards table. She was shocked by such unbridled thoughts, shocked but exhilarated at the same time.

She felt him draw away from her a little. His lips touched the hollow at the base of her throat and lingered in a caress that raised the goose bumps over her skin. He slid one hand into the bodice of her prim, businesslike gown and cupped her breast through her chemise, his thumb moving over the nipple. Lydia's knees weakened and she made a sound of supplication in her throat. Pure sensation skittered down her spine. Pleasure flowered deep inside her.

"You smell delicious. . . ." His tongue flicked the vulnerable curve of her collarbone. "Lemon and spices."

He turned her so that she was against the wall, cold stone at her back, her body trapped by the hard length of his, and he kissed her again, slowly, thoroughly and with such intent that Lydia trembled.

"We have to stop this." She wrenched herself away from him.

"Must we?" Johnny reached out to draw her back into his arms. He was breathing hard. "I find I rather like your plan after all."

"It's the wassail cup," Lydia said breathlessly.

Johnny laughed. "Are you saying that you need to be drunk to find me attractive?" He leaned closer. "Liar," he whispered. His eyes were dark with desire, so intense and concentrated it made Lydia's stomach drop.

She pushed him away. "Johnny!"

"Oh, very well." He loosened his grip. "If you insist."

Lydia steadied herself with both palms flat against the cold wall behind her. "If I misunderstood you, Johnny," she said, "what was it that you were going to say?"

Johnny hesitated. Then he took her hands in his. "I need your help, Lydia," he said. "I cannot turn the Newport estate around on my own. You know everybody. They trust you. I need you by my side to do this."

Lydia looked at him. "You need an estate manager," she whispered.

"I need a wife," Johnny said. "I need you." He was smiling a little. His eyes were clear, steady. "Lydia," he said. "Will you marry me?"

Chapter 3

Johnny knew at once that she was going to refuse him. That would be twice, he thought ruefully. Twice he would have laid his heart beneath Lydia Cole's feet and she would have kicked it aside. He wondered if he was mad to keep trying to win her. He wondered how many rejections a man was supposed to take. Then he looked at her. She looked flushed and ruffled and thoroughly kissed, and he realized that he would not give up, could not, until he had persuaded her that she could risk her heart on him.

"Johnny," she said.

"I've loved you for years." He had not intended to be so precipitate or so unpolished, but he thought it was worth trying to get in first, to try to make her see the truth. A moment later he saw that the words had been a mistake. She did not believe him.

"We can't talk here. It's not private." The clatter of the kitchen door opening emphasized her words.

"Where then?" He was not going to let her go before they had this resolved.

She looked hunted, afraid. "Johnny—" she said again.

"Where?"

She made a huffing noise at his insistence, but she took his hand and drew him down the flagstoned passageway to the private parlor he had occupied on the night he had arrived at the Silent Wench. A fire burned low in the grate though the room was dark. The air was scented with the sharp freshness of the pine branches that decorated the beams.

"We can talk in here." She sounded brisk, but Johnny saw her hands shake as she struggled to light the candle.

"I told you I loved you," Johnny repeated. "You seem determined to pretend that you did not hear me."

Lydia turned to face him. She looked pale and pinched, folding her arms across her chest as though to hold in her feelings or protect herself.

"I heard you," she said, with constraint. "But—"

"You don't believe me," Johnny said. "I wait years and years to tell a woman of my feelings and now, when finally I do, she does not believe me sincere." He wanted to take her in his arms and prove how much he loved her. He ached to hold her. But he knew that was not the way. He kept his fists clenched at his side.

"Four years ago I proposed to you," he said slowly. "You thought that was out of kindness. You were wrong."

Lydia's gaze fell. She looked so young, the nape of her neck a vulnerable curve beneath the fine strands of chestnut hair that curled from her chignon. She looked up to meet his eyes, and Johnny's heart clenched at the expression in her eyes. "I cannot marry you," she said in a rush. "Surely you can see that, Johnny? I am not a fit wife for a viscount."

Johnny felt so violent a rush of fury that it shocked him. If any man had spoken of Lydia so disparagingly he would have knocked him down. He grabbed her shoulders.

"Don't say that!" he bit out. "Don't ever say that. You are lovely; loving and generous and strong and brave." She had been so courageous, he thought. She had taken a life that had been in ruins and she had rebuilt it and turned it into something special. He released her, sliding his hands down her arms gently now in a caress that made her catch her breath.

"You care about people," he said slowly, "and they love you for it. You have carved out a life here for yourself and for Eliza, and nothing could be more admirable."

Lydia was watching him. A small smile curved her lips, but Johnny thought he saw the shimmer of tears in her eyes. "Why, Johnny," she said, "I do believe you may love me after all."

His heart bounded and he reached for her, but already she was withdrawing from him. Her smile had fled now, and in the rose glow of the fire her face was very grave.

"You don't understand," she said. "I am honored that you think of me in such a way, but it changes nothing." She put up a hand to quell the urgent words that jostled on his lips. "No, Johnny," she said. "You cannot marry me. Surely you can see that. My parents were disgraced, and I am ruined twice over."

Johnny was unimpressed. "Can you be ruined twice?" he queried. "I thought once was enough."

He was glad when Lydia was surprised into a giggle. "Stop it," she said. "How can I feel tragically sorry for myself if you make fun of me?"

"I'm not making fun," Johnny said. He took both her hands in his. "Darling Lydia, if you apply the same rules to me, then I am ruined more times than I care to remember."

"It's different for me," Lydia said.

Johnny shook his head. "Only in the minds of others. You made one mistake." His tone was fierce. "You were little more than a child. Are you to be punished for it forever?"

She tangled her fingers with his. Her eyes begged for his understanding. "You know that, rightly or wrongly, the rules are different for women," she said gently. "I transgressed society's code. I bore a child out of wedlock. That will never be forgotten. If we marry, my past conduct will tarnish your good name and your honor. People would forever be whispering about your wife and her scandalous past."

"You must think me a poor creature if you believe I would care for one moment what other people thought," Johnny said. "Lydia—"

"I'm doing this for the future," Lydia said. Johnny saw her swallow hard. "In the here and now it would be easy to be swept away by how much I love you." She warded him off when he would have taken her in his arms. "You need an heir, Johnny. You would want children from our marriage, and how would they feel to have an illegitimate half sister and to hear of their mother's disgrace? They could not escape the taint of the past. None of us could." She turned away so that he could no longer see her face. "I have to think of Eliza," she said. "If her real identity becomes known she will be the butt of gossip and scandal forever."

"So you hide away here," Johnny said, "and hope that no one will recognize you or discover your past."

He felt angry and frustrated, not just for himself but for Lydia and Eliza. He wanted to give them more of life and love and joy. He wanted to give them everything he had to give.

He saw Lydia's shoulders hunch. She looked so frail and so unprotected. Fury shook him again at the cruelty of fate that forced her to live a lie and an even greater fury possessed him that Tom Fortune had callously ruined the trusting girl Lydia Cole had once been; seduced her and abandoned her, and that she was the one paying the price.

"It's the only way," Lydia said. "For as long as people believe I am a respectable widow, Eliza is protected. Were I to wed you, I could no longer keep the secret."

"You can't live forever in fear of discovery," Johnny argued. "Lydia, you are both strong and brave. Surely it is better to be honest and tell the scandal-mongers to go to hell."

Lydia smiled ruefully. "There speaks a man who can afford to do such a thing," she said. "But I cannot."

Johnny could feel the situation slipping away from him, like water running through his fingers. "I'd protect you both," he said. "I would treat Eliza as my own, love her as my own. I swear it."

Once again he saw the sheen of tears in Lydia's eyes. She touched his cheek in a fleeting gesture.

"I believe you mean that, Johnny," she said, "but I can't ask it of you."

Johnny's patience snapped. "For God's sake, don't be so bloody noble, Lydia!" he said. "That is my decision, not yours. Are you to throw away any future chance of love because you are afraid of scandal?"

He caught her to him and kissed her hard, with all the need and longing that was within him. She yielded to him instantly, her body softening in his arms, her lips opening beneath his. For one endless, blissful moment she gave him back kisses that were passionate, sweet and hot enough to scald him to within an inch of control. But when he let her go he knew nothing had changed. He could feel it.

"Trust me," he said, pressing his lips to her hair, inhaling her scent and feeling his heart aching with the fierceness of his love. "Let me care for you both. You don't need to do this on your own anymore, Lydia."

He could see the conflict in her eyes. For a moment he thought she was going to agree and his heart surged with joy, but already she was drawing back. She shook her head, pressed her fingers briefly to his lips in a gesture of farewell and slipped from the room, leaving him alone with the dying embers of the fire.

Lydia lay in her bed watching the shadows shifting over the plasterwork of the ceiling and listening to the sounds of the Silent Wench settling for the night. She felt cold and alone, racked with misery. She knew she had been right to refuse Johnny, but it had been so painful. Yet she felt she had no choice. She could not expose Eliza to the scandal and scorn that would inevitably follow once the truth of her birth was revealed, nor could she bear to put Johnny's love for her to the test by asking him to spend the rest of his life defying convention for her sake. It was not fair to him or to any children they might have together. Nevertheless there was a hollow, aching feeling beneath her heart, and her future felt like a loveless void. She told herself it was the price of keeping Eliza safe, that nothing was more important than her child, yet a tiny voice in her mind whispered that she was a coward, hiding behind excuses because she was not brave enough to trust Johnny completely and risk everything for a life with him.

She rolled over and punched her pillows. Tomorrow, she thought, Johnny would leave for Newport Castle. He would not stay now that she had rejected him for a second time. She pressed her face into the coolness of the pillow and willed herself to sleep.

It seemed as though she had been asleep for no more than a few moments when she jolted awake again, all her senses alert to a feeling of danger. For a moment she lay quite still, straining to work out what it was that had disturbed her. Then she heard it again, the crack and hiss of dry tinder splitting apart, the unmistakable sounds of fire. She sat bolt upright in the bed and saw the leap of flame against the wall. Already there was the acrid taste of smoke on her tongue, and when she hurried from the bed the wooden boards of the floor were hot beneath her bare feet. She grabbed a robe and forced her stockingless feet into her shoes. The smoke filled her lungs now, stealing under the door, stinging her eyes, making them smart.

"Eliza!" Lydia flung open the chamber door and ran out

onto the landing. Terror filled her heart. If only Johnny had kept her room and she had continued to share with her daughter. She could have snatched Eliza up by now; she would have her safe. As it was she could barely see her way to Eliza's door. Thick smothering smoke coiled about her. The floorboards cracked beneath her feet. The Silent Wench was an old, old inn and it was being consumed already, folding in on itself, the fire ripping through the ancient timbers, crumbling them to ash. A beam fell in a shower of sparks. Lydia screamed until her lungs hurt. She fought the people who surrounded her now and who tried to pull her back.

"Eliza!"

"We can't reach her." Tydfil was holding her tightly, tears streaking the soot of her face. "We've tried and tried. The floor has gone."

"No!" Lydia wrenched herself from Tydfil's grip and ran, down the smouldering staircase, along the flagstone passage, out into the courtyard where the wind was laced with snow and ashes. If she could reach the outside stair and climb up to the gallery, then she might approach Eliza's room from the outside. But the outside stair was shattered and the gallery was in flames; the whole of the Silent Wench was alight, the blaze a livid blur against the black winter sky.

She felt despair then as deep as the pit and as dark as the sky. She who had sworn to protect her daughter had failed her now.

"Lydia!"

The shout came to her above the crackle of fire and the howl of the wind. She looked up. Johnny was running along the gallery, his figure no more than a black silhouette against the flames.

"Catch her!" The fire was at his back, snatching at him. Eliza was in his arms.

"Mama!" Lydia could hear her daughter calling; there

was nothing wrong with Eliza's lungs. She ran forward. There was no time to think. It was ten feet from the gallery to the ground. Johnny leaned over the balustrade and held Eliza out as far as he could, and then the child was dropping like a stone straight into Lydia's waiting arms, burrowing close, filthy, her hair smelling of smoke, but blissfully, blessedly alive. Lydia gave a sob and clutched her daughter so tightly that Eliza gave a squeak of reproach.

Johnny was climbing down the shattered stair, agile and sure-footed. He was not even out of breath. "I remembered how well you could catch," he said, his arms enfolding them both in a brief, hard hug. "You always won when we played cricket as children. I was going to rescue you too," he added, "but you didn't need me."

"Johnny—" Lydia said. She could not find the words. She felt as though her heart was going to burst.

Johnny smiled at her, his teeth a white slash in his filthy face, his eyes bright. "Later," he promised. He touched her cheek. "I have work to do." He glanced over her shoulder. "Let Miss Evans keep you warm and safe until I come back."

He raised a hand in salute and was away, across the yard to where the ostlers were leading out the frightened horses and the men were putting together a bucket chain with water from the well in a vain attempt to douse the flames. It had started to snow again, fat flakes hissing as they met the sparks of the fire. Lydia watched Johnny take control. This was a different Johnny from the indolent nobleman she remembered; direct, authoritative. She had underestimated him. She could see now how well he would take control of the Newport estate and bring it to order. He would do it because he had all the strength and determination that his predecessor had lacked. He would do it because he cared.

She pressed her lips to Eliza's silky black hair, and her daughter shifted in her arms, pressing her face against the curve of Lydia's neck. She was already half asleep again. Tydfil came over and wrapped a thick woollen blanket about them.

"Take this," the maid said. "Why don't you come back to the cottage with me? You need hot milk and a warm bed. You and Eliza will catch your death of cold out here."

"It's all gone," Lydia said, racked with shivers. "The Silent Wench, everything we worked for."

"We'll rebuild it." Tydfil squeezed her arm. She followed Lydia's gaze across the yard to where Johnny was directing the men to put out the last of the smouldering embers.

"There's a man who would walk into a burning building to save your daughter's life," Tydfil said slowly. "You should keep hold of him."

"I know," Lydia said. "I know. But it's too late."

Tydfil laughed. "I always thought you knew nothing of men. If you believe that you know even less than I had thought."

"I can't marry him," Lydia said in a rush. "Tydfil, I'm not a widow. I never was married."

"Bless you," the maid said. "Do you think we don't know that? Why should we care? Why does it matter?"

Lydia stared at her. "Because he's a viscount," she said faintly.

"And you're the daughter of a duke," Tydfil said. "But we still like you. Did you want to live in London, with all those snobs judging you?"

"No," Lydia said, realizing that it was true. "I want to live here in Newport. But—"

"You worry too much," Tydfil said comfortably. "See, here he comes." She smiled as Johnny started purposefully across the yard toward them. "Make sure you get it right this time," she added.

"I can't talk to him." Panic trapped inside Lydia's chest. "Tydfil—"

The maid took the sleeping Eliza from Lydia's arms and wrapped her close. "I'll take her home with me while you speak to him. She'll be quite safe. No—" She fended Lydia off as she made a grab for Eliza. "You can't use your child as a shield forever, madam. He wants both of you. Be brave. The hypocrites can go hang."

"Lydia." Johnny had reached her side now and taken both her hands in a strong grip. "You and Eliza are coming back to Newport Castle with me," he said, in a tone that brooked no argument. "At once. Dr. Griffiths has sent the horse and trap. And you're going to marry me and I won't take no for an answer."

"I thought that you said the castle was uninhabitable," Lydia said.

"I lied," Johnny said. "How else was I to persuade you to let me stay at the Silent Wench?"

"You should be ashamed of yourself," Lydia said, sliding her arms about his waist. She breathed in the scent of his skin mingled with the bitter smell of smoke. "Yes," she said, against his soot-streaked shirtfront. "Yes, we will come back with you. We have no roof over our heads now, and Eliza will enjoy Christmas at the castle."

Johnny put a hand under her chin and raised her face to his. He looked stern, his eyes blazing. "I want you for more than just Christmas, Lydia." He gave her a little shake. "Marry me."

"All right," Lydia said, smiling radiantly as Johnny's expression dissolved into relief. "I would like that very much, thank you." She rubbed her cheek against his chest. "I was a coward before," she admitted. "I could not take the risk until I saw what I stood to lose."

She felt Johnny's arms tighten about her. "You are the bravest person I know," he said softly. He kissed her, a long, slow kiss full of sweet promise that Lydia returned in full measure. "Thank you for entrusting yourself and your daughter to me," he whispered against her lips.

They broke apart as a ragged ripple of applause echoed around the courtyard. The Newport villagers, filthy and exhausted, had broken off from damping down the remains of the fire to salute their lord and lady's betrothal.

"Witnesses," Johnny said comfortably. "No going back now." He tucked her hand through his arm. "I hear that Miss Evans's brothers apprehended Mr. Roberts on the road. He was running away, having set the inn alight in revenge for his sacking."

Lydia gasped. "The blackguard!"

"I think he was hoping I would go up in flames along with the Silent Wench," Johnny said. "They have taken him to the magistrate."

"I thought Tydfil could run the Silent Wench for us once it is rebuilt," Lydia said as Johnny handed her up into the waiting trap.

"We had better rename it the Wanton Wench, then," Johnny said, swinging up to sit beside her and tucking the blanket around them.

Lydia poked him in the ribs. "The Joyful Wench."

And then Johnny was kissing her again, and it was the last either of them spoke for a very long time as the horse and trap rattled through the snow down the road to Newport.

WEATHERING
THE STORM

Cara Elliott

Lamplight pooled over the rough-planked tavern table, the tiny flicker of oily flame stirring a fresh wave of briny smells. *Dead mackerel, decaying seaweed* . . . along with several pungent odors that Sophie Thirkell did not care to identify.

Breathing shallowly through her mouth, she leaned into the glow and flashed a sweet smile. "Please, sir. It's a matter of *utmost* importance that I reach London by Christmas."

The grizzled figure seated across from her scratched at his salt-streaked beard, dislodging a shower of silvery fish scales. "Oiy, I wud of course like te help a damsel in distress. But . . ." His gaze strayed to the plump leather purse lying tantalizing close to his mug of ale. "But yer gentlemun friend makes an awfully compelling case fer his own needs."

Friend? A poor choice of words, to put it mildly.

Scowling, Sophie slanted a look at Bentley, Lord Leete. Despite the sudden Atlantic gale—a storm so violent that it had broken the mainmast of her father's merchant ship, forcing the captain to seek refuge in this remote Cornish cove—their aristocratic English passenger managed to look perfectly poised and polished in the raggle-taggle surroundings.

Or rather, perfectly irritating and infuriating.

The raging seas had swept away the schooner's gig and jollyboat, and the tiny fishing village had only one small sailing craft that the inhabitants were willing to sell to the stranded travelers. Despite his fancy title, the odious viscount was being extremely ungentlemanly about the situation.

"Oh, fie—where is your sense of noblesse oblige, sir?" she demanded. "I thought all you highborn lords were supposed to have a sense of chivalry."

"I'm afraid my personal feelings must be submerged in favor of my country's needs, Miss Thirkell," replied Bentley primly. Paying her no further heed, he turned back to the village elder. "As I said, Mr. Pengareth, I am a diplomat with the Foreign Office returning from an important mission in America. So much as I sympathize with the young lady's desire to celebrate the holidays in Town, I cannot help but insist that *my* request take precedence."

"Request—ha!" muttered Sophie bitterly. "It's your coins that speak with a golden eloquence."

"It is not my fault that your captain's sea chest was lost in the storm," said Bentley. Unfortunately, the iron-banded box containing her father's money had been moved to the jollyboat when the schooner was in danger of drifting onto the rocks, so it, too, had been washed overboard, leaving her with naught but a pocketful of pennies.

"Be reasonable, Miss Thirkell," Bentley went on. "I have a highly confidential report to deliver to Whitehall regarding negotiations between our two countries, and it must arrive in time for a special council meeting scheduled to take place on the evening of December twenty-fifth. In light of such circumstances, don't you think that you are being a bit childish to grouse over missing a Christmas goose dinner with all the trimmings?"

Sophie bit her lip to keep from uttering a very unladylike word in retort. His assumption was unfair and untrue, but somehow the elegant, effortlessly assured Lord Leete had the uncanny ability to make her feel like a scrubby little hell-fire hoyden.

This wasn't the first time they had met. The viscount had been in Boston for several months prior to embarking on the fateful ocean voyage, and as her father, a wealthy merchant who was one of the city's leading citizens, often entertained foreign diplomats with lavish suppers and fancy balls, the two of them had sailed in the same social circle.

And the waters have always turned choppy whenever the currents brought us together.

"Were my concerns merely centered around my stomach, you would have cause to rake me over the coals, sir," she responded. "However, they are not. I, too, have been delegated to deliver an important package. And while it may not have the same international repercussions as your mission, it is . . . it is . . ."

Arching an imperious brow, Bentley waited for her to go on.

Sophie hitched in another breath of the foul-smelling air, blinking back the sting of salt against her lids. "It is very important to me and my family, no matter that we make up a very tiny, insignificant part of your diplomatic world."

For an instant a ripple of emotion seemed to darken his gaze, but then he looked away and the curl of his gold-tipped lashes hid his eyes.

Pengareth blew out a regretful sigh. "Well, missy, I get yer drift, and yer story of kith and kin touches my heart." He thumped a callused fist to his chest to emphasize the avowal. "But alas, a boat costs money."

"Which I haven't got," she said softly.

The fisherman twitched a silent shrug of sympathy, but his eyes remained riveted on the viscount's purse.

"Then I assume the matter is settled," said Bentley. He spoke in a low tone, but to Sophie's ears, his words seemed to take on an insufferable thrum of arrogance as they echoed off the taproom walls.

Gathering her skirts, Sophie turned for the door with an angry swoosh of silk.

Swoosh, swoosh, swoosh.

"Just one last question, Lord Leete." She paused and looked back over her shoulder. "Who is going to sail your newly purchased vessel for you?"

The wavering flame caught a flutter of surprise flitting over his features. "Er . . ."

Ha! He could hem and haw all he wanted, thought Sophie. But no amount of fancy talking was going to change the fact that he was a complete landlubber. Indeed, during the ocean voyage, it had become abundantly clear that he didn't know a hawser from a ratline. While she, on the other hand, had been around her father's fleet of sailing ships all her life.

"I . . ." Bentley gave another small cough to clear his throat. "Why, it's very simple. I shall hire one of the *Bull-dog*'s crewmen."

"One of my *father's* crewmen?" said Sophie. It was her turn to waggle a brow. "Oh, I highly doubt that Captain Brewster can be convinced to spare any of his prime hands."

"But—" squeaked Bentley, for once losing his air of calm composure. However, he quickly inhaled a steadying breath and reassumed a self-assured smile. "Never mind. I am sure that Mr. Pengareth can recommend a local man who will gladly sail my boat for a handsome fee."

"All the way to *Lunnon?*" The fisherman make it sound as if the city were located on the newly discovered planet of Uranus. After carefully counting out the coins in the purse, he shook his head. "Besides, ye've only got enough here te cover the price of boat."

"I promise you that the man will be paid in full as soon as

we reach our destination." A pause. "Along with a extra bonus for the Holidays."

Sophie gave an audible sniff.

"One can't eat promises," pointed out Pengareth. "Nay, ye won't be finding anyone in this cove willing to abandon his nets on the word of a fancy stranger. Not with French privateers and the pesky Revenue cutters adding extra waves to the treacherous Channel waters."

Despite the shadows swirling in the salty air, Sophie saw the tic of a tiny muscle mar the smoothly shaven line of the viscount's jaw. "My good man, I assure you my word is gold." A rustling of cloth and oilskin rose above the sound of slurped ale. "Look, I have proof that I am a diplomat, engaged in an extremely important mission for the Crown."

Pengareth squinted at the document thrust under his nose.

"See, here are my official credentials from the Foreign Office," added Bentley, tapping a finger to the ornate wax seal and crimson ribbon attached to the paper, just below the elegant lines of copperplate script.

"I have a feeling that Mr. Pengareth can't read," murmured Sophie. "Which leaves you stranded in these isolated waters." She paused to let her words sink in. "That is, unless you care to negotiate."

"What do you have in mind?" he asked through clenched teeth.

"A compromise." Her mouth curled up at the corners. "Isn't that an essential element of diplomacy, sir?"

A faint ridge of color rose to his cheekbones. "One of them," he said tightly. "However, the key to a successful compromise also includes the ability to work in harmony with each other. I, for one, always look to forge a partnership with someone who understands the importance of prudence and restraint. A predilection for bold, brash behavior is likely to lead to trouble."

Touché. Sophie kept her smile pasted in place, though in truth his words cut like a knife. He was right to chide her for being a rebel against the strictures governing female deportment . . . but why, oh why, did he always seem to bring out the worst in her? From the very first awkward encounter, when she had splashed claret punch on his immaculate ivory-colored waistcoat while displaying a knife trick, to the horribly embarrassing moment when—

"Well?" he asked, breaking the stiff silence. "What is it that you propose?"

"You have the boat, and I have the skills to sail it," replied Sophie. She might be outspoken and independent to a fault, but no one had ever criticized her nautical expertise. "So, seeing as we both wish to reach London by Christmas, I am suggesting that we pool our resources, as it were."

A low hiss of air leaked from his lips. "Impossible! What you suggest is highly irregular—not to speak of highly improper. We can't travel together unchaperoned. Why, your reputation would be ruined. And so," he added grimly, "would mine."

"You can either stick to your rigid English rules and remain marooned here in . . . in . . ."

"Penpillickentish Bay," piped up the fisherman.

"Or you can throw caution to the wind," challenged Sophie. "Which is your only prayer of dropping anchor in the River Thames by December twenty-fifth."

Ebb and flow. The sound of the waves slapping against the stone jetty drifted in through the slatted shutters. The wind howled, its keening note thrumming with the echo of his earlier words.

Trouble, trouble, trouble.

"So, what's it going to be, Lord Leete?"

* * *

"By the rusty prongs of Neptune's trident! I must have been dangerously deranged to agree to this," muttered Bentley, as wind rattled through the rigging and a fresh pelter of freezing rain slapped against the sail canvas. He pressed a sodden sleeve to his dripping nose. "Or dangerously desperate."

"Did you say something, Lord Leete?" called Sophie from her perch by the tiller. "Any problems?"

"No, no—things are going along just swimmingly," he answered testily. Despite the oilskin jacket, he was soaked to the skin and the damp chill had seeped right down to his bones. *And I'm famished,* grumbled his stomach. Breakfast had been naught but soggy biscuits and a swig of cider.

"Tighten the jib sheet around the forward cleat," she ordered after peering up at the bow through the swirls of dark mist. "The sail is luffing."

Wincing, Bentley tugged at the rope, feeling the rough hemp scrape another layer of flesh from his palm. "My superiors had better appreciate the sacrifices I am making for King and Country."

"The *jib sheet,* not the pennant halyard!" cried Sophie as the little sloop gave a wild lurch, causing the boom to swing across the stern and nearly knock her into the sea.

"Sorry," he muttered, grabbing the right line and making it fast. "How the deuce can one tell the difference in the midst of all this chaos?"

"Oh, pish, this is just a passing squall. The wind is already changing." She shifted course slightly and the boat's motion became somewhat smoother. "You can come and take a rest in the cockpit now. It will blow over in another few minutes."

Tripping over one of the ringbolts, Bentley flopped unto the varnished bench, feeling as clumsy as a hooked flounder. "How can you tell?" he demanded, spitting out a hank of wet hair.

"The sky is lightening in the east."

"It is?" He squinted at the leaden clouds. "I see naught but unrelenting gray."

"I'm sure your treaty negotiations would look like a sea of mumble jumble to me." Shading her eyes, Sophie edged the tiller to the left. "It's all a matter of what you are used to, I suppose. When something is familiar, it seems easy."

An astute observation. Miss Thirkell clearly had a lively, intelligent mind . . . which was intriguingly apparent in the rare moments when she wasn't using her sharp, sarcastic tongue to flay him to ribbons.

The sloop took a sudden dive into the trough of a foam-flecked wave, sending Bentley's stomach sliding into his ribs with a sickening lurch. *On second thought, a spartan breakfast had probably been all for the good.*

"You seem, er, very comfortable with the vagaries of wind and water," he gasped, feeling himself turn a little green around the gills.

"Oh, I am," replied Sophie. "I've been sailing on my father's merchant ships since I was in leading strings." Grinning from ear to ear, she lifted her face to the howling gusts. "Lud, I always find it exhilarating to feel a flutter of an ocean breeze on my cheeks."

Breeze? It seemed like a great, thumping gale to him. But then, Bentley felt like a fish out of water away from land. While she appeared a gloriously happy sea nymph, a force of nature, confident and in command of the white-capped waves.

His gaze drifted down to her snug breeches and sea boots. He had never seen a young lady clad in male garb, and as she stood up and stretched to adjust a brass pulley on the boom, the full effect was . . .

"You," he said slowly, forcing his eyes away from the

shapely stretch of leg to the flight of a lone herring gull overhead, "are a *very* unusual female to enjoy battling the elements."

Her voice lost its sunny exuberance and turned grim as the shroud of fog ghosting over the bow of the sloop. "By which you mean I have none of the poise and polish of your highborn London lady friends."

Damnation. Bentley swore an inward oath. His fellow diplomats considered him extremely articulate, often lauding his skill in simplifying complex ideas and expressing them in a clear, concise manner. Yet around Miss Sophie Thirkell, his tongue seemed devilishly determined to tie itself in knots. *How else to explain how a simple observation had been interpreted a criticism?*

It hadn't been meant as such . . .

Well, not exactly.

Honesty compelled him to admit that he wasn't at all certain what to think of his companion. A part of him—the part that valued order and tradition—found her devil-may-care attitude defied all conventional notions of proper feminine behavior. After all, rational rules and roles were cornerstones of civilized society.

But the other part . . .

Bentley slanted a sidelong look at her sparking sea green eyes and red-gold curls, flying in unruly splendor on the swirling gusts of wind. There was no denying that something about her spirit was captivating.

"Oh, go right ahead and look down your long, lordly nose at me." Catching his glance, she lifted her chin to a pugnacious tilt. "I may be a rough-cut bit of New England granite compared to a smooth-sparkled London gemstone, but I am heartily glad that I know *practical* skills, however shocking they may be to your delicate sensibilities."

"Miss Thirkell—"

Ignoring his attempt to interrupt, Sophie expelled a loud huff. "At least I know how to be *useful*, rather than frittering my days away in idle indolence—"

"Miss Thirkell." He raised his voice another notch to make himself heard above the rattle of the rigging.

"—simpering, gossiping and stuffing myself with sweets."

"Are you finished?"

She opened her mouth, and then shut it without a sound.

"Excellent," snapped Bentley, his usual calm command of his emotions unraveling around the edges. "You are all afire to take offense over imaginary slights," he went on. "Yet you yourself are awfully quick to pass judgment on people you have never even met. There are a number of highborn ladies in London who are engaged in, as you call it, *useful* endeavors, like aiding the poor and establishing schools for orphans."

Sophie inhaled sharply but remained steadfastly silent.

"As for me looking down my nose at you, that accusation is also unfair. I have made every effort to be pleasant, only to have my civilities thrown back in my face."

Waves slapped against the hull, sending up a splash of salt spray. Blinking the mizzled drops from her lashes, Sophie squared her shoulders. "Civilities?" she repeated. "You were going to leave me stranded in the middle of nowhere, without so much as a thought to my predicament. But then, I suppose you had conveniently forgotten my father's kindness to you in your time of need. That he offered you passage on his speedy merchant ship, so that you might bring your government news of your secret negotiations in time for the special council, was the only reason you were able to reach England in the first place."

Bentley squirmed uncomfortably against the slatted seat, once again on the defensive. "Blast it all, Miss Thirkell, I have tried to explain the situation before and shall try to do so again," he said patiently. "As a diplomat, I cannot allow personal feelings to interfere with my duty."

"To the devil with your duty!" she exclaimed hotly. "You and your fancy words! Go ahead and pontificate all you want—no words will change the fact that you acted like a scrub."

He wasn't quite sure what a scrub was, but it took little imagination to guess it wasn't anything flattering.

"You must understand, a representative of the Crown cannot afford a whiff of scandal to attach to his name. It reflects badly on the Foreign Office." Gritting his teeth, he assured himself that he had done the right thing in following the letter of the law in regards to propriety. "And so I must always carefully consider all the ramifications of my actions."

Ye Gods, if his superiors ever got wind of this little interlude, his career would be sunk.

"Sometimes you have to think with your heart instead of your head, Lord Leete," countered Sophie. "Or don't they teach you that in your fancy bastions of privilege."

However tartly phrased, her words rubbed raw against his conscience, causing him to respond more harshly than he intended. "And sometimes you have to exercise a more ladylike restraint if you wish to sail along smoothly with other people. Or don't they teach you that in your free-spirited Boston schoolrooms?"

Her mouth pursed into a perfect "O" of outrage. "Oh, you odious, insufferable prig! How dare you lecture me on tactful behavior?"

"Because I am accorded to be an expert in it," answered Bentley rather smugly. He was now on more solid footing.

Or so he thought. However, her retort quickly rocked him back on his heels.

"For all your flowery platitudes on showing more consideration for the feelings of others," replied Sophie, "you never even asked why I was in such a helter-pelter hurry to get to London by Christmas."

Off-balance, Bentley steadied himself by repeating the familiar words about duty and the need for disciplined detachment. Satisfied that he had made a perfectly logical argument, he ended with an oblique challenge. "You truly think your reason could be more important than the negotiations between our two countries?"

"No." The answer rose above the crack of the canvas.

He started to smile.

"I think it *equally* important." For a moment, Sophie looked as if she wasn't going to elaborate. But after chuffing a reluctant sigh, she continued. "My father has long been estranged from his English family. There has been no contact between them for years—indeed, I don't even think my grandfather knows of my existence. But now that Papa is ailing, he wishes to end the feud. And so he has asked me to serve as an envoy of sorts."

Her hand strayed to the oilskin package stowed beneath the binnacled compass. She had, he noted, kept it close ever since coming aboard the little sloop.

"Let me guess," he murmured, falling back on humor to cover his confusion. Diplomatic meetings usually followed a very predictable script, but this encounter had fast drifted into uncharted waters. "A peace offering of your unusual New England treats—smoked cod, maple syrup and blueberry jam."

"Go ahead and mock me, and my father's provincialism, Lord Leete. I don't give a fig what you think of us." Fighting the force of the rising sea, Sophie brought the sloop a point closer to the wind. She went on, but in a far softer voice, as if she were speaking to herself.

"I've been delegated to bring the heirloom family Bible to London in time for Christmas, and come hell or high water, I mean to do everything in my power to carry out

Papa's wish." The tarred rigging thrummed, casting dark shadows across the taut white sail. "Given that it is the season of good will to all mankind, perhaps it will be accepted." Her expression, however, did not hold much hope. "Nonetheless I must try, though God knows—as you so kindly pointed out—my skills at diplomacy are virtually nil." A sigh puffed into the wind. "All my life, I've heard stories about my English relatives. . . . They sound far too stiff and starchy to welcome me as one of their own."

Was that an extra glitter of moisture in her eyes?

The queasy lurch of Bentley's insides had nothing to do with the choppy waves. He wasn't sure how to respond, but it was his stomach that saved him.

It gave a loud growl.

"You had better go below and have a bite to eat. There is a basket with ham, cheese and bread in the forward locker." She squinted into mizzled mist. "The wind has changed yet again, and a fresh squall seems to be headed our way."

"I'm not really hungry," he replied.

"Go below, and that's an order. I'll need your help with the sails shortly, so I can't afford to have you fall into a dead faint from lack of nourishment."

"Miss Thirkell, I . . ." Her point made perfect, practical sense, but he hated feeling so damnably helpless. "I am not used to taking orders from a lady."

Her flash of teeth was clearly not meant to be a smile. "At the moment, I'm not speaking as a lady, but as the ship's captain. And however little you like it, I am in command of this vessel."

On that note, Bentley retreated to the cabin, muttering darkly under his breath.

"I have enough swirling gusts to handle without having a pompous bag of wind blowing in my ear," grumbled Sophie as the hatch slammed shut. "A gilded tongue and clever phrases aren't worth a vial of spit in the real world."

Self-righteous indignation didn't quite quell the twinge of regret that things had turned so stormy between them.

Did I really expect a titled lord to admire a provincial hellion?

Her mouth thinned to a wry grimace. "I have been reading too many romantic novels," she added, feeling foolish for having secretly admired him. "It's easy to create a happy ending out of ink and paper. However, life is not a fairy tale. No knight in shining armor is going to swim up on a silver sea horse—"

A splash of salty spray hit her full in the face.

"Enough of daydreaming." Heaving a gurgled sigh, she glanced up at the thickening clouds and frowned. Things were going to get worse before they got better.

Sure enough, the wind shifted to north-northeast, its shriek growing louder, its force growing stronger. Hands aching, muscles tiring, Sophie hunched down and struggled to keep the sloop on its compass heading in the blustery seas. According to the charts provided by Pengareth, there were several small harbors on this stretch of coast where they could seek shelter. But first the sloop must round the dangerous jut of rocks up ahead.

"You must be famished." Echoing her own growling stomach, Bentley's voice floated up from below. He poked his head from the hatchway. "I made you a slab of bread and cheese. It's not elegant, but it's edible."

"Thank you." Sophie gratefully accepted the food.

"And Mr. Pengareth added a flask of smuggled brandy to the supplies—for medicinal purposes." Bentley passed it up. "A swig will warm your insides."

"W-warmth would be w-welcome," she said through chattering teeth. The brandy burned a trail of liquid fire down her throat, but as the heat radiated through her limbs, she felt it buoy her spirits.

"Is there anything I can do to help?" Ducking flying spray, he crawled across the cockpit.

"Not really," she answered. "It takes an experienced hand to hold course in this weather. One small slip and the sails will luff, spinning us broadside to the swell. That would make us vulnerable to a broaching wave."

"Which means?"

"Which means we would sink," replied Sophie flatly.

"Ah." Bentley scooted closer and watched for a moment as she worked both the rudder and the mainsail. "I know you think me a useless fribble, but I can tug on a rope. And I'm actually quite good at following orders."

"As you know, I'm not shy about bellowing commands. But in this case, it's best that I handle the sloop alone. Things happen quickly—I simply react instinctively to the nuances of wind and water."

Looking thoughtful, he nodded.

"You could, if you like, try to snug down those flapping sheets by the ratlines, before they tangle and cause trouble."

Moving alertly, Bentley began to wrap the ropes around the belaying pins.

Perhaps Lord Leete wasn't so starchy after all. Despite the drenching seas and biting cold, he toiled in uncomplaining silence.

Dragging her gaze away from his waterlogged form, Sophie concentrated on watching the clouds scud across the leaden sky. To the east, the color was lightening and taking on a tinge of pink. *Red sky at night—sailor's delight.* A good sign, according to the old maritime adage.

"What's that?"

She jerked around at the viscount's query and saw he was pointing at a dark shape off the leeward rail.

"Is it . . ." he began.

"Another ship," she confirmed. "And coming on fast."
Damnation.

Pengareth had privately warned her that a French privateer had recently been spotted in these waters. Small boats
were sometimes snapped up as prizes, with both the vessel
and the crew hauled off to France.

Sophie stared a moment longer, assessing the shape of
the sails and hull. "I think it's *Le Loup,* a twenty-two-gun
frigate out of Calais."

Bentley uttered an oath. "Aren't we too small a fish for a
privateer to hook?"

"Not according to Mr. Pengareth. He didn't wish to scuttle his sale, so he made no mention to you of the threat. But
that's why no fisherman was willing to sail this sloop to
London. *Le Loup* has apparently been feasting on the local
commerce, and given the dirty weather, we are likely the
only tasty morsel available."

"And you took on the task, despite the risk?"

"As you have pointed out, I'm a bold, brash hellion. And
stubborn to boot—I made a promise to my father, and I have
every intention of keeping it."

Through the swirls of fog she saw a flutter of sails as the
privateer tacked. It was now on a course to intercept their
small vessel.

"They've spotted us," she said.

"I must scuttle my documents," said Bentley grimly. "The
French can't be allowed to get their hands on those papers."
He made no mention of the fact that he would likely be im-
prisoned for the duration of the war once the privateer captain discovered he was no rough-spun local fisherman.

"How willing are you to take a risk?" she shot back.

"We can't outfight them, Miss Thirkell." His voice held a
note of humor, despite the direness of their situation. "They
throw a broadside of twelve fourteen-pound cannonballs,

while we have approximately eight oak belaying pins to heave at their hull."

"No, but we might be able to outfox *The Wolf.* According to my chart, there are a series of shoals sticking out from the rocky promontory ahead of us. We are a shallow-enough craft to pick our way through them, while *Le Loup* would smash itself to bits if it tries to follow." She gauged the distance to the shadowy ridge of land off the larboard bow. "It will be close, but I think we can outrun them."

"Then let us fly," replied Bentley without hesitation.

Sophie tightened her grip on the tiller. "Be advised that it's a dangerous choice, Lord Leete. They might blast us out of the water, or we may come to grief on the rocks. Surrender is the safest course—with your silver-tongued skills, I daresay you will be able to negotiate your release from prison without too long a wait."

He answered with a phrase that no gentleman would normally say in the presence of a female.

"Very well—uncleat the mainsheet," called Sophie, her mouth stretching to a grin. "And be ready to heave like the devil when I give the word."

"PULL!" . . . *"PULL!"* . . . *"PULL!"*

The little sloop darted through the dark waves, weaving a zigzag course toward the safety of the shoals. *Like a minnow fleeing the jaws of a rapacious Yankee bluefish,* thought Sophie wryly. She slanted a glance back at the privateer. It had closed the gap between them, but not by much. Her deliberate change of direction had kept *Le Loup*'s teeth at bay, for the frigate could not come about as fast as her vessel.

"Haul in the jib a touch, Lord Leete!" The viscount was fast becoming a seasoned sailor—she no longer had to point out the correct rope. "Just a little bit farther, and we should be safe."

BOOM!

The cannonball landed close enough to send a spout of gray-green water washing over her stern.

"Oh, fie, what a scrub the captain is to shoot at us." She stood up and shook her fist at their pursuer.

Another plume of smoke belched from the frigate's side.

"Duck!" cried Sophie as the missile whistled overhead, missing the mainsail by a hair.

The next shot fell a little short.

"Keep the sheets taut! We're nearly out of range," she called to Bentley. Just ahead, she could see a foaming line of surf breaking upon the shoals. "Look sharp—the leeward line needs another turn."

"Right." His broad shoulders were a dark, unflinching silhouette against the foggy gloom. Pulleys squeaked as he followed her orders. "I've never been shot at before. Have you?"

"Not with a cannon," she replied. "There was a harbor brawl in Kingston that turned a trifle hot. But the Spanish sailors were drunk, their pistols were damp and their aim was atrocious. They ran like rats from a sinking ship once I shot the lead fellow's earring off."

He gave a rumbled laugh. "Remind me not to cross swords with you."

"A good idea," she answered, smiling in spite of the danger. A sense of humor under fire said a lot about a man . . . or woman. "I'm quite skilled with a blade as well."

The sound of the waves churning against the rocks cut off all further banter. *Steady, steady.* Drawing a deep breath, Sophie concentrated on the menacing shapes ahead, looming dark and jagged as the teeth of a sea monster, waiting to eat them alive.

"Let us pray that I've chosen the right tack," she muttered under her breath, steering for the narrow gap in the churning seas. The chart showed no details, forcing her to judge the likeliest route by intuition alone.

The sloop shot through the opening, shaving past a sliver of barnacled rock by naught but the width of a razor. *So far, so good,* she thought . . . only to hear a sharp *crack* as the forward jib sheet snapped from the strain. As the wind spilled from the flapping sail, the little vessel yawed around, the force of the waves slamming into the hull and knocking Bentley head over heels into the bottom of the cockpit.

She, too, was thrown off her perch, but managed to keep a grip on the tiller. Struggling to her knees, Sophie brought the bow around, just as a cresting wave rose behind the stern. "Hold tight, Leete!" she cried, hoping that he had the presence of mind to grab onto a stanchion to keep from being washed overboard. An instant later, a deluge of dark, foaming water crashed into the cockpit.

To her horror, she saw her precious package—the family heirloom Bible—wrested from its shelter by the swirling sea. Caught in the current, it floated past her outstretched fingertips, followed by Lord Leete's official documents, which had been wedged in beside it at the start of the chase.

"Oh, no!" It was now the salt of tears stinging her eyes.

A jagged scrape, a shuddering shiver and suddenly the sloop was through the turbulence and into calm waters.

Safety.

"Oh, no," repeated Sophie with a choked sniff. The Bible was gone. *Gone.* She felt utterly defeated despite having eluded the French privateer.

The sea sluiced out through the scuppers, revealing a very bedraggled Lord Leete kneeling in six inches of water. His hair was plastered to his skull, his garments were dripping . . . and his hands were gripping her oilskin-wrapped Bible.

"B-but your documents!" she stammered. "W-what about your documents?"

"I daresay they are on their way to Neptune's locker," he replied. He had added a slab of the sloop's ballast to the wrappings, to ensure that they would sink quickly if capture was imminent. "I could grab only one thing."

"But your council meeting!"

"The words of mere mortals must yield to a higher good." A wry smile twitched on his lips. "Actually, I know the contents by heart, so the ministers will get all the details they need without the benefit of paper and ink. Whereas your family heirloom was irreplaceable."

"Thank you," whispered Sophie. "Thank you for saving my Bible, Lord Leete."

"Thank you for saving my arse, Miss Thirkell."

She swallowed a burble of laughter.

"You were magnificent."

Oh, surely the wind had distorted his words. "We're not quite out of danger yet," she cautioned as a sharp gust rocked the sloop. "If you can haul down the tattered jib, I'll get the mainsail under control and head for the lights up ahead. According to Mr. Pengareth's chart, that should be the harbor of Stony Creek—a safe port in a storm."

Bentley flexed his scraped hands, wincing at the burn of salt against his raw skin. *Dry clothes, hot food, mellow brandy*—no matter that the pungent smell of fish and pine tar hung over the ramshackle wharf, the moonlit land had never looked so delightfully appealing. It was late—very late—but he prayed that the local tavern would still be open.

"Be ready to jump out and snug the bowline around the piling when I drop the mainsail," called Sophie.

He nodded, taking up the heavy rope.

"Toss it here," called a gravelly voice. Bentley saw a half-dozen men step out from the shadows of the crab traps. "We'll help ye tie up here."

"Much obliged," Bentley replied, grateful for the offer. Smiling, he heaved the line to the waiting hands, relieved that he didn't have to fumble with making the unfamiliar nautical knots.

Echoing his thanks, Sophie threw over the stern line and set to furling the mainsail.

"Dirty weather out there," commented Gravel Voice.

"Aye," said Bentley. Following Sophie's orders, he set to tying down the jib and coiling the forward lines neatly on deck.

"An impressive display of sailing." Gravel Voice seemed to be the spokesman of the group. "Even the local men don't dare to cut through those shoals."

"We were in a bit of a hurry," said Sophie. After a quick check that all was shipshape, she took up her wrapped Bible and stepped onto the wharf.

"To put it mildly." Bentley gave a little laugh as he followed her.

"Ha, ha, ha," chorused the group.

Gravel Voice's raspy chuckle was the first to die away. "You're under arrest."

"On what grounds?" demanded Sophie.

"Smuggling," replied Gravel Voice, fixing her with a hard stare.

"You must be daft—"

Bentley gave her a swift kick in the shins, which thankfully surprised her into silence. "What my sister means," he said quickly, "is that you gentlemen are definitely mistaken. I assure you, we are innocent of any wrongdoing—"

"Innocent?" piped up one of Gravel Voice's companions. "Then why was a revenue cutter trying to blow you out of the water, heh?"

"It wasn't a revenue cutter," protested Bentley. "It was a French privateer."

"Hmmph." One of the other men spit in the water. "How d'ye know about *The Wolf* if ye ain't working hand in glove with the Frenchies?"

"Because—" began Sophie.

Another nudge cut her off. "Let me handle this," he whispered. "Diplomacy is my area of expertise."

She gave him a fishy look, but kept her mouth shut.

A promising start, he thought wryly. *My skills must not be too rusty if I've convinced Miss Thirkell to remain mum.*

"Actually, that's quite easy to explain, sirs," said Bentley in a louder voice. He went on to give a quick recount of the Atlantic storm and the broken mast that had forced the merchant ship to seek shelter. "So I purchased this little sloop from one of the locals, so that we could continue our voyage to London without delay."

"What's so hellfire important that ye and yer sister must go on ahead?" demanded Gravel Voice.

"I must reach Town in time for a special meeting." He squared his shoulders. "I am a diplomat for the Foreign Office."

There was a long pause as Gravel Voice eyed Bentley's bedraggled clothing. Pengareth had gifted him with the roughspun wool garments for warmth while working the sloop.

"And *I* am the Prince Regent."

Guffaws sounded from the group.

"Having met the Prince on a number of occasions, I can assure you that he is a great deal more rotund than you are," responded Bentley, hoping humor might soften the stony stare.

If anything, the man's face took on a harder look.

Bentley switched to a tougher tone. "And by the by, who are you, and by what right do you threaten to hold us?"

"I'm the local magistrate," answered Gravel Voice. "And I have full authority to imprison any criminals—especially smugglers."

He quickly regrouped and tried another tack. "If we are smugglers, where is our cargo?"

Gravel Voice made a rude sound. "Ye threw it overboard, o' course. Everyone knows that's wot smugglers do when the revenue men are about te catch them red-handed."

Sophie had been making little growling sounds under her breath but could no longer hold back her indignation. "Oh, be sensible, sir. If we were smugglers, we wouldn't be sailing such a small vessel. Why take such a big risk for a puny cargo?"

Silence.

"Hmm, the lass has got a point," one of the men finally murmured.

Gravel Voice looked unconvinced. "I've heard that the captain of *The Wolf* is working with a band of French smugglers when he ain't harassing our local fishermen and trading wherries. Nimrock, the magistrate up in Framington, says the cargo is off-loaded from the privateer into small boats, which land in the salt marshes."

"We're not French," pointed out Sophie.

Miss Thirkell was proving to be not only a very skilled sailor but also a very skilled negotiator.

"Ye talk funny," shot back Gravel Voice.

"I'm A—"

"Astounded!" said Bentley loudly. "My sister is absolutely astounded that you would find her accent odd. But then again, she's spent most of her time in Gloucestershire, while I've been living in London." He assumed his most official tone. "Surely you recognize the King's English when you hear it."

"Oiy, I was in London once," volunteered one of the men. "And he does sound just like one of them fancy toffs what struts down Piccadilly Street."

Gravel Voice narrowed his eyes. "I still say we haul them off to the gaol in Beecham and hold 'em until Colonel Markham returns from maneuvers."

"My good man, you really ought to consider the consequences of such action. If you are wrong about us, imagine how badly it will reflect on your authority to have impeded a government mission."

Bentley's words finally stirred the first flicker of doubt in the magistrate's eyes. Seeing it, he quickly forged on. "If I were you, I'd keep us here in the village overnight and send a messenger to the revenue cutter's home port. I assume it's somewhere close by, and that way any understanding can be cleared up quickly and discreetly, before any higher officials become involved.

"That makes some sense, Hawthorne," agreed one of the magistrate's companions. "We don't want te look like fools."

"We can lock 'em in the storeroom of The Saucy Wench," suggested one of the other men, pointing to the nearby tavern. "It's got a sturdy lock and no windows."

A murmur of assent rose from the group.

Gravel Voice—who appeared to be named Hawthorne—hesitated, and then gave a gruff nod. "Jem, you ride over to Neffington and bring back Captain Farraday while we secure the prisoners here." He turned and gestured for Sophie to hand over her package.

Scowling, she hugged it even tighter to her chest.

"That," intoned Bentley, "is an item of *utmost* importance to my government negotiations. I really must insist that it stays with us."

"It might contain pistols," argued the magistrate. "Or knives, or some other dangerous weapon."

"It contains nothing but printed words from a *High Authority*. Do you really wish to be held responsible if it goes missing?"

"How high?" asked Hawthorne after a barely perceptible pause.

Leaning a little closer, Bentley answered in a conspiratorial whisper. "The *Very Highest*."

"Hmmph." The magistrate thought for a moment. "Will ye consent to letting me have a closer look at it?"

Bentley held out his hand to Sophie and gave an encouraging little jiggle of his brow.

She didn't look overly pleased, but slowly handed the well-wrapped Bible to him.

"Thank you," he murmured, then offered it to Hawthorne. "Handle it gently, my good man," he cautioned.

A scowl, followed by a tiny shake and a few tentative pokes. "It seems harmless enough," growled the magistrate, passing it back. After hitching up his pants, he signaled his companions to surround Bentley and Sophie. "Follow me, and don't try any tricks or it's off te the county gaol with ye two, quicker than a kestrel can flap its wings."

"Wouldn't dream of trying to fly away," murmured Bentley.

The witticism didn't draw a smile. "March."

Blades of lantern light pierced the foggy gloom as the group tramped down the wooden wharf and across the puddled street. "In here," ordered Hawthorne, after leading the way through the tavern taproom and down a narrow passageway.

The iron-banded door opened with an ominous creak.

"M-might we be allowed a blanket and a candle," asked Sophie meekly, shrinking back from the dark-as-Hades blackness. "And perhaps s-something warm to eat and drink. I am f-feeling a trifle f-faint."

Miss Thirkell acting meek and fluttery? Bentley mentally added theatrical skills to her impressive arsenal of talents. If she gained them a hearty supper, he would see that she got a medal from Whitehall. Maybe two.

"Poor lass, she do look awfully pale." One of the barmaids had followed the procession to the storage area. "Shame on you, Harry Hawthorne, fer bullying a helpless female."

Bentley maintained a straight face.

"Wot if she takes ill?" muttered one of the men. "Then we would really be in hot water."

Hawthorne lifted his lantern. "It's not so very uncomfortable in there," he said defensively, casting his light around the packed earthen floor. "Once Sally fetches a couple of quilts and pillows, it'll be right homey."

"I'll also bring some Cornish pasties and a bottle of ale so they can wet their whistles," volunteered the barmaid. "It's almost closing time and there's still plenty left in the kitchen."

"My sister could also use a small nip of brandy to bring a touch of color back to her cheeks," said Bentley. He silently sketched the outline of a full bottle as the magistrate turned away for a moment.

"Oh, aye, I can see that," replied Sally with a saucy wink. "Don't ye worry. I won't let yer sister expire for lack of nourishment."

A flurry of activity soon had the temporary prison looking almost inviting. A small planked table and two chairs had been carried in by two of their captors, and the aroma of hot food perfumed the musty air. . . .

Bentley bit back a tiny groan. A plume of fragrant steam was rising up from a pewter platter of fresh baked Cornish pasties—a local specialty filled with beef and diced potatoes.

"Make yerself comfortable." Hawthorne fitted an oversized key into the heavy lock. "I can't say fer sure how long it will take to find Captain Farraday and his ship, so ye two may be in here fer a while."

"Ha." Sophie smiled as the door fell shut. "I highly doubt it."

Bentley cocked an ear and listened to a rapid-fire series of metallic clicks. "That," he said, "appears to be a rather formidable mechanism. I think Mr. Hawthorne is right—we aren't going anywhere."

"No," agreed Sophie. "Not until we fill our breadboxes." She reached for one of the pasties and took a bite. A sigh slipped from her lips as she savored the rich taste of meat and spices. "Oh, this is *delicious*. Really, sir, you should try one."

Bentley already had his teeth sunk into a mound of the flaky crust. "'Elishsus," he repeated around a mouthful of dough. A swallow. "Absolutely delicious." He washed down the other half with a swig of brandy.

"Thank you for saving my Bible. Again," she said. "That was very clever talking on your part."

"Not clever enough." He made a face and reached for another pasty. "I was hoping that our place of confinement would offer a chance of escape. But at least we may save precious time by being mere steps from our boat when we are released, instead of locked up in some distant inland gaol."

"You—" she began, only to cut off with a stifled giggle. "You have a dribble of juice on your chin, Lord Leete."

"Do I?" He stuck out his tongue and with an exaggerated slurping sound licked it up. "It's so good, it would be a pity to waste even a drop."

Sophie laughed, feeling the spontaneous sound add an oddly pleasant tickle of heat to the warmth of the food inside her. Strange how the dangers and discomforts of the voyage hadn't made the viscount snarly or sullen. On the contrary— he appeared to be enjoying himself.

"I confess, I am a little surprised that this adventure hasn't put your aristocratic nose out of joint," she murmured.

"Nearly every other body part is bruised and battered, but my nose seems quite undamaged," he quipped. "I'm sorry that it seems to offend you. This is the second time you have made a rather caustic comment about it."

"I . . ." Sophie looked away in embarrassment. "I have sometimes thought that you were looking down said appendage with disapproval."

"I don't disapprove of you, Miss Thirkell," he said quietly.

"But you always seem to stare at me with such a peculiar expression," blurted out Sophie. "And until now, you always act so . . . lordly."

"It's hard to act lordly when you are wet as a drowned rat," he replied. "Having cannonballs whizzing overhead and a hostile magistrate threatening arrest also tends to knock one down a peg or two."

"I'm sorry my plan subjected you to such abuse."

"Oh, good heavens, don't be!" exclaimed Bentley. "Without your intrepid skills, I wouldn't have a prayer of reaching London in time for the meeting."

He thinks me intrepid? Sophie had been sure he considered her the most horrible hoyden in all of Christendom.

"Besides," he went on. "I haven't had so much fun since the time at Eton when my friend and I nearly blew up one of the buildings trying to make stinkbombs."

"You have an awfully odd idea of fun, Lord Leete."

"As do you, Miss Thirkell."

A sigh slipped free. "True. I have very odd notions about a lot of things. Indeed, it often feels like I am a square peg trying to fit in a round hole."

"Then perhaps you just need to carve out your own niche."

"I . . ." Unsure of herself, Sophie found her voice trailing off.

"It isn't easy, I know," he continued. "We all doubt ourselves at times."

"Surely not you," she replied.

"Of course me." Bentley smiled. "I've been quaking like jellied aspic on the inside more times than I care to count.

But I have found that if you believe in yourself and your goals, then you can accomplish whatever you set your heart on." A pause. "So don't be nervous about the upcoming meeting with your relatives. Anyone who can outwit a French privateer and sail through dangerous shoals in a raging storm shouldn't be intimidated by *anything*.

To cover her confusion, Sophie carefully cut two wedges from the apple tart on the table. "T-this looks delicious as well. Are you still hungry?" she asked, offering him a piece.

"Good Lord, yes." He forked up a bite and took another swallow of brandy. "Talking works up quite an appetite—and thirst."

"You have a very devious tongue," observed Sophie, grateful for the change of subject. "I hadn't realized that diplomats could lie through their teeth."

"I did not lie," he replied with a grin. "I merely embellished the truth."

She arched a skeptical brow.

"Miss Thirkell, in the course of sailing, you employ whatever tactics it takes to keep your vessel safe, don't you?" he went on. "I simply use mental maneuvers to do the same thing."

"In other words," she mused, "you are saying that we are more alike than might appear at first blush."

"Well, er, yes." *Was it merely a quirk of candlelight that had his eyes aglow with fire?* "In a manner of speaking."

Sophie decided it must be the brandy talking. There was an odd little note in his voice. A rumble, redolent of smoke and salt . . . and sinful urges.

A tingling sensation danced down her spine. She quickly shook it off, and cleared her throat. *Concentrate!* She gave herself a mental scold. *Think of the Bible and your duty, not Lord Leete's beautiful blue eyes and sensuous smile.*

"If you have finished with your meal, let us get to work," she muttered.

Bentley popped the last morsel of tart into his mouth and dusted his hands. "Doing what?" he asked.

"Getting out of here."

"Miss Thirkell, unless you have a barrel of gunpowder hidden in your sea boots, I am afraid you must console yourself to the fact that we are stuck here for the night."

"No gunpowder," she replied. "Just a knife." Light winked off the thin-bladed length of steel. "Which is all we need to be on our way."

"But that lock—"

"Oh, piff—my father had a number of similar models in his Boston warehouses, until I showed him how easy they were to pick. They may look intimidating . . ." The knife-point jiggled into the iron keyhole. ". . . but there are very few levers inside, and those are simple to manipulate."

Click, click, click.

"Bring along the brandy and the bag of apples," said Sophie as she eased the door open. "We may need to avoid putting into port for the next little while."

"In that case, I had better take the cheese and bread too," said Bentley. "A pity the barmaid didn't bring more pasties. Perhaps we can check the larder as we leave."

"Let's think of our feet—and how fast we can move them—rather than our stomachs, shall we?" she advised, turning to take up the naval lantern Hawthorne had left behind. Metal scraped against metal as she adjusted the shutters to allow only a pinpoint beam of light.

The viscount chuckled as he buttoned up his worn wool coat. "You have already run me ragged—ha-ha."

Slanting a stern look his way, Sophie shushed him to silence. But in truth, his sense of humor was beginning to grow on her. That he could be both serious and silly was intriguing. What other hidden facets . . .

Sophie realized that she was staring and quickly looked

away. Seeing no sign of life in the passageway, she signaled for him to follow.

Crouched low, they hurried down its length and entered the taproom. A few dying coals crackled faintly in the hearth, and a cat padded across the wooden counter and disappeared into the deep shadows.

"Everyone appears to have retired to a nice, warm bed," whispered Bentley, as rain started to drum against the mullioned glass. He heaved a long sigh.

"Oh, show some bottom, sir. Sailors must be willing to brave the elements," she muttered.

"Rather than display my bottom, I would rather tuck it beneath a nice, thick eiderdown coverlet."

Shoving aside the intriguing thought of Bentley's bottom lying on softly rumpled sheets, Sophie moved to the side window and took hold of the heavy brass latches. "Put a cork in it, Lord Leete. And then help me get this open."

Mud squelched under his boots as Bentley dropped into the walled herb garden bordering the side of the tavern. Thankfully, the rain clouds had swirled away just as quickly as they had blown in. A half moon peeked through the mist-shrouded skies, its watery glow casting just enough light to pick out the path leading out to the street.

"Have a care, Miss Thirkell," he whispered, reaching up a helping hand. "The ground is slippery as a greased eel."

Sophie had already swung a leg over the casement. "Don't worry, I'm used to navigating all sorts of—" Her foot, clad in the heavy sea boot, suddenly slid over the slick stone, missing its toehold.

Whomp.

"Oh, I am *so* sorry, sir," she exclaimed in a wool-muffled voice as she squirmed to untangle herself from his flattened form.

"Think nothing of it," he wheezed. The force of her fall had knocked them both to the ground. "I am always happy to be of assistance to a lady, even when it calls for serving as a rug."

A breath of air—a silent laugh?—tickled against his cheek. "Oh, dear, the ground must be devilishly wet and cold."

True. His backside was mired in mud, and already the damp chill was seeping through his breeches. The rest of him, however, was experiencing a delicious flare of heat. *Friction causes fire. . . .*

"If you would remove your arm from my waist," said Sophie, redoubling her efforts to scramble free, "I could get up."

"Right." Bentley feigned a wince. "Just give me a moment to gather my wits."

"Dear Lord!" exclaimed Sophie in concern. "Did you hit your head on a stone?"

"It's nothing," he replied gruffly as she threaded her slim fingers through his hair.

"Stay still," she ordered. "Let me feel for any swelling."

Bentley gritted his teeth. A fast-rising lump of flesh was indeed forming, but it was located in an entirely different section of his anatomy. "No need for worry." With a huffed grunt, he managed to lever up onto his elbows. "I shall survive."

"Not so fast. Head injuries can be very dangerous."

So can the sweetly spiced scent of verbena.

Gently, gently, her hands explored his scalp in slow, circling strokes. Drawing in a gulp of air, he held it in his lungs, letting the sensation wash over him.

"You're lucky. You seem to have escaped injury," murmured Sophie.

Her face was hovering a hairsbreadth from his, and though the muzzy gloom hid her expression, his mind's eye could perfectly picture the exact shape of her cupid's bow mouth. *Dangerous—oh-so dangerous.* Hitching a notch higher, Bentley tilted his cheek just a fraction. Flesh kissed up against flesh, and he felt her breath quicken.

"Miss Thirkell, I . . ."

A dog's sharp bark interrupted the moment.

"I think we had better get moving."

"Yes, yes, we must. It's madness to linger here any longer." Scooting back, she hastily rose and tugged her coat into order. "The tide will be turning soon, and if we don't catch the ebb, we won't have a prayer of escape."

"What about the snapped jib line?" asked Bentley after levering to his feet.

"It will take only a moment to splice," answered Sophie as they crept along the line of the wall toward the front gate.

"Is there *anything* you can't do, Miss Thirkell?" he quipped.

"I can't waltz, as you so painfully learned in my father's ballroom. I was clumsy as the cow and must have squashed all ten of your toes."

"Only nine." Recalling how grimly uncomfortable she had appeared swathed in frilly silk and satin, Bentley chuckled. "I was sure you were deliberately seeking to cripple me, though I wasn't quite sure why." He ducked under a twist of ivy. "Had I offended you in some way?"

For a moment there was only the soft sound of their steps on the soggy grass and a flutter of air ruffling the wet leaves.

"Only by being so impossibly handsome and self-assured. In contrast I felt so awkward and provincial." Her murmur tightened to a rueful whisper. "Knowing I could never attract your attention through my graces, I suppose I chose the opposite tack."

Surprise hit him with all the force of an Atlantic gale. Knocked off his bearings, Bentley didn't notice she had come to a halt at the oaken gate. "I-I—" he stuttered, only to stumble and thump up against her shoulder, pinning her between his body and the unyielding planking. Dark twists of ivy swayed overhead . . . *no, no, it was mistletoe,* he noted vaguely as he managed to untangle his tongue. "As you see, in reality I'm naught but an awkward ox."

"Oh, it appears we are a rare pair of bumbling bovines, Lord Leete. How fortuitous that Fate has brought us together."

Her low, throaty laugh, a sound that seemed meant for his ears alone, sent a lick of heat spiraling through his chest. Emboldened by the intimacy, he added, "I can't believe that you, who are so attuned to every nuance of the ocean, didn't sense how nervous I was around you. I found you . . . intriguing. Alluring. Entrancing."

"Oh." Sophie swallowed a gulp of air. "Really? But you barely ever said a word to me."

"I was tongue-tied," he replied. "You were so exuberant."

"And you were so reserved."

"I couldn't help it. You had so many admirers circled around your skirts, all I could do was stare."

"And watch me behave like a hopeless hoyden." Scudding moonlight caught the pinch of embarrassment on Sophie's face. She bit her lip in momentary confusion, a little quirk that he found endearing. "Lively—ha! I'm surprised I didn't shock your very well-bred sense of propriety to flinders."

"I confess, your devil-may-care spirit was unlike anything I had ever experienced. I've never met a young lady with your sense of adventure."

A tiny tremor quivered along the curves of her mouth. "Proper young ladies aren't supposed to be adventurous. It's too dangerous."

"Dangerous," repeated Bentley, feeling a clench of lust take hold of his body. "Yes, I can see that." Even to his own ears, his voice sounded strangely smoky. "There's no telling what can happen when one ventures into the unknown."

"That doesn't frighten me," said Sophie. "I suppose it should. But instead, it makes my blood fizz and thrum." A sigh, soft as the tendrils of mist floating up from the harbor. "No wonder you were so opposed to having me sail in your sloop. I'm the sort of female who tends to cause trouble."

"I wasn't worried about what *you* might do, Miss Thirkell." *Trouble.* The word was reverberating inside his skull. *Trouble, trouble, trouble.* Bentley prided himself on listening to his voice of Inner Reason. But prudence, along with his official documents, seemed to have been swept overboard by the rogue wave.

She shifted slightly, the bump of the Bible tucked beneath her coat a chiding reminder that his intentions were anything but saintly.

To the devil with all the cursed, confining rules of propriety. In that instant, with frigid water dripping down his neck and raindrops freckling Sophie's delightfully pert nose, Bentley realized the only thing that mattered was *her*.

"The truth is, I was more afraid of what my own actions might be." He leaned in, their bodies kissing up against each other as he lowered his mouth to capture hers.

With a rusty snick, the latch popped open and the gate cracked open.

"Oiy! Wot's that?" A gruff voice pierced through the darkness.

Bloody hell. His hands, already gripping Sophie's shoulders, yanked her back from the opening. Keeping hold of her coat, he whirled around and sprinted for the back wall.

"Up you go," he whispered, lifting her off the ground. "And quickly."

Sophie scrambled to the top and reached down. "Here, grab hold of me."

Bentley didn't pause to argue the fine points of gentle-manly deportment. Boots scraping, scuffing against the rough stone, he pulled himself up to the ledge. Below them lay several narrow alleyways, twisting off into a haze of thick fog.

Which way, which way? Bentley hesitated, disoriented by the murky darkness.

"Follow me," said Sophie decisively. Dropping down to the ground, she chose the one leading off to the left.

He kept right on her heels, dodging piles of crab traps and tangled fishnets. It might only have been a quirk of the wind, but a burble of laughter seemed to echo off the storage sheds. After a quick dip and a sharp turn, the alley opened onto a rutted lane.

"You are enjoying this, aren't you?" he gasped, as they paused for a moment to catch their breath.

Sophie grinned. "Admit it—so are you!"

"There's something to be said for adventure," he replied with an answering smile. "Assuming the residents of Stony Creek don't shoot escaping prisoners on sight."

"If we keep moving quickly, we'll be long gone before the magistrate opens his eyes."

"Er, any idea of which way we should go to reach the harbor?" asked Bentley after a quick look around. "I'm completely lost."

Sophie rolled her eyes. "Good heavens, any mariner worth his salt can navigate by the stars. We're almost there." She checked up and down the lane before adding, "Stay close, and stay quiet. Like us, there seem to be a few fishermen up and looking to catch the outgoing tide."

Keeping to the shadows, they crossed the cart tracks and turned down a sloping side street that led past the back of several shops. Head hunched low, Bentley did his best to mimic her light step and lithe movements. Miss Thirkell might find the steps of a waltz intimidating, but clearly the racing through a strange town as a fugitive from justice held no fear.

The thought provoked a soft snort of laughter.

"Shhh." She turned and waggled a warning finger.

Drawing a steadying breath, he nodded—and then stopped short.

Frowning, she motioned for him to keep going.

"Wait," he whispered, inhaling another lungful of spiced air. *Gingerbread.* The sugary scent was coming from somewhere tantalizingly close by. Another sniff led him to a window several paces away. From inside he could hear the clatter of copper pots and pans. A bakery, beginning work on its wares for the coming day. Already a tray of nut-brown confections, formed in the shape of little men, were cooling on the sill.

"That's stealing," murmured Sophie as she watched him stuff a number of the pastries into the sack of apples.

"Since I'm already considered a criminal, I might as well add theft to my misdeeds," he replied. "But don't worry, I will send full restitution once we reach London."

"I think I'm a bad influence on you."

"Horrible," he agreed.

"Thank God." She flashed a pearlescent smile. "They smell absolutely delicious."

Bentley quickly retied the bag. "Lead on, Captain. The faster we shove off, the faster we can breakfast on our ill-gotten gains."

She started off, but no sooner had they turned the corner and slipped between a rack of spars and cordage when a gruff order brought them to an abrupt halt.

"Halt!" A burly figure stepped out from the hanging coils of rope, a wicked-looking eel spear punctuating the command. "Where do ye think ye two are going?"

"Umm . . ." For once, Sophie seemed at a loss for words.

"To London," answered Bentley. "It's a matter of life and death that we get there in time for Christmas."

The fisherman—Bentley recognized him as one of the magistrate's companions—frowned. "Ye told Hawthorne a different story."

"Ah, but Mr. Hawthorne did not strike me as a man with a heart, so I did not dare confide my sister's sad tale," improvised Bentley. A discreet nudge encouraged Sophie to give a watery sniff. "But *you,* my good fellow, look like a sympathetic soul. I am sure you are just the sort of man who would wish to aid a damsel in distress."

"Er . . ." The man coughed. "Well, naturally I'm always happy te help a female. Assuming it's fer a good reason."

"Oh, be assured it is for the very *best* of reasons," he replied. "Love and family—it's what the holiday season is all about."

The man nodded slightly, but the prongs of the spear remained hovering scant inches from Bentley's chest. "Family is important."

"Then I'm sure you'll understand my sister's—that is, my half sister's—heartfelt determination to fulfill a deathbed promise to her father. She has traveled all the way from America, braving heathen savages, Atlantic gales . . ." Warming to the task, Bentley launched into a long and admitted greatly embellished story of the perils they had faced.

The fisherman listened in wide-eyed silence. Sophie, on the other hand, was making a series of odd little noises in the back of her throat.

"Don't cry, my dear," soothed Bentley. "I am sure this fellow will do the right thing and not stand in the way of love."

The fisherman shuffled his feet. "The revenue captain should be here by noon. Shouldn't we wait fer an official te untangle all these misunderstandings?"

"The tide is turning," he replied. "If we miss it, we could

be stuck here until God-Knows-When. After all, there is no guarantee that your messenger will find the captain."

"Hmmph." The grunt was as raspy as the rattle of rusty anchor chain. "The thing is, yer under arrest."

"Not officially," pointed out Sophie. "We were merely detained until the proper authorities arrive." Another strategic sniff. "But by then, it might be too late."

"Hmmph." The new sound was considerably softer.

"Come now, do we look like dangerous criminals?" pressed Bentley, hiding the purloined gingerbread behind his back.

"Oh, fie." Swinging the spear away, the fisherman pointed the way to the wharf. "Be off with ye, afore I change my mind. Hawthorne would likely roast my cods along with the holiday chestnuts if he finds out about this, so let's just pretend I never saw ye."

"Happy Christmas," he murmured, taking Sophie by the arm and urging her forward.

"Happy Christmas," she echoed.

"Now let us run like the devil," whispered Bentley. "Before we encounter a less soft-hearted soul."

"Hold the tiller firmly and shift it right or left to keep the bow of the boat pointed north-northeast," called Sophie as she cast off the mooring lines. "It's actually quite simple. Just watch the compass. It will only take me a few minutes to splice the jib sheet."

"Do try to make it quick," said Bentley. He looked a little nervous at being put in charge of steering the sloop out of the narrow harbor. "I'd rather not run amuck at this point."

"Ha, there is little chance of that! There are no hidden hazards marked on the chart." Taking a marlinspike from one of the lockers, Sophie set to work repairing the snapped rope. Her fingers smoothed over the strands, weaving the two frayed pieces together. As a child, she had been amazed to see that two separate pieces could be made into one. It seems impossible, and yet the new was often stronger than the old.

Perhaps relationships are like that too. "At least I hope they are," she murmured to herself. Could past feuds be mended and her family made whole again? The question was a daunting one, but somehow Lord Leete's encouragement had her feeling more confident about the upcoming meeting. He had a way with words.

Repressing a laugh, Sophie looked around to tease him about the yarn he had just spun.

"You know, I've told some bouncers in my life, but that one was so outrageous that I'm surprised it didn't ricochet off the wharf and break your teeth."

He flashed a grin. "In moments of crisis, a good diplomat, like a good mariner, must improvise."

"Lord Leete, you—" The moonlight grew suddenly brighter as the wind kicked up and blew away the lingering clouds. "You should duck. And do it NOW!"

A block of iron came sailing across the water, struck the stern and then bounced up to land on the deck with a loud *thunk*.

"Stop them, stop them!" A hopping-mad Hawthorne skidded to a stop at the end of the wharf. "The criminals are getting away!" Grabbing up another piece of ballast from a barrow, he flung it at the sloop.

"Why, the skunk is trying to knock our rudder off its pins so we can't steer," exclaimed Sophie.

"Is he?" Taking up the spent missile, Bentley turned around and calmly pitched it back at the magistrate. It caught Hawthorne square on his well-cushioned belly, knocking him head over heels into the shallow, smelly water.

Sophie let out an admiring whistle. "For a frivolous fop,

you've got an awfully strong arm. And remarkably accurate aim."

"Cricket," he replied with a wicked wink. "Now and again, those asinine aristocratic games come in handy."

"So I see," she replied. A great many things had come into sharper focus over the last two days. To herself, she added, "Pride and pique tend to distort the view."

With a few quick twists of the marlinspike, she finished splicing the rope and raised the jib. Wind filled the sail and the sloop heeled over smartly, picking up speed and leaving a trail of white foam in its wake.

"Miscreants! I will see to it that you get your just deserts!" The magistrate's fast-fading bellowing was nearly swallowed by the surge of the open sea beyond the channel breakwater.

"I rather hope so," quipped Bentley. "I am very fond of Christmas pudding."

Sophie laughed as she came back to the cockpit and sat down beside him. "If the wind keeps up like this, we shall drop anchor in the Thames with time to spare." The stars were diamond bright overhead, and dawn was just beginning to dapple the horizon. After unfolding the chart, she studied the coastline in the shimmery half light. "There is a cove marked here just a few miles ahead. We ought to pull in and wait an hour or two for the tide to turn more favorable for our next tack."

"An excellent idea," said Bentley. "Indeed, I was just about to suggest that we do away with the evidence of our criminal activity, just in case we run into His Majesty's revenue cutter."

A short while later they were riding at anchor, the sails furled, the sloop rocking gently within the shelter of the cliffs. Bentley quickly found the bag and untied the strings.

The gingerbread was still warm, and as Sophie took a bite, the spicy sweetness melted on her tongue. "That," she said slowly, "could be the most delicious thing I have ever tasted."

An odd expression spread over his face as Bentley swallowed hard and went very still. "Actually, I think it's only the second-most delicious thing I've ever tasted."

She shifted, her hip bumping gently against his. They had stretched out side by side on the floorboards of the cockpit to shelter from the wind, a thick blanket from below providing a cozy covering to ward off the dampness.

"Oh?" Her voice turned a bit muzzy as a spun-sugar tickle of contentment teased over her limbs. "I ask you, what can be better than fresh-baked gingerbread?" she challenged, looking up to meet his gaze.

Strange—how had she not noticed those dancing flickers of fire-gold sparks in his eyes before now?

"This," he said, leaning down to capture her mouth.

He tasted of cloves and cinnamon, tinged with the salt of the sea. And some earthier essence she couldn't put a name to. A shiver of heat licked down her spine.

In contrast his lips felt blessedly cool as they broke off the embrace to trace a flutter of soft kisses over her flushed cheeks.

"Sweet, tart, tangy," he whispered. "I am usually good with words, but you defy description."

"Mmm. Then don't try to talk for a moment." With a tremulous sigh, Sophie drew him back and opened herself to a deeper embrace. Her hands slid along the slope of his shoulders, feeling the solid strength of chiseled muscle. "Bentley," she murmured against his mouth. It was a lovely name—elegant and aristocratic, yet stalwart and steadfast.

He groaned in response, his arms tightening and hugging her close. Their tongues twined, and for a dizzying, dazzling interlude, Sophie felt all rational thought skitter away in the breeze.

The bump of a wave finally broke them apart. "Sorry, I . . .

I seem to be sinking into depravity," he said in a ragged whisper. "Stolen gingerbread, stolen kisses."

"Oh, it is I who owe you an apology. I fear that I'm a bad influence on you," replied Sophie. "Not that I'm at all sorry for it," she added softly.

"Neither am I." He brushed an errant curl from her cheek. "But I mean to be a gentleman from now on—no matter how hard."

"I shall see that you won't suffer any consequences because of this," she said after a long moment. "I can sneak away before we reach—"

He pressed a finger to her lips. "Don't worry, I shall come up with a good story." A wink. "I've discovered that I am very good at talking my way out of trouble."

Laughing, she leaned back and gazed up at the heavens, where a bright twinkle was still visible against the fading night. "Oh, look. That reminds me of the tales about the Christmas star, the one that led the Three Wise Men to Bethlehem bearing gifts." She brushed a caress to the wrapped Bible, which was safely nestled beneath the slatted seat. "Perhaps it's come to be our own special guiding light to London."

"I can't claim to be Wise," quipped Bentley. "And while I'm bearing some useful tidings for the government, it is I who has received the greatest gift of all—your friendship." He crooked a smile. "For I do hope that we are friends."

Friends.

Sophie snuggled up against his warmth, feeling their closeness make her heart sing with joy.

"'Tis truly the season to give thanks," she murmured. "You have given me far more than you have received. Patience, kindness, counsel, and guidance on how to navigate the foreign waters of Society, with all its unfamiliar shoals. Because of you I can see a new horizon, with hint of new dawn lightening the darkness."

Bentley smiled. "And I, in turn, thank you for challenging me to explore new waters. Your bold courage and sense of adventure have reminded me that life is far more fun when there is a spark of unexpected excitement to it—not to speak of a frisson of danger."

She watched a hint of sunlight sparkle over a calm blue sea. "Don't worry. From here on in, it will be smooth sailing."

His brows rose a notch.

"Well," she amended. "There may be a few waves and whitecaps. But storms can be exhilarating."

"Very exhilarating," he drawled. "And somehow, together we seem to manage quite well in coming through them unscathed."

The curl of his mouth set her insides to turning topsy-turvy. "I-I hope that when we drop anchor in the Thames, our journey will not be over."

Bentley looked up at the twinkling morning star before answering. "My dear Sophie, I hope that our journey is just beginning."

THE MISTLETOE BRIDE

Anne Gracie

Chapter 1

HighTowers House, Scotland, 1814

"What you need is a dying woman."

Ronan McAllister stopped in midpace and swung around. *"What?"*

Adams, his lawyer, shrugged. "If you don't want to stay married, it's your best option."

Ronan frowned. "It's a bit . . . cold-blooded, don't you think? To marry a dying woman for the sake of an inheritance."

The elderly lawyer spread his hands in a philosophical gesture. "You said you didn't want to get married again."

"I don't. Still . . ." Ronan shook his head. "To be taking advantage of someone's tragedy . . ."

"Not necessarily. It might make things easier for her."

Ronan paused. "How so?"

"Dying women often fret about the people they leave behind; how they will live, the costs of the funeral and such things." Adams adjusted his pince-nez. "A payment in exchange for marriage could ease the way for such a woman to die in peace."

Ronan resumed his pacing. He didn't like it. It went

against the grain to use someone's death for his own gain. But . . . there was sense in what Adams had said.

He didn't want to marry again, didn't want to be saddled with a wife. He'd done that. The most miserable five years of his life.

A fee could ease the way for a dying woman.

Damn Great-Aunt Agatha and her fortune. And her blasted conditions. The cheek of a maiden aunt requiring him to marry again before his thirtieth birthday. *She'd* never bothered to marry. She'd lived a life of blissful freedom, doing what she wanted, going where she chose, living life as the whim took her.

If he didn't need the money so badly . . . He gazed out the window. His work on the estate had only just begun. Over the last twenty years the tenants and estate workers had suffered from his father's spendthrift ways, and Ronan had sworn to put things right. But for that he needed Great-Aunt Agatha's money, and the old witch had known it.

"How would it work?"

"My nephew lives in London," Adams said. "He would find a suitable woman of respectable birth, dying, but not of anything contagious. We'd have her condition certified by a doctor, of course. We wouldn't want any . . . errors." He gave a thin smile.

Ronan didn't smile back. The whole thing was repugnant. But he'd do it. He had no choice. Since he'd inherited the estate, he'd worked every hour God sent, bringing it slowly back to productivity after years of neglect. Great-Aunt Agatha's fortune would make all the difference in the world.

Adams continued. "She will have to travel here, of course, since your great-aunt's will specified an English-woman and marriage in the chapel on the estate, so we'd send her a ticket on the mail coach—"

"Hire her a post chaise, dammit—she's sick."

The lawyer raised his brows at this extravagance, but made a note. "Very well. As soon as we have a name, I shall procure a special license, and when she arrives the minister will perform a ceremony. After that it is a matter of . . . um . . . consummation and—"

"Consummation?"

Adams failed to meet Ronan's gaze. "It is a legal requirement."

There was a short silence. Ronan clenched his fists. He should have strangled Great-Aunt Agatha while she was alive.

The lawyer went on, "It has occurred to me that if the woman were a widow . . . and you simply shared a bed . . . nobody would be able to prove otherwise." He steepled his thin, white fingers and waited. Eventually he said, "All I need is your approval and I'll go ahead and make all the arrangements."

Ronan didn't approve of any part of the scheme, but he gave a curt nod. "Do it."

Traveling by stagecoach was even worse than the voyage home, Marguerite Blackett-Smith decided. She was just as sick from the constant swaying, lurching and jolting, but at least on the ship she hadn't been in constant danger of being squashed.

She discreetly shoved the large sleeping farmer beside her into a more or less vertical position. How he could sleep through it all was beyond her, but sleep he did, listing dangerously to one side—her side—smelling of stale sweat and onions.

She shoved him back up again.

Three days the journey had taken so far, and they were only halfway to their destination. Six days from London to Edinburgh, the coach company promised. Marguerite's destination lay just before Edinburgh.

Her destination. Her final destination. A twenty-five-year-old spinster with no money, no looks and no prospects ought to be grateful that any relative was prepared to take her in, Cousin Ida—who wasn't—had told her. Even if it was Uncle Alexander.

Uncle Alexander had sent Marguerite a ticket on the stage. Marguerite would repay his generosity by working for him, he informed her.

Her future was depressingly clear. There would be no chance of marriage now, no chance of a home of her own, or children.

Still, poor Mrs. Smith opposite looked even worse than Marguerite felt. She sat wedged into a corner, her face drawn, her skin so sallow it looked quite yellow. Her eyes were deep-set and exhausted and ringed with papery, bruised-looking skin.

As the only two women in the coach, they'd naturally been drawn together, keeping each other company during coach stops. They'd exchanged smiles at first, then a few comments on the journey and the bane of travel-sickness, for Marguerite noticed the other woman ate nothing during meal stops as well.

This morning, Marguerite had confided she was going to Scotland to live with an elderly uncle, and to Marguerite's surprise Peggy Smith had replied that she was going to Scotland to be married. She didn't look much like a bride, but then nobody looked their best traveling.

"Meal stop!" the coachman yelled. The other passengers eagerly descended into the yard at the inn, but Mrs. Smith did not move. Marguerite shook her arm. The woman's eyelashes fluttered and she moaned and tried to sit up, then fell back with a sigh.

"This lady's ill," Marguerite called to the coachman. "I think it's lack of food. She's hardly eaten in three days."

He came over and peered doubtfully in, then called to a couple of ostlers to carry the lady inside. "I don't like her color," he told Marguerite, "but no doubt a nice hot cup of tea and sommat to eat will revive her."

They carried her inside, placed her on a settle in the otherwise deserted coffee room and left her for Marguerite to care for. Marguerite ordered hot sweet tea and some dry toast—anything richer would be disastrous on a delicate stomach. She bathed Mrs. Smith's face and hands with vinegar, and by the time the tea and toast arrived she looked a little stronger.

With a shudder, she waved away the toast, but drank the tea slowly with her eyes still closed. When she'd finished she glanced warily around the room, then, seeing it was empty, placed a thin hand over Marguerite's. "Can I trust you?"

"Yes, of course," Marguerite responded without thinking.

"God, but I hope I can. There's nobody else . . ." Mrs. Smith closed her eyes again, as if gathering energy, and Marguerite wondered what on earth she wanted her to do. She already regretted her rash promise. She knew nothing about this woman.

Mrs. Smith reached into the inside pocket of her coat and drew out a folded card. She passed it to Marguerite. "My daughters."

Marguerite opened the card. Inside there was a pencil drawing of two little girls, the older, about five, a plain little creature with an endearingly earnest expression. The younger was still almost a baby, with a head of pale curls and a dreamy expression.

"Oh, how sweet they look—" Marguerite began.

"I'm dying," Mrs. Smith said in a hoarse voice.

Marguerite gave her a shocked look. "Oh, no, I'm sure . . . Once you've had a rest and something to eat—"

"No. It's my liver. . . . Jaundice. Doctor said . . . maybe a couple of months. I thought . . . enough time . . . but . . ." She sank back, exhausted.

Marguerite patted the woman's hand, knowing it was a feeble response, but what else could she do?

"Please . . . my daughters . . . my little girls. Will you take care of them?"

"Me? But surely your betrothed—"

"No. I've never met the man. All arranged through a lawyer in London." Peggy Smith's eyes were dull as she added, "He's paying me five hundred pounds to marry him. And then I can leave."

Marguerite wasn't sure she'd heard the woman aright. It sounded so bizarre. "I don't understand."

"He doesn't want a wife." Peggy Smith's voice was just a thread of sound. "Just a marriage certificate." She shook her head wearily. "Don't know why. Don't care. The money's all I care about. Cared about. Too late now." She broke off, coughing.

Marguerite poured the last of the tea into a cup and held it to Mrs. Smith's mouth. She swallowed a few mouthfuls, then pushed it away.

"My girls . . . he doesn't know about them. . . . Not interested in children. Just . . . marriage certificate." She fixed a desperate gaze on Marguerite. "The girls and I have no family. My little Jane is five and Amy nearly three. . . . I left them with a neighbor . . . gave her enough money for six weeks . . . but after that . . ." She shook her head. "She can't keep them. Doesn't want them. . . . If I don't return, she'll put them on the parish."

Her face crumpled. "I don't want them in the poor house, not my sweet babies. They'll die there." She clutched Marguerite's hand, rocking in distress. "Please, miss. They're good girls."

"I'm sure they are, but what could I do? I have no money

and I'm wholly dependent on the charity of my uncle." Thin and grudging charity at that. *You will make yourself useful in exchange for bed and board.* In other words, an unpaid servant.

Peggy Smith fumbled for the pocket of her skirt and drew out a cloth bag. "He sent me money to hire a post chaise and for meals along the way. I couldn't bring myself to waste so much money when I could travel on the stage so much cheaper. Take it. It's all I have in the world. Otherwise *they*"—she jerked her head to indicate the other people in the inn—"will steal it. There's a hundred pounds in there. Use it for my daughters. To keep them out of the workhouse."

"But—"

She gripped Marguerite's hand again. "Please. There's nobody else I can ask. No one in the world."

Marguerite bit her lip. She wanted to help, she really did, but she didn't see how she could. A hundred pounds was a substantial sum, but it would soon disappear with two little girls to feed and clothe and house. Not to mention herself.

It was madness to agree. She'd end up in the workhouse herself.

"Please, Marguerite." The desperation in the other woman's face was unbearable to watch.

Marguerite's gaze dropped to the portrait of the two little girls. Poor little mites, with no one to care for them or love them. How could she, who had nobody and nothing herself, refuse? She squeezed Peggy Smith's thin hand. "I promise I'll do whatever I can."

"Bless you, my dear." Peggy Smith sat back with a smile and closed her eyes, then jerked forward in a paroxysm of coughing that racked her thin frame.

"Water?"

Still coughing, Peggy nodded, and Marguerite went running to fetch a cup of water. She returned with it in a scant few minutes and stood stock-still, staring at Peggy Smith.

She was slumped over, her hand resting on the folded card. A small stub of pencil rolled from between her nerveless fingers.

Marguerite picked up the card. On the back, Peggy had scrawled, *I, Peggy Smith, give my darling girls Jane and Amy to the care of Margaret Blacket-Smith.* She'd signed her name below it.

Marguerite tucked the document and Peggy Smith's precious cloth bag into her coat pocket.

The coachman poked his head in at the door. "Coach leaving now, miss. Your friend need a hand?"

Marguerite turned to the coachman and tried to swallow the lump in her throat. "I'm afraid she's dead."

Chapter 2

Marguerite perched on the window seat inside the taproom of the Wench and Haggis Inn and peered out anxiously into the darkening sky. She'd been waiting for hours. Granted, the stagecoach had been delayed, not least by the death of one of its passengers, but still, Uncle Alexander had said Marguerite would be met at the inn.

Poor Peggy Smith. It had felt so wrong to leave her behind, her body not yet cold, but what could she do? The landlord of the inn and the coach driver had argued vehemently over Peggy's body, each claiming the other was responsible for dealing with the matter. The coach driver had settled it by collecting his remaining passengers and driving away.

Cold seeped in through the window. Marguerite shifted on the hard window seat and drew her coat more tightly around her. Who would bury Peggy? No doubt she'd be given a pauper's grave. Marguerite hoped it would not be unmarked; Peggy's name, at least, was known, even if there was no one to pay for a headstone.

Marguerite knew Peggy would rather her money was spent on her children than on her burial. She'd told nobody about the oilcloth bag Peggy had given her. She hadn't even examined it herself yet. She'd wait until she was alone and could inspect the contents in private.

"Can I fetch you anything, miss?" a tavern wench asked. "The stew's good tonight."

"Thank you, but I'm not hungry." Marguerite's stomach rumbled in contradiction. The aromas coming from the kitchen were rich and enticing, but she had no money to pay for a meal or even a cup of tea.

Only desperation would allow her to break into Peggy Smith's fund, and she was not desperate yet. Only hungry.

Where was Uncle Alexander? His letter was very specific. She was to alight from the coach at the village of Bedloe and wait outside the Wench and Haggis Inn. She was not to go inside the inn; it was not a fit place for a respectable woman. Someone would come to collect her directly.

But it was too cold to wait outside. She'd tried for a while, but the bitter wind had sliced through her thin coat, and when tiny flakes of snow began to swirl down, she'd retreated into the inn. She'd half expected to be rudely accosted, but apart from a few curious glances, the only person who'd approached her was the tavern wench.

Marguerite was dozing when the rumble of wheels on the cobblestones jerked her awake. An elderly-looking traveling chaise pulled up and the driver climbed down.

"Stage been through, has it?" she heard him ask an ostler. "Did a woman get off?"

At last! Marguerite grabbed her carpet bag and hurried outside. "Are you looking for me?"

The driver squinted at her. "The woman the master sent for? From London?"

"Yes, I'm Marguerite Blackett-Smith. And that's my trunk."

The man shrugged, opened the door for her and went to fetch her trunk.

The carriage was old and slightly shabby but it was clean and warm inside. As Marguerite seated herself, she stubbed her toe on a large oblong metal object on the floor of the carriage. She bent to examine it and discovered it was warm. A foot-warmer! And a soft woolen rug lay folded beside her on the seat. How very thoughtful. And luxurious.

The chaise moved off with a jerk and Marguerite settled back against the padded leather seats. Her toes were thawing nicely on the foot-warmer and she snuggled into the rug, her spirits rising at the unexpected provision for her comfort. For the first time in days, her future didn't seem so bleak.

The house was tall and cast in shadows, a gloomy-looking pile darkly silhouetted against the heavy slate gray of the sky. Just the sort of place she'd imagined her elderly bachelor uncle in.

A motherly-looking housekeeper neatly dressed in gray and white greeted her as she stepped down from the carriage. "The master sends his greeting, madam, but he's away with an ailing beast. But look at you," she exclaimed as she ushered Marguerite into the well-lit hall. "You're worn to a thread. You'll be wanting your bed, I'll warrant. And your supper on a tray."

"That would be wonderful, Mrs. . . . ?"

"Ferguson." As Marguerite turned to collect her bags, the housekeeper added, "Never you mind about your baggage. Tom will bring everything up. Come along, now."

She ushered Marguerite to a large bedchamber on the second floor. A fire was already burning merrily in the grate, and Mrs. Ferguson bustled across and tipped more coal onto it. "I expect you feel the cold something shocking, being such a wee bit of a thing."

Marguerite laughed and held her hands gratefully to the blaze. "I do, but it's more from living in India these last ten years."

"India, is it? Well, I never. Now I'll be off. I'll send someone up with hot water and a wee bit of supper. Would you fancy a spot of soup?"

"I would indeed, thank you."

No sooner had Mrs. Ferguson left than Marguerite's luggage arrived, followed almost immediately by a maidservant with a can of hot water. Moments later another girl arrived with a tray containing a bowl of thick chicken and potato soup, a warm bread roll, a pat of cool yellow butter and a generous slice of egg-and-bacon pie.

"Anything else you want, miss?" the girl asked.

"Nothing, thank you. This is wonderful." As the door closed behind the maid, Marguerite sat down on the bed with a huge sigh of relief.

It was going to be all right after all. Uncle Alexander was not the curmudgeonly old miser she'd been led to expect. He might be away from home, but he'd obviously instructed his staff to make her comfortable, and not in any grudging manner, either.

She removed her coat and felt the crackle of Peggy Smith's papers in their cloth bag. Uncle Alexander might even be willing to take in a couple of small orphaned girls. One could only hope.

The morning dawned gray and leaden, but Marguerite woke in an optimistic spirit. She dressed and went downstairs in search of breakfast.

A maid bobbed a greeting and pointed the way. "Breakfast parlor in there, miss. The master has already started. I'll bring you in some fresh tea."

Uncle Alexander. Marguerite smoothed her hair and

dress, then knocked and entered the room. A man was seated at a large square table set with fine white linen and silverware. At her entrance he looked up. Marguerite blinked. By no stretch of the imagination could this be Uncle Alexander.

He was young, perhaps twenty-nine or thirty, with an angular, attractive face, a bold nose and a stern-looking mouth. He was simply dressed in an old tweed coat over an open-necked, white shirt. A small vee of tanned skin was visible at the neck, and he'd quite clearly not yet shaved. His square, firm jaw was dark with bristle. His hair was brown, short, thick and tousled.

Had he not been taking his breakfast, very much at home at a gentleman's table, she would have thought him a farm laborer.

Over the breakfast dishes he stared at her with a frown that seemed to darken as she watched.

"I, er . . ." she faltered. His eyes were the blue of an Indian summer sky, and piercing. It was most disconcerting.

He blinked, then rose to greet her, a piece of toast in one hand. He was tall, perhaps six feet, with broad shoulders and long legs encased in well-worn buckskin breeches and high boots.

Marguerite stared. *Oh, my,* she thought. *Oh, my* . . .

So this was she. Ronan stared at the woman for a long moment. She was younger than he'd expected, a little bit of a thing, all big eyes and hair, with an air of fragility—well, that would be the illness, he supposed. It was an uncomfortable thought.

She gazed up at him with wide, gray eyes and a flush slowly crept across her face.

Damn, he must be staring. He dragged his gaze off her and realized he was still holding his toast. He dropped it on his plate. "Mrs. Smith, I see you got here at last."

"Yes, I—er, but I'm afraid it's not—" she began, her gaze

lingering on the open neck of his shirt, and he realized his dishabille must be causing her embarrassment.

He said brusquely, "My apologies for my attire, but I've been up half the night with a sick mare." And she wasn't out of the woods yet.

He pulled out a chair and the woman hesitated, then allowed herself to be seated. She looked worried. Her soft brown hair was drawn back in a loose knot, revealing a pale, slender nape. There were delicate lilac shadows beneath her eyes.

"You look tired. Did you get no sleep?"

"No, I slept well, thank y—"

"I was surprised when I received your letter saying you were coming by stage. Why choose the stage when you had a more comfortable option?"

She glanced up with a look of surprise, and seemed not to know how to respond.

"Never mind," he said. "It's done now. I suppose you had your reasons. Do you want tea? Or hot chocolate?"

"Tea, please, but—"

He yanked on the bellpull to summon a maid. The bell jangled in the distance. Still standing, he drained his cup and picked up his toast. He needed to get back to the stables, but he couldn't just run out on her the moment she'd arrived.

What to say? He'd never been much good with chitchat. How was your journey? No point. The stage had been delayed by several days and she was clearly still exhausted. How are you? She was dying. Not exactly comfortable breakfast conversation.

She, too, seemed not to know what to say. A faint frown marred her smooth brow. Several times she opened her mouth as if to speak, then seemed to think better of it, pressing her pale lips firmly together.

Ronan finished his toast. "The minister will be here at eleven. Will you need any assistance?"

"Minister?"

"Yes, for the wedding."

"Wedding?" The gray eyes widened.

It was probably crass of him to arrange it for her first day, but damn it, he wanted this thing done and out of the way. The sooner it was done, the sooner she would be gone. "Aye, Mrs. Smith, the wedding. It's the reason you're here, after all."

His voice sounded gruff. It was worse, now, seeing her obvious fragility, knowing what she faced and still taking advantage of it. No matter that she'd agreed to it.

"But—" Her jaw dropped. "I think—"

But he didn't have time to listen to what she thought. Jem was at the doorway, looking worried. "Sir, it's the mare again."

"Blast!" Ronan hurried toward the door. "Sorry, Mrs. Smith, I've got to go. If you need anything, ask Mrs. Ferguson or one of the servants. I'll see you at eleven."

The door banged shut behind him. It was as though a storm had passed from the room. Marguerite leaned against the hard chair back on a long, slow exhale, her mind in a whirl. *Mrs.* Smith. The first time he'd said it, she wasn't sure she'd heard him right—she'd been distracted by the faint burr of his accent, like rough, dark velvet—but now . . .

Did he think . . . ?

He did. He surely did. He'd called her Mrs. Smith and he'd spoken of a wedding.

Peggy Smith had mentioned Edinburgh Castle, so Marguerite had assumed Edinburgh was her destination and hadn't inquired any further. It would be too incredible a coincidence if they were both bound for the same small village.

But they must have been. And Marguerite had been collected at the inn in mistake for Peggy.

And now he—the man with blue eyes, whose name she didn't even know—thought she was Mrs. Smith. And he was expecting to marry her at eleven o'clock. She glanced at the clock on the mantel. Two hours.

And in the meantime, Uncle Alexander would be wondering what had happened to her.

What a terrible mix-up. If only she'd spoken at once, the moment the first question had risen in her mind. Instead, unable to take her eyes off him, dazzled by those piercing blue eyes, the stern, unsmiling mouth and the way his shirt had revealed a strong masculine throat, she'd mumbled and stammered like a ninny.

She hoped he hadn't invited many people to the wedding. How embarrassing if he had. But if he'd paid Peggy to marry him, he surely wouldn't want a lot of witnesses. She hoped not.

She sighed and reached for the teapot. She might as well have breakfast before she confessed.

"That'll be cold by now, miss. Besides, the master likes his tea terrible strong," the maid said from behind her. She set a fresh pot of tea and a silver rack of toast on the table.

Marguerite thanked her. "Would you know if there's a gentleman living hereabouts by the name of Alexander Murfitt?"

The girl gave her a curious look. "Old Miser Murfitt? Yes, he lives on the other side of the village, about ten or twelve miles from here. Do you know him, miss?"

"No, we've never met. I've heard of him, that's all. So he's a miser, is he?"

"Biggest skinflint in the county," the maid said cheerfully. She gestured to a buffet on which was arrayed a row of covered silver dishes. "There's porridge and eggs in the dishes there on the sideboard, and Mrs. Ferguson ordered kedgeree special for you, you having lived in India and all. Anything else you need, just ring for it, miss."

Marguerite thanked her and helped herself to kedgeree

and eggs. She wasn't particularly fond of kedgeree, but it was a kind gesture. She ate her breakfast slowly.

The thought of having to leave this cozy, friendly house and take up residence with the most notorious skinflint in the county made her stomach sink with dread. But there was no help to it—they thought she was Peggy Smith and—

And Peggy Smith was dead.

Peggy Smith, who'd promised to marry a man for money and then disappear from his life, no questions asked.

What if . . . ?

Marguerite bolted the rest of her meal, and hurried back up to her bedchamber. She pulled out Peggy Smith's cloth bag and tipped the contents onto the counterpane: a worn leather wallet containing some banknotes, a gold locket containing a miniature painting of a man in military uniform—Peggy's late husband, Marguerite supposed, the little girls' father—and a long lawyer's envelope with a broken wax seal.

Marguerite opened it and scanned the document rapidly. She closed her eyes, swallowed and read it again, paying attention to every word.

In it, one Peggy Smith agreed to marry Ronan James McAllister for the sum of five hundred pounds.

Five hundred pounds! It was a huge sum. With five hundred pounds Marguerite could purchase a small cottage and still have enough left over to support herself and two little girls for ten years at least, if she was careful. And if she could earn a little extra . . . They could keep chickens, grow vegetables . . . She could take in sewing, and washing . . .

All sorts of possibilities danced in her mind.

Marguerite Blackett-Smith, Peggy Smith. Peggy was another name for Margaret. Smith, Blackett-Smith—there was not a lot of difference. And they were both free to marry. It would not be such a great lie, surely? What had Peggy said? *He doesn't want a wife. Just a marriage certificate.*

She could give him his certificate. And his money could give her a future.

It was that or Uncle Alexander. *Miser Murfitt, the biggest skinflint in the county.* The bleak prospect of a life of unpaid drudgery and no love, or a home and two little girls to love and care for.

Put like that, there was no choice at all.

It seemed too easy to be true. All she had to do was to marry that tall young man with the stern, beautiful mouth and the summer blue eyes.

But could she do it? Make promises—sacred promises in front of God and His minister—that she had no intention of keeping.

It was what Ronan James McAllister wanted, she reminded herself. Why, she had no idea. That was his business.

And if it hurt no one. . . . Her gaze dropped to the drawing of the two little girls. And her mind was made up. She would take their mother's place in all ways. She would marry Ronan James McAllister.

Her eyes fell to the second part of the lawyer's document.

Following the wedding, Peggy Smith had agreed to live with Ronan James McAllister at HighTowers for thirty days, after which she would return to London and neither she nor any of her kin would make any further claim on Ronan James McAllister or his kin, and he would make no further claim on her.

She swallowed. Thirty days. What might he want of her in those thirty days? The document didn't specify. Would he expect . . . ?

And so what if he did, Marguerite decided. Only a few hours ago she'd fully expected to live out her life a virgin. If Ronan James McAllister wanted to consummate the marriage, she'd welcome him.

And if she fell pregnant as a result?

What did it matter? She'd be married.

And Uncle Alexander? Would she tell him where she was? No. Better to burn her bridges once and for all.

She sat down at the desk, took out a sheet of notepaper and began to write: *Dear Uncle Alexander, thank you for your offer of bed and board, however I have found a more suitable position . . .*

Marguerite rang the bell, gave the letter to a servant to post and requested hot water for a bath. It might be a sham wedding, but it was the only one she was likely to have and she was determined to make the best of it.

She went through her clothes. There was depressingly little choice. The light muslin dresses she'd brought from India were too flimsy for winter wear and she'd had no money to purchase anything new, so Cousin Ida had instructed her seamstress to cut down two of her old mourning dresses for Marguerite.

It was more than a year since Marguerite's father had died, but Cousin Ida was very strict about observing mourning. Cousin Ida also abhorred bright colors: *It is vulgar to drape oneself in bright colors, Marguerite.*

Marguerite's choice for her wedding gown was therefore one of two gray woolen dresses, both equally plain and unadorned. One she had worn on the coach, and it was a little travel-worn, so her wedding dress would have to be the other. It didn't matter—she hated them both.

The bath and hot water arrived, along with some scented soap and eau de cologne, for which she was very grateful. "And the master said to give you this, miss," the maid said, handing her a leather pouch.

A wedding gift? Marguerite opened it after the girl had left. It was a thick roll of banknotes. Five hundred pounds, to be exact. Marguerite had never seen so much money in her life. She hid it carefully in her trunk.

She bathed, washed her hair, dried it in front of the fire, put it up and dressed for her wedding. She put on the gray gown and pulled on her only pair of white gloves, rather worn and carefully darned at the fingertips.

Was it to be a church wedding? If so, she would need to cover her hair. She looked at her only hat, a plain gray felt thing. She plonked it on her head and stood in front of the looking glass. Her reflection stared back at her, drab and dull. A plain woman, in a plainer gown.

Rebellion bubbled up from deep within her. Her youth and any pretension to good looks might be in the past, but she would not be such a drab creature at her only wedding.

She lifted the lid of her cheap wood-and-canvas trunk and from the bottom pulled out a bundle wrapped in dark cotton and scented with cedar chips. It contained her treasures, the few things she'd brought back from India and hadn't been able to make herself sell.

She opened the bundle and shook out the shawl Papa had brought back from Kashmir when she was eighteen. Scarlet with a riot of gold embroidery, it was a bright splash of glorious color.

She draped the soft fabric around herself and twirled in front of the looking glass. The shawl covered her to the waist in front and fell almost to the hem of the hated gray gown at the back. More importantly, the scent of cedar and the faint hint of sandalwood reminded her of India, and Papa and the sandalwood soap he'd favored.

She searched through her bundle and drew out a scarlet gauze scarf threaded through with silver thread. She laid it carefully over her hair. How to keep it on? Of course, the silver headdress. Another one of Papa's impulsive marketplace buys, it was not real silver but some cheap imitation. Marguerite at sixteen had loved it. Marguerite at twenty-five loved it even more.

She lifted it up and a dozen tiny bells jingled.

You're not a gypsy, Marguerite, Cousin Ida intoned in her head. Marguerite laughed and settled the intricate, jangly silver headdress over the gauze scarf. It framed her face with tiny silver bells along her hairline and weighted the gauze scarf to the back of her head perfectly.

She glanced at her reflection in the looking glass. Oh, yes, that was much better.

Chapter 3

The wedding was to be held in the small private chapel that was part of the estate. Ronan would have preferred a civil ceremony in the house, except his aunt's will had specified a proper church wedding. His lawyer had also stressed that it should look, as far as possible, like a normal wedding. That would have meant dozens of relatives descending on him, and plenty of awkward questions, so he'd put it about that the bride was in mourning and it would be a small private ceremony, and no great reception afterward.

This morning she'd worn the plainest of sober gray gowns. Whether she was in mourning or simply some kind of puritan, he didn't care, as long as it gave the right impression. He just wanted to get the thing over with and get on with his life.

She'd surprised him when they'd met. She was younger than he'd expected, and with the kind of quiet assurance and unobtrusive manners that indicated she was gently born and raised. She was frail-looking and thin, but not obviously ill, which was a relief. For all Adams's talk of money easing the way for a dying woman, it still didn't sit square with Ronan's conscience.

Until she'd appeared in the breakfast parlor, he hadn't really thought about her as a person, not someone with thoughts and feelings and a history. But when she'd looked at him with those pretty gray eyes, and spoken in her soft English accent, he'd wondered what sort of a person she was, and what had brought her to this desperate pass—to be marrying a stranger for money in a country not her own.

Ronan glanced into the chapel to check that all was in order. It was a stark little building, plain stone, whitewashed inside and furnished with simple timber pews. Somebody had filled a couple of large vases with greenery—holly, juniper branches and mistletoe—and placed them on either side of the altar.

Ronan smiled. He had no objection to a bit of greenery, but it was nearing Christmas and he was sure Reverend Gillespie would have something to say about pagan customs being out of place in a good Scottish kirk.

Ronan pulled out his watch and checked the time. Half past ten. He hurried away to dress for his wedding.

She was late.

Had she taken the money and run?

Ronan paced back and forth before the altar, aware that his every twitch was under close observation. He'd informed his household that this was to be the simplest of ceremonies with no fuss and only a few requisite witnesses, but word had spread and the small chapel was filled. Apart from his servants, which he'd expected, half the village had turned out.

He tried not to mind. Adams had stressed that it should look like a normal wedding, and to that end, Ronan had dressed in the same clothes he'd worn for his first wedding—the same outfit he'd be buried in, no doubt—the

McAllister kilt, lace jabot and a short black coat with silver buttons.

He was absurdly nervous; why, he had no idea. He was marrying on his own terms, and in a month or so she'd be gone from his life. The ceremony was just a formality.

There was a stir in the church, then a sudden silence. He turned and there she stood, pale and still against the stark, whitewashed stone of the kirk; a slender gray candle wrapped in flame. The brilliant scarlet shawl was the brightest thing in the cold little chapel.

She walked slowly down the aisle, the hushed silence of the congregation broken by the silvery sound of tiny bells that jingled with each step she took. What on earth . . . ?

As she drew closer he saw the source of the sound, an intricate and exotic silver headdress that framed her brow with tiny silver bells.

Ronan glanced at the entranced congregation, and his lips twitched. So much for his bride-in-mourning. Behind him he heard the minister give a huff of disapproval, and Ronan's smile widened. The pagan vases of mistletoe, holly and juniper would pale before this *foreign* pagan display.

She reached his side and he took her hand. It was shaking. He held it firmly and gave Reverend Gillespie a nod.

The minister gave a loud sniff, then commenced. "Dearly beloved, we are gathered here in the sight of God, and in the presence of this company, to unite Ronan James McAllister and Peggy Smith—"

Marguerite took a deep breath. "Marguerite Elizabeth Blackett-Smith."

The minister stopped in midword, his mouth hanging open.

Ronan's black brows snapped together. "What?"

In a voice that shook only a little, she said, "Not Peggy Smith—Marguerite Elizabeth Blackett-Smith."

The summer blue eyes bored into her. "You mean you wish to be married as Marguerite, not Peggy?"

"Yes." Her palms were damp and her heart pounded as she prepared to explain the mix-up and offer herself in Peggy Smith's place. "You see—"

Ronan shrugged and turned to the minister. "Whether she calls herself Peggy or Marguerite, it makes no difference. Continue the ceremony."

"Yes, but—" Marguerite began.

"Dearly beloved . . ."

Marguerite hesitated, then decided to let it go. It was cowardly, she knew, but she wanted this wedding, wanted the money and the chance of a new life it offered her and those two little girls.

She listened to the drone of the minister, stunned by the ease with which Ronan James McAllister had accepted the substitution. He hadn't asked a single question or even let her explain. He really didn't care who he married.

Numbly she felt him remove her glove and slide a gold band onto her finger. He stood so close she could smell him—soap and cologne and a faint trace of woodsmoke. He must have bathed. He was freshly shaved, and his hair was damp and combed severely into place. No farm laborer now; he was an exotic mix of gentleman and . . . barbarian.

Bare knees. Strong, brawny legs clad in dark woolen stockings to the knee. A bright tartan kilt anchored with a hairy leather sporran slung low around his hips. It rested just . . . below his stomach.

Was it true that Scotsmen wore nothing under the kilt? She didn't know why the idea seemed so shocking, when she herself wore no drawers. Neither Papa nor Cousin Ida approved of the new fashion of ladies wearing drawers under their petticoats.

But it was different for a man. His skirts were so short. One good breeze and . . .

She felt her cheeks warm. It was not seemly to be thinking such things in church. Especially while she was getting married. *She was getting married.*

Dumbly she heard him promise to have and to hold her in sickness and in health . . .

As he spoke the words in a crisp, matter-of-fact voice, she couldn't help but think of poor Peggy Smith, whose life had been cut off so short and who should have been standing here, being joined to this man.

". . . and with all my worldly goods I thee endow."

Five hundred pounds, Marguerite thought. With five hundred pounds I thee endow.

She spoke her own vows parrot fashion. It felt quite unreal, like a pantomime or a play. And then . . .

"You may kiss the bride."

He turned her toward him and bent to kiss her, just as she put her face up to be kissed, a little anxious, self-conscious about kissing him with everyone watching, and in a hurry to get it over. Their noses bumped, she jumped, and his kiss missed, landing off-center, on the side of her mouth.

"Sorry," she whispered, agonizingly aware of the watching congregation.

He looked down at her a long moment, then gave her a slow smile. "I think we can do a little better than that." The sweetness of his smile dazzled her. Up to now he'd seemed so stern, but that smile . . .

His big hands cupped her face and he bent and kissed her, his mouth warm and possessive.

He smelled clean, like the scent of the moors, and at the first touch his lips had been cool. But when he came back the second time his mouth was hot and hungry. The taste of him was dark, masculine and enticing, like spiced port wine and gingerbread. It warmed her clear through to the pit of her stomach, and she surrendered herself wholly to the sensations that coursed through her, the hunger in him calling to something deep inside her.

The kiss drove every thought from Marguerite's mind, and when he released her, she staggered and might even have fallen had he not slipped an arm around her waist and steadied her.

She stared up at him. What had happened? She'd been kissed before and had never . . .

He bent and picked up the Kashmiri shawl, which had unaccountably slipped off her and lay in a pool at her feet. He settled it around her shoulders, saying, "I've never seen such a bold splash of color in the kirk. What, with that and the bells, the good Reverend is, no doubt, in shock."

She gave his red and green kilt a pointed glance. "You're not exactly drab yourself, sir."

He gave her a surprised look, and chuckled. He tucked her hand into the crook of his arm. "Now, Mrs. McAllister, we walk back down the aisle."

Mrs. McAllister? She suddenly realized the congregation was clapping and everyone was smiling.

She was married.

They walked back to the house. "So, Peggy—"

"I'd rather you didn't call me Peggy."

He gave her a dry look. "What then? Marguerite-Elizabeth-Blackett-Smith-McAllister? It's a bit of a mouthful."

She bit her lip. She wanted to explain, but there were guests close behind, their footsteps crunching the gravel of the path, and she was worried her confession would cause a scene. And she did not want to give up that fat roll of banknotes tucked away in her bag upstairs.

"Call me Meg." A new name for a new life.

"And Peggy Smith was what? Some kind of alias, in case you decided to change your mind?"

"Something like that," she mumbled guiltily.

"It makes no difference—the document you signed is still legal. As is the marriage."

"I know." The wedding might be a sham, but it was legal, all the same. And she'd added another layer of deception to it. Ronan McAllister still thought he'd married Peggy Smith.

They walked on. "I've arranged a wedding breakfast," he told her. "I couldn't really get out of one, but it'll be just a small gathering. I told people you were in mourning."

She gave him a surprised look. "According to Cousin Ida, I still should be."

He raised an eyebrow and she explained. "My father died in India just over a year ago." She gestured to her dress. "Cousin Ida decreed that only gray dresses are proper."

"You don't like gray?"

She hugged her shawl to her. "I've had a year in black. I would have preferred some cheerful colors. I like color, but Cousin Ida was paying."

"So I see." He gave her a thoughtful look. "But the gray suits you. It matches your eyes."

She sighed. "Dull."

"Not at all. Your eyes are the color of the morning mist on the moors."

Marguerite darted him a sideways glance. Was he flirting? Or making fun of her? But he was looking ahead with a pensive expression and a slight frown.

They walked on in silence. Behind them crunched the footsteps of the wedding guests. Marguerite tried to think of something to say. "Is the mare all right? The one who was sick?"

"Hmm? Oh, yes, she's recovering nicely, thank you. So your father died in India. How long had he lived there?"

"We went there when I was fifteen."

He looked at her with interest. "You lived there? What was it like?"

"I loved it. I loved the heat, the people, the richness of the culture, the colors, the food . . ."

"And yet you came back." There was a question in his voice.

"I loved India. Unfortunately India did not love me. I was ill almost constantly and in the end I had no alternative but to return to England."

"So that was it. I'm sorry." His voice was somber, and his big, warm hand closed over hers.

Only a dozen or so people attended the wedding breakfast, mostly neighbors from the district, but in a way the small numbers made it worse. Marguerite was the center of attention. Everyone was so kind, asking her about herself, making laughing but curious comments about how Ronan had kept her a secret.

Marguerite wanted to shrivel up and disappear.

The women exclaimed over the softness and beauty of her bright shawl, and made delicate inquiries about her mourning. She told them about Papa and the silver headdress, and when they probed her about how she and Ronan had met, she blushed and muttered something about having been brought together by a mutual acquaintance. And correspondence.

It was mortifying, receiving their kindness and welcome, knowing it was all deception, but finally the ordeal came to an end. Ronan declared he and his bride were leaving on a short bride trip. That prompted a bit of good-natured teasing and a few ribald jokes. Marguerite's cheeks were hot, but Ronan bore it with good humor and equanimity.

An open carriage was brought around. Ronan lifted Marguerite up into the seat and climbed nimbly up to sit beside her. He picked up the reins. "We're just going for a drive," he murmured. "As soon as this lot has gone, we'll come back."

They drove off to cheers and waves and well wishes drifting on the air.

"That went off all right," he said when they were alone. "You did well, Meg. You made it seem like a real marriage."

"It is a real marriage, isn't it?"

"A legal one, yes." He gave her a sideways glance. "Or it will be after tonight."

She swallowed. So it was to be consummated.

She looked at the strong, bare hands holding the reins, at the bare knees just visible beneath the line of the kilt. The strong column of lightly tanned neck was made somehow more masculine by the frilly lace jabot. She looked at the stern mouth that could smile so unexpectedly, and thought about those summer blue eyes. And she shivered.

"Are you cold?" he asked.

"No."

Chapter 4

Marguerite had little appetite at dinner. She'd eaten her fill at the wedding breakfast, but more than that, the tension in her had been growing all evening.

What did he expect of her?

The evening dragged on. After dinner Ronan excused himself—he had some important paperwork to complete. Ronan worked at the table on his papers while Marguerite sat on the sofa and pretended to read a book. It would have been quite domestic, except for the rising tension in the room.

Marguerite flipped pages, unseeing, aware of every small movement he made.

If only she *knew*.

Finally he blotted the last paper, closed the ledger, cleaned the pen, stoppered the ink bottle and tidied the table. "Time for bed."

The butterflies in her stomach turned into birds.

He escorted her to the door of her bedchamber, opened it and with a bow said, "Fifteen minutes?"

She nodded and closed the door behind her. Fifteen minutes.

She flew around the room, stripping off her clothes and pulling out her best nightdress. Another of Cousin Ida's gifts, it was thick and warm, shapeless and plain—perfect for a poor relation going to live in Scotland, but not exactly what a woman would want for her wedding night.

She pulled it on, shivering despite the fire that was already burning merrily in the grate. In a way she was grateful for the plainness of the garment. Dressed like this, there could be no pretense that this was anything other than a legal arrangement.

His soft knock almost made her jump out of her skin with fright. She flew into bed—the sheets were so chilly—lay down and pulled the blankets up to her chin. "Come in."

He was dressed the same as when he'd left her. She wasn't sure if she was relieved or not. She'd expected him to be in a dressing gown and nightshirt, not his kilt. She lay quietly, trying not to watch him, but it was impossible.

He shrugged off his short coat and hung it on the back of a chair. He removed his waistcoat and the jabot and then pulled his shirt over his head and laid it over his coat. Bare chested, he sat on the edge of the bed to remove his shoes and stockings. He set them neatly beside the chair.

Bare legged, bare chested. Marguerite's mouth was dry.

He stood, his back to her in the dim light of the fire and one bedside candle, and unfastened the buckle at his waist. There was a slither of fabric, and Marguerite swallowed. It was true what they said about what one Scotsman, at least, wore under his kilt.

Nothing.

She watched furtively as, nude and unembarrassed, he folded the kilt and laid it on the chair with the rest of his clothes. He turned, and she knew she should have shut her eyes, but . . .

She'd never seen a naked man before. He was bare, barbaric . . . and beautiful.

She couldn't help but stare, and then recalling she was supposed to be a lady—and ladies did *not* stare—turned her head away. But she could still see him out of the corner of her eye.

He paused. "I'm sorry, I didn't think. I always sleep like this. You're not offended by a man's body, are you? I thought, you being a widow and all . . ."

Oh, Lord, she'd forgotten she was supposed to be a widow. She made some sort of squeaking agreement noise and tried to look as though the sight of him had not near driven the breath from her body.

"I could fetch a nightshirt if you prefer."

"No, no, it's . . . It doesn't worry me." Worry wasn't the word.

The bed creaked and she felt a brief draft as he lifted the bedclothes. "'Tis just, there must be the appearance of consummation, at least," he said as he slid in beside her.

"A-appearance?"

"Aye, I assume you'll not be wishing to . . ."

Was there a hint of a question in that? She didn't respond. Her mind was a blank.

"That's right, isn't it? In your condition, I thought you'd not want to . . . But if you did . . ." He waited.

Marguerite had no idea what to say. Her *condition*?

"No, of course not," he said. "Well, it's been a long day and I had little enough sleep last night, so . . ." The bedclothes surged, and suddenly his naked body was looming over her. She stiffened, but all he did was reach across her to nip out her bedside candle between his finger and thumb.

He lay back down. "Good night, Meg."

"Good night," she whispered.

In a few minutes his breathing slowed to a deep, even rhythm. He was asleep. Marguerite lay wide awake, shivering, partly with cold, partly with . . . reaction? She was in bed with a large, naked, sleeping Scotsman whom she'd known less than a day.

He'd made it clear that he was willing to consummate the marriage, but he'd left the decision up to her. And he hadn't pressed her.

Did she want to consummate it? She thought about it. Her body tingled in strange places. She suspected she might. It was just . . . a bit too soon to be sure.

How could she possibly sleep? It was all so strange. She was cold. Last night they'd warmed the bed and given her a hot brick wrapped in flannel. Tonight all she had to warm her was a big naked man.

She was married. How peculiar.

Slowly his body heat permeated the bedclothes. His breathing was deep and even, and the rhythm soothed her skittering pulse. Slowly Marguerite relaxed . . .

Ronan woke at dawn rock hard with aching desire. A soft, sweet-smelling female body lay curled up against him. It took him a moment to recall who she was.

Peggy—no, Meg Smith. Meg McAllister now. Her silky brown hair was spread across the pillow.

His wife. But not his wife.

He breathed in her fragrance. Soap, a hint of cologne and warm, enticing female.

Thin, vulnerable female, he reminded himself. Too thin, too pale. And for a damn good reason. A man should feel ashamed of himself, lusting after a dying woman.

How long did she have to live? She had to be desperate to do this. What was she going to do with the money?

Not his business.

He lay in the warm bed, reluctant to leave it, leave the silent, sleeping woman. Five years since he'd last shared a bed like this.

Though it was never like this, never so quiet and peaceful and somehow . . . companionable.

Lenore had never been a peaceful wife. Nor companionable. Lenore was always wanting to be elsewhere, doing something different, with someone else, someone interesting. Someone exciting. Anywhere other than here. Anyone other than him.

He listened to Meg's gentle breathing. He should have felt lonely waking up next to a relative stranger, but the truth was, he'd never felt so lonely as those mornings when he'd woken up with Lenore, waiting for her eyes to open, only to see reflected in them her deep unhappiness with the husband she'd chosen.

There was nothing lonelier than the coldness of a failed marriage.

It was nobody's fault, Ronan told himself for the umpteenth time. They'd met in Edinburgh. He thought she was the love of his life. She thought he was . . . someone else. She'd imagined he'd be like his father, a rich sophisticate, an ornament of Edinburgh and Paris society.

When she'd learned Ronan's inheritance had all been spent, and that in any case Ronan was, at heart, a farmer with a deep and powerful love of his land, the disappointment had embittered her.

Looking back, he could see the signs were obvious even before he and Lenore had married—if he'd only bothered to look for them. But Lenore had dazzled him and he—well, he was blind to her faults. And stupid with lust.

The entire county had pitied Ronan when his wife ran off with another man, but Ronan had been quietly grateful. And, God help him, two years later, when he heard she'd died giving birth to that man's child, he'd felt some grief, but it was mostly relief, that she was never coming back.

The county would pity him again when this second wife

ran off, but it wouldn't hurt him. Not this time. That was the thing about marriage—it was all about expectations.

This time he had no expectations at all.

Apart from a bad case of inappropriate and misplaced lust, he thought, as the woman beside him stirred gently in sleep and his body responded.

He slid out of the bed, removing his lust from the object of its desire. He gathered his clothes and left, closing the door quietly behind him.

They met again at breakfast a few hours later. He'd had two hours of hard physical work in the stables to work the lust out of him.

She greeted him with a quiet "Good morning" and a shy smile that recalled him instantly to her flustered and not-quite-concealed blushes when she'd seen his nakedness.

She asked him about his plans for the day, and he'd responded with "Work," and then wondered if he'd sounded churlish. He hadn't meant to—it was the literal truth.

"What would you like me to do?" she asked.

"Whatever you want. You're a guest here."

She said no more for the rest of breakfast, but as he folded his napkin and prepared to leave she said, "What if I decorated the house for Christmas?"

"Christmas?" he repeated blankly. He'd never bothered much with Christmas. It was more of an English thing, the decorations, the celebrations. His English mother had celebrated it with gusto, but she'd died when he was a boy, and since then, Christmas was more of a solemn church occasion. New Year—Hogmanay—was the Scottish time for celebrations.

"I'd love to do it," she said eagerly. "I've never experienced a white Christmas. When I was a child in England we always lived in the south, and then we were in India. You've no idea how peculiar it is to have hot, sunny weather at Christmas. One of the things I've most looked forward to about returning to England is to have a proper English Christmas—well, a proper Scottish one—and now I'm here, and it might even snow for Christmas." Her face glowed at the prospect.

He didn't have the heart to tell her what a proper Scottish Christmas was like, particularly a Christmas of the sort that the Reverend Gillespie thought appropriate—all sermons and solemnity.

"Christmas decorations would be grand," he told her.

"Could I have a servant to help me gather the greenery?"

"I'll help you," Ronan found himself saying. He had mountains of work waiting for him, but this would probably be her last Christmas on earth, so why not make it the kind of occasion she'd dreamed of? She seemed a sweet little thing, and it was little enough to ask.

They donned their winter coats—Ronan saw how thin hers was and sent a servant up to find something warm from his late wife's clothing—he hadn't gone near her room since she'd left, and it was all still there. The maid brought down a coat in bright cherry red wool, a green and white scarf and a fur hat. Meg exclaimed delightedly over them, seeming not to mind that she was wearing cast-offs.

As for footwear, Meg wore the same sturdy black boots she'd worn to her wedding, perfectly suitable for tramping around in the cold and muddy outdoors. He wondered if they were the only shoes she had. They set off for the wood to the west of the estate, and Ronan found himself telling her about the estate and pointing out things of interest.

Lenore would have been bored rigid, but Meg asked him all sorts of questions as if she found the subject interesting. The brisk walk in the crisp, frigid air brought roses to her cheeks and a sparkle to those pretty gray eyes, and he found himself telling her more than he'd planned, explaining the vision he had for the rebuilding of the estate, something he'd never confided in to anyone.

Luckily they arrived at the edge of the wood before he'd spilled to her the reason for their marriage, Great-Aunt Agatha's damnable will.

They gathered greenery by the armful—fragrant juniper and spruce, long strands of ivy, prickly holly and mistletoe—Meg doing most of the selecting and Ronan doing the climbing and cutting. She was very choosy, directing him in a bossy, feminine manner that amused him.

"No, not that one, the other one, higher up. The branch above your head to the left—it's much more handsome, don't you think?"

"All I know is, it's higher up. Do you *want* me to break my neck?"

"No, of course not! Is it that dangerous?"

He couldn't help but smile. "Fearfully dangerous. But I'm a brave lad. I'll risk it."

She laughed. "What a hero you are, to be sure. And it's worth the risk. It's a much shapelier branch. You will see when I have it all arranged. It will look beautiful."

"It's all just green stuff to me," he grumbled, but he was enjoying himself, and they both knew it. And as they staggered homeward, half buried in greenery, she told him about Christmas in India, and Ronan reflected that he hadn't had so much simple fun in ages.

They dumped the greenery in the hallway and washed for luncheon. And after luncheon he left her to her decorating, telling her to call servants if she needed help.

It would have been fun to stay and help, but Ronan recognized the danger. She'd be gone in a month. And he was lonelier than he'd realized.

Besides, he had a mountain of work waiting.

* * *

When Ronan went to enter the back door that evening he found his way blocked by a maidservant. "Excuse me, sir, but we think you ought to go in by the front door."

Ronan raised his brows. This was the closest entrance to the stables at the back of the house. "*We* think?"

The maid blushed but held her ground. "Yes, sir." Her eyes were dancing. Something was afoot.

"Verra well, then." Ronan tramped around to the front door. As he expected there was a wreath of holly and ivy fastened above the knocker and tied with red and white ribbons. He knocked, feeling a little foolish. His own front door.

A footman opened it and stepped back smartly to let him in. The entrance hall was a riot of fragrant greenery and crimson ribbons. Meg was just tidying up the last of the offcuts. "What do you think?" she asked, brushing off her fingers. She was flushed and her eyes were shining.

"Very nice, very er, green."

She laughed. "Doesn't the smell make you think of Christmas?"

Ronan sniffed. The smell made him think of cold, muddy forests and splinters, but she was smiling with such a look on her face, he found himself saying heartily, "Indeed it does. Very, um, Christmassy. Well done. Now, I'll just wash up and change for dinner." He was cold, his clothes were damp and he was dying for a drink.

"Yes, of course. I must wash and tidy up, too," Meg agreed, and turned to leave. Two maids stepped into her path, smiling. Ronan frowned.

"Ahem!" The footman cleared his throat.

Ronan glanced at him, and the footman's gaze turned meaningfully upward. Ronan followed the man's gaze to a circle of greenery that hung suspended over the center of the hall. Mistletoe. And beneath it, though quite unaware, stood Meg. His new bride.

Suddenly Ronan knew why he'd been maneuvered there,

and why half his staff were unaccountably loitering around the entrance hall, smothering grins.

"I believe there's an old tradition we must honor," he told Meg, and pointed upward.

"Oh." She laughed a little, blushing, and lifted her face for the kiss.

He framed her face with his hands, feeling the delicate bones, the warm, silky skin. He intended to make it a brief, light kiss, but her eyes were shining and her soft lips parted in anticipation, and without thinking he covered her mouth with his and found himself tasting her deeply.

She tasted as sweet and potent as fresh bread and honey mead. He tightened his grip on her, moving closer, molding her body to his, and she pressed against him, her fingers spearing through his hair, her mouth warm and welcoming. The taste of her streamed along his veins like fire, igniting a response he wasn't prepared for. His hands dropped, running over her small body, marveling at the lightness of her, the delicacy, fine boned and dainty like a little bird—no!

Not delicate—ill. Dying. And he was mauling her in his own hallway in front of his servants.

He broke off the kiss, glanced around and found they were alone. His servants had melted silently away like wax. Or perhaps not. If a herd of elephants had thundered through, Ronan doubted he would have noticed.

He looked down at her and realized he was still holding her tightly. Her fragile shoulder bones were a silent reproach. He released her carefully and stepped back. He was breathing hard. So was she, but those gray eyes of hers were shining like polished silver and she was looking up at him as if he were . . .

No, he wasn't any kind of hero. He was an insensitive brute lusting after a dying woman.

He tried to think of something to say, but staring down into those wide gray eyes, and seeing the softly parted pink mouth, still damp from his kiss, all he could come up with was, "Time to wash up for dinner, then."

Dammit, how the hell was he going to get through another night in her bed?

Let alone the twenty-eight nights that would follow after that.

Chapter 5

Ronan arrived in his wife's bedchamber that night, dressed in a stiff new nightshirt and a brocade dressing gown. Meg looked at him in surprise and he said self-consciously, "I thought you might prefer this." Her gaze ran over him and, fool that he was, he felt it like a caress.

"I don't mind." She gave him a shy smile.

What did that mean? She wanted him to sleep naked? Or she didn't care what he wore to bed? Probably the latter. He shrugged off the dressing gown and slipped into bed beside her.

It took him forever to fall asleep. He was agonizingly aware of her, every breath and small movement she made. And the fragrance of her, the same sweetness as before with a faint added tang of juniper, spruce and mistletoe.

Now he'd think of her each time he went into the forest.

They were both being very careful not to touch. Once her foot grazed his calf. He must have made a small sound, for she said, "Sorry," in the darkness, sounding breathless.

"Your feet are cold. If you like you can warm them against me," he invited quietly, but she said nothing, pretending to be asleep. Wanting nothing to do with him.

Ronan turned over and tried to sleep.

He woke at dawn with the nightshirt twisted around his middle, bare from the waist down. Cuddled into the curve of his body, her backside pressed against his aching groin, was his wife, sound asleep and also naked from the waist down judging by the silky skin pressed against him. He wanted to lift the covers and check, but he was a gentleman. Nothing to do with the knowledge that the rush of cold air would waken her if he lifted the covers, he told himself. Liar.

He eased down his nightshirt and slipped out of bed, tucking the bedclothes around her so she wouldn't get cold. Two nights down, twenty-eight to go.

Marguerite kept her eyes closed as her husband of two nights slipped from the bed then tucked the bedclothes around her, carefully, sweetly man-clumsy, then left the room.

Why had she ever imagined this would be simple?

She snuggled into the warm space he'd left behind. Two days and two nights and she was already more than half in love with the man. How was she ever going to leave him?

But that was the deal.

Twenty-eight days was all she had. And twenty-eight nights. It wasn't much for a lifetime. She would waste no more of them. He desired her, she was sure of it. Every kiss, every touch, she felt the hunger in him.

He awakened an answering hunger in her.

The last two nights he'd been a gentleman, holding back, waiting for a sign from her. Tonight she would give him that sign. Tonight she would become Mrs. Ronan James McAllister in truth.

If only for twenty-eight more days.

The servants were conspiring against him, Ronan decided halfway through the next day. Sprigs of mistletoe kept sprouting in unexpected places. And every time there was some blasted maid or a footman silently prompting him to his duty to tradition and his bride.

He tried to pretend disapproval toward his servants—until recently they'd performed their duties with invisible efficiency—but he couldn't blame them. They thought they were welcoming a new bride to HighTowers, and romance was in the air.

But when that night he slid into bed with her and lay back on his pillow, he looked upward and groaned. She followed his gaze and exclaimed, "How did that get there?" She sent him an apologetic look. "I promise you, I had nothing to do with this. I don't know—"

"It's all right. I'll talk to the servants." He shook his head. "They mean well. The thing is, they like you and all this"—he gestured to the bunch of mistletoe hanging over their bed—"is because they want you to be happy here."

"I have been," she said quietly. "You cannot know how much."

Ronan contemplated the bunch of mistletoe. Servants usually knew all their master's secrets, but it seemed his hadn't yet realized his marriage was a sham. He sighed. When she left in the new year it was going to be a gloomy house.

What kind of a situation would Meg be returning to? None of his business, he knew, but still, he couldn't help wondering. And worrying. But she'd made it clear she didn't want to discuss her private affairs, and he had to respect that.

"Well, it's bad luck to ignore the tradition." Marshaling every shred of self-control he possessed, he leaned across to give her a light kiss.

She surprised him by pulling him closer, holding him tight and kissing him with an enthusiasm that dissolved all his good intentions.

Did she know what she was doing to him? "Meg? Are you saying . . . ?"

She blushed sweetly and nodded. "I'm saying yes. Please." She pulled at his nightshirt, dragging it up and over his head. It shattered the last remnants of his control.

Kissing her, he smoothed his palm along her body, bringing the hem of her nightgown with it. He drew it slowly up her body. She raised her arms to assist him, and he pulled it off her and tossed it aside, feasting his eyes on the sight of her, slender and silky gold in the light of a single candle and the glowing embers of the fire.

She was thin and small, but her breasts were high and firm and very, very sweet. He bent to taste them and she arched against him, murmuring with pleasure.

She ran her hands over his chest, along his arms, down his back, raining haphazard kisses over him, returning caress for caress. He ran his palm slowly down her stomach and felt her quiver, deep inside. He slipped his fingers between her legs and found her warm and wet and inviting, her thighs trembling and parting at his touch.

He lifted himself over her, braced at the juncture of her thighs. This is what he'd ached for every night and every morning, and each time he'd kissed her under the mistletoe.

In one slow, sure movement he entered her. She arched and cried out. Her nails dug into his shoulders, and in the firelight what he saw on her face was a grimace of pain, not of ecstasy.

He thrust again and she flinched, and he knew something wasn't right but he was too far gone and his body was out of his control, and he thrust and thrust and she arched and squirmed, and clung to him. And then he shattered. And was dimly aware she had not . . .

He held her close, panting as he tried to regain his senses, still buried deep in her body. She was a virgin. And yet she was a widow. A virgin widow? Impossible.

His breathing slowed. He slowly disengaged and she

flinched, and tried to hide it from him. "You were a virgin."
It was an accusation—and yes, he was angry. Guilty, too. If
he'd known it was her first time . . .

Dammit, she should have told him. If he'd known he
wouldn't have . . . He would have . . .

She pulled the bedcovers over her nakedness. "Yes."

"So how is it that a widow is still a virgin?"

She turned her head away.

"*Are* you a widow?"

"No." He barely heard her low admission.

"So, you lied about that?"

"Yes."

What other lies had she told him, he wondered. "And are
you dying, or not?" he heard himself say in a hard voice.

Her head whipped around and she looked at him in
shock. *"Dying?"*

"Yes. Are you?" Brutal, he knew, but dammit he felt like
being brutal. She'd lied to him.

"You *knew* she was dying?" She stared at him in disbelief.

Ronan frowned. Who was this *she* she was talking about?

Meg's mouth fell open in shock. "You did, didn't you. You
planned on marrying her even though she was dying." She
must have seen something in his face, because she gasped
and said, "You wanted her *because* she was dying? My God,
Ronan, how could you?"

"What are you talking about?" he demanded crossly. "I
married you." And was she dying or not? He needed—quite
desperately—to know.

"Yes, but you planned to marry Peggy Smith, knowing
she was dying."

"You're Peggy Smith."

"No, I'm Marguerite Blackett-Smith. I met Peggy on the
way up here."

"You what? Then where is she?" He found himself looking around, as if Peggy Smith might be lurking in a cup-board.

"She died on the way up, at an inn just over the border."

He stared at her, dumbfounded. "Peggy Smith—the real Peggy Smith—died?"

She nodded. "But before she did she told me what she'd intended to do. To marry you."

Now it was his turn to stare openmouthed. "And you thought you'd simply up and take her place?"

She had the grace to look ashamed. "Not quite. I was waiting at the Wench and Haggis Inn for my uncle to collect me. When your coachman came, I thought he'd come for me. I didn't realize the mistake until the next morning and found you in the breakfast parlor and not Uncle Alexander."

He didn't believe her. It was too simple. "But you knew all about our agreement."

She nodded. "Peggy told me. She gave me all her papers."

"You mean you stole them." Pain lanced through him. He'd been so wrong about her. She was worse than Lenore.

"I didn't steal anything," she told him hotly. "Peggy gave them to me. She wanted my help."

"What help could you give her if she was dying?"

"I'll show you!" Wrapping a sheet around her for de-cency—which annoyed him intensely—she was still his wife, dammit, even if she was a liar and a cheat!—she hopped out of bed and stalked to her trunk. He took the op-portunity to grab his nightshirt and drag it back on. His body still betrayed him. His body didn't care that she'd deceived him. His body still wanted her.

She pulled a small cloth bag from the trunk and marched back to the bed.

He watched her bitterly. He'd been such a fool. At least Lenore hadn't lied to him; she'd just found him dull. But Meg . . .

"Is Meg your real name?" he asked as she climbed back onto the bed.

She nodded. "Yes. My mother used to call me Meg. This is what Peggy Smith gave me." She upended the bag, tipping all the contents onto the bed, and in among a pile of bits and pieces he saw the long folded paper containing the lawyer's agreement. Also in the bag was the fat roll of banknotes he'd sent her on the morning of their wedding.

"You married me for the money," he said in a flat voice. "You seized the opportunity and you married me under false pretenses."

She flushed. "Yes, I did. But I never meant to cheat you. I read that agreement after I'd met you at breakfast that first morning. And I saw how similar my name was to Peggy's. And she'd told me you didn't want a wife, just a marriage certificate, that all she had to do was marry you, stay here for a month and then leave. And for that you were prepared to pay five hundred pounds."

"So you snatched at the chance to make some money."

"I did. I have none, you see, and no prospects. I never intended to cheat you." She eyed him shrewdly. "You married me for money, too, didn't you?"

But he wasn't buying into that. His motives and Great-Aunt Agatha's will were none of her business. He hadn't lied to *her.* He hadn't betrayed *her,* hadn't charmed her into wanting more than . . . He clenched his jaw and said nothing.

"But I didn't know you wanted to marry a dying woman. Peggy never mentioned that. It seems very strange to me. Quite . . . macabre."

"I needed to be married, but I didn't want to be saddled with a wife." It sounded as ugly as he'd thought it when Adams had first suggested it. He was even more ashamed of the plan now, but he'd done it, so he wasn't going to make any excuses.

He saw the moment she understood he'd expected his

wife to die. Her eyes widened with shock and she blanched, realizing the implications. "I've never heard of anything so cold-blooded in my life."

"You were quick enough to step into the shoes of a dead woman."

"And now you're stuck with me."

"That's right. And you're stuck with me." They were each as bad as the other, he thought.

They sat glaring at each other across the rumpled bed. "If it was a 'misunderstanding,' why didn't you tell me before the wedding?"

She hunched a thin shoulder defensively. "There wasn't much time—you were busy with that mare. And then in church I started to explain, but you brushed that aside and told the minister to get on with it, and I thought . . . why not?"

"And you had my five hundred pounds by then."

"Yes. I did." She made no excuse, simply looked at him with those wide gray eyes, chin raised, guilty but unashamed.

Her refusal to defend herself infuriated him. He didn't want her to admit it was all about the money. He wanted her to fling his accusations back in his teeth. He wanted her to say . . .

Pain twisted inside him. He was a damned fool. Blinded by lust. Again.

Only this time—No, he was a damned fool.

"I'll leave first thing in the morning."

"You damned well will not!" he snapped. "You'll stay till after Hogmanay. You have a contract to fulfill."

"Very well." She pulled the bedsheet tighter around her, which infuriated him all over again. "And now, please leave."

He rose and stalked toward the door. And hesitated. She'd been a virgin. "Are you . . . are you all right?" he said in a voice that came out gruff. "I mean . . ."

"I know what you mean." Her face was turned away from him. "And I'm quite all right, thank you." Her voice wobbled.

Ronan hesitated. Damn it, she was going to cry. He hated hearing women cry. "Ach, Meg—" he began, and took a couple of steps toward her.

"P-please leave."

Swearing under his breath and feeling like a complete brute, Ronan left.

For the next few days Ronan went about his business, trying to ignore the blasted situation, but it was impossible. His wife stayed right out of his way so that he never saw her.

And dammit if he didn't miss her. The lying little cheat!

His servants had resumed their efficient, invisible ways. There was no smiling and whispering in hallways, no attempt to send him to inconvenient corners where he'd just happen to bump into his bride, and there was not a sprig of mistletoe anywhere to be seen in the house. Ronan knew. He'd looked.

The house felt like a cold and empty barn.

The only time he saw her was at meals, and then the conversation was polite and banal and utterly impersonal. He hated it. Why the devil had she lied? If only she'd been Peggy Smith.

No, for then she would have been dying, and he didn't want her to die.

He wanted her to stay here with him forever. Or he would, if she weren't such a cold-blooded little liar. If she would just offer him some reason, some excuse . . .

Ronan spent the days working himself to exhaustion, trying to drive out the questions that plagued him. He'd asked her her plans and she'd told him quite willingly. After Hogmanay she would return to London. She would abide by the terms of the contract and never bother him again.

She would bother him the rest of his life. No matter where she lived.

And who was she running to with his five hundred pounds? Some man?

He'd found out about "Uncle Alexander." Old Miser Murfitt. He wouldn't wish a dog to live with that old man. If that's where she was bound, he could understand why she'd snatched at the money.

Not that he forgave her. He could see her reasoning, that was all.

On the morning of the third day at breakfast she asked him for the address of the man in London who'd arranged the contract with Peggy Smith.

"Why?"

"I was going to tell you that night when . . . But you were so beastly I never got the chance. And I didn't think you'd care, anyway." She showed him a drawing of two little girls.

Ronan frowned. What had these children to do with her?

"Peggy Smith had two little daughters. She paid a neighbor to look after them, but I want to ensure that the children are all right. I've been worrying about them."

"She had children?"

"Yes, two little girls, aged five and three. I hoped your man could check on them and inform the woman caring for them that I'll be down to collect the children after the New Year."

"You'll collect them? Peggy Smith's children? Why?"

"They have no one else." And at those simple words the hurt and guilt he'd carried around like a hard lump in his chest started to unravel

"Yes, but why you?"

"When Peggy was dying, I promised her I'd do whatever I could to care for her children. That's why she was marrying you—to provide for her children's future." She turned over the card to show him the scrawled note on the back. "I'm going to raise them as if they were my own. We will be a family."

And suddenly Ronan realized he'd been an even blinder fool than he'd thought. Yes, she'd lied, and married him for the money. But she wasn't cold-bloodedly stepping into a dead woman's shoes—and he could talk, plotting to marry a dying woman. Suddenly it didn't seem to matter that she'd pretended to be someone else.

Who could blame her, when Miser Murfitt was the alternative?

His heart full, he folded his napkin and for something to do, poured himself another cup of coffee. "I'll write to Adams's nephew. He drew up the contract." He stirred in a lump of sugar. He never took sugar. He pushed the coffee cup aside. "He'll be coming up to Edinburgh at Christmas. If you wanted, he could bring the little girls with him."

She gave him a startled look. "Bring them here?"

"They've just lost their mother. Better they be with you for Christmas." He looked at her and added, "With us."

"Us?" She fixed those wide gray eyes on him, and he felt his last defenses crumbling.

He cleared his throat and said, "This house has been too long without children."

There was a short silence. Meg's heart was beating so loudly she thought he must hear it. Did he mean what she thought he did?

With a shaking hand, she set her napkin aside. "Ronan, what are you saying?"

He pushed his chair back and walked around the table to her, six feet of brawny Scotsman looking down at her with troubled blue eyes. "Ach, Meg, I've been a damned fool. I'm sorry I said all those hurtful things to ye." His Scots burr deepened, as it did when he was moved.

"And I'm sorry I deceived you," she said, her heart full.

"Meg, if ye want to stay—after Hogmanay, I mean—ye can." He ran his fingers through his hair, rumpling it, and said awkwardly, "No, not ye *can*—I mean, I *want* ye to stay. Here. With me." He swallowed and fixed on her a gaze of painful intensity. "So, will ye?"

Meg rose and set her palms lightly against his chest, over his heart. She could feel it thudding almost as fast as hers. "Tell me, Ronan James McAllister, why do you want me to stay?"

He swallowed again, and couldn't seem to find the words. But the love shone from his eyes.

"Is it perhaps because I love you?" she said softly. Her eyes blurred with tears. "And because it would break my heart to leave you? Because it would, Ronan, it would."

He nodded, his heart full. "Aye. That would be it." He pulled her into his arms and kissed her with all the pent-up grief and hurt and love in his heart. "I love ye, Meg McAllister. And I don't ever want ye to leave me. Will ye stay, Meg? Will ye be my wife in truth?"

"I will," she told him on a sob. "Oh, Ronan, I will indeed."

Epilogue

"Christmas is all verra well, but Hogmanay is a lot more fun."

"More fun than Christmas?" Amy said, wide eyed.

Meg smiled. It had been a Christmas to remember, better than anything she'd ever dreamed of back in India. Almost perfect.

Almost.

She sat by the fire, knitting. Outside, snow fell gently. Ronan sat sprawled on the hearthrug, peeling an orange and tossing chunks of peel into the fire. Peggy Smith's two little girls, dressed for bed in nightgowns and dressing gowns, sat on either side of him.

Ronan smiled and ruffled Amy's fair curls. "Aye, sweetheart. For a start, children get presents."

Jane frowned. "More presents?" Ronan had showered presents on them all that Christmas.

"Aye. And there's a feast, and Mrs. Ferguson will bake a black bun." Amy wrinkled her nose, and he chuckled. "And at night we have the best thing of all."

"What's that?"

"A great big bonfire, and we sing and dance and tell stories, and we roast potatoes in it, and eat them hot with lashings of butter and salt. Och, ye'll love Hogmanay." He handed them each a wedge of orange.

Amy ate hers straightaway and immediately held out her hand for another one, but Jane waited until Ronan ate a piece himself. Peggy Smith's oldest girl never asked for anything, was wary, almost silent and overly polite. She endured hugs with stiff courtesy, and she tried to keep her younger sister quiet, a feat which was getting more difficult; Amy was settling in beautifully.

Meg watched as Ronan fed the girls chunks of orange and told them the tale of Hector Owl and Timothy Mouse. Amy leaned sleepily against him and, when he put her arm around her, she snuggled up happily.

Jane sat straight and still, paying grave attention to the story.

Meg ached for her. From the moment the post chaise had arrived and Jane's plain little face had peered warily out, Meg had loved the child. Loved both of them, poor bewildered little lambs.

Meg had explained that she was their mother's friend and that they would live with her and Ronan now. She showed them their picture and the note from their mother on the back. Amy was too young to understand, but Jane did. She'd traced her mother's name with a finger. And had said very little else since.

Jane resisted everything, and Meg knew why; she expected everything to be snatched away at a moment's notice.

It would take time, Meg knew. But it was Christmas, and she wanted everyone to be happy.

"Time for little girls to go to bed," she said as Ronan finished the story. She bent and scooped up Amy, who was already half asleep.

And as he had every night, Ronan picked up Jane. So far

she'd raised no objection, but had suffered herself to be carried up to bed like a stiff little doll.

But tonight . . . oh, tonight her arms came up and twined around his neck. Breathless with sudden joy, Meg met Ronan's gaze. His summer blue eyes smiled back at her. It was a start.

They carried the children upstairs and placed them in the big bed that the girls shared. And as Ronan bent to put Jane in the bed, she hugged him and planted a sleepy, sticky, orangey kiss on his cheek and murmured, "Night."

"Night, Janey-girl." His voice was deep and gravelly, and he turned away, blinking.

Meg tucked them in and kissed both girls good night, and again Jane's skinny little arms emerged from the bedclothes and she held Meg tight for a long, long moment.

When Meg straightened, her eyes were awash.

Ronan led her from the room. He carefully closed the girls' bedroom door, then swung Meg into his arms. "Because sometimes big girls need to be carried to bed, too. So, Mrs. McAllister, has our Christmas come up to expectations?"

"Perfect, just perfect," she murmured, planting kisses all along his jaw. And it was.

A WILDER WENCH

Susan King

Prologue

Scotland, the Highlands—1800

Hearing the fierce pounding on the door in the night, Cristina knew what it meant: men looking for her father again, either rascals or gaugers. But Johnny Shaw was not at home, nor was Mama just then. Da was running the whisky, for the moon was high; and Mama had hurried out in her shawl and sleeping braid to take the pony and warn Da about something important.

"I will be back soon, Kirstie," her mother had whispered. "Stay with your brother. If anyone comes to the door, you must hide!"

The pounding increased, and shouts followed. Cristina leaped from her narrow bed and ran to the box bed in the wall, where Patrick lay asleep. He sat up, rubbing his eyes, and she drew him close, pulling a plaid blanket around both of them. He was warm, solid, and sleepy against her, and even so young, he knew to be silent.

Outside the dog barked and someone shouted again. The dog quieted, perhaps led away by someone—or worse, simply silenced. Cristina shuddered.

"Johnny Shaw!" a man called, beating on the door. "Open up!"

Cristina held Patrick tightly. He was five, trembling with fright, and she was ten, old enough to watch him. Later Da would sing to them while Mama served hot tea with extra sugar. The midnight trips brought sweets along with laces, baubles, whisky, and coin for the coffers.

"Hush, now, hushabye," she sang to Patrick.

"I'm not a bairnie," he pouted, but tucked his tousled head under her chin. Moonlight gleamed over his golden curls and clear blue eyes, so like hers, like Johnny Shaw's.

Da was running the whisky in casks stacked under hay in pony carts. He and others often guided such loads across the hills to the river, where men took the goods by boat to the sea and to England and beyond. Smugglers traveling in large groups were rarely stopped by the excise men. Only two gaugers would be on patrol tonight against thirty or more smugglers, she knew.

"We may be fools," Da had once told his wife, "but bold fools, and rich fools one day, love. And then I will run the peat-reek no longer, I promise."

What her father did was dangerous, but otherwise he was laird of his lands and also the glen's dominie. A kind and interesting teacher, he especially loved history. The students enjoyed learning from him, and all who lived in the glen loved the songs Johnny Shaw would sing in his mellow voice. And so they looked the other way when their freebooting schoolteacher and others moved goods to and from the glen, especially ankers of free-trade whisky. Cristina had only tasted whisky in small doses when she was sick. But once she was grown, she would sip a dram each day if she liked; that was done by even the finest Scottish ladies.

One day she would be a fine lady, so Da had promised, along with an education for her and her brother. Johnny Shaw also promised to earn a fortune to keep his family happy and safe, with no more fear of the risks in the night. And he said Cristina would marry well someday.

But tonight the risks for him were great. Earlier, a neighbor had come to the door and then Mama had gone out, leaving her children guarded by the dog outside until she returned.

More knocking, more shouting. Cristina huddled with Patrick, and touched a locket round her neck, an heirloom once worn by her great-great-grandmother, Lady Grisell Cochrane. Just now Cristina wished she could be as brave as that lady, who had faced danger to save her father. Cristina's own father, John Heron-Shaw—his true name—descended directly from Lady Grisell. Even if Cristina could not help her father this night, she could protect her brother.

"Johnny Shaw!" Furniture scraped over the floor, and cupboard doors snapped open. Hobnailed boots pounded on the wooden steps in the two-story stone house. "Come out, ye coward! Pay the fee you owe the Crown—or be arrested!"

"No one is here, Rutledge," another man said.

"Then we'll take what we like, since Johnny owes the government so much in whisky taxes. If we cannot earn our fee by arresting him, we'll take it from his home and later his hide."

Cristina pulled the plaid higher over Patrick. On the ground floor she heard dishes smashed, doors slammed, boots stomping and voices everywhere. Mama had some good things that she treasured—suddenly Cristina was so angry that she wanted to run down and tell the men to leave, tell them that Da was a good man and better than any gauger.

Her father and his comrades said the English government demanded fees for whisky even though every Scotsman deserved the right to use his barley as he pleased for bread and drink, and to sell, too. But gaugers earned their pay by the arrests they made and the goods they confiscated, so they sometimes raided homes to take their fee there.

Shadow and light filled the doorway. Cristina went still.

A man walked into the bedchamber, holding a lantern high as he turned. Light reflected on window glass and around the room, then streamed into the box bed where the shutter door gapped, revealing the red plaid and illuminating Cristina's face.

She stared at him, her hand clamped over Patrick's mouth. The intruder moved closer. She pressed against the wall with her brother.

"Hey, Ned!" the one called Rutledge said from the hallway. "What have you found?"

This Ned was young, Cristina realized, an adolescent like her cousins, just seventeen or so. He might be an apprentice gauger or a young kinsman joining the raid. Even so, he was helping to ransack her house. She glared at him. He watched her in silence, head tilted.

"Whatever you find is ours," the other man said. "Hey! Is that a gleam of gold there?"

Cristina's long blond braid had caught the light. She shrank back, holding Patrick close. Ned placed a hand on the shutter and turned, blocking the other man's view.

"Just the lamplight shining on . . . a yellow curtain rope," he answered.

Muttering, the other man walked away. Cristina breathed out.

"Girl, what are you called?" Ned asked softly.

"Kirstie," she said, giving her familiar name.

"Is that your wee brother, Kirstie?"

She looked up. His eyes were clear green in the lamplight. Dark curls framed a lean face beneath a battered hat. He smiled. He was bonny. She wanted to trust him, and nodded.

"Stay there until we're gone. You're both safe, lass. I'll see to it." He closed the shutter, leaving Cristina and Patrick in darkness.

She waited until the men left, until birdsong cut the silence, while her brother slept on her shoulder. Finally she heard footsteps and Da's voice calling out. Her mother called, too, anxiously, and then the dog barked and loped up the stairs.

"Here!" Cristina shouted. "I am here, and Patrick is safe with me."

Chapter 1

All she had to do was hold up a coach.

Just that, Cristina Heron-Shaw thought, twisting her fingers in the folds of her gown, a creamy silk embroidered with pink rosebuds. Was she mad? Wickedly so, but she had no choice. Da would have understood her decision, were he still alive.

Her uncle, Reverend Heron-Shaw, would not approve, of course; he had disliked his brother's free-trading lifestyle. But the vicar of Craigiston did not know that his nephew was currently locked in the town tolbooth as one Patrick Kerr, using his mother's surname.

Seated at the supper table, Cristina smiled and nodded at whatever her aunt, Mrs. Mary Heron-Shaw, was saying as she exchanged pleasantries with Edward Armstrong, Lord Dunallan, the newly inherited viscount and sheriff. Something about the Christmas Eve supper they were sharing; something about pie.

Cristina smiled, mind racing. Just before supper she had overheard Dunallan speaking to his sheriff-deputy, Mr. Rutledge. What they said had nearly spun her into a panic. Mr.

Rutledge often made her teeth grind; the man's grudge with her family went back to his days as a gauger, when her father had constantly eluded him. If Rutledge knew that young Patrick Kerr was actually Johnny Shaw's son, there would be hell to pay.

And now she sat across from the sheriff and deputy, secretly plotting a crime.

All evening, she had endured Mr. Rutledge's insufferable politeness. He enjoyed her discomfiture, for he knew too much—and not enough—about her kinsmen. She wondered if he had informed Lord Dunallan yet about the shameful origins of the vicar's niece. If not, the deputy would detail it soon enough.

"Indeed, madam, the apple pie is delicious," Dunallan answered the vicar's wife. His deep voice was velvety and compelling. Cristina stole another glance at him.

He was astonishingly handsome, as her Cousin Lilias had whispered earlier. True, he had a long, lean, muscled physique, well-balanced features, dark curls and hazel green eyes of such striking beauty that whenever he glanced at her, her heart set to wild beating.

Stop that, she told herself. She had no time for the swoony behavior that younger Lilias, seated at the far end of the table, favored. Cristina had too much on her mind.

"My niece made the pie herself," Aunt Mary was explaining. "She is so gifted in domestic arts, and she has a kind heart. Why, she sent our cook home to family for the evening in case of bad weather tonight and finished the baking herself. And her pies are as excellent as her charitable nature. We are so proud of Cristina."

"As you should be." He smiled, the corner of his mouth dimpling. Cristina wished she had not noticed that. "Such charity and skill are commendable."

How mortifying! She cringed at her aunt's matchmaking attempt. Every local matron was pushing eligible girls at the man. He was titled, rich, handsome, and unmarried—a rarity in this region on the fringes of the Highlands. But she would not be shoved at him, or anyone.

Still, she glanced again at the viscount as he spoke with her aunt. She wished that he would resume his conversation with Rutledge; she needed to hear more of his plans.

"I do know that Highland Christmas is celebrated tomorrow, the sixth of January," he was telling Mrs. Lindsay, the miller's wife. "Although New Year's—Hogmanay—is just past."

"Aye so. We call our later Yule the 'Old Style,' a holiday followed long, long ago." Mrs. Lindsay, an elderly lady in black taffeta, smiled. "You will remember it from visiting your grandparents. I remember you as a wee lad, sir. Very bold, you were," she said, shaking a finger.

"Sometimes, madam." He laughed.

Cristina felt that rich, low chuckle melt through her. "We consider ourselves Highland in this region, just below Stirling, and we do celebrate the second Yule, which is not often done in your Lowlands, sir." Did she sound haughty? The man unsettled her thinking.

Green eyes met hers, lingered. He nodded, and it seemed almost intimate. "Not my Lowlands, exactly, but I enjoy living there."

"We are Highland and proud of it," the miller's wife said. "In the south, the Lowlanders celebrate Christmas with little tradition and less merriment, I hear. They are very dour about the day, with solemn kirk services and then the shops are opened, with a bit of greenery over the doors. It is all the merry they can summon!"

"It is not so bad, madam. I do remember excellent Highland Christmases as a boy, when I visited my grandparents." He smiled.

"Very merry indeed, with parties and dances," the lady agreed.

Rutledge leaned over to murmur to Dunallan then, and Cristina wished she could hear it more clearly.

"The delivery should be tonight," Dunallan murmured in response to a question.

Tonight! Was she mad to cross the new sheriff? She did not know what to make of him yet. She remembered the new Dunallan's grandfather, who had also been sheriff. The old man had spoken well of her father, admiring his cleverness—and he enjoyed the smuggled spirits Johnny Shaw had brought him. His grandson seemed unlikely to forgive such unlawful activities.

Rumor said the new viscount would not remain in the area despite his appointment. According to Aunt Mary's friends, he would sell the estate, resign his office, and return to Edinburgh, where he had a law practice, a town house, and a fortune.

Unwilling to admit it, Cristina had been intensely aware of him all night—naturally, since her brother was locked in the man's tolbooth. But watching Dunallan now, she was caught by an attraction she could not explain or wholly understand, and did not want to feel.

Luckily her inadvertent eavesdropping had inspired a solution to the very dilemma she faced. Her impulsive plan could save Patrick, if she could summon the courage to see it through.

Earlier she had listened as Dunallan confirmed to Rutledge that certain documents would be delivered that night containing orders to transfer the prisoner to Edinburgh for trial. The government meant to make an example of him, Dunallan had explained grimly, while Rutledge had seemed pleased.

All she need do, Cristina told herself, was disguise herself, halt the coach, wave a pistol about, demand the documents, and ride off. The resulting delay would give her time to free Patrick and get him to the Highlands, where he could hide until his innocence could be proven.

The wild deed had precedence. Her great-great-grandmother had played highwayman to stop a coach and steal documents ordering her father's hanging, thus saving him with the gift of time. If Lady Grisell Cochrane could do it in the seventeenth century, Cristina told herself firmly that she could carry it off now. At twenty-one, she had an independent nature, though she wondered if she had the backbone to see this mad scheme through.

She straightened her shoulders, draped in a pale green shawl, and touched the little golden locket at her throat, for she wore Grisell's own pendant, passed down, and felt that it lent her courage. Then she smiled, pretending to follow what her aunt was saying.

"An excellent plan, Cristina. It would please Lord Dunallan so!" the lady said.

"W-what would please him, Aunt Mary?" Cristina asked, startled.

"Were you not listening again? I said you should serve him some of the jam trifle yourself, since you made it," her aunt whispered. "He would surely appreciate it!"

He does not look easy to please, Cristina thought. Just now he looked stern as he spoke to Rutledge. He might be a divine catch, but she did not want to attract his attention tonight.

"That would be too forward, Aunt." *Not as forward as robbing a coach,* she thought.

"We do not follow strict rules here in the Highlands, dear, especially at the holidays. We treat guests like family. And you know every cap will be set—"

"Hush," Cristina said desperately. Of course she wanted a husband one day, but not now, not this man. She wanted to love deeply and enduringly, but not yet. Besides, the surly viscount would never consider a bride whose brother sat in his tolbooth and whose father had been a smuggler. Nor would he ever marry a girl who schemed to steal his documents.

"They do say," Aunt Mary murmured, persistent, "that he has a considerable income, a house in Edinburgh, and an estate in the Borders. He visited here often as a boy. Now that he owns the castle, perhaps he will restore it. Such a handsome old place!"

"It is absolutely crumbling," Cristina murmured. "It would take a fortune to fix it."

"But so picturesque! I wonder," Aunt Mary whispered, "if he will take a Highland bride now that he is a Highland laird."

"More likely, he will open the castle only for shooting parties," Cristina said sourly.

She did not recall meeting Edward Armstrong as a boy at his grandfather's home during her visits to Craigiston, though he did seem strangely familiar. Perhaps there was a family resemblance. What mattered far more just now was that he was the sheriff.

She had learned of Patrick's arrest while she was staying with friends in the Highlands and received word from a cousin who had been with her brother. Hastening to Craigiston, she discovered that Patrick had given the name Kerr to protect his family. She had not seen him yet, and had no good excuse to go to the tolbooth alone. She had also learned that old Lord Dunallan had died recently, leaving the estate to a Lowland grandson who had been quickly invested as sheriff in his grandfather's place. Although the position was no longer hereditary, the new viscount was an Edinburgh advocate called to the Bar, and so the government had offered him the appointment.

Now Mrs. Lindsay, the miller's widow, was praising the

pies and Cristina's domestic abilities. Inwardly groaning, Cristina wished the evening—the whole of it—was over.

Her uncle leaned forward from his place at the head of the table. "Sir, your grandfather spoke highly of you, and mentioned your interest in Scottish history. My niece Cristina is enamored of history as well."

"I read it avidly, as many do," Cristina said. "I am quite fond of Scott's poetry as well as his scholarly work."

"Aye, his work is fascinating," Dunallan agreed. "I find his epic poems excellent, particularly in their historical aspects."

History and Scott and dimples and dark curls, and there she was melting again when she should think only of her mission. "So you are familiar with Mr. Scott!"

"My mother is personally acquainted with him, and he has kindly given me some advice, even though my own work is amateur," he went on, sounding sincere. "I am working on a history of the Armstrongs, as my ancestors enjoyed some notoriety as Border reivers."

"I have read of the bold Lowland reivers," Cristina said.

"Our family tree boasts rogues, too," the vicar said. "My great-grandmother—"

"Uncle, Lord Dunallan would not find that very interesting," Cristina said hastily.

"But I do find it intriguing," Dunallan said. "The vicar mentioned his bold ancestress earlier, when we were in his library."

"Their family has current rogues even more notorious," Rutledge began.

"Oh, but we never speak of them!" Aunt Mary said. "Do we, Mr. Heron-Shaw?"

"No, indeed, my dear. Some we never mention."

Dunallan glanced at Cristina, his brow wrinkling. She tried to look innocent. "Do tell us about your Border rascals, sir," she said impulsively.

"I would be glad to do so sometime, Miss Heron-Shaw," he answered. His gaze was arrow-keen, thoughtful. In the candlelight, his eyes were green, astute, focused on her.

"Please," she said, and knew she sounded desperate.

Wrapping long fingers around his wine glass, he raised it slightly in half toast. *Miss Heron-Shaw,* those eyes and lifted hand seemed to say, *I know your secrets, and we will talk, you and I—alone.*

She blinked. Guilt and anxiety fueled her imagination. Surely the man thought only of apple pie and clotted cream, and surely cringed at yet another young woman pushed blatantly toward him. He could not guess her secrets, unless Mr. Rutledge had already ruined her in his regard. Tonight, that would not be far wrong.

Cristina glanced away. *All she had to do was stop the coach. . . .*

First she needed a pistol, a disguise, a horse, a reason to leave the house that night—and a good deal of courage.

Chapter 2

All he had to do was survive the holidays. . . .

And for now, supper at the vicar's, Edward thought. But the meal was over, port sipped, cards played, and some hot, baked, salted potato slices were enjoyed with a steaming brose of cream, honey, and whisky. Now the gigs and carriages were being brought round and the ladies were donning bonnets and cloaks. Soon a servant would bring his greatcoat to him and his horse would be walked to the post.

He sighed. He had not expected to enjoy the evening, but he had liked it, not the least reason the vicar's niece. Lovely, intelligent, forthright, with an appreciation of history—the combination was hard to resist, but he meant to do so.

Even though he was now viscount and owner of a ramshackle castle and sheriff of a quaint Highland village, he did not intend to linger in the area. Nor was he eager to find a bride and sink into domesticity here or anywhere. He rather expected married life to be dull, and he considered himself dull enough already.

He had a lamentable love of history, books, and solitude over cards, racing, and parties. Sought after in social circles, he rarely accepted, which suited his bookish nature. His current research about the Armstrong Border clan played more on his mind than marriage, to the everlasting frustration of his mother in England and his siblings on both sides of the Border.

"Merry Yule to you, Lord Dunallan, and good night," Mrs. Lindsay said. She was the widow of a local laird—no, she was the miller's wife, he thought; the lady fussing with her fur pelisse was the laird's widow. Only one face and name had captured his full attention that night.

Cristina Heron-Shaw, standing with her aunt, glanced at him again. And so it had gone all evening: stolen glances, little smiles, some frowns. Hooked like a fish, he was, though the girl had not acted deliberately. That was even more alluring, he thought.

"So good to make your acquaintance. Safe journey home in this weather," he told the older woman, and repeated it again and again as he took gloved hands to say farewell. He knew the ladies in particular were curious about him: a titled bachelor with a decent yearly sum, a civic office, and a castle, however decrepit. But he was not as marriageable as they thought, being in no hurry.

Even his St. Andrews friends had made bets that he would be the first of them to marry, which he found laughable. He felt sorry for the eager mums hauling their daughters and nieces about on his behalf in Edinburgh, and now here. There was no point, he sometimes wanted to tell them. Not yet.

Since his arrival a fortnight ago, he had attended three country dances, five supper parties, a funeral, and a christening, all while learning his duties as sheriff and viscount. Much of his time was devoted to going through his grandfather's library and papers. Then Rutledge had produced boxes of documents and excise officers' reports to review, along with other issues to consider—including a young prisoner in the tolbooth soon to be transferred.

Enough to keep anyone busy, surely, particularly since the area was a hub for the manufacture and smuggling of illicit spirits and the free-trading of goods. He knew that before arriving, as he had gone out on patrol with his grandfather and others, years back—but he had never expected to be sheriff.

He intended to return to Edinburgh as soon as another sheriff could be named. He had a law office to think about, and a comfortable, well-ordered George Street house with staff who knew to leave him be. He had a few trustworthy friends and reliable relationships with his mother and siblings. His life was peaceful and dull, and he meant to keep it that way.

Besides, he had been engaged once and jilted. Youth, idealism, and poor judgment on his part—and some conniving on her part—were to blame. He was not bitter, having gained maturity and perspective, and now he scarcely remembered why he had loved her. Currently free of encumbrances at twenty-nine, he enjoyed life as an advocate, an amateur scholar, and quiet bachelor. He also enjoyed the discreet acquaintance of a few lovers over time, leisurely savored without ties.

But his grandfather's death and will had left him unexpected responsibilities—not only the castle and civic duties, but boxes of old family documents. The prospect of the research made him happy as a child with pots, shovels, and dirt. He could not wait to resume it this evening.

"Lord Dunallan, do take an apple pie home with you, sir," Mrs. Heron-Shaw said then. "We have so much food left, as the poor weather kept some of our guests from coming."

"Thank you, madam, but I could not accept." Politeness dictated that, though he wanted to accept; he had sent the housekeeper home at Hogmanay, and there was little left in the larder.

"The crust is perfection, the filling sublime. My niece made it, as you know."

"I do." He saw Miss Heron-Shaw blush like a peach—which he preferred to apple—as her aunt touted her accomplishments. He felt a bit sorry for the girl, paraded by others when she clearly did not want it.

"I hope you enjoyed the meal," the aunt persisted. "We are so happy you could join us."

"An excellent Scottish country supper! It reminded me of my boyhood," he said heartily, knowing it would please his hostess. "Roast lamb, seasoned vegetables, crusty breads, wonderful desserts—a grand feast." He had not had a decent meal in a fortnight. But if he said so, the whole glen might know by morning, and platters would appear on his very doorstep.

When he had arrived at Dunallan Castle, the place boasted an elderly housekeeper, a groundsman, and one dim maidservant. Edward had sent them off to their families for the holidays, wanting peace and quiet for his research. The shabby old castle had character but lacked the order of his well-appointed town house. The larder held a store of bannocks, cheese, and apples, and he had relied otherwise on the plain cuisine at the Drouthy Wench Inn down the main road. And in the castle he had discovered a supply of whisky so fine that a long sip would satisfy any man's drouth, or thirst, as was said here.

"If you have more pie, Mary, you could give it to neighbors," Mrs. Lindsay suggested.

Mrs. Heron-Shaw had already directed a servant to bring some pies wrapped in brown paper and string. "Here, Lord Dunallan," she insisted. "Apple custard, jam trifle, rhubarb, and a cheesecake, too. Perfect for a hungry bachelor."

He accepted the pies clumsily stacked to his chin, their smells enticing. "Thank you, madam," he conceded, slightly embarrassed by the familiar generosity he remembered from his boyhood days here.

"Aunt, I could bring something to Mrs. MacDonell down the road," the niece offered.

Edward peered over the pies. The girl looked up at him. Heaven-blue eyes and long lashes made his heart leap. A turn of the golden head, curls whipped to marzipan froth, made him hungry again, but for something other than rich food.

In fact, his breath caught and he felt as if his heart opened, warmed somehow. But he could not, would not, be smitten.

"Remember, Mrs. MacDonell is infirm and could not join us tonight," the niece said.

"Snow is falling now. It could be dangerous, Kirstie."

"It's just flurries and it's only down the road. I could stay for company, and if the weather worsens, I could stay the night." She smiled, sunny, dimpled, lovely and impish.

Watching in silence, Edward might have agreed to do anything for her.

"Well . . . Yule is traditionally a time for charity," her aunt considered.

The vicar's fetching niece smiled up at Edward. "Charity should extend to everyone at Christmas, even prisoners, do you not agree, sir?"

He blinked. "I never thought about it, to be honest."

"You ought to," she said bluntly.

"Miss, the fellow in our tolbooth cannot be released," Rutledge said, stepping toward them. "Perhaps the young lady has forgotten that smugglers are the criminal sort."

"They deserve charity as much as anyone." She glared at the deputy.

Puzzled by that sudden spark, Edward lifted a brow. "It is not usual custom to grant holiday privileges for prisoners," he told her. "But we could take it into consideration."

She began to answer, but her aunt drew her by the arm to bid farewell to other guests. Edward stared after her, then rebalanced the leaning pies.

"Do be careful, Dunallan," Rutledge murmured. "That bonny thing has notorious kinsmen. Her father was Johnny Shaw. The good reverend has a wicked branch in his family."

Frowning, Edward hid his surprise, but his mind whirled. He had met Johnny Shaw's daughter years ago. Surely Cristina Heron-Shaw was not—

Kirstie, her aunt had called her. Stunned, he glanced toward the girl who stood nearby, her back to him, the lamplight spilling gold through her hair. In that instant, he knew.

"Indeed," he said softly.

"Her uncle and aunt took her in after her father's death, and made sure she had an education and was brought up properly," Rutledge explained. "A younger brother stayed in the hills with his mother and uncles, I think. Rogues and lawbreakers, that lot."

"Her father was never caught or formally accused."

"Shot by a lawman while smuggling is accusation enough. You went with us on a raid to his house once, when old Dunallan was away. Remember, Ned?"

"I do recall that," Edward murmured as he watched young Kirstie. She had grown into a beautiful young woman. With her back to him, she turned her head just so. Lovely indeed.

He felt a tug again, her familiarity now understood. Eleven years ago he had encountered a child protecting her small brother. What he felt tonight was but a response to a dim memory, he told himself. Only that.

"Be warned, sir," Rutledge repeated.

"Of course," Edward agreed. "Arthur, may I remind you that I am expecting a parcel delivery this evening from Edinburgh. I have another parcel to send off as well."

"Aye. Odd for Yule Eve, sir, if I may say."

"The court considers the matter to be pressing. The documents contain orders for . . . our guest," he said carefully, "drawn up last week, as you know, though they could not be delivered sooner due to the winter weather south of here."

"I am glad he is being transferred for trial. Too much smuggling goes on in this area of Scotland. May the rascal's fate serve to deter others."

"His guilt is not yet proven."

"I caught him at it myself, and that's enough for me. The foul weather has cleared in Lothian, so I hear," Rutledge went on. "The vicar mentioned that an acquaintance of his could not travel here until today, due to the snow to the south."

"The Stirling road is adequate for travel now, so I am told."

"But those thick flurries outside may be the beginning of the snow for us. Sir, I had arranged for Mr. Gordon to relieve me at the tolbooth this evening so that I could spend Old Yule with my wife and our family. But now it seems I must wait upon your courier."

"No need, sir. I will watch for the courier—the road runs past the castle. Let Mr. Gordon keep watch at the jail if he is willing. Go home to your family." Edward felt a twinge of regret, but he had chosen to be alone for the holidays this year. He felt quick sympathy for the young lad shut up alone in the tolbooth this night.

"Patrick Kerr seems a decent lad," he told Rutledge. "Perhaps I will bring the pies over for him later." He shifted the wrapped packages in his hands.

"He should have no privilege, sir. He and his comrades were free-trading. The others ran off and left him to take the blame. Any punishment is deserved."

"Perhaps, but he insists that he was on his way to Edinburgh for his first year of university, happened to visit his cousins, and that he is no smuggler."

"And you believed him? I saw cause to arrest him and so I did. You mentioned two parcels?" Rutledge asked, changing the topic.

"Aye. The other is for a friend. The courier can take that one tonight. Sir, I bid you and yours a merry Yule." Edward turned to take final leave of Reverend Heron-Shaw and his family, looking around for the niece—Johnny Shaw's daughter, he corrected himself—who had been standing there only moments ago.

"Please give my compliments to your niece," he then told her aunt and uncle.

"Oh, do say farewell yourself!" The aunt smiled. "There she is, coming out of the library." She practically pushed him in that direction. The girl paused in the hallway, where an oil lamp on a table gave off a flickering light.

Miss Heron-Shaw looked startled as he approached, tucking something under a black cloak slung over her arm. "Lord Dunallan! I was just going out—"

"I was just leaving—" he said at the same time.

"What a pleasant evening," she went on politely, yet sounded nervous.

"Flurries have started," he replied, glancing toward the open front door. "May I escort you to your neighbor's house?" He had not planned to offer, but it felt natural. "It would be on my way."

"I will be fine . . . but thank you," she added.

"Well." He hesitated, not wanting to leave, suddenly. "I must be going. I . . . very much enjoyed the evening, too. The apple pie was delicious." She would be delicious, too—sweet and curvy and soft beneath his lips and hands. He stopped that wicked thought, but could not keep his gaze from dropping, lifting.

A glint caught his eye. What had she tucked under the cloak? The object looked like a gun with a flashing of brass over wood. But the light in the hallway was dim; surely he saw only the gilded spine of a book. "Taking some reading to Mrs. MacDonell?"

"Oh—aye! Good night, Lord Dunallan." She stepped past him, a graceful golden creature in lamp glow and shadows. He went with her, and she paused to shake his hand at the door, forthright about that, like many Scotswomen. He loved the exquisite feel of her slim, soft hand in his. Then he departed, carrying the pies.

Riding through the darkness on the road back to Dunallan, he mused that if he had been looking for a Highland bride—which he was not—then Johnny Shaw's golden-haired daughter would be his first choice, no matter what her father had done. Briefly he wondered if she would even consider a dull and bookish viscount who was not a very exciting gentleman.

A moment's dream on a snow-dusted night. First, many things needed his attention—starting with parcels and a coach.

Chapter 3

Bitter cold air, the moor washed pale by moonlight and snowfall, the horse restive on the frozen track—and Cristina shivering in the saddle, thinking herself a lunatic to be waiting here to rob a coach. She patted the neck of her uncle's chestnut mare, borrowed for the ride to Mrs. MacDonell's, and sighed. After she had brought the meal and visited briefly with the lady, she had changed her clothes in a barn and had struck out along the Stirling road.

Whatever did one say to halt a coach? *Your money or your life,* the English highwaymen of old had called out, Dick Turpin and Sixteen-string Jack and the like. Scottish history had few of those, boasting a greater number of whisky smugglers and cattle reivers than highway robbers—except for her own legendary great-great-grandmama.

Johnny Shaw would have applauded her courage this night. He was never a thief, simply a peace-loving teacher and a charming, clever free-trader for the benefit of his family and his glen. And he had been killed by gaugers on a moonlit night before he could hang for his beliefs.

Her own life would be at risk tonight, for the sake of a document intended for the sheriff. After clearing her throat, she lowered her voice to rehearse. "Hand over the parcel," she said gruffly. "Give me the mail pouch, if you please, sir."

She sighed. She sounded like an adolescent schoolboy. Her breath puffed outward in the cold air, and she tucked the black paisley shawl, one of her own, snug around her face and throat. Otherwise she wore male clothing—a black woolen greatcoat, knee breeches, waistcoat, and jacket of black superfine. She wore black leather boots as well, tall for her and folded at the thigh. A broad-brimmed black hat covered her giveaway golden hair.

The things belonged to Patrick, who was tall and slender; she had brought them to Craigiston in case he needed decent clothing for a trial, or a burial. Although she had not anticipated this impromptu use, so be it.

Tucked in a pocket of the greatcoat was the antique wood-and-brass pistol that had once belonged to her great-great-grandmother. Clean of powder and shot, it was missing a latch, which rendered it unusable. She had taken the heirloom from its brace on the library wall—Dunallan had nearly seen her with it—and she intended to return it soon.

Her sins that night were many, she thought, but all for Patrick's good. With luck, her aunt and uncle would never know that the tolbooth prisoner was their own nephew until he was free. Let any blame fall to her.

She did not question Patrick's innocence, knowing how he despised the smuggling trade that had caused their father's death. He had been traveling to Edinburgh for the Candlemas term at the university to begin his law studies. A cousin had brought word of Patrick's trouble, reporting that the lad had stayed the night with some cousins still involved in the free-trade, and he had been caught in their midst. They had fled, but he had been arrested.

All this had transpired before Dunallan's arrival, and the court orders to transfer Patrick were already on their way. Tonight she would steal them, and tomorrow convince Rutledge to allow the prisoner to visit the vicar's home for the holiday. Then she intended to spirit her brother back up to the Highlands without involving her uncle.

That was the whole of her scheme. Now that Dunallan, stern and astute, had come to Craigiston, her best chance to help Patrick was now or never. Silently she blessed the new sheriff for mentioning the documents and inspiring her new plan.

Snow fell peacefully through the darkness, calming her. She watched her frosted breaths, listened to the wind, the whicker of the horse, the creak of leather. Her gloved hands and booted feet were cold. She desperately wished this night was over.

Finally she heard hoofbeats and wheels. She straightened, heart pounding, sitting tense upon the horse hidden by trees along the roadside. Soon she saw a vehicle and two horses rounding a curve in the road, coming closer at a good pace.

She wanted to turn and run—but thought of her great-great-grandmother's bravery and felt fresh resolve. Lady Grisell Cochrane had waited like this, too, and had accomplished her goal. That gave Cristina hope. With a gloved finger, she touched the small locket for luck.

Now the snow mixed with sleety rain, pelting the ground, the trees, her hat, her shoulders. She saw that the approaching vehicle was just a gig drawn by two horses, with two men on the crossbench. She narrowed her eyes, judging the distance to the road, waiting.

Now, Kirstie, she told herself. *Now!* Drawing a breath, she urged the horse into the path. "Hold!" she shouted, deepening her voice. "Hold there!"

The lead horse neighed, her mare sidestepped nervously. The driver pulled on the reins.

"What is this!" he shouted. "What d'ye want, there?"

She pulled out her riding whip, brandished it, reluctant to

reveal the old, useless gun unless necessary. "Please, sir, give over your valuables!"

"Be damned! A highway thief, here?" the driver said.

"Where's me pistol—" The second man reached into his coat pocket.

"Stop!" Cristina snapped the whip, which only fluttered. "You carry something of worth, I hear! Please give it over and go safely on your way!"

"We carry papers, not coin!" the driver said.

"It's a lad," the other muttered. "Or a girl, I swear. You! Go home to Mama and suckle some milk!" The driver laughed at that.

She had expected resistance, but not rude dismissal. Suddenly a pistol appeared in the second man's hand, its long, fierce barrel glinting. Terrified, she wanted to race away. Her horse sensed that and pranced anxiously.

She drew out the antique pistol, hands trembling. "Put that down or I will shoot," she called, trying earnestly to deepen her voice.

"You put *that* one away! Does yer da know you have it? Let us pass or you will be hurt!" the driver called. "It's a wee brat what ought to be sleeping," he growled to the other man.

"Toss your valuables to me now!"

"'Tis papers, ye nitwit." The driver waved a leather satchel. "What d'ye want with these?"

"Best run off before I shoot!" the man with the gun shouted.

"I do not want trouble," she said hastily. "Just the papers, if you please, sir."

"Please, it says, with its fine wee manners," the driver mocked. "Go on!"

"Give me the papers and save yourselves!"

"What, from a wee bairnie?"

"Aye!" she shouted, training the pistol on them, praying her bluff was convincing.

The men muttered, shrugged, and then the driver launched an object at her. She reached out for it, balancing pistol, whip, and reins. As the missile brushed her gloved fingers, she realized it was a bottle, not the packet of documents she wanted. What she had believed was a gun was in fact this very bottle. She leaned back quickly, but it clipped her brow and grazed the horse's flank before falling to the ground. Startled, her horse sidestepped and reared. Cristina slid out of the saddle, then hit the ground hard, the wind knocked from her. She rolled away just as the mare dropped its hooves and spun, bumping into the lead horse, which neighed and lurched.

The gig careened off suddenly, the men shouting. Cristina's own horse cantered away.

Standing, tripping on the greatcoat, she saw a packet lying in the road and threw herself on it, snatching it up, cramming it inside her waistcoat. As she got up again, her foot turned sideways in the overlarge boots, and sharp pain shot through her ankle. She ran, wincing, desperate to catch her horse and get away while the gig rattled down the road.

She limped after the mare, which hesitated for a moment. Cristina hurled herself forward and grabbed the dangling lead before the horse could take off again. Bouncing on her injured foot, she scrabbled into the saddle, grabbed the reins, and turned the horse's head toward Craigiston.

The weight of the parchment-wrapped packet tucked inside her waistcoat was reassuring. Despite all, she had grabbed the documents intended for the sheriff. Now for home—

She glanced over her shoulder just as another horse and rider emerged from between the trees and thundered toward her.

Chapter 4

What the devil?

Edward guided his black stallion through the darkness, intent on pursuing the thieving rascal he had just spied along the highway attempting to hold up the courier. But the gig's horses had startled, running off with the vehicle in tow, and the brigand's own horse had thrown its rider to the ground. The fellow had grabbed something up from the road, then regained his mount and took off in the opposite direction.

He was astonished to see a highwayman here, of all places, of all nights. Swearing under his breath, he followed at a brisk pace. Not only was he sheriff, but likely the one robbed.

The thief was rapidly vanishing into the shadows. Passing the spot where the encounter had happened, Edward saw a leather satchel on the ground. Halting the horse, he leaped down and snatched it up. The thing was empty.

Bloody hell. His papers were gone. They were irreplaceable documents—not the court papers safely tucked in his pocket now, but the packet he had given the courier not a half hour earlier. Knowing the recipient expected it forthwith, he had paid dearly for its quick transport to the Lowlands, adding something extra for the two couriers to enjoy a good supper and rooms for the night at the Drouthy Wench Inn along the Stirling road.

Then he noticed the pistol lying in the road. After snatching it up and noting its old-fashioned shape and the fact that it likely could not fire, he dropped it into his coat pocket. Then he remounted and went after the brigand. He wanted those papers back, and he meant to make an arrest for the crime that had been committed under his very nose. Best hurry, he told himself; the insolent rascal was far along the road despite a mix of snow and sleet.

Edward urged the black onward over a surface hard-packed but not slick where earth and stone roughened the way. Ahead, he saw the dark, fluid shapes of horse and rider.

Cold wind, the horse surging powerfully beneath him over the frozen turf, and the excitement of the chase invigorated him after the wine and rich food. He followed as the thief turned off the highway onto a moorland track that he knew led past Dunallan.

All had gone awry, from the arguing couriers to the stumbling horse and her own fall and injury. Now she was being followed. Was one of the drivers chasing her?

At least she had the documents. If she could escape into the darkness, the highway thief and the orders for her brother's trial would vanish with her. And then this Yule Eve would be best forgotten, Cristina thought, leaning forward, encouraging her horse to a quicker pace.

The highway was too open, so she left the road for the shortest route, a track over the moor past Dunallan toward Craigiston. Then she glanced back over her shoulder—

Her pursuer was still there, lessening the gap between his horse and hers.

Heart pounding, she leaned close, knees tight, feeling the

horse thunder ahead, mane brushing her face. If she was caught, it would go badly for her and Patrick, too, if their kinship was revealed. She had to lose the persistent rider behind her.

A cluster of trees to the right would provide cover, she thought, and a place to hide the parcel. Urging the horse down a dip in the moorland where the pursuer could not see them, Cristina slowed the horse to enter the thicket of pines. Sliding from the saddle, she winced as her ankle took the weight. Then she pulled the parcel from her waistcoat and stuffed it under a carpet of pine needles at the base of a tree. The fragrant piney smell came away with her.

She waited, patting and shushing the horse. In the quiet, she heard the distant rhythm of hooves over the moor. The rider was there. Heart pounding, breath held, she waited as the thudding faded. Relieved, she knew he was taking the moorland track onward.

When she was sure he was gone, she used a stone to remount. She was glad that her father had fostered independence in his daughter as much as his son. He had even taken her on smuggling runs that he deemed safe enough, and proudly told her the story of Lady Grisell. Cristina had loved the stories, the adventure and excitement, and Da's attention, too.

What would Da think now? She thought he would understand. He had always told her to take care of her little brother—and that was precisely what she intended to do.

Guiding the mare out of the pine break, Cristina felt again the anticipation of earlier days, a breathless sense of balancing on the dangerous edge of life. She never truly enjoyed demurely sewing or serving tea to friends in the parlor. She wanted adventure. The only other place that lent her a sense of freedom, boldness, and risk existed in books, where her imagination could keep pace with stories and histories.

Riding once again over the dark moor, she hoped that the

spirit of Lady Grisell was proud of her, too, and hoped the lady might even look after her great-great-granddaughter this night.

Perhaps so. The sleet had ended, though snowflakes still floated down, and the pursuer was gone. Cristina headed for the village, satisfied that she was safe, with the documents in hand. Soon Patrick would be free, and no one would ever be the wiser—

Out of shadows and nowhere, the rider appeared, a black form winging alongside her. She urged the mare faster, just as a wickedly strong arm whipped out to hook her about the waist and drag her out of the saddle and toward him, though she struggled.

Edward reached, but the thief, nimble and lightweight, twisted free and clung to the other horse. Then the fellow slipped, plunging to the ground between the moving horses.

Deftly sidling the stallion to avoid a hoof strike, Edward peered down. The thief lay still, a slight shape with great-coat, hat, sprawled legs. The other horse cantered away, but then stopped to graze nearby. The animal would have to be captured; Edward would not leave it to wander in the cold and the sleet, which had resumed, icy and slick.

First, the brigand. Edward dismounted and prodded with a foot and got no response. He knelt in cold muck to shake the fellow's shoulder and tap his cheek. The face was pale and soft beneath the black hat and concealing scarf.

A beardless lad, Edward thought, up to mischief on a holiday eve—but why? Scooping the boy into his arms, he carried him back to the stallion, lifting him easily over the saddle pommel. Setting a foot in the stirrup, he leaped up after him.

Concerned that there might be a head injury, he leaned the unconscious lad against his shoulder. Thinking of his own nephews, his brother's children, Edward felt a twinge of compassion. What had driven the lad out tonight of all nights, when most people were with their families?

Well, he had no family himself this holiday—but now he had a lost soul in his keeping. Knowing he ought to toss the lad in the tolbooth with the other young prisoner, he paused due to a sense of caution as well as compassion. The ride to Craigiston could cause more harm if there was indeed an injury.

Through pelting snow and sleet, Edward rounded his stallion, caught the second horse's lead within moments, and headed for Dunallan Castle.

The brigand stirred, moaned, set a gloved hand to his head. The eyes opened, beautiful in the snowy light—and familiar. Seeing Edward, the thief gasped and subsided in a faint.

Edward frowned. He knew those eyes, that face.

The vicar's niece—Johnny Shaw's daughter—was a highway robber.

Swearing low, riding fast as he dared while cradling his charge, he took the castle's slope carefully as he guided the horses over a long swath of frozen grass toward the entrance.

The girl woke and began to struggle, thrashing, kicking to get away. She half slid from the horse, forcing Edward to dismount with her. He managed to land on one knee, still holding the girl. Then the packages roped to the back of the saddle burst free, jostled by the ride, strings loose and contents dumping.

He had forgotten about the pies.

As the sweet fillings dripped in dollops over his head and shoulders, he hauled Miss Heron-Shaw to her feet and tossed her unceremoniously over his shoulder.

Chapter 5

He kicked the door open, rusty latch giving, and strode across the hall and up the stairs. She was a featherweight, this troublemaking girl, he thought as he pushed open the door of his bedchamber. The intimacy of the location hardly occurred to him. He was preoccupied with the horses still waiting to be stabled, the wicked weather, the pie sliding over his brow, the fact that the vicar's niece was a blasted bandit.

He dumped her on the red satin coverlet, muck and pie on her coat making a mess that the housekeeper would likely fuss about later, and he stood back. His grandfather's dogs bumped against his legs, for the white terrier and old deerhound had followed him up the steps.

The girl sat up, setting a hand to her head. She had lost the hat somewhere, and her hair fell in a golden tousle, smeared with apple custard. Turning, Edward lit an oil lamp on a side table, then snatched a linen towel from the washbasin stand and returned to hand it to her.

In silence, she wiped the glop from her hair. He fisted hands to hips. "There's crust over your ear," he said.

She reached, but the piece dropped to the floor and was snatched by the terrier. The girl looked up at Edward. "I am sorry about the pies. I'll make more for you."

He huffed. "The tolbooth lacks a kitchen, and that's where you'll be."

She blinked, eyes wide and blue. "You've custard on your nose."

"Miss Heron-Shaw," he said, rubbing his face, "first, are you hurt? How is your head?"

"Aches a bit." Touching her brow gingerly, she winced. "I am fine. I should go—" She began to stand, but sat abruptly.

"Rest a moment," he advised. "Then explain yourself. What the devil—"

"I cannot tell you, exactly," she said, rubbing her brow. "Please do not swear."

"Pardon. We will stay here until you are ready to talk."

She glanced around. "But this is . . . a bedchamber!"

"With the servants away, this is the only heated room in this blasted—sorry, this old—castle. Just what were you about tonight?"

"The servants are gone?" She picked the desserty bits from her hair and let them drop to the dogs. They gobbled up and eagerly awaited more.

"Aye. Now talk."

"If I do, it might go badly for others."

"Worse than for you?" He hooked his foot around a chair, drew it to him, and sat so close that his knees nearly touched hers. He reached up to extract gooey pie from his hair and brushed at clumps on his coat sleeves. "So, you rode out this evening with a plate for a neighbor, and then decided to rob a courier. Do not deny it," he said, when she was silent. "I saw you."

"I did bring something to Mrs. MacDonell."

"Dressed like a brigand?"

"It is cold outside."

"I see. Perhaps the scarf about your face gave you an irresistible urge to waylay a gig."

"I am not a thief! I only meant to help someone."

"By taking my papers?" he asked abruptly.

"P—papers?" She ran her fingers through her tangled hair.

Impatient, Edward plucked a wedge of crust from her hair. His fingers smoothed over curls so fine and soft that his heart bounded. "You took a valuable parcel that belongs to me, and I want it returned," he said.

Silent, she touched his cheek to wipe away a sweet drizzle, and her touch nearly made him jump. He took the cloth from her hand to scrub it vigorously over his hair, where glop and crust were caught in the insufferable curls. Tossing the cloth aside, he reached into his greatcoat pocket and produced the pistol. "What did you intend to do with this?"

"Nothing," she said. "It is old and broken and does not shoot."

He grunted. "I saw it in your uncle's library. He said it had belonged to an ancestor."

"Yes. Lady Grisell Cochrane."

"I know of her—the brave young lady who once saved a man back in the days of the Covenanting army. So there is more than one virago in your family. But which is the wilder wench . . . bold Lady Grisell or troublesome Miss Cristina?" He cocked a brow.

She frowned. "Are you going to arrest me?"

"I caught you in flagrante delicto. I am the sheriff. I daresay it's done." He shoved the pistol back into his pocket. "I intend to find out what this is about, Miss. And I want my deuced parcel back."

"Sir," she said, "may I use a washbasin?"

"Shall I draw a bath and fetch clean clothing, too?" He felt growing frustration.

"I do have a change of clothes packed on my horse, if you allow me to get them."

Damn! "The horses! I will be back. Do not leave this room, I warn you."

He hurried for the stairs, pie bits still shedding from his greatcoat. The dogs trotted after him, licking the floor.

Cristina stood quickly, wincing at the sear of pain, and looked around. She needed to escape, but could barely walk. Nor would Dunallan let her go—if she ran off, he would go straight to her uncle. Frantic, she wondered what to do.

Without the essential papers, the sheriff had no order to send Patrick away. Dread decided her: she could not stay. If she could reach Craigiston and the tolbooth before the sheriff thought to go there, she might be able to claim Patrick for the vicar and get him free that way. Removing the heavy greatcoat, slimed with mud, custard, and pastry, she hobbled to the window to tug on the casement. Through the thick glass, she saw snow swirling in fat, white flakes.

"Leaving already, Miss Heron-Shaw?"

She whirled. He stood so close that she sidled away, limping, her back to the wall. He had removed his outer coat, and the dogs had returned with him.

"Let me go," she said desperately. The deerhound crowded close, sniffing at her hand.

"Poor weather has stranded us both for now. Sit," he said. "Not you—the dog," he added.

Cristina looked down to see the deerhound licking at the sweet filling that still clung to her wrist.

"That will make her ill," Dunallan said.

"It is just cream and jam from the trifle. She likes it."

He huffed impatiently as the dog wandered off to sit with the terrier. Then Dunallan slapped a hand, each one, on the wall beside her head, trapping her there. "No more pies, dogs, or delays. What were you doing out there tonight?"

She closed her eyes against a wrenching urge to tell the truth, wanting to trust him, but caution made her hesitate. Still, she had best explain some of it. "I meant to save my brother."

"Patrick," he said softly. "Patrick Shaw."

"How did you know?" Had Rutledge discovered Patrick's identity already?

Dunallan's strong, straight arms trapped her. He sighed and nodded half to himself. "Kirstie," he said, "I am Ned. We met once, years back."

She stared at him. Recalled, gasped. Then tears pooled. "N-Ned, who saved us when—"

"When you and your brother were children hiding in the box bed." He spoke gently.

A sort of relief washed through her, and hot new tears trickled free. This was not Dunallan, the stranger—here was Ned, who had guaranteed safety. She studied him for a moment and saw indeed that same Ned, grown handsome and sure—but quite possibly dangerous.

"So, Patrick Kerr is indeed Patrick Shaw. He looks like you," he said, brushing his fingers over her hair, then placing his hand quickly on the wall. "What else should I know?"

"Nothing else. Will you put me in the tolbooth?"

"Just tell me the whole of it, Kirstie."

She sighed. His hands pressed near as he leaned toward her. She could smell lemon sugar, buttery crust, and the good scent of him, too, soap and wool and horses. Still silent, she looked up. His face was so close that she could see the dark sand of his beard and the dimple hiding beside his mouth. He waited. Cristina finally nodded.

"At supper, I heard you tell Mr. Rutledge that the documents were coming tonight."

"Go on."

"I thought if the document went missing, there would be a delay, and I would have time to help Patrick. He was not smuggling that night, but traveling with cousins who were known to Mr. Rutledge, who saw them out together."

"Can you prove his innocence?"

"My cousins can verify it. But Rutledge never asked them, never looked for anyone else. He seemed eager to lay the blame on Patrick, since he was already in his custody."

"Interesting. Why the disguise and the robbery?"

"There was so little time, I had to do something quickly. My great-great-grandmother saved her father from a hanging this way. I thought to do the same."

"Bold lass," he murmured. "And a foolish risk."

"Without proper documents, you cannot transfer the prisoner." Her heart beat fast. She might be risking her brother's life by saying too much, trusting so much.

He smiled, the dimple forming. Watching his mouth, she felt a surge of feeling—fear, anticipation, hope. And she felt deeply stirred, distracted by his closeness, his solid warmth. When he moved a hand to cup her cheek, she leaned toward him, pressed close, wanting something she could not define.

"Sweet and foolish," he murmured, his fingers shaping her chin. Then he moved toward her, touching his lips to her brow, tracing down. Her heart quickened as his lips met hers, and in that deep, warm, sudden kiss she tasted lemon and cream and something new, manly, intoxicating. When she should protest, she felt herself melting, giving in—

He drew away, stepping back, raising his hands. "Pardon. That was not good of me."

She did not mind, though knew she should. But her body thrummed, lips hungry, heart pounding: She only wanted more, despite all. "What now?" she asked breathlessly.

He reached into his waistcoat and drew out a slim packet wrapped in brown paper and string, fixed with a red wax seal. "These are the documents," he said, "from the Session

Court regarding Patrick Kerr, who is to be brought from Craigiston to Edinburgh for trial—"

"Where did you get those!" She reached, he avoided.

"The courier delivered them to me over an hour ago," he said calmly. "What you stole is the parcel I gave them in return. And I want it back."

Reaching out, Cristina shoved at Dunallan with all her might.

Chapter 6

Edward grabbed her hands, pulled her toward him, while she half sobbed, so angry that she pushed at him again. Aware of her frustration, he wanted to understand the rest but had to know more.

"Easy," he said, batting her hands down. "Go easy. Listen," he said, as she pounded a fist on his arm. "Kirstie, have some sense. Help me sort this out."

She subsided, breathing hard. He guided her to the bed to sit her there and noticed she was limping. When she sat, he took the chair opposite and leaned forward, beckoning. "Your foot—let me see."

Allowing him to take her by the ankle and tug the boot free, the girl leaned back. He noted the lovely curves beneath breeches and waistcoat, the same womanly form he had admired in silk and satin earlier. The linen shirt, without a neckcloth, gapped to reveal the glint of a delicate gold necklace and an embroidered corset supporting her lush breasts. He glanced away, his body responding too well to the sight.

Removing the long boot, he cradled her slender foot in its silk stocking. "You turned it?" He flexed it this way and that;

she winced. "I doubt you will be running off this evening," he said. "Let me remove the other boot."

She nodded as he tugged. He would need to find the girl some slippers, as well as a nightshirt and a bed for the night, he thought. And he frowned. Regardless of sheriff and would-be brigand, this situation was more than scandalous.

No matter what happened tonight, the girl was ruined. If the truth was discovered, Cristina Heron-Shaw would be done for in good company. Already her father's reputation worked against her, although her uncle's standing countered it. But if this got out, she might never have a suitor, might be shunned in social circles, and the vicar and his family might suffer, too. Edward contributed to social disaster by detaining her here, alone with him. He sighed, unsure what to do quite yet.

"These are my brother's things," she explained as he took off the second boot and examined her other foot, small and fine-boned and without injury. "I brought a gown to change back before returning to my uncle's house."

"'Oh, what a tangled web we weave,'" he quoted softly, setting her foot down.

"'When first we practice to deceive,'" she finished. *"Marmion."*

"You know your poetry."

"I admire Scott. And I have made quite a tangle," she admitted.

"I will not argue that. Nor do I know how to escape this tangle."

"I suppose I am ruined." She watched him, eyes summer blue, her meaning unsaid. But he understood her wariness.

"I might be lost as well," he murmured. "You are in no danger here. I promise."

"I know. Lord Dunallan—"

"We are long past polite acquaintanceship, do you agree? It's Ned."

She nodded. "Ned, if you already had the court orders, what is in the other parcel?"

He stood. "Come—can you walk? Good. Careful." He took her hand to assist her in crossing the room, and opened a doorway. "This was my grandfather's study."

Entering, he turned up the wick of an oil lamp. Bookshelves covered the walls from parquet floor to painted ceiling. In the center, an oak desk was littered with papers, ink bottle, pens.

"I came here as a girl, with my uncle," she said, looking around. "I remember this room."

"Grandfather respected the vicar. He greatly admired your father, too."

"Lord Dunallan—your grandfather—told me that once, when we visited."

"He was a fair-minded sheriff, and thought the whisky tax unjust. He considered your father a friend. I've spent the last fortnight going through papers and found mention of your father."

"I hope it was favorable." She limped toward the desk. "Is this where you are writing your history of the Armstrongs?"

"For now. I discovered some papers here that Grandfather had intended to send to a family friend for an opinion. So I sent them—or tried—tonight. Sir Walter Scott," he said, "is waiting for those pages."

She lifted her brows in surprise. "The other parcel is for the poet himself?"

"It is. My grandfather found some original handwritten ballads composed about our Armstrong ancestors, some of whom were notable thieves and rascals, and knew his friend would appreciate seeing them."

She laughed. He loved the sound of it. "But your ballads were stolen by a highway rascal. How ironic!"

"I did notice that," he drawled.

She took a paper from the desk. "Is this a copy of one of the songs? My father sang this very one to me when I was a girl. I know it well, along with others about the Armstrongs. The songs are local to this area, I suppose."

"Indeed!" He went to her side to look at the page. "I did not find any written music for the songs."

"Da taught the songs to me. Like this." She began to sing in a light, clear voice.

Listening, Edward was enchanted. As a man, he found her enthralling, a revelation; as a scholar, he was nearly as thrilled. "If you know these old songs, you must sing them all for me. The rest of the verses are in the missing parcel, which means—"

"You want it returned," she finished.

"I do," he murmured.

"Very well . . . we will make a bargain," she suggested, tapping a finger on his chest, where the legal documents were tucked in his waistcoat. "I want these papers, and you want the other set. I could be persuaded to reveal where they are hidden."

"If your brother goes free? I cannot promise that." He wished, suddenly, that he could.

"But you could promise to look into the matter most sincerely."

"I could," he agreed. "But . . . it occurs to me that these orders may be useless."

"How so?"

"They are made up for Patrick Kerr, as Rutledge requested. But we have a Patrick Shaw in custody." He had thought about that detail earlier, as soon as he knew the name for sure. Now the solution seemed logical.

She gasped. "So simple as that?"

"Well, it is at least a reason to delay the proceedings, and that will give me time to find the truth. About the other issues, such as your unlawful actions tonight—"

"I did not steal any legal papers, since you already had them," she pointed out. "Nor did I steal the other parcel, really. The courier dropped it. I only picked it up."

"You scared the devil out of the coachmen."

"I, scare them? They frightened me to my wits' end—they threw a bottle at me!"

"Likely they thought the ghost of Dick Turpin was upon them." He smiled.

"Hah! They thought me a wee bit lad who should go home to his mum."

He nearly laughed. "Luckily they did not think you a threat, or you would have been shot dead. That parcel of songs must be delivered. I will take it to Sir Walter myself," he said thoughtfully. "Perhaps I could bring along the lovely Miss Heron-Shaw to sing the ballads authentically for him. He would be delighted to meet the daughter of a notorious smuggler."

"My uncle would never allow me to travel with you. But my aunt might persuade him, if she thought the scandal would—" She stopped, blushed.

"Would throw us together in compromising circumstances? That is already done."

"So it is." She tilted her head. "While I would love to meet Sir Walter, I cannot go with you, I think. I would rather avoid such a scandal for my family's sake."

"Certainly." He blew out a breath, thinking about a detail that had puzzled him for days. "I found something recently among my grandfather's papers but haven't known what to make of it. I'd like you to see it." He reached down to open a little cubby in the desk and took out a folded letter, its red wax seal broken. He offered the page to her.

* * *

Time seemed to slow in that moment. Cristina could not explain why—nor did she know quite why her heart beat so insistently, or why her fingers trembled as she took the page from his hand. His fingers brushed hers gently and withdrew. He watched her in silence as she opened the folded paper.

The note was inked in old-fashioned script with the spikiness of an elderly hand. "Did your grandfather write this?" she asked.

"That is his handscript. The letter is dated seven years ago."

"'To my good friend John,'" she read aloud. "'I have thought more about the conversation we had during your last visit when we shared a bottle of the finest Highland whisky I have ever tasted. I agree, sir, it is high time for you to forgo your current enterprise and take up the venture we spoke of—the manufacture of Highland whisky to be legitimately sold rather than illicitly distributed. I am willing to invest in this new venture as your business partner, supplying the funds, while you—as you expressed—contribute the work. When next you visit, we shall discuss the prospect further and may come to a pleasing agreement. Yrs, Dunallan.'"

She glanced up. "What does this mean? Who is—oh! My father!"

"I believe so. Read the postcript," he said.

Cristina unfolded another crease. "'Post scriptum,'" she read. "'If you recall, sir, we spoke of a possible match between your daughter and one of my grandsons. Lately I met the young lady, who visited here with her uncle. She is bright and thoughtful, lovely, too, and you have cause to be proud. She possesses a spirit that would match my grandson well, were she older. He is at university, a serious lad who has taken his father's passing to heart and finds solace in his studies. We shall talk more of this when you come to Craigiston. Yrs, D.' "

She looked up, her heart quickening. "Do you think he meant . . . us?"

"I do. I was the grandson who was at university that year. My brothers had graduated. But something else puzzles me. The letter was locked in the desk, its wax seal unbroken."

Cristina nodded. "This is dated just two days before my father was killed by an excise man," she said.

"So Grandfather never sent the letter," he said. "Your father never knew."

Her breath caught in her throat. "It must be. My father would have been so glad, had he known. This news—your grandfather's wishes—might have changed his life."

"And ours." Dunallan took the letter from her fingers and set it aside. "Had he lived, and had the two of them talked about this and made an agreement . . ."

"Then Papa would have gone into business with your grandfather," she said. "It was always his dream to open his own distillery. He never had the chance."

"If he had, Cristina, we might be married now," he said quietly.

She took in a quick little breath as hope and wonder and something deeper, finer, rose within her. Looking into his eyes, she nodded.

Taking her by the shoulders, he drew her toward him. "So," he said, voice soft and low, "what do you think?"

"About what?" she asked, breathless.

"Brigands and parcels and pies," he said, "and this snowy night—"

"Which has stranded us alone," she added.

He gave her a little smile. "Do you mind?"

"Not at all. We have a good deal to sort out. What shall we do first, Dunallan?" she whispered, resting her palms on his chest, over his heart.

"For now, we could begin here." He pulled her closer, into the circle of his warmth, his strength, his safe presence; a safety she had not forgotten in all this time. "And here," he whispered, cradling her face in his fingers, touching his lips to hers.

"A fine place to begin," she murmured, returning that kiss, letting it deepen. She drew back, though she felt eager for so much more. "And tomorrow, we will go together to the tolbooth—"

"Hush you," he said, and kissed her again. "Time enough to sort that out, I promise."

Time enough for all of it, Cristina thought. For now, this snowy holiday eve brought an unexpected gift of peace— and love—that she willingly, gratefully, accepted with all her heart.

Books by Bestselling Author
Fern Michaels

___The Jury	0-8217-7878-1	$6.99US/$9.99CAN
___Sweet Revenge	0-8217-7879-X	$6.99US/$9.99CAN
___Lethal Justice	0-8217-7880-3	$6.99US/$9.99CAN
___Free Fall	0-8217-7881-1	$6.99US/$9.99CAN
___Fool Me Once	0-8217-8071-9	$7.99US/$10.99CAN
___Vegas Rich	0-8217-8112-X	$7.99US/$10.99CAN
___Hide and Seek	1-4201-0184-6	$6.99US/$9.99CAN
___Hokus Pokus	1-4201-0185-4	$6.99US/$9.99CAN
___Fast Track	1-4201-0186-2	$6.99US/$9.99CAN
___Collateral Damage	1-4201-0187-0	$6.99US/$9.99CAN
___Final Justice	1-4201-0188-9	$6.99US/$9.99CAN
___Up Close and Personal	0-8217-7956-7	$7.99US/$9.99CAN
___Under the Radar	1-4201-0683-X	$6.99US/$9.99CAN
___Razor Sharp	1-4201-0684-8	$7.99US/$10.99CAN
___Yesterday	1-4201-1494-8	$5.99US/$6.99CAN
___Vanishing Act	1-4201-0685-6	$7.99US/$10.99CAN
___Sara's Song	1-4201-1493-X	$5.99US/$6.99CAN
___Deadly Deals	1-4201-0686-4	$7.99US/$10.99CAN
___Game Over	1-4201-0687-2	$7.99US/$10.99CAN
___Sins of Omission	1-4201-1153-1	$7.99US/$10.99CAN
___Sins of the Flesh	1-4201-1154-X	$7.99US/$10.99CAN
___Cross Roads	1-4201-1192-2	$7.99US/$10.99CAN

Available Wherever Books Are Sold!
Check out our website at www.kensingtonbooks.com